THE GREEN YEARS

Also by Genevieve Lyons

SLIEVELEA

GENEVIEVE LYONS

THE GREEN YEARS

Macdonald

A Macdonald book

First published in Great Britain in 1987
by Macdonald & Co (Publishers) Ltd
London & Sydney

*All characters in this publication are fictitious
and any resemblance to real persons, living or dead,
is purely coincidental.*

British Library Cataloguing in Publication Data

Lyons, Genevieve
The green years.
I. Title
823'.914 [F]   PR6062.Y627

ISBN 0-356-12062-7

Reproduced, printed and bound in Great Britain by
Hazell Watson & Viney Limited,
Member of the BPCC Group,
Aylesbury, Bucks

Macdonald & Co (Publishers) Ltd
Greater London House
Hampstead Road
London NW1 7QX
A BPCC plc Company

This book is for Michele, a very special person,
and Neal, her husband. It is also for all those at the real
Mount Rivers which bears no resemblance to the Mount Rivers in
this book except insofar as it, too, is lovely and contains the room
I wrote a lot of this book in and where I was looked after with
wonderful kindness by my dear Liz, Granny Dot and Helen,
children, cats and dogs.

Prologue

THE limousines sat like black bugs in the driveway. Death had come to Slievelea. Big Dan Casey's death.

Samantha could see the huge cars through the library window, the dark-suited drivers lounging and smoking, leaning on the bonnets or against the sides, trying to look subdued, unanimated in the face of death.

The hearse was like a giant cockroach, she thought, the whole scene observed through the glass of the French windows was remote. The bare branches of the trees blew and waved against the silver-grey of the sky and the shadow of the mountains sleeping in the distance. Samantha looked at the brilliant platinum sun that shot golden shafts of light through the trees wherever it was free of the clouds and wondered why it wavered like a reflection in the lake. Then she realised that her eyes were full of tears. She blinked and looked down, then grimaced at her black-stockinged legs. A hiccup caught her throat and a sob escaped her as engulfing loneliness and rage made her shiver.

'I loved you so much, Grandpa. I'm gonna miss you so much,' she whispered.

She hugged her thin body tightly, arms reaching round her back. She could have been a boy. Sometimes people thought she was and it confused her. Her feelings at thirteen were very ambiguous about her sex. She had short golden hair and large brown eyes in a sharp little face. Her heart-shaped aggressive visage seemed permanently ready to fight, to defend, to weep.

She knew she would never be as beautiful as Aisling, her mother, and was afraid of the time when, as was bound to happen, they would be compared. She vaguely hoped time would stand still and she could remain indefinitely hovering on the brink of adulthood.

At least she didn't have pimples. Had her mother ever had pimples? she wondered. No, she felt sure not. No blemish had ever flawed her mother's perfect beauty. She wondered how

Aisling felt about her father's death. Big Dan Casey and his daughter Aisling had had a stormy relationship, there was no doubt of that. And now? Her mother was upstairs in her room. She would be down shortly and the ritual of laying her father to rest would commence.

Her mother was a survivor and Samantha herself was good at accepting life's vicissitudes and the illogical behaviour of adults. She'd had plenty of experience. Her mother's dreadful drinking and her father's affairs with other women had left her bruised but gallant. 'You're a great little fighter,' Big Dan had told her. 'Like me. You and I are survivors.'

'Mom is too,' she had said, sadly thinking of Aisling's terrific battle against her addiction. Big Dan had looked at her, his eyes full of sympathy. 'It runs in the family,' he replied. 'Surviving.'

Samantha knew now that her mother had been successful, had fought, had won. She was glad the battle was over, and that her parents had divorced; they were much better apart. Samantha was glad to see them separately; she did not feel so responsible for their misery now. Indeed, they both seemed very happy. Her mother had never been so tranquil, so content. Samantha knew something had happened recently to her mother. She was not sure what it was, but whatever had occurred was something momentous, an overwhelming event beyond Samantha's imagining. She could feel the excitement and joy and a curious sense of expectancy radiating from her mother.

If only her grandfather had lived a little longer, Samantha thought, everything would have been quite perfect. She supposed she was lucky that he had lived for the year after her arrival at Slievelea. At least they had had that time together. Her mother had told her that death was part of life, but how could that be? Samantha did not understand. Love, the feeling she had for Big Dan, so new, so special, should not be cut off so abruptly. If only she had known him longer. If only ... But it was useless to speculate. Death was something that separated, destroyed, removed and devoured, consuming the one you loved and leaving only ashes or dust. What had life to do with that? Life was sun and rain and tears and laughter, not dust and ashes.

She heard the crunch of wheels on the gravelled drive. People were arriving at Slievelea. Samantha shivered, curled up

8

in Big Dan's leather chair in the library. She heard car doors slam and ran to the window, pressing her nose against the pane. It was raining now and the undertaker's men were in the limousines. You could see the blurred outlines of their faces wreathed in cigarette smoke. Then she saw a woman in black hurrying across the driveway, protected by a large black umbrella held for her by a tall silver-haired man.

It was very quiet in the library. The grandfather clock ticked monotonously, calming her. She could hear Sheilagh, the maid, weeping noisily somewhere; she stopped for a beat of five and then let out a long keening sound, a moan that settled uneasily on the air. Samantha turned as the door behind her opened. Devlin, the butler, stood there, his eyes swollen from crying. He cleared his throat and opened his mouth to speak but no words came. The woman following him came into the room, removing her black gloves. It was the woman she had seen a moment ago, outside the house. She was followed by the tall silver-haired man whose face, close to, was surprisingly young. The woman spoke as she entered. Her voice was soft and kind and Irish.

'You must be Samantha. How nice to meet you at last. My name is Camilla Fitzgerald, and this is Julian Harcourt — a friend of your mother's. How pretty you are, and so slim. Oh, my dear, you're so lucky. At your age — thirteen, isn't it? — I was a pudding.'

She crossed to the window, holding out her hand to Samantha. Samantha came towards her to shake it but found herself in the woman's arms instead.

'Off you go, Julian,' she told her companion. 'Find Aisling, and get that poor weeping maid outside to make us some coffee. I want to talk to Samantha.'

Camilla removed the black hat she wore, pulling out long lethal-looking hatpins. She shook out hair bright as a copper coin, red as the autumn leaves outside. The rain suddenly stopped and the sun shot a blinding ray into the room, illuminating the auburn halo around Camilla Fitzgerald's head. The woman's eyes were green lightly flecked with grey, her skin pale pearl dusted with freckles. Samantha liked her. She was warm and vivid, sympathetic and friendly without being effusive.

'How do you feel?' Camilla asked when the door closed behind Julian.

'Sad — very sad. I loved him very much.'

9

'Your mother told me. How is Aisling? Is she all right?'

'Mom? Oh, yes. She's fine. She's been wonderful.'

Camilla smiled.

'You find her changed? Better?'

Samantha nodded. 'Yes. She's changed completely.'

They stood at the window together. Camilla put her arm gently around Samantha's shoulder, feeling the sharp bones beneath her black sweater. Samantha said,

Samantha said, 'I had nothing black to wear, so Mom lent me this. The skirt's too big.'

'It doesn't matter, Big Dan won't mind. He'll understand, and he's the only one who matters today.'

Samantha looked up at her. 'Do you think he ... that he's ... ?'

Camilla nodded again. Her movements, Samantha noted, were quick and decisive. 'Of course, my dear. He's here now. With us. Within us.'

Samantha wondered if this friend of her mother's was lying to comfort her or if perhaps it could be true. Her brain felt like cottonwool. She had not slept at all the previous night. The woman's hand still rested gently around her shoulder. They were quiet for a moment. A log fell in the grate but Camilla did not move. She was a very relaxed person, Samantha thought, as if they were old friends.

Camilla sighed and smiled at Samantha. 'You are quite beautiful, you know.' Then, as Samantha turned an anxious face up to her, 'No, you're not like your mother. You're quite different but just as delightful. Your beauty is uniquely your own.'

Samantha couldn't speak, her throat felt tight and her eyes stung, but for the first time that day she felt a resurgence of some of the confidence Big Dan had instilled in her. A feeling that somehow she would cope and that things would be all right.

They looked through the window silently at the rain. As they looked it stopped abruptly and the sun came out again from behind a thunder-dark cloud. The rain-washed scene sparkled for a moment full of irridescent gleamings.

'Who's that over there in the trees?' Camilla asked suddenly. Samantha shaded her eyes against the sun's fierce light, seeing nothing.

'Look, over there.' Camilla pointed to a place where a cluster of trees, elm and beech, were swaying in a sudden gusty breeze.

As the branches were pressed back by the wind, Samantha saw the face of Derry Devlin. He was probably looking for his uncle, but Michael Devlin was too distraught at the death of his beloved employer to keep any appointments today. Well, Derry would just have to wait, she thought. After the funeral she would sneak down to the lake and take him some food and drink. It must be cold down there today. The sun had disappeared behind a dark and angry cloud that looked as if it threatened more rain.

'It's Derry Devlin. Michael Devlin's nephew. He's the butler here, you know. It's all right really.' She saw that Camilla was perplexed.

'Why is he hiding then?' she asked.

'Oh, he's watching all the activity, I suppose. Grandfather didn't like him,' Samantha lied, and had the funniest feeling that the lie was seen through. But Camilla did not pursue the subject. She walked away from the window and sat on the old leather sofa.

'Leather is so cold to sit on, don't you think? It's for men in trousers, not women in skirts,' she said, patting the place beside her for Samantha to sit.

'We could go into the music room if you like,' Samantha said anxious to please, but Camilla shook her head.

'No. No, it's fine here. Let's put some more logs on,' she suggested. 'You know, this is the first time I've been in Slievelea that everything was not "just so" for comfort.'

'Yes, but Devlin's so upset, and Sheilagh ...'

'Oh, I'm not complaining. It's odd to see, that's all.'

'You know Slievelea well?'

Camilla nodded. She had replenished the fire and the flames licked the logs, curling over them in a burst of energy.

'I grew up with your mother. The Vestrys, my people, live in Mount Rivers a couple of miles away. Your mother and I have always been friends.'

'I'd love to have a friend like that. I have Charlie Clerkenwell, but it's not the same. I'd like a girlfriend to confide in, have cosy chats with, you know?'

Camilla laughed. 'Oh, it wasn't like that. I think that's strictly for books like *Little Women*. But even in *Little Women* they quarrelled. No, your mother and I had a fierce love–hate relationship. Happily it resolved itself into a real, loving friendship but it took a long time.'

Samantha's voice shook. 'It took me no time at all to love Grandfather. I'm going to miss him so much.'

Tears shook her frail body and sobs tore harshly from her chest. Camilla wrapped her arms around the girl, holding her tight. She let her cry herself out and, when she had done, gave her a tissue from her bag.

At that moment the door opened and Julian Harcourt came in, carrying a tray.

'Here's some coffee,' he said. 'It's chaos downstairs. The staff are busy preparing for afterwards and the hordes they're expecting — half Ireland by the looks of it. Cook made this coffee, very grudgingly until I told her it was for Miss Samantha. I brought it myself for half the servants are weeping and wailing and in no condition to do anything at all. I'll leave this with you.'

He exchanged glances with Camilla who nodded. 'I fancy a drink myself. A large brandy would fit the bill. See you anon.'

'There are drinks here,' Samantha called after him but he seemed not to have heard. 'Oh, how rude of me,' she whispered. Tears welled in her eyes again.

'Don't worry. Julian was just being discreet,' Camilla reassured her. 'Now, I want you to have a little rest. I'll bet you haven't slept?'

Samantha shook her head. 'How did you know?'

'I guessed. Besides you've got eyes like a raccoon. Oh they're very beautiful, but very, very tired. We'll sit here quietly till your mother comes. We have plenty of time. Relax now, Samantha. Remember your grandfather loved you. You made him very happy. Think about that for a while.'

The fire crackled in the grate. Camilla poured two coffees, put in milk and sugar with calm, slow, restful movements. She gave one to Samantha. The young girl started to speak but Camilla shushed her gently.

'Rest,' she said.

They sat, allowing the silence to envelop them. Camilla sighed. She watched covertly as the girl beside her relaxed. She had drunk her coffee thirstily and then seemed to let go. Slowly, each tensed muscle relaxed. Her head slipped sideways against

12

the sofa, and Samantha slept.

Upstairs in the great house, insulated from the sombre bustle of the funeral preparations, Aisling Casey Al-Mulla knelt at her prie-dieu. A few weeks before it had been unearthed for her, on Big Dan's instructions, from the store room where it had lain unused and gathering dust since her great-grandmother Deirdre Renett's day. It and the old Russian icon, brought from St Petersburg by a great-uncle of Deirdre's countless years ago, had been placed in the corner of Aisling's room for her use.

Today, as every day, she followed her invariable routine. Sheilagh woke her with coffee then, having donned her velvet *robe de chambre*, Aisling knelt at the prie-dieu. Gazing at the Byzantine face of the Madonna, she meditated for half an hour. Afterwards, refreshed, calmed, strengthened, she would be able to face the day ahead. It was her habit now, no matter where she was, to begin every day thus, even the day of her father's funeral.

She cleared her mind of the turmoil of clamorous thoughts and prayed. 'No matter what happens, help me accept, accept, accept.'

Calmed, she sighed and rose, filled with the peace and emotional balance needed for the day ahead. Seeing Big Dan laid to rest would be an ordeal in itself, but another event loomed larger in her mind.

Alexander. When had her health, her sanity, her only happiness not revolved around his name? Her whole past was Alexander. She had never stopped loving him — not for five minutes, not for a split second. Not when she thought him dead, even when she married Ali and bore Samantha. He was her other half, the skipped heartbeat, the shadow on her mind. All those years she had loved him, mourned him, missed him, ached for him, and now, at this point in time, outside her control a momentous decision was being made.

She fought to keep the serenity she had achieved through her meditation but thoughts of Alexander tantalised her, ruffling the calm pool of her consciousness. Today she would know. Today she would have her answer.

'God help me, I want you, Alexander,' she whispered. 'Commit any crime, break every rule, be as cruel as Herod but come to me, come to me! I cannot have journeyed so far, lost so much, fought so hard not to win now.'

When she had dressed in black, she studied her face in the mirror for the marks of grief. Only Alexander would see the dreadful fear she struggled to conceal.

Camilla listened to the ticking of the clock and felt the magic of Slievelea steal over her, a magic composed of rich surfaces well tended; mahogany and rosewood, silver and brass, the shimmer of crystal, chandelier and glass, the soft pile of luxurious carpets; the silk-covered chairs, velvet curtains, the linen and the tapestries and the elegantly framed works of art.

She had always been jealous of Slievelea. But most of all she had envied Aisling the library. How she had coveted this room with its hundreds of books, leather-bound, sweet-smelling. How detrimentally, in those dim days of long ago, she had compared her own home, Mount Rivers, with Slievelea. She had hated the girl she called her friend for her beauty and wealth and the grandeur of her home. But that was all over now, all behind them. There had been good times and bad and they had survived both. Now they were friends in truth rather than in the polite fiction which the proximity of their homes and families had imposed.

Their friendship had been full of misunderstandings and separations. It had blown hot and cold over the years. Sometimes they had been very close and sometimes a huge gulf had separated them. But deep down love had always been there and at the worst moments of each other's life they had helped and comforted, and now, in the fullness of time, they had reached a plateau of understanding, a unity that was rare and precious.

Camilla looked at the small, sleeping Samantha, who for some reason reminded her of herself all those years ago. Growing up could be so painful, she thought, and was glad she had told the child that she was beautiful. She had done it impulsively and now she remembered the agony of her own childhood realisation, made clear by an uncomprehending father, that she would never be as beautiful as her mother. That had been his considered opinion and she had not realised then that he could be wrong.

She shivered and covered Samantha with a mohair rug she found on the back of Big Dan's chair. Outside the wind swept the leaves off the trees and sent the clouds scurrying across the sky. The sun was obscured and the world seemed black and threatening, the mountains in the distance pewter-dark.

Those days, the days of her childhood, had always seemed green, she thought. They had seemed so long, too, long in misery or in joy, time trickling slowly. For a moment, outside the window, she imagined the ghosts of two small girls playing on the lawn, and the virile figure of Big Dan in his prime swinging Aisling high in the air, their laughter blending, the high bird-call of the child, excited, shrill, the full bass of the man.

And Livia, Big Dan's wife, exquisite and high-strung, pouring tea from a silver pot, heaping strawberry jam on hot scones. The sun always seemed to shine on Slievelea while the Mount Rivers of those days had been a dark, cold place.

Camilla saw the pale face move in the thicket again and thought how like that she had been; afraid to approach, always lurking in the wings, an outsider to the Casey family. Big Dan and Livia, David and Aisling. It was all so long ago: another time, another world.

PART ONE

Chapter

1

CAMILLA'S first memories were of long days spent playing in the buttercup meadows, chanting fairy-tales aloud to herself and acting them out in the waist-high grasses. She would turn her face to the sun as she cried: 'Welcome, Prince. Alas, alas, I have waited a long and weary time for you.' And then she would sigh deeply and sink back into the sweet-smelling grass, clutching Minny, her kitten, to her chest.

She ran too beside the silver streams galloping an imaginary horse and using a make-believe whip as she clicked her teeth and *wahooed* loudly.

She played with a broken-down doll's pram in the patch of shade behind the laundry at Mount Rivers where dandelions and nettles grew on a little strip of grass. The pram squeaked when she pushed it. It was rusty and rickety and had lost one wheel but she did not mind for then she had not learned to compare.

Caitlin was always there, watching over her. She wore a floral print cotton cross-over apron and black shoes, and she trailed after Camilla everywhere she went, carrying a half-finished piece of knitting. She sat while Camilla played, the needles clicking together rhythmically. Minny liked to catch the wool and Camilla would pluck it quite cruelly from the kitten's paws, dragging the thread from the sharp little claws while Minny spat and scratched and tried to hold on to the wool. In a surprisingly grown-up voice the little girl would admonish the cat: 'Naugh-ty. Oh, naugh-ty Minny.'

She spent a lot of time outdoors, wandering the big estate. Caitlin, her shadow, never stopped her even when she crossed streams and small tributaries, balancing on the stepping-stones, skipping on the verge, and she not able to swim.

Mount Rivers was a jewel of a place, set at the Meeting of the Waters: little rivers and waterfalls, small green lakes and tributaries, dales and mysterious pools. Well-named, the house was two-storeyed, of hard grey stone, sitting high on its hill, the river flowing front and back. The sound of hurrying, scurrying water, its babble and call, its perpetual murmur, filled the rooms of the old house with its constant melody. The house was draped in ivy, which clung to the crumbling stone and seemed almost to support the neglected old building. Nevertheless the tough well-constructed domicile faced the soft rains and winds of Wicklow with gallant fortitude. It was good for another hundred years but the Vestrys, frightened of its seeming fragility and disrepair, struggled hard to fight the damp and decay that was so obvious to them, although hardly noticeable to visitors.

Charles Vestry, Camilla's handsome father, was eaten up with the frustration of trying to keep Mount Rivers in what he considered an acceptable condition on the very limited income which was all that remained of the family fortune. He lived constantly on the edge of nervous irritability, comparing his lot unfavourably to that of his more prosperous neighbours, deploring Fate's unfair treatment of him, his family and Mount Rivers.

Camilla grew up in the edgy atmosphere of stress and strife between her parents. Her mother was a great beauty whose charms had been lauded in Wicklow, Dublin, London and Paris society before her marriage when she was Caroline Jeffries. A true product of that wealthy high-living clan at Usher Castle, she had broken hearts across Europe. Some said her father was only too glad to wed her before she brought scandal and shame on the proud family name.

Caroline had done whatever she wanted all her life, disobeying everyone, including her quite formidable father, going her own headstrong way. She adored her father, who had sired six sons and one daughter, whom he called the 'runt of the litter' and did not quite know how to treat, so he behaved to her exactly as he behaved to her brothers and she responded by conducting herself just as they did. She rode hard, played hard, gambled and flirted indiscriminately. Her mother, an ineffectual little woman, deplored the hoydenish way her daughter carried on, but she was incapable of imposing her will on her fiery offspring, and Caroline, having been brought up as a boy, brooked no criticism of her behaviour and went on doing just as she pleased. They sent her to finishing school in Switzerland but it made no difference. She was expelled for staying out all night and refusing to explain why. She returned home in disgrace, saw the twinkle in her father's eye and carried on as usual. Her mother clucked and remonstrated with her but to no avail.

Caroline had taken to the music and the life style of the Jazz Age like a duck to water: smoking, drinking cocktails, flirting, and later taking lovers in Paris where that sort of thing was condoned.

Finally, in desperation, her mother pointed out that Caroline was *not* a boy and her behaviour could land them all in deep trouble, casting a slur on the family honour, and though he was slow to get the message the penny finally dropped and her father decided it was time she got married.

Charles Vestry had spent most of his life outside Ireland. His mother had died at his birth, and his father sent him first to public school in England, then Oxford. Later he had returned to Mount Rivers — the damp, the leaking roof, the ageing plumbing and the rusty pipes — and the penny-pinching, and assumed his place at his father's side without complaint. It was his duty. Just as Caroline was influenced by her father, so was he.

Both fathers, the hell-raising autocrat and the honorable gentleman, had one thing in common: an unshakable belief that their opinions were the only correct ones and that anyone who disagreed was misguided and totally wrongheaded. Both children had been indoctrinated in the belief that there was only one way of life: for the Jeffries the hedonistic pursuit of pleasure, for the Vestrys martyrdom to duty.

It was precisely because her father had not wanted her to marry Charles Vestry that, contrarily, Caroline did so, bringing about a breach with her family that she paid for dearly all her life.

Charles's and Caroline's families were part of the same society and therefore well acquainted with each other, as indeed were all the important families of County Wicklow, Wexford and Dublin. The fact that Jeffries and Vestrys led totally different lives, lives whose aims and goals were widely disparate, was not relevant; County families stuck together and in general

21

were tolerant of each other's characteristics and life styles.

Both Charles and Caroline had been out of the country a lot, and although they had known each other as youngsters they had not met in adulthood. Charles, a serious-minded but extremely handsome young man, with secret hopes of marrying someone rich who could help with the terrible financial problems at Mount Rivers, was predisposed to fall for Caroline, and she had flirted with and grown tired of all the available and suitable men in the district. In any event, when she returned from Europe most of her contemporaries, both men and women, had married and settled down, so the cream of the County was now unavailable. She was moreover no longer a teenager and her freewheeling life style had left her slightly shop-soiled in the eyes of the best society, so when Charles Vestry appeared in her life she seized on him with eagerness and determination. Smarting from a recent lecture from her mother about her future as an old maid, and her father's suggestion that she was anyway totally unsuited to marriage, she was ripe as a plum for the attractive young man who suddenly appeared on the scene, and he, after years of loneliness that the English public school system had imposed upon him, was scorched by the bright flame of her personality.

Their first meeting was highly romantic and propelled them into each other's arms.

Charles had attended the hunt that day reluctantly. He was not a sportsman and as he spent long hours in the saddle anyway and hated killing, hunting was not exactly his cup of tea. His father, however, urged him to accept all social invitations. He wanted his son married and settled down, preferably to an heiress who would pour money into his beloved Mount Rivers.

The hunt had gathered on a day cold and sharp-aired, brisk and autumnally crisp. Noses were red, breaths came in puffs of condensed air. The horses champed restively, dogs barked, and Charles felt a charge of exhilaration. Suddenly at one with the bright crackling day he felt energetic and expectant.

It was at that moment that Caroline Jeffries had come thundering around the corner barely holding her seat on a huge grey mare. She struggled with the reins whilst dogs scattered, grooms tutted, and other horses and riders, scarlet-coated or black-garbed, set their mounts side-stepping swiftly, frowns of impatience on their faces. The Master called out a sharp reproof to the newcomer and Charles saw her face for the first time.

Perfectly dressed in her riding-habit, a crisp white stock at her throat, in the struggle to control her horse her hat fell off and her red hair escaped, flowing around her face like a bronze banner. She was in an ill humour, cursing her mount, her face flushed and her eyes diamond-hard.

Charles had drawn in his breath sharply and his heart had stopped at the sight of her. He fell in love instantly with the red-haired vision, swearing on her horse, wind tearing her hair across her eyes. He was fascinated and bewitched. Caroline was like a wild thing, exotic and seductive, and he longed to possess her.

Caroline's horse, in a particularly foul mood that morning, had begun to tremble violently and then risen on her hind legs, pawing the air with her forefeet and whinnying wildly. Her eyes rolled in her head, and she deposited her rider on the gravel at Charles's feet. He dismounted and rushed to help.

The others had laughed. Caroline's temperament, her superb seat on a horse, her pride, her high-handedness and her stubborness being legendary in the hunt, most members were glad to see her take a tumble.

Alone out of all that crowd only the handsome, serious-faced Charles Vestry had rushed to her aid. Tenderly he helped her to her feet, brushing her down and enquiring solicitously whether she was hurt.

He treated her like a delicate Victorian maiden. Touched and utterly disarmed, to everyone's astonishment she allowed herself to be helped and in the most womanly way let herself be led, limping and leaning heavily on his arm, back to the house.

Thereafter Charles pursued her singlemindedly. He was not on intimate terms with the young bucks of the county for his lack of funds had always been a restriction, so he heard none of the gossip, the snide remarks, of the more socially aware families. It is doubtful that he would have paid the slightest attention if he had heard them for he was head-over-heels in love. He was Caroline's slave; he idolised her. His father backed him to the hilt, seeing only the advantages to the family in such a union, but Caroline's father opposed the match vigorously. Nevertheless, against the combined energy of the Vestrys and Caroline herself he stood no chance.

Caroline had decided that here was exactly the husband for her. He had all the qualities she required in a man: he was tall and good looking, he had long legs, graceful, sensitive hands, strong wrists, a neat head, soft hair and passionate eyes. He was undeniably well-bred. She reviewed the same points she would in a horse, except that in a husband she looked for a more biddable temperament. The most attractive thing about Charles was his obedience to her every whim, his desire to please her. Here, she thought, was a man she could twist around her little finger, a man who would behave as she wished, would obey her slightest command, a man she could control. She did not see that this could be construed as weakness. She was not to find out until after her marriage how right and how wrong she had been. She was right about Charles being her adoring slave, except when her requests clashed with his sense of duty. Duty ruled everything the Vestrys did.

She had also mistakenly thought that Charles was rich, or at least had enough money to enable her to continue living as she was accustomed to. She was to find out how totally wrong she was. No one in those parts was completely honest about their financial situation. Most families implied that they did not have money to throw around, gentle self-deprecation on the subject of money was considered the polite attitude. The families often were quite short of money, and there was no stigma attached to that. For most of them, however, such straits were temporary, whereas at Mount Rivers the condition was constant and chronic.

The exception was Slievelea. Everyone knew that there was never any shortage there, and everyone was profoundly jealous. It made them more inclined to plead poverty, almost as a reproach against the splendours of Slievelea. In any event, being straightforward about one's financial position was not the behaviour of a gentleman, so because of this Charles Vestry's exact situation was unclear. People speculated, of course, but while a lot of people guessed correctly an equal number were quite wrong. Caroline was one of them.

Charles was deeply in love with her but he too had made a fundamental mistake. He thought she would make a wonderful wife, one who if not exactly biddable would at least be a good companion and a helpmate. He visualised them strolling the estate which the Jeffries' money had improved beyond belief, restoring roofs, refurbishing the buildings, an army of workers around them polishing and weeding, dusting and revarnishing. He imagined the hustle and bustle, he ordering the extensive estate repairs, she busy with housewifely things — the upholstering, the cooking, the linens and jam-making and such-like — until Mount Rivers shone again, a jewel at the Meeting of the Waters, windows winking in the light reflected from the dancing rivers, prosperous, restored to its former glory. In Charles's rosy visions Caroline always wore a long skirt and an old-world high-necked bodice, with a bunch of keys at her waist and a pack of bright-faced children clustered about her. She would encourage him, look up to him, and they would live happily in love with each other forever. So Charles Vestry foolishly dreamt.

Their wedding was a big society affair, their honeymoon idyllic. The honeymoon was Caroline's father's present to them and Charles saw it as the shape of things to come. They went to London where they stayed at Claridges. In town they were wined and dined by many friends, Charles's old Oxford chums and Caroline's society acquaintances, who were more than willing to show the newly-weds a good time. They danced under great chandeliers to the music of the day, the Black Bottom and the Tango. They heard Hutch sing at the Colony Club and drank cocktails and saw 'Chu Chin Chow'. Caroline was delighted and surprised by Charles's passion and skill in bed, and for that month they were superbly happy.

It was inevitable that disillusionment would follow when they returned to the reality of Mount Rivers. The frugality of life there appalled Caroline. She soon discovered the paucity of funds; that Mount Rivers was a shell, falling apart from lack of money for essential repairs. The hot-water system did not function properly. The draughts were cruel in winter and chilling in the summer. The smell of damp everywhere sickened her, and the penny-pinching life she now faced depressed her, sapping her once abundant energy and vivacity. Furthermore Charles had no sympathy for her in her dilemma. He thought her desire for Paris dresses frivolous, her cravings for the social round the mark of an adolescent rather than a married woman.

He was to find out that she had been spoiled by money and the best it could buy, and that she did not take kindly to the lack of it. She found it impossible to adapt to a disciplined mode of life, particularly one where the restrictions imposed were financial.

Her father refused to help them. 'You've made your bed and now you must lie on it,' he said smugly. He always liked to be proved right. Caroline had gone against his explicit instructions in marrying that ineffectual idiot. Nevertheless he had dutifully handed over her dowry which Charles promptly put to good use. Plumbing was fixed, the roof repaired, but the money was soon swallowed up without a trace and Jack Jeffries saw no reason why he should throw good money after bad. Perhaps if Caroline had approached her father more gently, perhaps if she could have controlled her temper, she might have found him more generous. But after her marriage, as soon as they met she rubbed him up the wrong way. She was on the defensive, had lost forever her ability to manage him, so she got nowhere.

She never forgave her husband their lack of financial security. Charles soon found out how vindictive his beautiful bride could be if not given her own way. She was not at all what he had fondly imagined. He found out how impatient with and uninterested she was in the running of the house and her role as mistress of Mount Rivers. Spoiled and cossetted all her life, the comparative poverty of Mount Rivers brought out the worst in her character instead of the best.

To give her her due Caroline tried to come to terms with her position, but nothing in her life had prepared her for it and she received no help from anyone. There was no one else at Mount Rivers except Charles's crusty old father who resented the fact that she had not brought bags of Jeffries' gold with her and showed her at every available opportunity how disgusted he was at the way things had turned out, as if she and she alone was responsible for the disrepair of his estate. He harangued his son about his wife's inadequacies and Charles, exasperated, felt trapped between the two people, both of whom sang him a daily song of complaint.

Camilla was born, not the son desired and expected by Charles and his father for Vestry first-born were always male. They made Caroline feel a failure over that, too, humiliation heaped on top of a very painful experience she had no intention of repeating. Child-birth had horrified her. Instead of feeling fulfilled, as she had been led to expect, she felt scared silly of the pain and awkward with her child. She who had never spent a day sick in her life was restless to leave her bed after her confinement, and to Charles's horror quite explicit in her refusal to bear any more children. If she ever got pregnant again, she told him, she would go to Switzerland to a doctor she knew of who would terminate the pregnancy, and if this happened she would never sleep with him again. If he wanted to make love to her he had to make sure it was safe.

Charles was forced to give in to her ultimatum. That was the one area of their lives that was a success. Their lovemaking fulfilled them both, smoothing over their jagged differences of opinion, taking the sting out of the bitter words and ugly recriminations hurled back and forth as they struggled to overcome their mutual disappointment. There was a sexual undertone to their sometimes vicious battles and often they ended a row in bed, hot and angry, driving into each others bodies with a fury that spent itself in shuddering orgasm, after which they slept deeply, all tension gone. It was a struggle of wills that they both deplored, yet at bottom, though neither would admit it, they gained a vicarious excitement from their warring. Now after the birth of Camilla, that pleasure, that mutual communication was in jeopardy.

Chapter

2

IT was an uneasy childhood for Camilla, the lone offspring of this ill-matched pair, a childhood shadowed by the slamming of doors and thundering silences, of angry voices and solitary evenings in ill-lit, badly-heated rooms, of broken promises and loneliness. Her parents would return from Caroline's family at Usher Castle, or Kilcrony, from dinner with the Blackwaters, or a grand ball at Slievelea, and their harsh voices and shouts would rouse Camilla from sleep and grate on her nerves.

'Oh hush, hush, hush,' she would cry, covering her ears with her hands and burying her face in her pillow. She bitterly envied her friends their comfortable welcoming homes which were so unlike hers. She resented them, the 'haves', and pitied herself, the 'have-not'.

In company, her parents gave the impression that they were as unconcerned and affluent as their County friends, but within Mount Rivers the pretence collapsed, the tension erupted, and she was caught in the eye of the storm. As will any small creature intent on self-preservation, she became adept at taking cover, concealing herself and her emotions.

She was shaken by passionate feelings that had no outlet. She disliked the greed she discovered within herself and was appalled by the strength of the resentment she bore her parents. Yet she loved them. Her mother's beauty delighted her and was a constant source of joy. Alone together, she and her mother had the most wonderful conversations. Caroline, understanding the role of parent no better than her own father had done, tended to treat Camilla as she would a friend, and to the lonely young girl this was bliss.

She pitied and understood her father's dilemma from an early age. He had explained it to her simply once. She had been very small and had wept because she had only one dress to wear, and all the other girls seemed to have a new dress for every party they attended. In a tantrum, not because she craved a large wardrobe of clothes but because she hated to be the odd one out, she had screamed at her father. Instead of being angry, this one time he had soothed her.

'I haven't the money, my dear,' he had explained quietly. 'It simply is not there. We have nothing to sell but our land, the beloved land of Mount Rivers. Every time I let that go, a bit at a time as I have to, I know that eventually we'll have nothing and Mount Rivers will have to be sold. I love Mount Rivers, my dear, as I know you do, but there is a price to pay if we are to stay here.'

Camilla would not have minded leaving Mount Rivers at all, but she did not think it was the right thing to say to her father at that moment. She felt privileged to have been taken into his confidence so said instead, 'Oh, Father I'd hate to leave Mount Rivers. I do understand, really I do.'

'Well, I don't think it will ever come to that, my dear, not so long as I have breath in my body, so don't worry. But try to understand the economies we have to practise. New dresses are a luxury we simply cannot afford.'

There were always to be economies at Mount Rivers just as there was always abundance at Slievelea. And Slievelea held Aisling.

The two most profound emotions that shook Camilla Vestry during her childhood were resentment of Aisling Casey's situation in life, and frustration at her unconditional generosity towards Camilla herself. Aisling's graciousness sprang from her own generous nature, but it was helped too by the unlimited wealth that enabled the Casey family to be so open-handed. Camilla's best impulses were curbed by her family's lack of funds. She felt she had been placed in a false position for her mother and father had impressed on her that she must never allow anyone outside the family to know how broke they really were.

'If my father knew how penniless we are how he would gloat ... Oh, how he would gloat!' Caroline told her. 'And the County families ... How could we hold up our heads in company again?'

'People would feel sorry for us, my dear, and that would be too dreadful to bear,' Charles assured her.

Camilla could not see why. She would have found it a relief to be honest about their lack of money but the need to cover up had been instilled into her and eventually she stopped querying the rightness of the stance they took.

Aisling Casey took for granted her affluence and the accessibility of anything she wanted or needed. She had no glimmer of understanding of what it was like to want. If it was chilly a fire was instantly lit, and in its glow the chill fled. If she was hungry a servant brought a snack on a silver tray. Camilla resented the inequality of fate which had made her poor and Aisling rich. She could not understand Father O'Brien saying that worldly goods were unimportant. She thought him stupid for didn't he realise how money or the lack of it was reflected in one's every gesture?

Aisling took for granted the toys she got and gave as presents with generous abandon. Her clothes were always in transit; old ones being given away before the full use had been got out of them, new ones tried on and altered for perfect fit. Camilla bit her lip as Caitlin let out or let down the blue dress yet again, and prayed that a miracle would happen.

She suffered in her blue dress, and she suffered not being able to give freely as Aisling Casey was able to.

They had known each other all their lives. They went to all the children's parties in the County, their sibling social life starting with invitations from their mother's and father's friends asking them to birthday parties, teas, and pony afternoons which would lead eventually to tennis parties and dances when they grew up. They went to the Blackwaters, Camilla Jeffries' cousins at Usher Castle, to the O'Sheas and the Gormans.

Aisling was always driven in the Bentley by a uniformed Devlin. Camilla, arriving in the pony and trap with Marty Tullough handling the frisky little animal, a clay pipe in his mouth and a cloth cap on the back of his head, often saw her pass by, an exquisite doll, sitting on the big back seat with her Nanny, neat and shining clean in a dress of the latest fashion made in the most exquisite fabric. She carried a parcel on her knee wrapped in festive paper with a ribbon binding it neatly and tied in a bow. As soon as she spied that beautiful parcel on Aisling's knee, Camilla coveted it. She knew she would love

30

what it contained, and she desired it sight unseen with all her might. The car would purr past, throwing Marty Tullough into confusion and the use of bad language, his temper put out by the power of the big car and the insultingly proprietorial attitude to the road shown by Devlin in his peaked cap.

'That great monstrosity of a thing,' Marty Tullough would splutter. 'Yerra sure God never meant for ingins to take over the boreens of Wickeleh, 'an He giving us in His mercy the gift of the horse! Downright ingratitude,' Marty would say, removing his pipe at the beginning of his tirade and rattling it against his yellow teeth at the end. But Camilla envied the little girl in her solitary state on the back seat of the car.

Aisling was then full of joy, like a bottle ready to pop. She wanted to share, to give, to bestow the abundance of her happiness on all those around her. It seemed strange that no one wanted her extravagant gifts of loving kindness; they drew away and were embarassed by a generosity that asked nothing in return. The other little girls were suspicious of her niceness, jealous of her beauty and wealth, grudging in their approval of her presents, so neatly and beautifully wrapped. These perfect offerings always made the other presents seem ordinary and mundane beside their magnificence. Aisling was totally unaware of the undercurrent of feeling against her. The centre of her world was Slievelea where her parents adored her, and money bestowed on her all that was beautiful and best. She had been rightly set in Slievelea for nature as well as her father's wealth had showered her with blessings: the gifts of physical beauty and a charming and generous disposition.

But the gods are jealous. During Aisling's childhood no one except Camilla Vestry seemed to understand this.

'She has too much,' Caroline said to Charles one day while Caroline listened unobserved. 'It makes me frightened for her. Oh, I hate Dan Casey as you know — a jumped-up peasant, a nabob, an upstart. I'll never forgive him for turning you down, Charles, humiliating us by refusing a loan when he could easily afford it. And I was jealous of all Livia Rennett had, even before she married Dan. Her family always had an abundance, then she marries Dan Casey and gets even more! She does not realise what it's like to want, to need anything.

'But I would not wish their child ill. She's lovely. I only wish Camilla had her potential, or even half of it. That child of ours is beyond me. She does the most extraordinary things! You know, Charles, I found her the other day actually *sneaking* a pair of your socks into her room. She must have got them from the laundry room in some underhand way, from the Kilty twins, though why I cannot imagine.

'No, I wouldn't dream of anything but good for Aisling yet I feel in my bones that it is all too good to be true. She'll have to pay for her plentitude. She has too much.'

It was natural that Aisling should go to St Dymphna's when the time came. All the best Wicklow and a lot of Dublin families sent their girls to be educated there. What was remarkable was that the Vestrys who could not afford it, nevertheless went ahead, out of pride, Camilla knew, and sent her there too. Livia Casey had been so enthusiastic about St Dymphna's at a children's party at Slievelea, calling it the most fashionable school in Ireland.

The children sat on the floor of the nursery playing Pass the Parcel. It was a big bright room, freshly painted, containing a blackboard, dolls of every description, children's books on white-painted shelves. Winnie the Pooh and Beatrix Potter books nestled in unspoiled covers next to *Tales from the Brothers Grimm* and *The Golden Treasury of Nursery Rhymes*. There were painting books and overalls in red-and-white checked cotton on the back of the door; teddy bears, golliwogs and beautiful dolls, some china, some raggedy-Ann, neatly sitting in a row on a sofa covered in flowered chintz.

It was neither too hot nor too cold in the room, Caroline Vestry noted, but just warm enough, the perfect temperature. Everything was so sparkling clean and fresh that she felt such a wave of resentment rise within her she had difficulty in concentrating on what Livia Casey was saying.

'It's a delightful school. Sacred Heart nuns, you know. I was at the Sacré Coeur in England, Caroline. You remember, I told you? They're a lovely order, gentle but very firm. They teach manners, produce ladies, and are academically sound. The grounds are extensive. They have tennis-courts, of course, facilities for riding, basket-ball, a superb gym — in fact, all the necessities. Of course it's expensive, but it *is* the best.'

Caroline looked at Livia sharply, but the latter's face was devoid of malice. She looked very lovely. She was pregnant and wore a wonderful dress of lilac voile. It was frilled at the neck and fell loosely about her body, but the material was so soft and fluid that instead of looking cumbersome she seemed to be swathed in wisps of gossamer.

Someone was crying. Livia picked up little Georgina Jeffries who constantly grizzled.

'There, there, darling.'

'But I *want* it,' the little girl in the stiff velvet dress was sniffing petulantly.

'Well, we'll get one for you, never fear.'

'What?' Caroline asked.

Livia turned to her enquiringly, the lavender frill fanning over her cheek.

'What does Georgina want?' Caroline repeated.

'Oh! It's the chocolate bar that Emmit has. I'll fetch another. Georgina is going to St. Dymphna's too,' Livia said.

That had decided Caroline. She told Charles, and although reluctant, worried about the cost, he agreed. There was no choice really.

'It's the village school otherwise,' he said bitterly. 'Good God, she'd be with the servants' children! Imagine it.'

'It's not only that, Charles, it's her speech and manners. She would sound like a peasant and lose whatever veneer of social polish I could manage to instill in her. Heavens, she's the most extraordinary child! She sat apart from the other children at that party and would not join in. I felt a fool, I can tell you. Sometimes I don't know what to do with her.'

Camilla did not remember that party but she remembered Aisling's dolls-house, seen for the first time that day. It was displayed in a little alcove in the room, all on its own. It was the most glamorous affair with miniature furniture, cabinets and cupboards that you could open and close using tiny knobs. The kitchen drawers were full of minute tin knives, forks and spoons, and the beds had itsy-bitsy pillows the size of your finger-nail, and frilled coverlets. Camilla thought it was the most marvellous thing she had ever seen, and stood in front of it open-mouthed, agog with amazement.

She jumped when she heard Aisling behind her and looked around guiltily.

'I didn't touch it,' she said, blushing. Aisling laughed, her small rosy face creasing and her violet eyes dancing like water in the sun.

33

'Oh, it doesn't matter,' she said, full of six-year-old import-ance. Play with it if you want, please do, I'd like you to.'

But Camilla could not bring herself to touch it. It was too perfect, too beautiful. Imagine if she spoiled or broke anything, how horrendous it would be. Camilla felt certain that she would mess it up somehow, her fingers were so large and clumsy. Rendered tense with nerves at the mere prospect of breaking anything, she knew she dared not play with the exquisite toy. She had been brought up in a house where if something was destroyed it could not, for lack of funds, be replaced. She was too frightened to accept Aisling's generous offer.

Her first impression of Aisling had been on that day. She always remembered her gentle, joyous face smiling at her, generously offering her the beautiful dolls-house to play with.

At Mount Rivers a week later Camilla overheard her parents arguing again. 'How we're going to pay for St Dymphna's for Camilla without going broke I simply don't know!' Charles was protesting.

Caroline's nerves, taut at the best of times, snapped. 'Oh, shut up about it Charles. Just shut up. All I've thought about, day in, day out since we got married, is money. Money, money! I'm sick, sick, sick of it, do you hear?' And she left the room, slamming the door behind her.

Charles sighed. He nodded his head. He agreed with Caroline, felt exactly the same. Money had dominated their thoughts, was their priority, their main topic of conversation since their wedding day. He too was fed up, totally bored by the subject. Yet what could he do? How could he avoid it?

He pressed his fingers to his temples. The pain there was fierce. He had been getting blinding pain just behind his fore-head for years, the result of tension and worry, he knew. Some-times, to his horror, he felt like putting his head in his arms and weeping but that was unthinkable. That was something not even to be contemplated. No, the bills must be tackled, the administration of the estate dealt with. Even when it seemed impossible to find the basic running expenses he must soldier on. That was a gentleman's duty, irrespective of reversals, of impossible debts incurred through no fault of your own, of a malign fate and a total absence of help. A gentleman's duty was a sacred trust. He shuddered to think of the stocks and shares sold over the years since his father died, of the stretches of land here and there auctioned off of necessity, of the money and recourses dribbling inexorably away. And the worst nightmare, the fear that dogged his every waking moment: of losing Mount Rivers to the Bank. The thought of losing his home, the home of his family for generations, robbed Charles of the last vestiges of courage and left him at the mercy of an anxiety too deeply ingrained to leave him a moment's peace. The struggle to preserve the house left him short-tempered and a martyr to splitting headaches and indigestion. Without Mount Rivers he would have no identity, he would lose his position in the world, be without substance or dignity. He could not contemplate even for a second the horror of being Charles Vestry without Mount Rivers.

He rubbed the heels of his hands into his tired eyes. He would go on juggling the books, robbing Peter to pay Paul, the constant nightmarish struggle that exhausted him and rendered him an ineffective husband and an unsympathetic and edgy father, spoiling the flavour of his life as the bruising on an apple ruins its taste. He thought of the short, sharp violent coupling with Caroline the night before, and sighed. He still loved her, and knew that deep down under all her shrewishness she loved him too, or rather would love him if only he could find a way out of this numbing poverty. Then their love would have the opportunity to blossom and develop.

But that was only a dream. He had to be very strict. Electricity must be rationed. They should think twice about every light they burned. Camilla who lived for her books, read by torchlight under the bedcovers.

'She'll go blind, Charles, and it'll be your fault,' Caroline rebuked him.

'It's no use blaming me. I've tried so hard but there is no more money. I'm doing my best.'

'Well, your best is simply not good enough!'

Camilla would sit meekly by, listening, eyes downcast to avoid drawing attention to herself. She hated those tight-lipped altercations, hated family meals when she would sit in the middle of the long table, her parents at either end, the interminable ritual of servants waiting on them, pulling back their chairs as if they were the King and Queen in Buckingham Palace or the Caseys up at Slievelea. It was ridiculous, Camilla thought. The food served was plain, mostly stew. Caroline

35

called it peasant food. It was not so much a scarcity of food at Mount Rivers — there was always bread and butter, always cheese and eggs, always enough — but the attitude to it that Caroline hated, and that made her greedy. Everything must be eaten up; every scrap must be finished, even the gristle, an appalling rule of her father's that revolted her.

If you did not finish what was on your plate you got no pudding. Camilla loved pudding. Sometimes she closed her eyes and swallowed a ball of gristle, fighting nausea, and all for a piece of treacle tart. She would have swallowed much worse to relish the succulent golden slice.

She knew her mother and father loved her. She knew the cause of their quarrels was a simple lack of money. Yet sometimes understanding was not enough. Lonely, she wandered the green woods around Mount Rivers, dreaming of a miracle, fantasising about a fairytale ending to the tension and struggle within her home. She spent hours by the river watching the silver fish leap, chewing an apple, alone with her thoughts. If only ... If only ...

She made up stories with herself as the heroine. She met a prince and fought a dragon. She talked to herself and her mother scolded her for muttering under her breath.

While Aisling Casey in Slievelea was adored and cossetted, wrapped around in a cocoon of the best that money could buy, Camilla Vestry in Mount Rivers dreamed of escape, of adventure, and learned how to cope by fair means or foul with an unkind fate.

Chapter

3

CAMILLA was too young to attend dinner parties, the one time in Mount Rivers that food was interesting. She would be allowed to eat the left-overs next day, which she loved, but she could never wait until then.

Her father spent as much as he dared on entertaining his friends. Roofs might leak but it was important to keep up with the social commitments, not allowing anyone to divine the extent of their poverty.

'As if the rest of Wicklow were eejits and fools,' Tansy Tullough said in the kitchen, resenting the economies to which she was subjected in her administration of the kitchen.

'Sure the whole of the County from Slievelea to Usher knows he hasn't got sixpence to bless himself with. Why doesn't he cut down all the unnecessary entertaining he does like some jumped up Johnnie-come-lately? What's he tryin' to prove? Sure there's no disgrace in being poor, so why does he have these delusions of grandeur, the poor man, that everyone knows are all sham and covering up? I ask myself, and as usual with no reply I'm stunned to silence.'

She could not know how wrong she was. The servants from Slievelea to Usher might know for sure the Vestrys' plight, but the gentry could only speculate.

Tansy Tullough would purse up her lips and bash the pastry she was making with the rolling pin, her face flushed angrily. She was a good cook but the flavour of her dishes might have improved if she had not vented her spleen with such a heavy hand.

Camilla loved the kitchen at Mount Rivers. It was very large, with pantries and larders and a buttery and store rooms running off it. It was the warmest room in the house and always filled with the most delicious smells. Black and white flagstones paved the floor and there was a huge unbleached pine table down the middle on which everything productive seemed to happen. Pastry and bread were made on it, meat and vegetables chopped, chickens and game plucked, and the staff ate their meals there. It was scrubbed down nightly by Caitlin and in the morning shone whitely, waiting and expectant, in the glow from the range. There were copper pans and iron saucepans shining on the shelves. Herbs and onions sat in big porcelain bowls and knives glittered in the warm dusky light. There was a huge old-fashioned range that Tansy Tullough complained constantly about, setting up the modernity of Slievelea and Usher and their gas and electric installations as the shining examples of how a 'treasure of a cook' like herself should be catered for.

Camilla spent as much time in the kitchen as possible, but when her father or mother found her there was trouble. How dare she spend so much time with the servants? No one else they knew did. What a funny child she was.

So she would hover and loiter around the room, a small noiseless shadow, creeping about and dipping in here and there. There'd be a chicken bone, the meat hanging from it, succulent and dripping, put apart while the breasts were coated in aspic for Chicken Galantine. She would nibble away the tender meat with small milk-white teeth then, sitting at the table, her fingers would roam till they rested on a piece of bread to dip in the gravy, a freshly baked biscuit, or whatever else was available. Anything and everything was manna to the small greedy hungry little girl.

When left-overs were not easy to come by, she stole food that was specially set aside. She was a thief, she knew. The thought of going to Hell frightened her in the far reaches of the night as she lay in bed, cold and hungry, her mother's and father's quarrelling voices in her ears. On one particular day she had stolen a small tart from the kitchen. It must have been autumn because the apples were in and Tansy Tullough was making *tarte aux pommes* for dessert for the dinner party that night.

There were two *tartes aux pommes* and two plates of *petites tartes aux fruites* — little tarts filled with custard topped with juicy chunks of plum, apricot, apple and damson, glazed and left to cool. Camilla should have known they were counted. Previously she had always been clever and cautious enough to take only what could not be traced or missed. But she could not resist those tarts. So she took one when Tansy Tullough's attention was on the aspic for the chicken, snatched it up and fled to her room.

She came out of the kitchen through the swing-door, quiet as a mouse. The hall was warmer than usual, a huge log fire burning in the grate at the side. The hall was polished and burnished for the guests that night, but it was dark and the little girl a fleeting shadow among shadows. She crept up the wide staircase unnoticed. Her mother and father would be dressing. She went down the corridor to her room. It was very cold on the landing. The guests would use the toilets and anterooms below.

When she reached her room she did not eat the *tarte* right away. She thought she would keep it in the top of her great heavy chest of drawers and have it as a consolation later on when the dinner party was in full swing and she was all alone up here in her big cold bed. She put it carefully down on the coverlet and looked at it. It was pale gold. Pastry delicate as tissue paper that would crumble at a touch, apricots, marigold in the dim light of her room, shining under the coat of glistening glaze. The *tarte* looked alive and warm on the patchwork quilt on her bed. Camilla put it carefully away, standing on tiptoe to reach the top drawer. She looked forward to nibbling it slowly, savouring each delectable mouthful. She undressed, shivering with cold as usual but happier tonight at the prospect of her feast to come.

Her mother came to say good night. She looked so beautiful it made Camilla's heart stop. Her red hair was a fiery halo around her pale oval face, her eyes ice-green like Nordic skies. She wore a green chiffon dress in the Grecian style, like the dresses in the illustrations in Macaulay's *Ladys of Ancient Rome*. It was draped across her full white bosom, girdled at the waist and falling to her knees, softly pleated, flowing about her like water.

She sighed and said, 'Oh dear, it *is* cold in here. Poor Milla, how you do suffer. I'll have to tackle Charles about the heating. You really should have a fire.'

'Oh could I, Mummy? Could I?' The thought of a fire here in her bedroom was magical: logs burning, pictures dancing in the flames, the sweet smell of burning turf, and above all warmth.

But she knew, deep in her heart, it would never happen. Her mother would speak to her father and there would be a quarrel.

Sure enough her mother said vaguely, 'I'll speak to your father. Good night now, Camilla. Sleep well.'

She kissed her daughter and went to the door. She turned as she got there and said, 'Perhaps you could wear some socks in bed. It would help you, darling.'

Camilla nodded. She did not bother to tell her mother that she was already wearing a thick pair of her father's socks pinched from the laundry and hidden in her school case, transferred from place to place in order not to be discovered.

'Goodnight, Mother,' she said.

She drowsed in the bed, making a snug little tent of blankets around herself and rubbing her knees and arms to speed up circulation and help keep her warm. She heard the sound of her mother's high heels receding down the corridor and sighed, looking forward to the *tarte*. Suddenly, just as she was getting warm and sleepy, the door burst open and the light was turned cruelly on. Her father stood there, tall and handsome in his evening clothes, his face like thunder.

'Did you steal a tart? Tansy Tullough says it could only have been you.'

'Old bitch. Old cow,' Camilla muttered under breath.

'What was that, Camilla?'

'Nothing, Father.'

'Well, did you?'

'Yes, I'm sorry. I was hungry.'

'Nonsense, you have plenty to eat. How dare you imply that you are kept short? It's downright impertinence. That tarte is one of a set carefully arranged by Tansy! It could have ruined the whole table. This dinner is most important to me, and to your mother. What will people say, what will people think, if the dessert is half eaten, for God's sake? Would you see it at the Caseys? Would you see it in Usher? No, of course not. It takes me all my time to keep up our place in society. We cannot have people thinking we are inferior. Our family, Camilla, is one of the oldest families in the area.'

Oh God, here we go, she thought.

'I keep telling you that Dan Casey is nouveau riche, an upstart. He has no breeding, only money. We are one of the best families in the region and you would have us made a laughing-stock.'

Camilla listened to the familiar refrain, uncaring. She thought about Aisling Casey, her wealth and plenty. She didn't care about Mr Casey being nouveau riche, or think it terrible, she just envied them all that money at Slievelea. It provided warmth, food aplenty, and books, Camilla's idea of heaven. She didn't care what the neighbours thought of her at all. She didn't think you could call them neighbours anyhow. Neighbours were people who lived close to each other, popped in and out of each other's houses, were comrades, shared confidences and stood by each other in times of stress. You couldn't call the people of Slievelea or Usher Castle neighbours, isolated as they were in their extensive grounds, miles away from each other. Camilla fantasised about small-town life in a James Stewart movie she had seen.

Her father broke in on her reverie, 'And what did you do with it?'

'What?'

'The tarte! What did you do with it?'

Some malicious impulse invaded Camilla. 'I ate it.'

Her father struck his thigh with his hand in exasperation, staring at her angrily.

'I'm sorry, Father. I didn't mean to be bad.'

'You're just like your mother,' he said.

'Oh, Father, she's so beautiful.'

'I didn't mean that,' he said impatiently. 'No, not that. You'll never be as beautiful as your mother, anyone can see that. It's just that it's your mother's favourite sentence: "I didn't mean to". Well, if you've eaten it Tansy Tullough will just have to find another way of arranging them, perhaps on one big tray with decorations, cherries or nuts . . . Oh, I don't know. She'll think of something.

'But you, Miss, you'll have to mend your ways! You're always sneaking about, looking as if you're up to no good even if you aren't. You're to turn over a new leaf, do you hear? Pull your socks up and behave, otherwise it'll be a sad day for you. I mean it.'

He left, banging the door behind him. Camilla lay in her little bundle of bedclothes and wept.

She could hear his voice saying over and over in her head:

'You'll never be as beautiful as your mother, anyone can see that.'

How sad that was. She had been so sure, had fully expected

41

to grow into a carbon copy of her mother. Now her father had shattered her dream. She did not blame him for it. He was not a malicious man. Any cruelty he had perpetrated was unintentional. Her mother, too, never meant to hurt her. It was just that they should never have been parents, Camilla thought.

Her father would not lie. He never lied. In his book, lying was the worst crime and she had just committed it. She extricated herself from the bedclothes and crossed the threadbare carpet to the tall oak wardrobe, opening the door to look in the full-length mirror inside. She studied her reflection: the tubby body, sturdy legs, the little freckled snub-nosed face, blotched and red-patched from crying. She was disgusted with herself. She was a liar, a thief, and ugly.

Ah, well, she consoled herself, at least I have the *tarte*. She opened the drawer and carefully took it out. She put it on her pillow, then climbed into bed and pulled the bedclothes around her in a warm cocoon. She left her hands free. In one she held a torch to the open pages of *Eric: Or Little by Little*, and with the other she crumbled the apricot *tarte* and ate it, mouthful by delicious mouthful, until every crumb was gone.

Chapter

4

CAMILLA was sent to Aisling Casey's expensive school, and was reminded regularly by her father of how much she was costing them and how ill they could afford it and what sacrifices they were making to send her to one of the best schools in all Ireland. She did not tell him that she knew he sent her because of public opinion and his pride rather than for her own good. She wished anyway that he hadn't bothered. Life at school was a nightmare for her.

St Dymphna's was housed in an old building further inland than Slievelea or Mount Rivers. Set in the soft green fields of Wicklow, the lush lands around the Convent lent truth to the title 'the Garden of Ireland' that had been bestowed on it. It was a pretty place. Unfortunately neither Aisling nor Camilla thought so. It was a factor that was to unite them. They did not really see St Dymphna's, could not look at it dispassionately but viewed it through the eyes of dislike and never gave it a chance for very different reasons: Aisling because she was so happy at home she could not bear to be away, Camilla because her parents could not afford the necessary paraphernalia she needed for school.

It was September in her burnished cloak, leaves falling, chestnuts roasting, light fading, the time of the year for endings not beginnings, Camilla thought when she arrived at St Dymphna's for the first time. She and Aisling were both born just after the outbreak of World War II, so they were the same age, six-going-on-seven, when they started school which meant they were in the same class. Aisling arrived in the back of the big Bentley, driven as usual by the uniformed Devlin, and Camilla, also true

43

to form, came in the trap with her luggage strapped behind.

And that was the first humiliation. Her luggage was a collection of battered old cases she was ashamed of, and some of her things were tied up in parcels. Caroline had told Caitlin to 'pack up Miss Camilla's things', and to the best of the maid's limited understanding that was exactly what she had done.

So the cases and the parcels were precariously roped on to the vehicle from which, much to Marty Tullough's annoyance, they kept falling off, bursting open and scattering their contents into the boreen. He insisted on Camilla's helping him to replace them and she was bending down retrieving her possessions, towels and face-cloth, soap and toothpaste, from the dusty ground when, to her horror, she saw the little green school bus rapidly approaching, screaming girls dangling out of the windows like bunches of grapes in their plum and grey uniforms.

They jeered when they saw her St Dymphna's uniform, starting the shameful sing-song cry: 'We can see your knick-ers ... we can see your knick-ers ...' The bus steered around the trap and careered off down the country road, sending amber leaves scudding. It racketed tipsily out of sight leaving Camilla and Marty angry and red-faced, stuffing her things back into the case and retying it with the string that Caitlin had not succeeded in making secure.

It was weekly boarding and after that Camilla came early each week, before the other girls arrived, so that they should not see her cases and the bags she carried. She hid them under the bed.

Her uniform was a constant shame to her. Intended to last longer than the most optimistic life expectancy it was far too big and not of regulation material. It had been 'run-up' by Caitlin on the Singer sewing machine and in it Camilla looked indefinably different from the other girls, the 'odd one out'. Later, as she grew, it got shorter and shorter, tighter and tighter, as she did not develop in the expected mould. In the clinging uniform the chubby girl became agonisingly aware that the others thought she looked ridiculous and unstylish. She pretended not to care but inside she was in turmoil.

Her blazer turned shiny at the elbows and around the edges, and the nuns suffered for Camilla and tried to do what they could to help her. They got no thanks from the proud little girl who resented help of any kind.

44

She was ashamed, too, of her underwear. Aisling Casey's was silk. All the girls knew that and they hated her for it, for if Camilla was mocked for her shortcomings, Aisling was loathed for the abundance of her clothes and possessions. The other girls had fresh white cotton or soft cream wool underwear of an identical brand, with new sets each season and neat little name-tags on, it looked lovely! Camilla's was old, well-worn and holey, and she hated it. She tried not to let the other girls see it. The machinations she had to resort to to dress and undress under cover would have alarmed a contortionist! It was all very complicated and filled her life with anxiety and tension, just like her father. The strain of trying not to be the odd girl out creased her forehead, addled her mind and rendered her incapable of learning.

Aisling and Camilla were thrown together, sat beside each other at class, were bed-to-bed in the dormitory. Because they knew each other so well, lived close to each other and had visited each other's houses, everyone, nuns and girls, expected them to be friends — so they were. Besides, Aisling liked Camilla in so far as she showed any real interest in anything outside Slievelea. She adored her home. For her life really only happened there. She said once to Camilla, 'In Slievelea everything is like Technicolour. Outside is black-and-white. You know?'

Camilla didn't but she knew how happy Aisling was at home. The family closed around her, wrapping her in their love. The house itself welcomed, was full of laughter and life.

One weekend, a smiling gilded Sunday of gentle breezes and sunshine, Aisling and Camilla made a chain of daisies on the lawn at Slievelea and Aisling crowned Camilla with the wreath. The flowers drooped almost immediately. The sun shone and Camilla screwed up her eyes and saw Big Dan approaching from the house. Behind him strode Devlin, carrying the table for tea, and Sheilagh shaking out the linen tablecloth while she sang in a high sweet voice:

My young love said to me,
My mother won't mind . . .

Big Dan whooped, his laughter rich and loud as he saw Aisling. She jumped to her feet and ran to him. He scooped her

45

up and she curled her legs around his waist and buried her face in his neck.

'Pappy, Pappy, Pappy,' she crooned. Then, as Camilla watched, he looked at her. His right arm supported his daughter but he held out his left hand to her.

'Camilla,' he said, but she rose and turned away from him, shaking the now-dead daisies from her hair.

For a while Camilla was afraid to grow too close to Aisling. A deep core of pride forbade her to become too friendly with anyone at the convent in case they discovered the true extent of her penury. She was extraordinarily good at covering up but one day Aisling said to her, 'You mustn't worry about things so, Milla. If they break, they break. We can get another, honestly. You were so worried about my dolls-house, remember? At my party.'

Camilla looked into her friend's candid blue eyes and realised that Aisling truly did not want her to worry. She tried to explain. 'Don't you see, Ash, that's the difference between us? You see, we don't have any money to replace things, and you ... Are you really as rich as they say?'

Aisling blushed and nodded. She pushed her fine blonde hair away from her face and tilted her head proudly. She would have looked arrogant but for the anxious expression in her eyes, an anxiety not to hurt. 'I'm afraid Pappy has pots but I'm not going to apologise for it, Camilla Vestry. It's not my fault and, anyhow, I like being rich, I think. I've never known it any other way. Do you mind?'

'Sometimes. I'm sorry, Ash. Sometimes I mind for Father who has to worry and scheme to get what comes to you without any trouble at all.'

She thought guiltily of the tides of hate that washed over her when she thought of all Aisling Casey's advantages and many possessions.

'You musn't tell anyone, Ash, about me. You wouldn't, would you?'

Aisling shook her head solemnly and crossed her heart.

'Never,' she whispered. 'Never.'

Camilla looked at her friend with green eyes swimming in tears and said dramatically: 'We are destitute, Aisling.'

If you were going to be something distasteful, like poor, she thought, you might as well capitalise on it.

'Gosh, wouldn't it be wonderful if our families could share? I'll share with you, Milla, really I will. Anything you want.'

And, tactfully, she did share how and when she could. They were both outsiders by virtue of their financial situation; Aisling Casey because of her fabulous wealth and Camilla Vestry because of poverty. The extremity of their positions brought them even closer together. They became protective of each other's frailties. The horn of plenty and the dearth of privilege drew them irresistibly towards each other and they became inseparable. They were forced together also by the other girls' unmerciful teasing.

'Lookit Aisling Casey, will you, in her fancy gansey, all la-di-da. Who does she think she is — Betty Grable?'

'Poor old Camilla Vestry, holey, holey, holier than anybody.'

And they would screech with laughter, then run away as if expecting to be pursued.

Camilla kept well away from her Jeffries cousins, particularly Georgina, for they were the worst. They had the added advantage of knowing Mount Rivers and the state it was in, although in all fairness they knew of it only through their parents' unguarded remarks. They themselves would not have noticed the missing slates, the desrepair of the furniture and the general down at heel atmosphere of the place. The Jeffries girls delighted in rubbing Camilla's nose in the fact that she was their poor relation, her mother — their aunt — having come down in the world by marrying a Vestry.

They were a wayward bunch, full of sauce and taunts, and they loved to jeer and make fun of their shabbier, poorer cousin. Every so often, when least expected, with unabashed cruelty of children they would chant: 'Who wears last year's clothes and lives in a BARN?'

Why the children slid into Dublinese when they were baiting each other was a mystery. Normally well-spoken, angelic-faced youngsters would wrinkle up their faces gargoyle-like and lapse into the language they heard at the pantomime and the Jimmy O'Dea shows at the Gaiety Theatre. In a mindless chorus they would torment the friends mercilessly.

Aisling Casey's Daddy was a barrow-boy,
So why is she so hoity-toity?

Milla Vestry wears old vests,
And THE ELASTIC IS GONE ON HER KNICKERS.

They would not be able to finish sometimes for laughing, 'Sheeeeee uses a p-p-pin,' they would gasp before collapsing in hysterics.

Georgina Jeffries was the bane of Camilla's life. A tall, thin girl, pretty enough but afflicted with spots, she loved to jeer at Camilla and Aisling, and took every opportunity of insulting her less fortunate cousin.

Tears would burn Camilla's eyes. Pride forbade them to fall, and with head held high she would walk away, the chorus pursuing her down the corridor. But she did not lie down under the barrage of taunts. Whenever she could trust her voice, control her tears, she gave as good as she got. A lot of the time she was well able to stand up for herself, calling Georgina a 'stuck-up moran', which was right on target, and 'a long string of a bean-pole', and worst of all a smug taunt, delivered with a saintly smile on her face, her eyes wide and ingenuous: 'Anyhow you say all those things because you're jealous, 'cause Aisling and me have lovely skin and YOU'RE ALL SPOTTY!'

This drove Georgina to fury for it was accurate. Whereas no one could actually verify the allegations Georgina and the Jeffries made about Camilla's home and Aisling's Daddy, the girls could see for themselves how apt Camilla's comment was and fell about the corridor laughing at the infuriated girl. Nevertheless, after a few minutes' fury Georgina could walk away from the confrontations and forget all about what had been said and join immediately in the general hurly-burly of life at school. Camilla was deeply distressed by such encounters, ruffled to the core and left seething and angry for days afterwards.

Aisling passionately defended her friend, standing up for her and Camilla was grateful.

'Don't pay any attention to Georgina,' she would say, her violet eyes filled with tears of sympathy for she could not bear unkindness. 'She doesn't mean it, really she doesn't. She's jealous of you because you're so pretty, Milla.' She would slip her hand under Camilla's and arm-in-arm they would march away from the jeering group, heads in the air.

All this took place against a backcloth of wide green fields and the song of birds. The gentle tones of the nuns, the plain chant in the chapel, the smell of beeswax in the corridors the girls liked to slide down, and the murmurous drone of repeated lessons were tranquil sounds, but the girls' emotions were passionate, their side-taking ardent, their denunciations fanatical. All except Aisling. She was happy, had everything she wanted at home. At school she waited patiently, doing all she was bidden just well enough not to get into trouble, living only for weekends and holidays when it was back to Slievelea, to Big Dan and Livia and David, the sweet content of the haven she loved.

Camilla, at the other extreme, was happy neither at Mount Rivers nor St Dymphna's. She felt at home nowhere, was filled with unrest wherever she was. Her feelings for Aisling compounded her unease. The girl was her champion and friend, and Camilla was deeply ashamed that sometimes she hated her so much.

The discovery that she needed spectacles plunged Camilla into deeper gloom. She found herself having more and more difficulty in seeing the blackboard properly during lessons. The writing was fuzzy and unclear. She told Aisling her worries.

'Tell Sister Marguerite and Sister Denise. They're lovely, they'll understand,' Aisling said.

'But they might be cross.' Camilla was always afraid to draw attention to herself, preferring to say nothing rather than cause a fuss.

Aisling laughed. 'They would never be angry, Milla. I'll tell Sister Marguerite at break, I promise.'

In the playground the girls stood about in groups, hunching their shoulders under their cardigans. They were not allowed to put on their coats or blazers for break in the hope that the cold would force them to run about and take exercise. It was frosty that day and the girls' noses were red, their breath clouding the clear air. Some ran about or jumped up and down with their hands under their armpits. Sister Denise was turning one end of a skipping rope while a queue of girls waited their turn to hop over it. Her face under her wimple was creased in smiles though her nose was damp in the cold. She kept rubbing it, and when she did the rope missed a beat and the girls screamed in anger.

Camilla could see Aisling talking to Sister Marguerite. The nun's face, dark and intelligent, was serious as she listened to the girl. They crossed the playground together, Aisling running behind the nun. Camilla noted that of all the girls Aisling alone did not look cold. She wore fluffy ear-muffs and her cardigan was cashmere.

Sister Marguerite took Camilla's hands in hers and rubbed them as she spoke. 'Oh Camilla why didn't you tell us? For heaven's sake, child, do you think we are monsters? I'll let your mother and father know immediately.'

Camilla's heart sank. She knew that glasses cost money; her father complained often enough when he had to get new ones. She dreaded the trouble her need would cause.

'Don't look so glum, Camilla,' Sister Marguerite said, 'I'm only sorry we were cross with you, but we didn't know the reason for your slowness. Off you go now. Run along and play and I'll write to Mount Rivers.'

To Camilla's astonishment there was no trouble at home, perhaps because her parents got the news mid-week and therefore had had time to get over their initial irritation and worry by the time she came home for the weekend.

Camilla dreaded that the day she first wore the glasses in school would be the worst day of her life. She hated them, hated herself with the nasty alien things on her nose. They made everything so clear. She glowered at herself in the mirror, muttering, 'This is *all* I need. This is *all* I need.'

Anything new, anything different at all, made the girls burst into giggles or sniggers, and that was what Camilla dreaded when she first wore the glasses. She put them on in the classroom before her first lesson on Monday morning. She was in for a ribbing, she knew, but just as she put them on Aisling cried loudly: 'Milla, they're *wonderful*! You look just like Ginger Rogers in that movie where she played a schoolgirl. She wore glasses just like those. Remember?'

Everyone had seen the movie. Their attention was diverted at exactly the right moment. It passed, and the danger with it. They had seen Camilla in her glasses and been told she looked like a movie star. She knew she wasn't in the least like Ginger Rogers, but Aisling Casey had said so and even if only one person had seen a likeness the others were forced at least to entertain the possibility. They paused for thought, and in pausing missed the chance to inflict the first telling barb.

Camilla felt a surge of relief. Every bone in her body had been tense and now she relaxed. After class she hugged her friend. 'Ash, that was so nice of you.'

Aisling laughed, her face full of warmth. 'I'm quite good at it now, putting them off. They can be hateful. And, Milla, I did mean it. Glasses suit you.'

'The optician says I won't need them for too long. He says my eyes will get better.'

Aisling shrugged. 'It doesn't matter, Milla. I like you, no matter what.' She gave a whoop and raced down the corridor, sliding to a halt as Sister Denise appeared.

'Aisling Casey, this is not the Wild West and you are not a cowboy! You are supposed to be a lady.'

Sometimes at night Aisling heard Camilla weeping into her pillow, and would slide into her bed though it was forbidden. Her friend would push her aside, reluctant to accept sympathy, too proud to admit pain, but Aisling would persist, and eventually Camilla would allow herself to be hugged and comforted. They would snuggle up together and whisper in the night.

Once Camilla said to Aisling, 'Oh Ash, let's run away.' Aisling was delighted. They would go to Slievelea at once, she said, but Camilla pushed her aside sadly. Aisling just did not understand. Camilla was thinking of the names she read in books: Samarkand, Istanbul, Venice, Siam, Port Au Prince. Such names, such places. That was where she dreamed of going. Home was the last place she wanted to be.

There were lots of holidays and long weekends when she had to do just that. Then, sadly, on her own, she would wander the grounds of Mount Rivers, sitting beside the rivers running so near the house, listening to the murmur and gurgle and looking deep into the water at the swaying ferns just beneath the surface.

The sibilant whispering, the lapping monotonous sigh of the water of the two rivers would lull Camilla into a kind of trance. She would forget school, forget her parents, forget her home and her problems, and daydream herself into a land of make-believe. It was a curious land made up of all the divergent things she had read, fairy-tales mixed with classics, Greek and Irish mythology mixed with Dickens, Balsac and Sir Walter Scott, Hermann Melville and the poems of Yeats:

All the words that I utter,
And all the words that I write,

51

Must spread out their wings untiring,
And never rest in their flight,
Till they come where your sad, sad heart is,

Tears would trickle down her cheeks, yet she was not really
unhappy. She was the writer and the sad, sad-hearted one as
well.

And sing to you in the night,
Beyond where the waters are moving,

She would gaze at the eddies and whorls of the silver-grey water
and sniff, indulging in her emotion:

Storm-darken'd or starry bright.

On other days, leaning against a tree, she would whisper over
and over like a chant the words written in an opium dream by
Samual Taylor Coleridge:

In Xanadu did Kubla Khan
A stately pleasure-dome decree:
Where Alph, the sacred river ran
Through caverns measureless to man
Down to a sunless sea.

'A sunless sea,' she would whisper to the crows above. 'A
sunless sea,' she would call to the changing clouds. 'A sunless
sea,' she would breathe to the turbulent jade water, to the
laplets at her feet, and she would pull off her socks and dangle
her legs in the ice cold water, quite content.

During the holidays Camilla was often invited to Slievelea.
There, with Aisling, she roamed the bluebell wood under a
canopy of lustrous green trees, wet grass glowing azure blue,
reflecting the drifts of flowers. The lake, when they reached it,
was a mysterious place, ever-changing in colour from peat
brown to jade green to a shimmering cobalt on a sunny day.
The Greek-pillared gazebo rested in the middle mere like an
enchanted temple to Aphrodite. She loved the rose gardens,
the cold statuary, the old uneven steps from garden to garden,
the elaborate ceremony of tea on the lawn, white damask,

Georgian silver, fragile china, the myriad cakes, scones, breads, the wondrous jams: gooseberry, green as emerald, strawberry, thick as porridge, plum, dark as wine. Everything about Slievelea seduced Camilla and set her dreaming.

The lavishness of Slievelea itself never ceased to delight her. The thick-piled carpets in freshly-painted bedrooms, gilt never allowed to tarnish or dim, packs of tissues opened for visitors in bright bathrooms, bath crystals and sweet-smelling toiletries left for them to use. There were warm fires in rooms not currently in use, magazines laid out for anyone to read: *Vogue*, *Queen*, *Tatler* and *Sketch*, *Punch* and *Ladies' Home Journal* from America. The warmth of the house enveloped you, food aplenty awaited you at every turn: elevenses, lunch, tea, dinner. Camilla felt the luxury of Slievelea as a palpable thing, a welcoming thing, an infinitely seductive thing. So what if Big Dan Casey was a gangster, or nouveau riche as her parents suggested? If this was how gangsters lived, she only wished her own father could be one.

She could stand in front of the paintings at Slievelea, gawk in amazement. Most of the good paintings at Mount Rivers had been sold to pay debts, to keep the house going. At first sight the books in Slievelea's library made her gasp and she was meticulous in her care of the ones Aisling lent her with Dan's permission. She fell for him, thought him the personification of the heroes she read about in her novels: dark, handsome, wicked in an utterly charming way. She admired the ruthlessness that had enabled him to make the money to maintain Slievelea, improve it and show the open hand of abundance.

She found Livia, Aisling's mother, remote, nervous, incredibly beautiful, charming, and as distant as a star. She envied Aisling her home and the accessibility to her parents, the family feeling emanating from their proximity to each other. She loved David, Aisling's little brother who had been born during their first term at St Dymphna's, drawn to his obvious high-strung sensibility and gentle sweetness.

Camilla was amazed and not a little gratified that Aisling, proud possessor of all this magnificence and easy camaraderie in her family life, should love Mount Rivers so. Inevitably, and in fear and trepidation, she had asked her friend home. Aisling had been enchanted. She said she found the crumbling mansion mysterious and exciting. She loved the old kitchen, declaring it

53

infinitely superior to the more modern one at Slievelea. Tansy Tullough, overhearing, snorted loudly.

'Ours is all chrome and shiny and *straight*,' Aisling said to Camilla. 'Yours is like the one Cinderella was in in the Walt Disney film. Nooks and crannies and magic could happen.'

They wandered through the house, exploring odd corners of it. One entire wing was closed. No one went there any more. It smelled of dust, disuse and damp, but the girls loved it. They would creep through the doors that separated it from the rest of the house. The furniture, what there was of it, was draped in white dust covers and the rooms were shadowed, echoing and faintly creepy. They played hide-and-seek through the empty place, concealing themselves in cupboards, crouching with bated breath in the dark as the seeker called, her voice ricocheting from the ceilings and hollow spaces.

'Milla ... Milla ... Milla ...'

'Aisling ... Ash ... Ash ...'

The lonely cries shattered the silence, then there would be shrieks of laughter from the quarry as she was found or even if she was not, to signal her whereabouts, for her nerve was going in whatever dark nook or cranny she had chosen. The laughter was terror-laden although they had no intention of revealing the depth of their fear. The boards creaked, the wind whistled and cried through the ill-fitting window frames, there were sounds of moaning and groaning from the very movement of the house itself. Peggy Kilty said it was mourning its past grandeur, sighing for its present state of neglect.

There were portraits on the walls of other Vestrys, lace at their throats, be-wigged and velvet-garbed. One had a turban on his head though he looked not in the least Eastern, but Peggy Kilty, who was a mine of information said it was the fashion in those days to dress up to have your portrait painted in some fancy attire. Everything was covered in dust and cobwebs. The place was alive with spiders and their undisturbed webs and Peggy said a fly stood no chance in there. The shutters were permanently nailed to windows which rattled constantly, and the flickering wavering lights from the waters below crept in through the slats of the shutters and cast eerie patterns on the ceilings and the walls. They shifted and moved and sometimes gave the impression that the house was under water.

The girls roamed the wood together, sitting on fallen logs

covered with lichen and moss and searched for mushrooms. They dabbled their feet in the icy waters of the rivers and shrieked with the coldness of the waves that washed over their toes.

Aisling liked Caroline, admiring her easy sensuousness and her uncensored conversation. She never seemed to talk down to the girls, treating them in her absent-minded way like contemporaries. She kept nothing back, withheld nothing, was explicit while discussing sex in a way that Aisling found utterly riveting though it embarrassed Camilla almost as much as Caroline's other chief topic of conversation, the money situation at Mount Rivers.

Camilla felt the burden of her mother's frankness — too much knowledge brought fear of the uncertain future. Aisling, returning to the security of Slievelea, found it exciting, felt privileged to be party to such adult confidences.

'I don't think it's as bad here as you make it out to be,' she said to her friend, sitting cross-legged on the worn Persian carpet in the slant of brilliant sunlight which fell from a long window into the brown and shadowed room. They were playing Cat's Cradle, squirming with the heat of the sun on their backs.

Camilla said, sadly, 'You don't know the half of it, Ash. You only know what you see. Have you ever seen Mother or Father laughing? Yours do all the time.'

Aisling had a sudden vision of Big Dan's head thrown back on his strong neck, loud, warm waves of laughter rumbling through his giant frame. She saw, too, in her mind's eye Livia's small beautiful face giggling as she covered her mouth with her hand, tears slipping sideways from her streaming eyes, trying to stop the stem of her mirth. And, no, she had never seen Charles or Caroline Vestry laughing.

'Aisling, what do you want to do when you grow up?' Camilla asked.

Aisling surprised her with the violence of her reply. Usually gentle-voiced she replied loudly and emphatically, 'I don't want to! Grow up, I mean.' And then in a softer more normal voice she added, 'I want things to stay exactly as they are. Exactly. I want time to stop quite still, for it always to be like this.'

There was silence in the room. Outside they could hear the meadow-lark calling and the hum of bees, and the drone of bluebottles in the sleepy sunny day.

'Sometimes, Milla, I want to open my arms and gather up Slievelea and Mount Rivers and all of us, especially you, dear, dear Milla, and hold it all tightly forever, just as it is. But I can't, can I? It won't always be like this, will it?'

She shivered in the warm sun, her hair shining golden in the shimmering light. 'Sometimes, Milla, I'm so afraid of growing up and going out there.' She waved her hand towards the window. 'I'm afraid of what it will be like.'

Camilla never forgot Aisling's intensity as she said this. It surprised her for she could not imagine anyone in their right mind desiring such a thing as that time should stand still. She wanted to hurry it along. She sighed, got up, and stood on one leg looking out of the window. She was plump as a partridge in a puff-sleeved faded cotton dress, her red hair scraped back in two stiff pigtails, her green eyes squinting behind her spectacles in the sun. She looked down at her freckled arms leaning against the windowsill.

'I don't think I'd like that at all, Ash,' she said. 'I want to grow up, for life really to start. I feel I'm just hanging about waiting for it to begin. There's so much to find out. So much excitement out there.'

'Like what, Milla? What?' Aisling stood up, too, and stood beside her at the window.

'I dunno. I s'pose we'll have to wait and see.' She didn't know what she looked forward to, she just felt it out there, somewhere, on the edge of her life, waiting to take over. She was impatient for it to arrive.

'I think you're very strong, Milla,' Aisling said, putting her arm around Camilla's shoulders, and looking across the fields of daisies and buttercups, down to the gurgling river. 'Much stronger and braver than me.'

They ran down to the cherry-orchard where Marty Tullough had fixed up a swing. The orchard was enclosed by a hawthorn hedge six foot high from lack of tending. There was a duck-pond hard to the hedge and the wild ducks came to swim there. Camilla sat on the swing and Aisling pushed her. Camilla held her legs out in front of her and her head back so that her body was almost horizontal and her hair swept the grassy green ground. Camilla squinted at the sun which was trying to glint and glimmer through the branches.

'Would you like to get married, Ash?'

'Oh, yes.' Aisling nodded her head. 'I'm going to get married in Slievelea and I'll wear a beautiful white dress and we'll have a party on the lawn and Pappy will give me away, of course, but I'd far rather marry him.'

'Well, he's your father so you can't. So there, Aisling Casey.'

Aisling sighed. 'I know,' she said 'Pity. Can we go to the laundry, please? And have tea with the Kiltys?'

Aisling loved the laundry room at Mount Rivers and spent hours there arm in arm with Camilla, watching the Kilty twins working in the steam and damp of the big converted barn half a mile away from the house. At Slievelea more modern methods and machines were employed in the kitchen complex, and to Aisling the big barn was almost as seductive as the old Forge along the Dublin Road where she and David and Camilla would peer into the hellfire interior, mouths ajar, at the sight of the horses being shod.

Here in the vast laundry room bars hung with dripping sheets suspended from the ceiling over the earthen floor. Worked by pulleys, they could be raised or lowered as required. The pot-bellied stove in the corner gave out a mighty heat; huge tubs like vats stood full of steaming soapy water, each with its own corrugated washingboard and a wringer with wooden rollers to squeeze the water out. The Kilty twins, two middle-aged spinsters who lived in a thatched cottage on the Mount Rivers estate, washed everything from the big house, laundry that incorporated socks, sheets, coverlets, blouses, petticoats, shirts, curtains, kitchen cloths, tablecloths, pillow-slips *et al*. It was blue-rinsed, scrubbed and tubbed by Nellie Kilty and starched and ironed by Peggy, her alike as a pea-in-a-pod sister. The smells of the place, and the merry seamed faces of the twins held a fascination for the girls.

The Kiltys' whitewashed thatched cottage, sitting on the river's edge near the Meeting of the Waters a stones throw from Mount Rivers, was a place the friends loved being invited to. A turf fire blazed in the hearth, the kettle hanging over it from a hook was always kept on the boil. There was a spinning-wheel in one corner and a harp in the other. A scrubbed table, old and uneven, covered with a crocheted tablecloth, sat lowly in the middle of the room. The smell of new-baked brown soda bread filled the kitchen with its fragrance.

The girls sat in the window-seat by the tiny cottage window full of red and pink geraniums and Peggy sat on one side of the turf fire and Nellie on the other. The twins were small and apple-cheeked, fat, fresh-faced, and full of laughter. The fine skin around their eyes had wrinkled from their constant hilarity; there were chuckles just below the surface of the most serious conversation. The Kilty twins stepped outside the cottage door each morning and laid the flat of their hands in the dew-drenched grass and pressed the damp palms on their cheeks and foreheads. They had skin like silk but 'twas said they never saw a man they liked. Bright, bonny, in tune with each other and the simplicity of their world, they often invited the girls to spend a short evening listening to Nellie play the harp, plucking the sweet sadness from the taut strings, while Peggy sang an Irish song high in her head, nasal, trilling and strangely oriental, rolling the notes around and around in the back of the nose, letting go on a high sweet note that hovered on the air as if reluctant to leave.

They were a musical family indeed. Tom Kilty, their father, beat the Devil himself at fiddling. The violin sang under his fingers. The jigs and the reels he played had more life and energy than a school of jumping fleas. He had married Maisie Molloy, the maid up at Mount Rivers, on his strolling way across Ireland and, as he said, got bogged down forever. He spawned the twins on her. She, not the full shilling, was not too sure what was happening, not too sure she liked it at all. At any rate she died in childbed nine months later through ignorance and stupidity and not asking the simplest questions. Tom Kilty brought up the twins haphazardly, and when they were pushing twelve he left them to fend for themselves which they did very well, self-sufficient unto each other they were.

'Me Da was never able to resist the call of the open road or the lure of the open door or the offer of a pint o'porter, and that's the truth. And sure, God bless him, who's to blame him?' Nellie Kilty would say.

'Didn't he have to follow his nose wherever it led him, and he unable to see the happiness that's here at Mount Rivers?' Peggy would add.

She would sigh and Nellie would look up and laugh and say, 'To be searchin' the length and breadth of the world for the happiness that's in it, and wouldn't you be findin' it under your nose.'

They would drink black tea so strong that the spoon nearly stood up in it, eat barm brack and soda bread with lashings of salt butter and loganberry jam. Then Nellie would pluck her harp and Peggy would sing 'The Tubbercurry Bride', the girls would listen and watch the ginger tom lap up the milk and hear the turf sods fall in the grate and notice the blue dusk come down over the hills and know then that it was time to leave.

They would cross the little wooden bridge over the stream and linger over it, leaning to watch a while the water curling over the flat grey stones and sharp rocks and listen to its murmurous song. Then they would climb the hill to Mount Rivers, passing the waterfall and the big bridge that led over the now swollen river to traverse the unkempt field to the neglected avenue up to the house.

They would get a cup of cocoa from Tansy Tullough and scarper through the huge cold shadowed hall, frightening themselves and each other with stories of ghosties and banshees and imaginary movement in the deep dark recesses there. They would climb the creaking stairs holding tight to their mugs, and run down the corridor not a little scared of the brooding silence, hastening to Camilla's big room where Caitlin waited. She would help them undress in the cold and tuck them in and blow out the candle and leave.

The girls would snuggle up to each other in the large bed to try to get warm, and they would whisper and giggle and exchange confidences late into the night, then fall asleep exhausted.

Aisling found enchantment in some of the things and people Camilla took for granted or even derided. The life she led at Slievelea was ordered and elegant, stable and secure. Here in Mount Rivers life held a curious promise of magic, a dangerous sense of insecurity, the lure of the unpredictable and the unexplained. Here life was an adventure.

Chapter

5

LIVIA and Aisling, in wordless conspiracy, sought to help Camilla. Once, when she had stayed overnight in Slievelea, she was told that Marty Tullough was waiting to take her home, and on leaving she saw the case strapped to the back of the trap. It was a big beautiful leather suitcase with shiny clasps and binding. She drew in her breath, flushing under her pale skin, and was about to say something when Livia broke in in her soft voice: 'Oh dear, Camilla, you must forgive me. I've had to replace your case. It's shocking, I know, but Marie said your old case slid down the back of the store room floorboards and neither she nor Devlin can reach it. We'll retrieve it when we can, but it's too bad, my dear, really very careless. So I hope you don't mind having this one of Aisling's instead? Don't blame us too much, will you?'

What could Camilla say? What could she do but accept? She had neither the sophistication nor the maturity to let Livia see she knew what was going on. And, besides, she wanted the case. Already she loved it. She just hated having to accept what she knew in her heart was charity.

'Oh, it's all right,' she said dismissively, and climbed into the trap, her heart full of conflicting emotions. Above all she hoped Caroline and Charles would not make her return the beautiful shiny case, but they did not even notice it. Camilla had become adept at concealing things from them.

Then, as time passed, her parents surprised her by accepting the Caseys' offer of a lift in the Bentley for Camilla, from Slievelea back to school at the beginning of each week. If Marty Tullough could take her to Slievelea in the trap, the Bentley would take both girls from there to St Dymphna's.

'It'll save the pony and Marty a long journey, and we have to do it anyway,' Livia said. And, clinching matters, 'Besides it'll be company for Aisling.'

Her logic was irrefutable. It would be churlish to refuse, so Caroline and Charles reluctantly agreed. Charles especially hated to be, as he put it, 'indebted to those upstarts'. But Livia played her part too well, seemed blissfully unaware of the Vestrys' attitude.

At school Camilla's chief joy, her one friend and champion besides Ash, was Mother Felix. The nun had a brilliant mind, and taught Camilla English. She loved the language to such an extent that she worried in case it divided her from her spirituality, which as a nun must be her primary concern.

To be so much in love with a language, and the manifestation of that language at its best in Shakespeare, Marlowe, Keats, was a passion which she sensed should be restrained. But, like St Paul, not today, not yet. And in the meantime the little Vestry girl kept pace with her page by page, volume by volume. It was quite remarkable. Mother Felix, a tall gaunt woman with a pince-nez, took great delight in feeding Camilla's bright curiosity with books of all descriptions. Sometimes she worried about the scope and content of the volumes she entrusted to the girl. Nevertheless, when Camilla was sixteen and seventeen she gave her Rousseau, Proust, and Graham Greene's *Heart of the Matter* which was banned in Ireland. Afterwards Mother Felix would run to the Chapel to pray to the good Lord to protect the girl from the ideas that she, Mother Felix, His handmaiden, was feeding her.

Dear Lord, she would pray, you and I know that ideas are good, that censorship is destructive. Grant Camilla Vestry the grace to pick out the good and not to be corrupted by the evil therein.

'After all it's not Boccacio or de Sade,' she added, consoling herself.

As time went by and the girls grew older, their work-load became heavier. Mother Felix was the first to encourage Camilla in her writing. She helped to guide her away from her more excessive and basically romantic ideas.

'Your essays and stories have imagination and verve!' She thumped her fist into the palm of her other hand. She gestured a lot, throwing her arms about, a legacy from her French Mama, a trait deplored by her Mother Superior.

'Mother Felix, *please*. We have to show the girls a good example and how can we hope to do so if you behave like a windmill?'

Mother Felix prayed that she might cure herself of the habit but the Good Lord was too busy seemingly to help her achieve her aim and in moments of excitement she was wont to flail her arms around like pistons.

'Your poems are *lurid*,' she told Camilla, knocking a pile of books off her desk which the girl bent to retrieve for her. 'They are deplorable! Leave those alone Camilla and listen to me. You have written purple passages that would make the more fevered Pre-Raphaelites sit up and take note. Leave poetry for the moment and concentrate on your prose. It is good, Camilla. It is very good.'

In all her other subjects Camilla was always in trouble. Aisling said her father helped her with the difficult subjects and that made Camilla envy her even more. Aisling had extra books, beautiful illustrated books on *The Mountains and Lakes of Ireland*, a copy of the *Book of Kells* with glorious scale reproductions of the monks' illuminations, paintings and elaborate script. She had a wonderful illustrated book called *The Vatican and its Treasures* which had pictures so beautiful they took your breath away, but Camilla was beside herself with jealousy when Aisling brought in the most marvellous book yet, *Japan: Its People and Its Culture*. She became obsessed with the book. She thought of it night and day. She crept into the classroom after prep every evening to open Aisling's desk and look at it. The illustrations were gloriously coloured on thick heavy paper, glossy and seductive. She gazed enraptured at Mount Fuji's rising peaks, at the little wooden bridges over narrow rivers, at paper houses with painted screens and exquisite vases containing one bud, one single blossom highlit and perfect. The sight of giant Buddhas took her breath away.

Japan entered her dreams and when the week was nearly over she decided, quite coolly, to steal Aisling's book. She had become used to taking what she wanted by fair means or foul at home. Now she decided to do it here. Aisling had so much she wouldn't miss it. So Camilla went to the classroom as usual after prep on Friday, and instead of simply looking at the book she carefully wrapped it in the brown paper she had used to carry her plimsolls to school that week. She was trembling when she put it in the beautiful suitcase Aisling had given her, and with beating heart stowed the case beneath her bed until next day. She felt awful, mean and slimy, but triumphantly in possession.

At home she sat on her bedroom floor, clutching the book to her breast. She had it at last. It was hers. She did not think of the consequences but she did not feel good. She did not feel the joy of possession that she had felt when Mother Felix told her to keep a tattered copy of her favourite Keats poems. Still, she consoled herself, the book was hers now. She could take it out in the semi-darkness of an evening and look at the pagodas and the golden buddahs, the mixture of snow and cherry-blossom that fascinated her. That weekend she pored over the illustrations, but her heart was leaden and uneasy. Before she went back to school she put it with the growing collection of loot in the toy-chest under the window of her room.

The following Monday Aisling came up to her during recess. Camilla was, as usual, alone, and as usual had her head in a book, oblivious to all around her. She did not see the sunny green fields, the laughing gym-slipped girls knocking balls to each other on the tennis court. She did not see the wind in the trees, the flight of the birds across the sun, the buttercups at the side of the meadow. Nor did she hear the raucous laughter, the high-pitched chatter of the group on the gravel driveway where Georgina Jeffries was showing off again, nor the far-off squeals of the tennis players or the high grand sound of the nuns, remonstrating, admonishing. She did not hear the bird song, or the call of the gulls or the school bell calling them back to class.

She did not see or hear Aisling who called out 'Milla, Milla', skipping over the grass, but she felt her arm being shaken and blushed deeply when she saw Aisling's lovely face before her. She felt the same charge of jealousy she often felt when that face was close to her, so perfect, so beautiful. She pulled her arm away defensively, feeling guilty.

The dimple above Aisling's mouth came and went which meant that she was nervous. Her enormous violet eyes were full of concern.

'Camilla, why did you do it? she asked without preamble. Camilla's heart sank. She felt a terrible panicky sensation in the pit of her stomach. She knew what Aisling was talking about but she pretended ignorance.

'What, Aisling?' She looked blank, peering through her glasses.

'You know, Milla, I'm not cross. I'd have given it to you if you'd asked.'

'I don't know what you're talking about, Aisling Casey, really I don't.'

Aisling flushed a dark pink under her pale skin. She looked levelly at Camilla, her eyes not condemning but sad.

'All right,' she shrugged, 'if that's the way you want it.' She turned away and Camilla watched her go, the pleated uniform neat on her slim graceful figure, the long legs still shapely in the gross lisle regulation school stockings. Camilla had a sudden impulse to follow her, to call out, be honest and tell her the truth, but she did not have the courage. She bit her lip and dashed the tears away with an angry gesture, and returned to school alone, lagging behind the others.

Aisling did not talk much to her after that. It was their first real break. She was nice and polite, but then she was nice and polite to everyone. It was her habit. The nuns loved her but the girls said she was stuck-up. Camilla missed her company more than she could have imagined but went on stealing. It was the only way she ever got anything of her own. She stole other girls' rubbers, pencils, rulers, pens, elastic bands, slides.

Aisling went her way and Camilla was lonely. She made an excuse when Camilla asked her to Mount Rivers that weekend. On the way back to school, after what had been for Camilla a lost and miserable few days, Aisling was polite but remote.

School life went on. Camilla became quieter, ducking and dodging trouble rather than meeting it head on. The nuns were puzzled about her split with Aisling. Mother Felix asked her about it but Camilla shrugged and said nothing.

Nowadays she was always to be found in the shadows somewhere, reading a book or writing. She loved the cloisters, a quiet walkway around the four sides of a grassy green square, with a fountain playing in the middle and pillars wound about with ivy supporting the grey slate roof.

The other girls were uncomfortable in the cloisters. There were always nuns about and they felt constrained by the sisters' observation. It squashed their exuberance and put a damper on their behaviour and speech. But Camilla loved it, the sweet smell of the grass, the peace of it and above all the quiet, the opportunity to read undisturbed. Winter or summer she often sat there. She would stare at the gentle rain falling from the pearl-grey sky, or bask in the golden rays of the sun, her face turned upwards to its warmth. The nuns, seeing her, hoped. They thought she looked so saintly, her face in profile pure and serene, that they felt sure that eventually Camilla Vestry would become a Bride of Christ, would join the Sacred Heart Community and bring glory on St Dymphna's.

They little knew that far from entertaining the spiritual, prayerful and lofty thoughts indicated by the ardent expression on her face, Camilla was thinking of the passion generated by Greto Garbo in 'Marie Waleska' and how she would love Charles Boyer to hold her, Camilla, in his arms, a far cry indeed from the line of thought the nuns in their innocence thought she pursued.

Chapter

6

A new torment had entered her life at Mount Rivers. Her mother had taken to making her wear torn strips of sheet as sanitary towels as every available penny was being channelled into the new roof for the west wing and the Hunt Ball at Mount Rivers. Caroline was driven to distraction, she told Camilla, as there was not a farthing over.

'I've asked my father and he refuses to give us a penny. "Paddle your own canoe," he says. It's a terrible thing when a Jeffries sinks to this, Camilla,' she said, tearing up the sheet into neat ruler-length strips and deftly folding them over.

'At least the linen is good. You can punch two holes, one at each end, and put the elastic through and knot it at the side. That bastard Dan Casey has turned down Charles again for a loan, and they swimming in money, up to their necks in it.'

Her mother sighed as she bent over the linen, the lovely white curve of her throat gleaming like pearl and a wing of red-gold hair caressing her cheek.

'Oh, Camilla, if only you knew how much I long to be wasteful! Not much, not very, just a little wasteful, like Tansy Tullough throwing the skins of the potatoes out of the kitchen door and saying "Thank God we've full and plenty", that kind of extravagance. I'd like to wear my best clothes every day and not care if I break something, have fat fluffy towels and enough perfume to drown in.'

'Oh, Mother, some day I'll make it up to you, you'll see.'

Caroline smiled. 'You funny little thing, what can you do? Dan Casey could have lent Charles that money, though, but he refused. Nicely but firmly, your father says. You have no idea

66

yet, my pet, what it's like to be constantly aware of the lack of money. When one has it one can ignore its existence. Aisling and her brother David have never had to think about it. Livia, too. They are blissfully unaware of how much they have. They take completely for granted the patina of ease that money coats everything with. Like honey it sweetens. It gives a gloss to daily living.'

Caroline tugged at the sheet, worn in the middle, now to be used as dusters, polishers and sanitary towels for Camilla. She put the linen between her teeth and yanked it in half. She ran her pink tongue over her full upper lip to moisten it. She continued, her low musical voice whining a little under its soft modulation, the complaining note inaudible to anyone but her daughter and husband: 'Oh, it's not fair, Camilla. It's just not fair.'

Camilla said nothing but vowed that some day, somehow, she would grant her mother's wishes.

Camilla took to going into Dublin City. Riding her bicycle, a second-hand affair rickety on its wheels, she would whizz down the narrow lanes to the railway station. She loved the free flying sensation, the feel of the cool wind in her hair and the soft rain on her face. She would catch the train for Dublin, never paying. She either avoided the conductor altogether by hiding in the lavatory, or made some excuse in a grand accent. At the drop of a hat, the first smell of disbelief, she was quite capable of bursting into tears so heart-rending and fearful — which was the truth — that the scene invariably ended with the poor official helplessly consoling her.

The train stopped at Amiens Street station and she would wheel off her bike, saying to the official at the exit when he asked her for her ticket 'I gave it to the man on the train, an' he kept the whole of it', looking at the official with wide green eyes shining with honesty. Then she would drag the bike down the station steps with a sigh of relief and an excited lift to her heart.

Bicycling down Amiens Street she would arrive breathless in O'Connell Street, and turning into Abbey Street would chain her bike to a lampost. Sighing with joy unconfined she would face the main street, expectancy making her heart beat fifteen to the dozen. Mouth dry she would walk the length of the pavement, up one side to the Parnel Monument, down the other, listing the wonderful names in her head and closely examining what was playing in each: The Savoy, the Metropole, the Capitol, the Grand Central, all in O'Connell Street, and sometimes up to St Stephens Green, to the little Green Cinema. The picture palaces contained riches for a lonely little girl's imagination. Her favourite occupation, next to reading, was sitting in a darkened cinema watching films.

While she was in the cinema she could forget the painful realities of Mount Rivers. She lived in another world, but they had her custom without payment. She discovered ways of sneaking in at the back, through an emergency exit or sometimes the door of the ladies' loo. Once she was in she found a means of staying through two performances.

Inside the cinemas she gazed at the screen letting all her worries slip away, all her apprehensions vanish, all the envy and pain and insecurity disappear as she laughed at the Three Stooges, marvelled at the exotic places visited by James A. Mitchener: 'And so we say "Farewell" to sunny Hawaii, where grass-skirted dusky maidens sway to the beat of the drum, and as the sun sinks slowly in the West we say "Aloha" and wend our way home, content with the wonders we have seen.' Then came the trailers, and with sudden concentration she would become as selective as any connoisseur, deciding which films she wanted to go to and which she should miss. She did not like war films, never being able to distinguish the goodies from the baddies. She disliked Westerns on the whole, preferring dark moody Edward G. Robinson movies with Joan Bennett and Gene Tierney, or James Cagney gangster stories backed by the music of a lone saxophone and full of brooding fatalistic women, Veronica Lake, Lauren Bacall, Bette Davis and Joan Crawford, who rarely smiled and wrought havoc on the men who admired them.

She loved, too, exotic Sabu films in glorious technicolour with Maria Montez, Yvonne de Carlo, and Jon Hall, or Dorothy Lamour in a hurricane and a sarong. She pondered words like 'lotus blossom' and 'lagoon' as if they were lush pieces of fruit. She liked the classics, Freddie Bartholomew and C. Aubrey Smith in Dickens, Frederick March in 'Les Misérables' and Laurence Olivier as Hamlet or with Vivien Leigh as Nelson and Lady Hamilton.

She adored the musicals, movies where they all lived in

hotels with vast rooms that had shiny floors and Fred Astaire never walked across them like an ordinary man (her father ploughed across the echoing rooms in Mount Rivers like a man in the teeth of a storm), but swaggered, or danced like a dream, or ran. The girls wore feathers and weird and wonderful hats, and music played all the time. The girl was usually Ginger Rogers, who held her shoulders up just a little (Camilla tried to copy her until her mother noticed and said 'Stop doing that, Camilla. You'll end up a hunchback.'), and wore wonderful satin dresses. She dealt with financial problems with a shrug, and won Camilla's admiration by refusing to kow-tow to anyone.

Camilla lived in a world inhabited by Jane Eyre and Mr Rochester, a world of dark moody hills and windy places where Cathy met Heathcliff and Olivia de Havilland's heart palpitated for Errol Flynn who died with his boots on, or was an outlaw in green swards, living beneath trees, singing minstrel lays and rescuing maidens in distress. Tyrone Power and Rita Hayworth were more real to her in 'Blood and Sand' than her mother and father or the nuns in school.

She fell in love with the English Milord who thought he was an Arab in E.M. Hull's book *The Sheikh* which she purloined from Webb's second-hand bookshop on the quays. She had extended her stealing to that establishment which she loved more than any other place in the world.

Real people did not exist for her any more. They were a shadowy background to her intense inner life. In her imagination she was the heroine of all the sagas she read and saw. The realities of life in Mount Rivers, the daily grind at school, the inconveniences, embarrassments and deprivations engendered by lack of money did not touch her any more. She no longer heard her mother's and father's quarrels, hardly heard them when they scolded her for her bad reports or lectured her on how much she cost them.

Sometimes she shivered superstitiously at the unbroken run of luck she had had in her thievery. Odds were she would one day be caught. But not yet, she prayed, not yet. Like an addict she was hooked and would take the necessary risks to feed her habit.

Then one day something happened that was to have a far-reaching effect on her life. This particular day in August, cold as

October, the wind whipping the brown Liffey, she propped her bicycle against the lamp post and sauntered into the Aladdin's cave of Webb's to see what magic it held for her that day. She ached to find new delights, something different to feed her imagination on. She had finished *Anna Karenina* and was feeling withdrawal symptoms at the lack of a fictitious place for her imagination to dwell in. She browsed around finding nothing until she suddenly saw *Gone With The Wind*. She stared at it, coveting it with all her heart. She had longed to see the movie which had been shown at the Savoy Cinema but could never manage to get in. It was an extra long film and Camilla could not contrive to slip past the uniformed ushers, so on the alert were they during the special presentation. Then the film had moved elsewhere and she could no longer feast her eyes on the large advertisement in front of the cinema which showed Clark Gable's shirt-clad figure larger than life leaning over a prone Vivien Leigh. How Camilla had longed to penetrate the mysteries unfolding behind those velvet-curtained doors with the red-uniformed usher standing impassively in front of them, coldly eyeing the bespectacled girl in her shabby school uniform and tatty raincoat.

And now here it was, up on the shelves in two volumes. Two volumes, that was the problem. She had never tried to take two books before. One seemed safe enough. You could conceal one quite easily. But two? Could she leave one volume behind for another day? Suppose it went? Suppose when she came back it wasn't there? The nightmare of not knowing the end! Suppose, heaven forbid, the shop decided the second half without the first was useless and threw it away and it was gone when she returned? There was a pile of tattered discards left in a heap for the dustmen to remove around the side alley to the left of the building. Camilla had gone through it many times but she never found anything of any value. The dogs peed on the pile and made the print run. Once she had taken home a book that had had the last few chapters missing. She stayed awake at nights for a month agitating about what happened, unable to rest until she found out, unable to find out. It was a ghastly frustrating business she had no wish to repeat.

She looked at the twin volumes, avid as an alcoholic in front of an unopened bottle of whisky. As she stared she felt someone looking at her. She glanced around and saw one of the assistants watching her. He was an earnest young man, polite and helpful any time she had asked for information. But she realised now he must be becoming suspicious of her many visits to the shop and her minute number of purchases. Commonsense told her not to worry, that this little gem of a shop allowed unlimited browsing and understood the needs of literature lovers. Nevertheless, he made her feel nervous.

She gazed again at *Gone With The Wind* then, looking around, saw that the assistant was serving someone. Quick as a flash she took the two volumes off the shelf and quickly tucked them under her blazer. Her arms crossed she walked slowly and with great dignity towards the door, her heart hammering in her chest, pausing to glance at a book here and there. She smiled at the earnest assistant who looked at her in what could only be described as a suspicious manner, keeping her arms firmly folded across her chest. She left the shop and crossed the pavement to where her bike stood propped against a lamp-post.

She forgot as she went to mount it that she had taken two volumes. She held the first under the blazer with the elbow of her left arm as usual, but reached for the handlebars with her right hand. Out fell the second part, plonk on the pavement, white leaves fluttering like a wounded bird in the wind.

Camilla's stomach lurched in fear as she felt a strong hand on her shoulder. She looked up into the triumphant face of the pimply assistant as, horror of horrors, the other volume joined its companion in the gutter. Keeping a firm grip on Camilla's shoulder, the pimply assistant picked up the books.

'Well, I guessed it — I knew it all along, Miss Slippery Fingers. I've had me eye on you for a wee while now an' I've been proved right!' He sounded overjoyed. 'Mr Klein over there said no, ye were too young, but I sussed ye. I can smell the likes of you a mile away.'

He hauled her into the shop. Camilla was sweating and crying and she had widdled in her pants with fear.

'Ah, Mr Klein, there ye are — I was right, ye see. *Gone With The Wind* under her gansey. I was right. I told you I was. This gentleman said I was wrong. Well, I'm not, Mr Klein, am I?'

Camilla began to sob.

'Ah, hold yer whisht and quit bawlin', it'll have no effect on me. This is a case for the Gardi,' the assistant said with relish.

Camilla thought she would faint. The daughter of Charles

and Caroline Vestry of Mount Rivers, County Wicklow, in Mountjoy Jail! They would kill her, their place in society blasted forever, the family name disgraced. Her father would kill her for sure.

She looked up into the face of an old Jew man. He wore a little skull-cap on his head, and a dusty embroidered waistcoat under a maroon velvet jacket. Grey ringlets fell on either side of his face which looked faintly greasy in the dim lights in the bookshop. But his eyes, behind steel-rimmed spectacles not unlike her own, were kindly and understanding and wise as the good God himself. She gazed steadfastly into them and knew she could trust him, knew that for some reason she couldn't fathom he was on her side.

'Ah, now, of course you are right, Mr Brody,' the old man said. 'You are a very clever fellow and destined to go far, I feel, but in this case — isn't the Gardi a little extreme? Sure she's only a schoolgirl and they hardly count. The Gardi might feel somehow — and, mind you, I'm not saying they would be right — that you had caught a tiddler that should be thrown back, you see? She's hardly a desperate criminal, now, is she? And the Gardi have their hands full with trigger-happy bank robbers and Machiavellian swindlers and the like; they just might find the fellow who delivers into their hands a schoolgirl who has stolen *Gone With The Wind* a wee bit of an eejit.'

Camilla knew Dublin was peculiarly free of bank robbers and swindlers but tucked her hand into Mr Klein's, trusting him to get her out of this mess. She could not believe her luck when the pimply-faced youth stammered, 'Ah — yes — Mr Klein, sir, you may be right, but . . .'

'I know it was a wicked thing to do and evil deeds must be punished. She cannot escape scot-free, that I see. So leave it to me, Mr Brody. Leave the young lady to me. I'll deal with it, never fear.'

Camilla's heart lurched again. She'd been through so much in the short space of ten minutes that she felt shell-shocked. Perhaps Mr Klein was a Fu Manchu, a white slave trafficker. But, no. Reason told her that then he would have to look like Basil Rathbone or Peter Lorre and he resembled them not one whit.

'I'll pay for *Gone With The Wind* as it's slightly damaged and I'll take it home for Martha.' He paid two and six per volume, five shillings in all, an exorbitant price that made Camilla gasp. Afterwards they left the shop together.

'Leave it there,' Mr Klein said, nodding at Camilla's bike, 'it'll be safe enough. I live just down the quay a few steps.' And fair enough he had hardly finished speaking when they were there outside the most fascinating shop Camilla had ever seen.

'Hymie Klein, Jewellers. Honest Business Done Here' was written over the door, and there were gold balls swinging above it, creaking in the wild wind off the Liffey. The windows bulged a little, round and pot-bellied, as if from the press of the contents within: clocks and vases, rare cups rimmed with gold, engraved silver jugs and crystal decanters. There were little rosewood writing companions, gold chains, engravings of ancient ladies with old-fashioned hairdos, gay hunting prints, and framed caricatures from *Punch*. Mirrors set in gilt frames surrounded by bunches of gold grapes. Fire-irons of brass. Stuffed birds, owls and falcons. A tiger skin with yellow teeth bared in a petrifying snarl, and yellow and black eyes. A tray of butterflies pinned under glass.

Camilla's round eyes surveyed it all, mesmerised. It was gloomy inside but not like Mount Rivers. This was the gloom of oil-lamps, mellow wine, starched damask, of friendly fires and shadows. It was a welcoming gloom.

The old Jew man told Camilla to sit on a velvet-covered stool that wound up or down. He called into the inner recesses of the shop for a cup of hot chocolate and some biscuits, put *Gone With The Wind* on the counter in front of them and locked the shop door, turning the sign that read 'Open' to 'Closed'. Camilla knew a moment's fear but the old man looked at her over his spectacles, eyes merry. He pointed to the rimmed glasses on his nose. 'We read too much,' he said. 'It takes one to know one.'

A steaming cup of chocolate was brought by one of the prettiest women Camilla had ever seen. Used to the sleek, well-groomed good looks of her mother's set or the sturdy handsomeness of the servants, farmworkers and peasants about Mount Rivers, she was sadly ignorant of the middle classes of women. This one's hair was thick and curly, black as a raven's wing, and her eyes were lustrous as the midnight sky. The voluptuous body defied the fashion for slenderness. It was warm and comfortable as Mother Earth, the body of an Irish heroine,

73

a warrior queen like Maeve.

'This is my daughter Jessica, young lady. I don't know your name?'

'I'm sorry, Mr Klein. It's Camilla. Camilla Vestry.'

'Ah, good, Miss Vestry. Now drink up.'

Camilla needed no prompting. She gulped the steaming liquid greedily. It was the most luscious drink she had ever had in her life. She carefully opened the Club Milk and nibbled on the biscuit.

Mr Klein watched his daughter leave then said, 'Now, Miss Vestry, perhaps you can tell me why you, shall we say, purloined Margaret Mitchell's great saga?'

Camilla put down her biscuit and started to explain. To her surprise the whole story of her life tumbled out: the bitter humiliations heaped on her by her father's lack of money, how she was jealous of her friend who was so kind, the petty little privations and deceptions made necessary by Charles Vestry's insolvent position, last of all her stealing, the full story. She held nothing back. It flowed from her, gushing out in a sudden deluge, surprising both her and her listener by the vehemence of her pent-up emotion and long-harboured resentment.

When she had finished there was a long pause, then Mr Klein said, 'You'll never survive if you fight it so. Acceptance is the secret of life, you know.'

'No,' Camilla said doubtfully. 'I didn't. I suppose I am fighting it but I'm not sure I know what you mean by acceptance.'

'Well, Camilla — I may call you Camilla, may I not?' She nodded. 'Well, Camilla. Your father cannot help, shall we say, being hard up. It's tough on the old families being left with crippling debts by a past, more profligate generation who could not imagine a decline in the power of the moneyed ruling class. But you must not allow the change in your family's circumstances to destroy you. It will if you allow resentment to gnaw at your soul and poison your emotions. It will blight your life, limit your vision and hurt you beyond saving. Roll with life, Camilla. This may not last forever. Perhaps when you grow up you will find the money to put your home back where it belongs, re-establish your social position. You could at least try.'

'But Mr Klein, how? I've never thought of earning money. Girls from our school just don't.'

'Why not?'

'It's not considered ladylike.'

'Does that matter so much — not being ladylike?'

'Oh yes, Mr Klein. It's the most important thing for Mother and Father.'

'What about for you? You're going to have to live your own life, Camilla, you know.'

Hymie Klein cocked his head and looked down at the girl's intense face. Without her glasses she had the strangely defenceless look common to all wearers of spectacles when they are removed. There were two red marks on the bridge of her nose where the glasses pinched her. Red hair fanned around her shoulders in a firey aureole.

'You have hair like the sun setting on a field of corn,' he said.

'Yes, but I'm not beautiful.' She stated the fact calmly, accepting it.

'Who told you that?'

'My father. He didn't mean to. He let it slip.'

'Well, he's wrong.' He took her chin between his fingers. She felt the hard skin of his hand rasp against her cheek. He turned her face first one way then the other.

'No, he's right. You are not beautiful now, not now. But then, what girl is at your age. What is it, fourteen? Hmmmmm. Yes.'

Camilla's eyes filled with tears as she thought of Aisling Casey.

'But you will be. You can be sure you will be. Not a raving beauty, no, but you have very remarkable bones and marvellous colouring. You are going to be a stunner in a few years, young lady. The beauties will have to look out — you'll catch the eye with that hair.' Then he thought of the thing most likely to please her and give her confidence.

'Like Rita Hayworth,' he said.

Camilla flushed with pleasure, eyes sparkling. 'You really think so?'

'I don't think, I know so.'

She sighed, deeply contented.

'Think over what I have said, Camilla. And while you are about it — with all this love of literature and the pictures, — of adventures and romance — did you never think of writing yourself, creating your own adventures, your own romances? Drawing on the world you know and weaving stories from the fabric of your own life?'

Camilla didn't answer. She was too overwhelmed by the thought.

He saw her confusion. 'I'm going to leave you alone for a moment and get your bike.'

Camilla heard the shop door bell tinkle and he was gone. She thought over what he had said about writing, her head in a whirl. She thought of Mother Felix and what she had said. She thought of the fantasies she had created in her cold dark bedroom and how she had acted out her dreams, fantastical tales of horror and romance. She thought of the scribbled poems, the essays she had written for school but had always had to cut for they were too long, her flights of imagination unwillingly curbed. Suddenly it all made sense. Like a jigsaw pattern magically put together, the pattern of her life became clear, its purpose revealed.

She smiled contentedly, more relaxed in this moment than she had ever been before in her life. She heard the doorbell jangle and Mr Klein stood before her.

'Come on, young lady. I'm going to say goodbye to you now. I'll expect you to call on me weekly here. We'll go to Webb's and you can choose whatever books you want within reason. You must, however, return *Japan* to your little friend.'

'Aisling,' she said.

'Yes, Aisling. Give it back and be big enough to apologise. I'm not saying it'll be easy but it has to be done. Is that a promise?'

She nodded. She tried to speak but her heart was so full that she felt it would crack in two. He put a finger against her lips.

'Young lady, I've a feeling you're going to be a very good investment.'

Chapter

7

THE meeting with Mr Klein changed the course of Camilla Vestry's life: she began to write. Everywhere she went she took a jotter with her. She was perpetually scribbling. She still found it hard to forgive her parents, and the deprivations at home and school still touched a raw nerve within her, but life was so much better these days. She met Mr Klein once a week at Webb's and to Kevin Brody's chagrin carefully chose a book, sometimes two, and paid the full amount at the desk. Mr Klein always gave Camilla the money so that she could conduct the transaction herself. It felt very good to be paying, as if she was earning the right to the precious literature. She could not resist winking at Kevin occasionally which discomfited the youth and drove him near mad with frustration.

'He's waiting for me to do it again so he can pounce,' Camilla told Mr Klein.

'Well, you won't, so he's doomed to failure,' Mr Klein laughed. They often went back to the Kleins' shop for a cup of cocoa and a blini, a bagel or a Club Milk. They would sit behind the counter, Camilla on the high stool she had sat on the first time, and talk for an hour. Then she would put on her blazer, or coat and beret, and off she would pedal to the station to get the train for Bray and ride thence to Mount Rivers.

During term-time she saw Mr Klein every third Saturday. He helped her with her essays, guided her a little, steered her from her more lurid flights of fancy towards writing about the situations and environments she knew and understood.

The wild romance she had written heavily influenced by E.M. Hull's *The Sheikh*, and hesitantly submitted to his amused perusal, he criticised gently. The tender tale of a small child in a big Irish house whose only friend is her little mongrel dog, he praised so much that Camilla went around in a daze of happiness for a week. She listened to everything Mr Klein said, paying more attention to him than to any of her teachers, except Mother Felix.

'It's a waste of time hating someone for what they've got and you haven't,' he said. 'It's not going to change the facts, just consume your time and energy and attention. Don't compare yourself with others, Camilla. You have too much to do to waste precious energy on things like that. Remember, no matter how much you have, there will always be somebody else with more.'

She loved and listened to him and did what he suggested. First, she apologised to Aisling, as he had asked her. It was not easy. She wanted to get it over with so she chose a Monday morning which was silly as Aisling was always in a bad mood then. She hated so much leaving Slievelea and her mother and father that she called Monday the Black Day.

Usually Camilla could not wait to quit Mount Rivers after the weekend, though contrarily she did not look forward to arriving at St Dymphna's. The journeys recently had not been fun, the atmosphere in the car full of uneasyness. She had thought she would speak to Aisling in the Bentley on the way back to school but when she arrived at the house it was to be told that Aisling had a cold and would not be returning that day. She waved to Camilla from behind a window. Camilla went alone in the big car, feeling relieved at having been let off the hook for today. She enjoyed the solitary journey, waving to an invisible populace as she pretended to be Marie Antoinette before that unfortunate lady's fall from grace.

The following day Aisling was back. Full of trepidation Camilla whispered to her friend at Assembly that she wanted to see her alone after Prayers. Aisling followed her to the locker room off the gym where Camilla silently handed her the book on Japan.

'I'm sorry Ash,' she said, meaning it.

Aisling took it, then looked into Camilla's eyes.

'It's all right. Thanks. You can have it if you really want.'

I wish she wasn't so nice, Camilla thought, and said aloud, 'No, Ash, no. It wouldn't be right.'

78

Aisling walked over to the window that overlooked the hockey pitch and the tennis courts.

'Why did you do it, Milla?' she asked. 'I'd like to know — to understand.'

'We have no money, Ash, I told you. There's no money in Mount Rivers to mend the roof let alone buy books for me. I love books, and sweets, and movies, so as I couldn't get the money for them I stole them — or in the case of the movies, sneaked in the back way without paying.'

Aisling was gazing at her with admiration, Camilla saw.

'Did you really, Milla? How brave of you! I could never — I'd be too afraid. Oh, Milla . . .'

Camilla said nonchalantly, 'I nearly got arrested.'

Aisling's eyes were huge as Wedgwood saucers. 'Oh, you never, Milla,' she said.

Camilla could not help rising to the bait and gave Aisling a slightly exaggerated and dramatically highlit version of the fracas at Webb's. Then she looked at Aisling.

'I've missed you, Ash,' she said.

Aisling smiled and nodded. 'Me too. Me too. Oh, Milla!'

She opened her arms and they hugged each other, crying a little and laughing too. Then Aisling tucked her arm around Camilla's waist and the two girls wandered out to the playing fields instantly engrossed in conversation.

It was hot the summer the girls were fifteen. The sun shone and the nuns' faces were pearled with sweat under their wimples. The girls were restless and found work impossible. They sat about in their summer frocks, pink and white striped, their knee socks at half-mast. The nuns had to relax discipline as they too were affected by the heat. It seemed a long slow-motion time, everything suspended, everyone drowsy. The butterflies danced around the roses and the bees set up a constant cacophany in the orchard. The flies died in their thousands on the long sticky papers the nuns hung from the ceilings. The air simmered over the countryside and the girls became lethargic. Teasing had become a bore, it required too much energy. They could not think up anything new, could invent no more cruelties, ran out of original taunts. They felt soporific and too drained by the warmth to be their usual inventive selves. They were growing up. Reason had begun to enter the area of their thinking. The old mindless chanting began to seem babyish.

They liked Aisling as a doubles partner for tennis, you were sure to win playing with her, and Camilla was a great help with English. Aisling was generous with the wonderful books her father gave her, and the Caseys gave super parties. Besides, they felt, all that jibing, jeering and yaabooing was for babies. They were grown up now, and anyhow it was too hot.

It was the last summer Aisling Casey and Camilla Vestry were to spend in each other's company, though they did not know it then. When the holidays came they were in each other's pockets, at each other's houses all the time. There were days at Slievelea when the sprinklers sprayed the thirsty lawns, green and verdant despite the sun, rolling down to the sea.

Aisling coaxed Camilla into a swim-suit purporting to be an old one of hers, but with an immaculate manufacturers' label revealing a size at least two larger than Aisling's. Camilla, far less on the defensive with her since their conversation about the book, was persuaded to accept, if not eagerly then with a little more grace than was her wont.

They cavorted in the cove, laughing and calling to each other, then Aisling, who was a superb swimmer, would leave Camilla splashing about where the breakers crashed to clouds of white foam starred by the sun with pinpoints of sparkling gold, and striking out would swim away until she was a dot on the horizon. Then Camilla who had never learned from embarrassment over her holey swimsuit would watch her till she disappeared. Afterwards they would go to Aisling's pink bedroom, where the fourposter bed had gossamer white curtains strewn with rosebuds and was looped back with gold-tasselled velvet ropes. There was a dressing table frilled and flounced in the same fine material. Aisling's wardrobe was not like the huge mahogany affair in Mount Rivers but of panelled sliding doors, cream paint lightly gilt-edged, that slid back to reveal frocks, coats, pure wool jumpers on neat little shelves, twin-sets in neat little piles. Just like a shop, Camilla thought. There were shoes in rows on rails at the bottom of the wardrobe, stockings and socks, underwear and ribbons, gloves and hair-slides in lined baskets, everything one could wish for, could dream of, to suit every occasion. They were beautifully arranged, perfectly kept, ready to put on immediately; it was luxury beyond belief. It was impossible for Camilla, despite Mr Klein's advice, not to compare, not to think of her own dark room. That great heavy monstrosity of a wardrobe and its meagre contents, the threadbare wine-coloured carpet, the plum velvet drapes so full of dust they made her sneeze when she closed them. How could she not compare her lot to Aisling's?

This summer day, however, she felt too full of fun and life to entertain the poison in her head for long. She showered, a fabulous invention to be found only in Slievelea where Big Dan had installed all the newest facilities from America. It was like bathing in a heavenly fountain, the water as hot or as cold as you liked.

After her shower Aisling threw Camilla an apple-green and white dress in Liberty print, with a square neck edged in pale green zig-zag braid. The dress tied at the back in a bow and was crisp and cool to the touch.

'You wear it, Milla, Green is grim on me and your dress is all wet.' And then she was gone, giving Camilla no opportunity to reply. She did not want to refuse. She stood a moment, holding the garment Aisling had thrown at her. It smelled cottony and new and the temptation was too much. She put it on, estatically twirling in front of the full-length mirror. The dress was a bit tight across the chest, she was at last developing there, and a little taut over the tummy, but to Camilla it was the most fabulous garment she had ever worn.

She followed Aisling down the grand staircase and out on to the lawn for tea. Behind them the pearl-grey house seemed to stretch contentedly in the sun, and bask deep below the mountains, windows winking in the reflected light and little darts of silver twinkling from the granite stone.

Livia awaited them as always, cool in her linen or silk frock, some airy confection by Captain Molyneux. She chatted with the girls on the lawn, cool in the trees' shade. She poured tea, and Camilla noticed that her wrist curved like the neck of a swan. Camilla had seen the scones and clotted cream and the dish of chunky strawberry jam. Her mouth watered. The sun shone through the leaves like green lace and Livia said, 'What wonderful eyes you've got, Camilla. I'll swear they are mint green. Hasn't she lovely eyes, Ash?'

Aisling smiled and squeezed her friend's arm. 'I think they're like emeralds and her hair is like fire.'

Camilla felt a well of happiness rise within her. But they must be joking! Or her father had lied. Or perhaps, for no one could doubt Livia and Aisling's kindness, they were saying it to make her feel better. But then, Mr Klein never lied either, and she remembered what he had told her very well. It was confusing. Camilla waved away the flies and stuffed herself with scones and cream and jam, and when finished she heaved a contented sigh.

Afterwards they strolled through the bluebell wood and came out into the sun at the lakeside. The lake in summer was indigo blue, shushing and whispering at their feet. Swallows darted here and there and in the distance a lark sang over the meadow. A kingfisher cleft the water in a shower of silver droplets and swans moved over the radiant surface like pale ships. The gazebo seemed to rest on the water like a mirage, cool and white, a magic temple from a fairy tale.

For the first time of her own accord, Camilla reached out and took Aisling's hand. She felt the answering pressure of her friend's warm fingers and smiled, knowing now what happiness was and what Aisling meant when she said she loved her home, was content there and never wanted things to change.

'It's so beautiful Ash,' she breathed. Aisling nodded and shook herself as if to break a spell.

'Come on, Milla. Let's get back. Devlin will be waiting.'

He drove her back to Mount Rivers. She sat on the back seat of the car swanking and pretending she was Chèrie de la Rue — a name she thought exotic — a millionairess on her way to a ball.

When she saw the chimneys of her home appear and the car moved downhill, her heart sank. In the setting sun Mount Rivers rested like a jewel in green velvet; trees, oak, ash, elm, chestnut and aspen, all crowded the hill and woodland behind, and the water, jade-green and black, gurgled along in the warm light of the setting sun. The rushing water, the trees, the crooked foot-bridge and the house leaning into the land, old-stoned and lichened, mossy and ivy-clad, held an incomparable beauty Camilla did not see.

She was going back to the constant irritations heaped upon her by fate. Once again, like little drops of poison, the bitter refrain echoed within her. Why does Aisling have so much and I so little?

Chapter

8

A week later Aisling was at Mount Rivers, admiring the old house no matter what Camilla said. It was another hot day in that summer of unbroken sun and Camilla wore her new dress. She had had to tell her mother the truth about how she had acquired it.

'Mine was wet and spoiled and Aisling and her mother insisted I wear it and, oh, Mummy, she's got *hundreds*. It would look so gauche, as if I was overwhelmed by their money, if I refused. Such bad manners! To them it is a little thing, nothing at all.'

This last shaft was slyly aimed. She was confident her mother would not want the Caseys to think, horror of horrors, that a Vestry lacked social grace. And it was a little thing, Caroline thought bitterly, to the Caseys. She allowed Camilla to keep the precious dress.

Tansy Tullough had fed them stewed beef and dumplings, which Aisling loved though Camilla could not think why, and apple pie to finish. Afterwards they walked through the trees, so much closer together than in the wood at Slievelea. Branches met overhead, and they could hear water somewhere, gurgling and rushing along. The land sloped upwards, but the incline was so gradual the girls did not notice they were climbing. It was dark and cool under the tangled boughs. They sat on a fallen log and talked.

'Do you believe in God, Ash?'

'Of course. Don't you?'

'I dunno. He's not very fair if there is one,' Camilla said, then added. 'It's like you and me, Ash. God gave you Slievelea.' And as Aisling was going to protest — 'No, Ash, listen. He gave you all that, *and* a lovely mother and father who chat with you and take you out and don't fight all the time, *and* He made you beautiful. And then, well, He gave me nothing really, nothing at all.'

Aisling jumped to her feet. 'Oh, Camilla Vestry, how can you *say* that. He gave you Mount Rivers, and your mother and father. They don't beat you, do they? And the Kiltys are blissful, and you have a warm bed and food and you are at St Dymphna's. And you have nice straight teeth, and gorgeous hair and eyes and skin.'

'I've got freckles.'

'Freckles are lovely. Oh, Milla, I'm ashamed of you!' Camilla was beginning to be ashamed of herself as Aisling continued: 'You're so ungrateful. Look at Angela Cunningham. She has no mother or father, lives with an old aunt who *hates* her . . .'

'Never! I never knew that. How do you know?'

'I found her in the orchard one day, crying. I put my arm around her, you know, for comfort, and she told me.'

Camilla remembered the many times that reassuring arm had encircled her. There was a brief silence that Camilla broke when she asked, 'Is it true, Ash, that a man puts his, you know, into a woman's . . . into you to get babies?'

Aisling's eyes opened to their widest extent. 'Of course,' she said. 'Didn't you know? Your mother often talks about sex, doesn't she?'

'Oh yes. She talks about affairs and romance and adultery and periods, but never the *details*. I just wanted to be sure I had it right. Who told you?'

'My mother. She said it was beautiful because you loved the man. She said women get as much pleasure from their husbands as their husbands get from them.' She shrugged. 'I can't imagine it myself, Milla. I don't think I'm too keen on that sort of pleasure. It's a bit weird, don't you think?'

Camilla nodded, absorbed in thought. Then she said: 'Well, I think if my husband wants children, I'll adopt.'

She rose and they started walking again. The leaves were dark and jungle thick. Fallen stumps of tree trunks were everywhere, covered in lichen and moss. Mushrooms and toadstools clustered at the base of the trees and the ferns were waist high. Thick tangles of bracken grew everywhere, making progress slow. The smell of the dank earth was strong and Camilla realised that they must have ventured further than she had ever gone before.

'Let's go back, Ash,' she said, and at that moment her foot stepped out into thin air. She felt a sickening sensation of emptiness beneath it, then lost her balance and fell.

She heard Aisling shout her name. The fall seemed to go on a long time. Like Alice in the well, she thought. Then, with a sickening jolt, she crashed into the river, sinking like a stone to the bottom. Terrified, she felt the brackish water fill her mouth, trickling down into her throat, gagging her, filling her lungs. There was thunder in her head, and the pressure in her nose and ears was unbearably painful. Her heart felt as if it would split her chest. She thought, 'I'm going to die. Dear Jesus, forgive me. I didn't mean . . .'

Then she rose, spluttering, to the surface to inhale a breath of God's sweet air, only to sink again, heavily and slowly, agonisingly, to the foul depths of a weed-filled nightmare. Her heart was going to explode, and the weeds and gently swaying ferns had suddenly turned vicious. They curled, snakelike and tenacious, around her legs and arms, pulling her insistently to the bottom.

Her lungs fought. She felt as if her chest would burst, and the agony and terror were such as she had never known. She tried to struggle, but the more she fought the worse the suffocation got. Her hands clawed the water groping for a stick, a branch, anything to hold, but grasped only weeds, slimy and intangible; her fingers met nothing. All she could feel now was her madly thudding heart and the filling of her body with foul water. Then she lost consciousness.

Afterwards she remembered that in that short sweet moment when she had risen to the surface she had had a vague impression of Aisling, poised high up the cliffside in the trees above, then dropping like an arrow into the river beside her.

When she came to she realised she was naked and wrapped in warm blankets. She remembered, as if in a dream, lying on the grass while someone pumped her chest. Aisling's face floated above her, foggy, blurred and unreal. There was pressure on her ribs, green bile in her mouth.

'My dress,' she whispered through stiff lips. 'My beautiful dress.'

'Don't worry, Milla. We'll get you another easy-peasy. I promise.'

Aisling's face swam into view again and Camilla felt the reassuring pressure of her hand. She focussed on the white walls and the scarlet geraniums, the glowing peat fire, the unmistakable accoutrements of the Kiltys' home. She knew that somehow, miraculously, she was in their kitchen.

'How'd I get here? Her voice sounded harsh and low, her throat felt sore.

Peggy Kilty's fat apple-cheeked face thrust itself into her line of vision. 'Cluny O'Rourke saw, the good God be praised, saw Miss Aisling dive offa the cleft, where the cove is. It's sheer there on the edge of the wood, an' a terrible drop down to the water. An' what were you doin', may I ask, in that neck o' the woods, an' it a dangerous *ait*, an' your da always tellin' you, *na teigh that d'airde*, don't go beyond your depth? Did ye know there are wolves sometimes in that part o' the woods, an' the Fir Bolg haunt the darkness of that place.'

'I didn't realise we were so high until . . .' Aisling said.

Camilla looked at her. Her hair, darkened by the water, clung to her neck, and she too was wrapped in a towel. Camilla couldn't understand why. She was overwhelmed by weariness, her eyes wanted desperately to close.

Nellie Kilty said, 'The woods rise up steep behind the big house, Miss. They march right up the mountainside to near the top, and at the river's side it's sheer cliff. The rock drops down into the water like a wall.'

'Well, anyhow, Cluny saw Miss Aisling dive offa it and thought she'd lost her mind,' Peggy continued.

'Why did she do that?' Camilla queried, still dazed.

'To save you, acushla. Only for her, sure, wouldn't you be at the bottom of the river or floating down-stream on yer way to the sea.'

Nellie clasped her fat red hands together. 'Like Ophelia drowned!' she said.

Peggy gave her a push. 'Och, get away wi' your mush,' she said briskly. 'Much like Ophelia she looked, an' her choking and thrashing about like a landed fish, an' gasping something awful!'

Camilla shuddered.

'What was Cluny doin' there?' Nellie Kilty asked her sister innocently.

'Will ye hold yer whist,' Peggy Kilty said through her teeth. 'Sure wasn't he gettin' some hazel faggots offa the ground fer firewood. An' why not, may I ask? It isn't the time of the Sassanach any more, praise be, an' the trees is free.'

'But it's forbidden,' Nellie Kilty said, her lips tightening primly.

Her sister gave her a belt across the shoulder. 'Yerra yid try the patience of a martyr, so ye would. Didn't Cluny get Miss Camilla and Miss Aisling here in the trap, an' if heda been someplace else doin' the *right* thing, wouldn't they still be sat there shiverin' like skinned rabbits and wet as drowned rats an' well on their way to pneumonia?'

'Yes, well, why didn't he take them up to the big house?' Nellie asked.

Camilla was vaguely wondering that herself.

Peggy Kilty sighed, her patience sorely tried. 'As ye said yerself, wasn't he doin' something he shouldna? An' it was six of one an' half-a-dozen of the other an' he preferred to bundle the two of them into the trap, not have to use the bridge, and come here where he *hoped* —' she eyed her sister malignantly — 'where he *hoped* he'd not have to answer a lotta stupid questions an' be hauled over the coals when all he did was a good turn.' She cast her eyes up to heaven. 'It'd put anyone off doin' a kindness, so it would.' She looked at her sister bitterly and added, 'Like the bloody Gestapo!'

Aisling suddenly began to cry. Tears splashed down her cheeks like rain.

'I was so afraid,' she cried. 'I thought Milla was going to die.'

'There, there now *a gra*,' Peggy said and turned on her sister anew. 'Now see what you've done.' She glared at poor Nellie, who hung back shamefaced, then folded Aisling in her plump raspberry-coloured arms, cradling her to her ample bosom.

'Didn't you only save Miss Camilla's life? Didn't you only jump in the water and rescue her? It can't have been easy diving offa that cliff. Don't you talk about being afraid. Haven't you the courage of Queen Maeve herself? You're a brave little colleen, so you are. She's quite a weight —' Camilla squirmed — 'an' you rescued her and got her to the shore and then did first aid on her, so you did now.'

Camilla was distracted, as were they all, by the sound of a huge outburst of blubbering masculine sobs. She realised that

Cluny, a big freckle-faced boney lad, had been lurking in the corner of the kitchen all the time. Unable to control his emotion any longer, he sounded like a frightened six-year-old or a bullock in pain.

'An' what's the answer wi' you?' Peggy Kilty asked.

And Nellie, to everyone's surprise, suddenly burst out. 'Aw shut up! Fellas make me sick! Supposed to be a man an' blubberin' like a sheep,' she muttered contemptuously, and gave him two belts across the head with her fist which shut him up instantaneously and gave Nellie the satisfaction of meting out the same treatment to him as her sister had to her. She nodded briskly and glared at the cringeing boy.

'I don't wanna get into trouble,' he hiccupped. 'I don't wanna get into trouble, I don't.'

'Aw shut up. Nobody is going to get you into trouble. You know us better than that, Cluny, me lad. What do ye think we are? Haven't ye done a great thing this day?'

Cluny was bewildered. 'I have?' he said brightening.

Peggy nodded vigorously. 'Shouldn't you be proud of yourseln? Stop hitting him, Nellie.' Nellie had given him another belt, not a strong one but a firm clip nevertheless. She loved the opportunity of giving a fellow a belt when she could. It showed them their place!

'Leave him alone Nellie,' her sister said firmly. 'Cluny, I wouldn't wonder if it's a reward ye'll get. I wouldn't wonder at all. An' if yer asked what ye were doin', why ye were commin' over to us to ask if we wanted anythin'. Doin' us a kindness, ye were, an' who's to know otherwise?'

Cluny was nodding happily. Camilla had the whole picture now. She had fallen from the cliff into the river, and without a thought Aisling had dived in after her. She had got her out of the water, pumped her out, given her the kiss of life. Aisling had saved her life. She felt the tears stream weakly out of the corners of her eyes and over her temples, into her hair. She caught her friend's hand.

'Oh, Ash,' she said feebly. 'Ash.'

Aisling put her arms around Camilla. They clung together, sobbing in each other's arms, while Cluny puzzled over the rights and wrongs of the affair and ducked out of Nellie Kilty's way for she kept swinging her arms, fists clenched in an alarming manner, and Peggy decided it was time for some nice hot tea.

Cluny got a reward. Charles Vestry gave him twenty pounds, and everyone said how generous he had been. Camilla knew, however, that an envelope had come from Slievelea with two £10 notes inside it and a request that it be given to the young man who so promptly took the girls to the Kilty cottage, thereby saving them from double pneumonia or heavens knew what complication brought about by cold and shock.

There were no more visits that summer. The Casey family went to Italy and France where they were staying with friends, the de Beauvillandes, and having a bit of a break, Livia said in a note to Caroline. Camilla spent a week in bed. She felt hot and cross and the time passed slowly. She wrote a lot and read. She felt sick when she thought of the twenty pounds and her father taking the credit for it. Sadly she watched the swallows sitting in rows on the slanted boughs of the trees outside her window. They know that summer, the golden days, are over long before we do, she thought.

Chapter

9

TIME passed. As the girls grew older and turned seventeen, Aisling grew startling in her beauty, awesome in her glamour. Camilla found it very difficult. The lovelier her friend grew, the more jealousy reared its ugly head.

Now Aisling went abroad in the holidays to the de Beauvillande family in France and the d'Achettas in Italy. Her absences had the effect of alienating them even more, for Aisling, try as she might, could not share her cosmopolitan experiences and Camilla, prickly at the best of times, was acutely aware of the gulf that had opened up between them, and envious of her friend's travelling. She remained stuck at home, a plump seventeen. But always on her trips to Dublin Mr Klein was there, helping her with her writing, encouraging her.

The girls were beginning to be encouraged to go out with such eligible offspring of their parents' friends as were available.

'A crowd of pimply youths has suddenly crawled out of the woodwork,' Caroline said. 'They're hopping around like fleas at a cattle fair.'

In those early days the boys and girls were still wary of each other, tentative, ready to retreat at the slightest affront to their dignity, unsure of themselves and shy. Caroline was anxious that Camilla meet the right young man. It was her dream that she should marry the scion of one of the old moneyed families. Then, in their generosity, the boy's family would take Mount Rivers under its wing, debts would be paid, repairs done, and she, Caroline, could at last buy some decent clothes. Charles Vestry was very keen on the scheme too, completely forgetting his own mistake. He often suggested a little get-together, encouraging Camilla to bring her friends home for a drink and a buffet meal for the young people, and, because of money, asked Camilla to keep it simple, which she did. But he was anxious that as soon as possible she marry well. 'It would be an end to all our problems,' he said.

Aisling was to have a huge coming-out party at Slievelea on her eighteenth birthday. Until then the girls had managed to steer fairly clear of the boys. They played tennis with them, and listened to records, but their parents were always around and although there was a lot of horseplay, sly glances and sniggers in corners, neither sex had really taken stock of each other. All that changed at Aisling's party.

Livia Casey had written to Caroline on a small card enclosed with the invitation to the ball.

Please allow me to make Camilla a present of her first ball-gown. I would deem it an honour if you could see your way to indulging my great desire to do so.
  Ever Yours,
    Livia.

To Camilla's horror, Caroline and Charles refused even to entertain the idea.

'Be under an obligation like that to those Caseys? They'd never let us forget it.'

Camilla wished her father would get it out of his head that everyone else behaved and thought as he did. She was aghast at the thought of a lovely creation chosen by Livia slipping through her fingers.

'Oh, Daddy. Mrs Casey and Ash aren't like that, I promise you. They have never once mentioned that Ash saved my life that day by the river. Never once.'

'There, you see,' Caroline joined in. 'We are under an obligation to them already. *And* Dan Casey refused your father's request for a loan.'

'Oh I'm *sick* of hearing about that. The Caseys have been lovely to me, and I think you could ...'

Charles interrupted her. 'Don't you *dare* speak like that again. And don't you lecture us about the Caseys. We know more about them than you do, young lady. So they think I can't buy my own daughter a dress for their blasted ball ...'

91

'Well, you can't. Not like the one Mrs Casey would have got for me!' Camilla screamed at him, and ran out of the room before he could say any more.

Secretly Caroline would have loved to accept Livia's offer, and knew, as Camilla did, that it came from the kindness of her heart. If their situations had been reversed, she would have done the same for Aisling. But it was no use arguing with Charles, he had no such generous impulses.

Caroline drew in a deep breath and decided to allow Caitlin to slightly alter her best green chiffon Schiaparelli gown. It was her favourite dress but she would willingly make the sacrifice, although she knew it would not be appreciated by her daughter. Well, she thought, why should Camilla appreciate it? She saw only that a brand new dress was available for her, and thanks to her parents' pigheadedness she could not have it.

Camilla was scathing about the altered dress. The fabric was sea-green and matched her eyes but the dress, the one that Caroline had worn that night long ago when Camilla had stolen the *tarte* seemed curiously old-fashioned. It had an elegant Grecian line instead of the wasp-waisted, strapless look in fashion.

'Jasus, I look like a granny,' Camilla wailed, tears in her eyes.

'Nonsense,' her mother said. 'Come along, Camilla. No dramatics. It's a beautiful dress and you look lovely in it.'

'It's a cast-off, so it is. I wonder just how many girls tonight will be wearing their Mammy's old dresses. They'll all have lovely new ones and I could've had if you'dve let me! I don't want to go at all.'

But she went. Marty Tullough took her over in the trap and she arrived in stony-faced fury among the slamming of the doors of Bentleys and Daimlers and Model Ts. Down she jumped off the trap, her head held high, her cheeks bright red with anger, her mother's old beaver jacket over her shoulders.

Devlin greeted her and a maid took her coat. There was an orchestra under the great staircase in the hall and dancing had started. Livia looked exquisite in a black sheath, cut low, with two narrow diamanté straps over her pale shoulders. Big Dan stood beside her, handsome, tall and smiling, flashing his teeth in a wicked grin. And Aisling ... Camilla gasped. She looked more beautiful than ever: tall, slender, her blonde hair straight and full of light, like spun-gold. Camilla saw how excited she was, luminous with joy and anticipation, but, Camilla thought, she had an aura that somehow isolated her.

Her gown was ivory satin, quite plain. The stiff material billowed from the narrowest of waistlines, the boned bodice curving over each breast. She wore cream gloves to her elbows and her great-grandmother, Deirdre Rennett's pearls at her throat and in her ears. She looked like a Princess waiting for the inevitable happy ending. It had to happen for Aisling, Camilla thought, as Big Dan put his arm around his daughter and led her on to the floor for a slow fox-trot. She had everything else. Her life had been like a fairy tale, and it would in all probability end in the same way. But her expectations were so high!

Camilla had no expectations at all. She hung back, hating her dress and her shoes, cheap ones that pinched. But she wasn't going to let anyone see. No one was going to know how she felt, Cinderella coming to the ball in her mother's cast-off dress. No one must see how furious she was. She drew in a deep breath, tossed back her red hair and walked defiantly to the edge of the dance floor.

'I'll show them,' she thought, green eyes flashing. She was so angry that her cheeks glowed pink. She sparked with rage and tension as she stood there alone for a moment, sweeping the room with a bold glance. Her smile was wide and mischievous, unconsciously seductive as she tapped her foot impatiently on the floor. She was unaware of the effect she was having on the boys as she looked at them, bright challenge in her eyes.

She was alone only for a moment, then they came from the four corners of the hall, eager to dance with her. They came as if drawn to a beacon, a magnet. She stared, astonished, at the circle of tuxedoed young men who suddenly swarmed around her, not understanding the effect she had on them. She was completely unaware of her own vitality, the challenging sparkle in her eyes. But she was very grateful. She sent up a prayer of profound thanks to whoever was looking after her, and thanked the good Lord that these boyos knew no better.

'Milla, give us a dance?'

'Can I book one, Milla?'

'Milla, let's hop.'

'Milla, care to cut a rug?'

'Milla, don't leave me out.'

Tossing her red hair she played up delightedly. She looked at them from beneath provocatively lowered lashes as she had seen Rita Hayworth do in 'Gilda'. A whole battery of tricks she didn't even know she knew came to her aid. She quick-stepped with one admirer, fox-trotted with another, sambaed with a third and jived with a fourth. The band played 'Slow Boat to China'.

'I'd like to get you, on a slow boat to China, All to myself alone,' Alan Maguire sang in her ear. It didn't matter that he had a boil on his neck.

'You're breaking my heart 'cause you're leaving. You've fallen for somebody new,' wailed Emmit Riley to her, looking at her with passion-filled eyes. It didn't matter that he had a cast in one.

'I want some red roses for a blue lady, send them to the sweetest gal in town,' Andrew McNamara warbled at her, breathing whiskey fumes and the heavy smell of nicotine all over her. It wasn't important. What mattered was that this shining night held for Camilla the discovery that men liked her. They loved her. She moved from one dinner-jacketed bryl-creemed youth to another in a daze of joy at the discovery of her power over them. The band played 'My Resistance is Low' and 'Ballin' the Jack'. Saxophones sobbed, drums rolled, and Camilla floated on in a dream. Every shining moment saw not one, but two, three or four swains at her side. They were her slaves, her slightest wish their command.

Meanwhile, Ash danced with Big Dan. Then a stiff line of young men bowed formally and asked her for their duty dance, a courtesy to the daughter of their hosts, the 'birthday girl'. She held herself stiffly in their arms, and the sparkle and the glitter of her became hard and glazed. Camilla observed her only off and on, fully occupied as she was, but eventually she realised Aisling had stopped dancing. She was sitting there, a fixed smile on her face, a slightly desperate look in her eyes. All the other girls were having a good time. Even Georgina Jeffries, looking awkward in her long shocking pink taffeta and showing off as usual, was hopping merrily in Emmit Riley's arms. She was shrieking with laughter and seemed oblivious to the fact that she was at least three inches taller than he.

Camilla could not understand it. Aisling was the most exqui-site girl in the room. Perhaps that was the trouble, that and her intimidating dignity, her inability ever to be just one of the gang, to fling herself about as the others were doing. Perhaps it was because she was so rich.

'A group of young men surrounded Camilla. ''Scuse me, fellas. Hold on tight, I'll be right back,' she said, in a passable imitation of Mae West. She made her way to Aisling's side, noticing that her friend's eyes were enormous and dark with unshed tears.

'It's a lovely party, Ash, and you look beautiful,' she said. 'Just gorgeous.'

Aisling nodded. She seemed tense and nervous. 'Yes,' she whispered. She seemed to sag, her body drooping in the lovely satin dress. 'So do you, Camilla.'

'Are you okay? Is there anything I can do?' Camilla felt awkward. For once the words wouldn't come.

Aisling shook her head, looked at Camilla and said 'I was right, wasn't I? It's horrid growing up.' Then she sighed and added, 'For me, that is. For me.'

At that moment her mother came along with Emmit Riley in tow. He struggled to conceal his reluctance as Livia said, 'Darling, Emmit wants to dance with you.'

Aisling rose obediently, all her usual vitality gone, her move-ments stiff and self-conscious. Camilla could not help thinking that what Aisling had lost she had somehow gained.

'I'm worried about her, Camilla,' Livia confided. 'Why do you suppose those boys are so tardy?'

'It's not Ash's fault, Mrs. Casey. She's so lovely and the boys are a bit crass, a bit juvenile. She scares them. As a family, you're rather overwhelming and the boys are afraid.' Camilla felt herself blush as she tried to choose her words carefully. 'I wish there was something I could do.'

'How kind you are, Camilla,' Livia said.

And Camilla thought, I'm not. If only you knew ...

'Your mother was clever to dress you in that green chiffon,' Livia said. 'It suits you so well. Go off now and join your admir-ers. They are getting impatient.'

Camilla felt a surge of gratitude towards her. For the first time in her life she was pleased to be herself. She looked to where a clutch of young men awaited her and, pressing Livia Casey's hand gently, went to join them. As she crossed the dance floor they rushed towards her. Her red hair clustered in damp fronds on her brow and soft curls on her milk-white shoulders. She laughed at a joke of Alan's which was not *that* funny, and Andrew, his arm about her waist, smiled at her as she removed a shoe to ease her foot, wriggling her toes and wrinkling her small freckled nose, giggling up at them both.

'She has the knack of making them think they're kings,' Livia thought and her heart swelled with pain when she saw her daughter's white face and hurt eyes. She was dancing a quick step, stiff in the arms of the reluctant Emmit Riley.

Camilla saw Aisling stand alone and isolated as the night wore on. Part of her wanted Ash to see her success, and part of her was sorry for her friend. For Aisling the night must seem endless.

At last, after some hot soup at three o'clock, the guests started leaving, thanking Livia formally for a lovely evening, their laughter shattering the peace of the night as they piled into their cars and headed for home.

Camilla was the last to leave. Something held her back, sympathy for Aisling, a wish somehow to help her friend. She paused in the doorway and looked back over her shoulder as Devlin helped her on with her coat.

She saw Big Dan standing at the foot of the staircase, put his arm around Aisling,

'You beat them all hollow,' he said. 'You were easily the most beautiful woman in the room. Except, of course, for your mother.'

He doesn't see what has happened, Camilla thought. This is not a simple matter of being the prettiest, this is a heartbreaking thing.

She saw him kiss Aisling's forehead, heard her murmur, 'Oh, Pappy.' Camilla knew that Aisling would not let him see how hurt she was.

Don't you see? she thought. If anyone is to blame for this, he is.

Livia was calling instructions to the tired servants and complimenting them on a job well done,

'Tell Cook the chocolate soufflé was sinfully wonderful, and she surpassed herself with her crab mousse. Sheilagh, well done! You are to be congratulated. Tell Mary and Oonagh, too.'

Devlin said. 'Goodnight, Miss' and moved away from Camilla.

Livia noticed him. 'Devlin, everything went beautifully. Tell Paddy he has earned his increase. You all did very well indeed.

Breakfast can be late tomorrow, say from nine instead of eight. Aisling, my darling ...'

Camilla saw her friend move gracefully over to her mother. She looked weary and pale-faced. Livia spoke to her softly but Aisling shook her head.

'Mother, please don't say anything more. I couldn't bear it if you did.'

She kissed her and ran lightly up the stairs. Camilla slipped away, ashamed of her own happiness, sad for her friend's pain.

That year passed quickly. Aisling and Camilla went to the same parties, coming-out balls, dances at Kilcrony, in Dublin at the Shelbourne and the Gresham, hunt balls and tennis hops. They danced to Phil Murtagh and his eighteen-piece orchestra while the Bing Crosby sound-alike, Frankie Blowers ('Your favourite and mine'), crooned 'Heartbreaker' and 'Sentimental Journey'. They drank gin-and-it, and ate suppers of chicken and ham and fruit salad, and clung to their partners when the band played 'Good night, Sweetheart', and were grateful that scope for more amorous action was taken out of their hands by the proximity of their friends as they piled in, six at least to a car, for the home-ward journey. They kissed and cuddled a bit — an exploratory hand might find its way to an uplift bra — but nothing much happened. And truth to tell they were relieved, both boys and girls, that it didn't.

Camilla saw Aisling's continuing misery, saw how wary the boys were of her, how isolated she was by her wealth and beauty. She understood her friend's agony very well. She had suffered the same pain so often herself. The feelings were familiar, but it was as if an invisible barrier held her from Aisling, immobilised her and prevented her from sharing her friend's pain.

She had discovered that boys were interested in her and that she was the most popular girl in town. She did not wear her spectacles to the hops and balls they attended, and she had fined down and become slimmer. Maybe, she thought, maybe Mr Klein's prediction has come true. Her mother went on adapting her dresses to fit her daughter and somehow Camilla, lending her youth to the chiffon and the taffeta, with her halo of flaming hair and her vitality, her devil-may-care attitude triumphed over the cast-offs and won. She discovered boys admired her and that discovery changed her from a shy quiet girl to a real woman. She had a flirtatious manner and a sassy turn of phrase that made the boys laugh and put them at their ease. She unwittingly laid siege to the males of their set, and conquered while Aisling failed.

Camilla danced, had supper, drove hither and yon in battered cars and beaten-up jalopies, full of laughter and joking and hot hands exploring, surrounded by her admirers. They were not a very personable bunch, and she did not fancy any of them. Acne-ridden, inexperienced youths, yet familiar from the houses of her parents' friends, they were united by a similar background, could speak of people, places and experiences they all understood and shared. It was reassuring and gave her confidence. For once in her life she had the upper hand and the more she succeeded the more sure she became.

They always had hip flasks, her little group; they carried the 'tincture' wherever they went. The drive to Dublin was long, and a trip to Kilcrony took half-an-hour, and even the short spin over to neighbouring estates warranted a nip or two. They careered across country, sipping the fiery Irish whiskey until they reached their destination and more orthodox drinks were available. On the way home they popped into a bona fide where, so long as you were outside a three-mile limit (and weren't you always?), you could get a drink at any time of the day or night.

Aisling arrived and left in her father's Mercedes or the Bentley, driven by Devlin. She dazzled and intimidated through no fault of her own. Sometimes Camilla wanted to put her arms around the stunning girl as she sat alone, head held up proudly, tears swimming in her violet eyes unshed. Always unshed. If she had shed one tear, all the boys of Wicklow and Dublin would have been at her feet. But she never did.

Camilla's generous impulses were stifled at birth as Andrew or Emmit whispered in her ear or asked her to dance or lit her cigarette. They all smoked 'coffin nails' and said 'Match me' whenever they needed a light. She was so busy with boys she had no time to think of an answer to her friend's problem.

Then Aisling left Wicklow. Overnight, it seemed, she was gone. No one missed her except Camilla. No one had ever been conscious of her pain except Camilla. They heard she had gone to England to be in a film. They drank a toast to her and wished her luck in absentia.

Aisling sent Camilla a brief note.

Guess what Milla? I'm making a film!! Glam, don't you think? Wish me luck! I'll write soon.
   Love,
      Aisling.

But she didn't. Camilla never replied to the note. And anyway, she had lost Aisling's address. And anyway . . . and anyway.

Chapter

10

FOR the year after Aisling left Slievelea Camilla wrote seriously, about herself, her feelings, and the strangeness of human behaviour as she saw it. She finished her first book, *Requiem for Eithne*. It was a bitter little book, but then bitter little books were fashionable. It was redeemed from being trite by a depth of understanding for human frailties remarkable in so young an author.

Camilla took the manuscript to Mr Klein, written in longhand in exercise books filched from her father's study. She took it in fear and trepidation. He was not in his shop but his daughter Jessica was. She saw at once the young girl's distress.

'My father has gone into the country for an auction. I'm minding the shop for him today,' she said, pushing her wild black tresses away from her face.

She looked beautiful, Camilla thought. She must be the same age as Camilla's mother but she was lovely, and her manner, serene and humorous, seemed to imply that nothing really bad could possibly happen to her or anyone. Camilla knew she had a son studying painting in Italy. She had seen him once or twice in the shop, a tall handsome intense young man who did not look as if he could ever have been a child, this woman's baby.

Jessica Klein was asking her if she wanted some tea.

'Sit down a tick, do. Have a cup. The kettle's on the boil and there's some of your favourite Club Milk biscuits. We haven't seen you lately. I hope you've been well?'

Camilla obediently sat. 'No, I was busy. I was writing this . . . er, this.' She thrust the brown paper parcel out in front of her. She had wrapped the exercise books up carefully. Jessica took

100

the parcel and put it beneath the counter.

'I'll give it to Papa when he comes home.'

Camilla looked anxious. 'You won't forget, will you? I mean, it's very important. It was, well, a lot of work. I don't know what I would do if it was lost.'

Jessica smiled at her. 'Don't worry, poppet. It's safe here. Papa will get it the moment he returns, never fear.'

'You're very kind, Miss Klein.'

'Oh, call me Jessica. You're grown up now. Let's have tea and we can chat. I never get a chance when you're with Father. It will be nice to talk to you.'

She brought the tea out on an ancient lacquered tray. It was a beautiful object with a golden trellis pattern and delicate handles. On it were two cups, wide and shallow, with egg-shell blue borders and gold rims. The tea was Chinese and tasted funny but Camilla loved it; it made her feel elegant and mature, and the fine cups were so delicate you had to treat them with grace.

'It's Sèvres. Eighteenth-century,' Jessica said as they drank. 'My father came by the set accidentally. Half of the pieces were broken or damaged. Still, they are very valuable. Museum pieces really. I refused to allow him to sell them, I loved them so. My tea tastes so much nicer drunk from fine porcelain.'

Jessica held the cup to the light. It looked fragile enough to break in her fingers yet she never once told Camilla to be careful. She was profoundly honoured by the trust placed in her and did not feel in the least nervous of handling the exquisite porcelain. She looked at the colours, blue and gold, admiring its beauty and thinking how right Jessica Klein was; the tea did taste nicer. She felt very grown up to be sitting here chatting with this woman. She nibbled her Club Milk and said to Jessica in a manner she thought was sophisticated, 'And how is your son?'

'Alex? Oh, he's fine. Working hard. He's really a very nice person, you know.'

Camilla thought it an odd thing for a parent to say, but Jessica explained.

'Most parents love their children, and I love mine, but not many are friends — chums, as the English say. Do you have a chum?'

Camilla nodded, then shook her head. 'I used to. But not

101

really any more.' She thought of Aisling, wondered where she was now and how she was doing.

Jessica shook her head. 'Pity. It's sad to lose friends. Shared experiences are so precious. This friend, did you share secrets, confidences?'

Camilla nodded again.

'Well, that's how my son and I are. We are good friends as well as being mother and son.'

Camilla was silent. She had never asked about Jessica's son's father. Who was he? she wondered. Jessica wore no ring. A situation like that was beyond Camilla's experience and she did not quite know how to behave about it. For her, women were either good or bad. Good women were those like her mother and Livia Casey, Seidh Jeffries, and — yes, Jessica Klein. She did not belong with the bad ones, the 'good time girls' who always came a cropper. Anyhow that sort wore six-inch heels, red rouge, showed a lot of cleavage and dyed their hair. Jessica Klein did none of those things. Good girls got married and bad girls had bastards. Jessica Klein had a bastard, so what did that make her? It was very confusing and Camilla shelved the problem.

When she had finished her tea she thanked Jessica and left, begging her again not to forget to give the parcel to her father.

Hymie read it with mounting excitement. He was stunned by its clarity, its poetry and pain. He decided to enlist the help of Kieron Kineally.

Kineally was a successful playwright and novelist, lionised by Dublin society. He was forty years old, had a flat in Georgian Merrion Square, a French wife, Nicole, two sons, two Irish Wolfhounds and a Persian cat. He was a good friend of Hymie's and the two spent a companionable hour talking about Camilla Vestry in the Country Shop on the Green, drinking tea and nibbling fruit cake.

'She's a fine writer, Kieron, I promise you. I would not ask you otherwise, you know that. She's uneven and the book wanders a bit but it's got style and originality.'

'I believe you, Hymie. I've never known you wrong in a matter of taste. You could put your finger on quality blindfold.'

'Well, I know nothing of editing, but it seems to me the book is not in a fit state to be sent to a publisher. Please read it, see her for me and give her a helping hand.'

Kieron sighed inwardly. He hated being asked this kind of favour, but he and Nicole had benefited from their acquaintance with Hymie, adding considerably to their collection of *objets d'art* with his knowledgeable assistance. He had never asked anything of them before. Really, Kieron thought, he had no choice.

'Sure I'll see her,' he said. 'Delighted to.' And that was that.

Chapter

11

THE sun shone through the long windows on to the pale green
thick-piled carpet in the spacious drawing room of Kieron
Kineally's home in Merrion Square. He had the two top floors
of the elegant Georgian house. A brass plate on the door
indicated that B. Solomons MD, Gynaecologist, had his surgery
and rooms below. A faint disinfectant smell redolent of hospital
further testified to the medical presence.

Camilla sat, ankles crossed, looking intently at the man
seated opposite her, her heart wildly out of control. The room
was full of sunlight but as it was a March day a coal fire crackled
in the hearth. Camilla felt warm and at ease, much more so here
than she ever did in Slievelea or Mount Rivers. The style of the
room indicated a more manageable type of wealth. Salmon-
coloured silk damask curtains were drawn back from the long
windows through which the trees in Stephen's Green were
visible, new buds and tender leaves decorated the bare brown
branches. A clavichord stood in one corner of the room, a
carved eighteenth-century desk in another. The chintz-covered
sofa was deep and comfortable. Over the marble fireplace hung
four Jack Yeats paintings.

Camilla hardly tasted her tea, light gold, with a slice of
lemon, in a big delicate cup. She didn't touch her Bath Oliver.
Kieron, opposite her, dipped his biscuit neatly into his tea and
nibbled the damp part with relish. He was a big square-built
man in his forties with crinkly brown hair liberally sprinkled
with grey and strong, even, ivory-coloured teeth. His face was
tanned and scored with long lines that made furrows from his
nose to his chin and across his brow. His nose was wide and

104

straight. His eyes, brown and merry, twinkled at the tense young woman opposite him. He wore a leather-patched tweed jacket, heathery-coloured, rough-textured, and beige cavalry twill trousers, a fine-checked Viyella shirt and a wine-coloured silk tie. He had shining polished brogues on his feet. As she watched he swung one leg over the other and seemed to examine the toe of his right shoe, though in reality he was closely scrutinising Camilla Vestry. It was their first meeting.

He noticed her fine pale skin, the colour of buttermilk, and the dappling of freckles across her nose. He marked the strong curved mouth. It held a hint of pain, of endurance, of anger and perhaps cruelty? The chin was determined, the jawline firm. He looked with frank admiration at the riot of red-gold hair tumbling over her forehead and clustering at the nape of her neck. The eyes too, light green and pale-lashed, were enigmatic, cautious as an animal's, wary but hopeful.

He spoke when he had finished the last morsel of his Bath Oliver.

'Aren't you going to drink your tea? Would you prefer milk in it?'

'Oh no, no, it's lovely,' she said hurriedly.

'Then I expect you must want me to get down to business.' Her face lit up but she nodded eagerly and apprehensively. He said kindly: 'Don't worry, the news is good. In my humble opinion you are a gifted writer . . .'

It seemed to him that all the life left her body. She stared at him a moment, what pale colour there was leaving her face and her eyes becoming cold and lifeless in her head. She slid forward in slow motion and collapsed in a heap on the carpet, upsetting the cup and saucer in her fall.

Kieron jumped to his feet, startled, and rang the bell. He went over to Camilla and picked her up, laying her on the sofa as the smart young maid in her black dress and white frilly cap and apron came in. She had brought in the tea and Camilla had thought she was like a waitress in Bewley's.

Her name was Fidelma and Kieron asked her to help him with the 'child', as he referred to the visitor, though Fidelma felt she was far from childish in her behaviour and looks, and in years was at least eighteen like herself. Thanks be to God Kieron Kineally was an honourable and faithful husband to Nicole, his pretty French wife, away in Paris visiting her parents at the moment. If this was a faint then she, Fidelma, was an Indian squaw! But then, she thought, as she undid the top buttons of the redhead's cream *crêpe de chine* blouse, didn't he have to deal with actresses and the like in the Abbey and Gate Theatres, and weren't they, she felt certain, the kind of people who would lead such a handsome man a merry dance with their seductive ways and boldness and sauce, so surely he could deal with this teenaged amateur?

'Could you bring some cold water, please, Fidelma?' he asked, and she left the room reluctantly. She had no sooner gone than Camilla started to stir, sat up and then quickly fell back as the room spun about her.

'Sit still,' Kieron said. 'Here.' And he tucked a cushion behind her back.

Fidelma came in with the water and Camilla sipped it gratefully. The maid noticed spilt tea and insisted on getting damp cloths to prevent the carpet staining. Camilla tried to pull herself together and stop the buzzing in her head and the dizziness that assailed her each time she stirred.

When at last Fidelma had gone, Kieron, who was sitting at the end of the sofa, asked her when she had last eaten. Camilla looked shamefaced.

'Was it that that did it?' she said innocently. 'Oh, I'm sorry, Mr Kineally — I don't know what you must think of me. I was so excited, so nervous about meeting you and what you might say about my book, I couldn't eat for days.'

He had seen the hero-worship in her eyes when she came in. Now he took her chin in his hand and said gently, 'I'm not God, you know, but I'll tell you now you must have no more apprehension. It's a good book. It will be published and it will be a success. It needs a lot of work first, though, hard work. You're not afraid of that, are you?'

She shook her head.

'Well, that's good,' he said briskly. 'Now, I'll tell you what we are going to do. You will rest here. I have a few things to attend to, letters to write, phone calls to make. I won't, I promise you, be long. Then I'll take you to lunch in Jammet's down off Grafton Street.'

'Oh, I know where it is,' Camilla said quickly. She did not want him to take her for an ignoramus. He smiled and continued, 'We'll talk about your book then. How's that?'

Camilla gazed after him as he left. She heard him out in the hall talking to Fidelma, telling her he would be out to lunch. Later she heard him talk to several people on the phone in the hall. He cancelled an appointment at two in the Gate Theatre, apologising and saying he would be there later. He spoke in French to Nicole, whom she knew was his wife, calling her *ma chèrie*, but Camilla did not care. It didn't matter. She loved him. He was the most wonderful person she had ever seen, ever met. She knew she had met the love of her life. He was every-thing. There was nothing else. She stared into the fire and smiled a blissful, determined smile. It never dawned on her for a moment that she would not get him.

That night when she got home to Mount Rivers she was rest-less as a butterfly, hopping here and there, jumping up, sitting down, moving about the old house unable to settle. She could not sleep and got up after twenty minutes in bed. She opened her window and leaned out, gazing up at the tender sliver of a moon silvering the world, bathing it in irridescent light.

They never told me it would be like this, she thought, and felt her heart thudding within her as she remembered the hair curling on his neck and the blue veins that ran in dual lines inside his strong wrists. She remembered as a child deciding she would never have sex with any man. She blushed now, knowing that what she wanted more than anything was this man's hands on her body, this man's mouth to her's. Heart to heart, limb to limb. She remembered Aisling telling her 'Mother said it was beautiful', and knew now that must be right.

She shivered in the moonlight and leant her forehead against the cold glass at the side of the open window. Her brow was burning as if she had a fever.

'Oh Kieron, Kieron, Kieron,' she whispered to herself and the night, then she pulled down the window and shut it out. She went to the battered old escritoire and took out an exercise book.

'I must write down how I feel,' she said to herself. 'Exactly how I feel.'

In the late Fifties and early Sixties, the Dublin theatre was in a ferment. Exciting new productions were being staged and a crop of new playwrights was emerging, startling the theatregoer, provoking a new freedom of thought and challenging old moralities. In England there were John Osborne and Arnold Wesker, and in Dublin Kieron Kineally. Excitement and euphoria gripped the theatrical circles of the town and this perhaps led to his downfall. Everything seemed possible then. Guilt and remorse, honour and faithfulness, were words that had lost their meaning, gone out of style. The old plots, where justice was not only done but seen to be done, were defunct now and the theatrical conventions overturned. The 'angry young man' used four letter words and now the hero (they called him anti-hero) or lead was far from heroic. The well-dressed gentleman were out of date on stage. 'Anyone for tennis?' became a joke, and well-pressed flannels, dinner suits, evening dress and white trousers, one-time essentials, disappeared from the actor's wardrobe. Enunciated accents were discarded and regional burrs suddenly became fashionable. Jeans and tee-shirts became the accepted clothing. The theatre was never the same again.

The changes spilled over into real life, changing patterns of conduct forever. Little bars and cafés opened up and down O'Connell Street to accommodate the overspill of artists, actors, writers and intellectuals. People gathered to talk and the talk was rich.

In another climate commonsense might have prevailed, but this was a bonnets over the windmill era. And in the last analysis Kieron had been married a long time, and Camilla was very young. It was her youth, her innocence, that finally undid him.

She hung on his every word, which was flattering, but others had done that before. What precipitated the affair was the excitement released into the atmosphere, the sudden permissiveness that descended on the islands.

Camilla was in the grip of madness. Unable to sit and look at Kieron without her knickers becoming moist, her stomach churning, her knees refusing to hold her up, she hardly knew what was happening to her.

She behaved stupidly, hanging about outside his house, sitting on a bench in Merrion Square of an evening watching the guests drive up and enter his home, catching a glimpse of him at the doorway or silhouetted against the window. Just the sight of him caused her heart to pound and an ecstatic shiver to course through her body. She loved mooching about in the dark, knowing he was there at home, not far from her. She was lurking again as she had when she was a child, watching the grown ups in Mount Rivers from the top of the staircase. She felt close to him, united, but quite content to stay outside. She felt no jealousy at not being included on his guest list, content to wait, holding her breath in the wings, until he was ready to be hers. She never doubted for a moment that this would eventually happen. She never thought of his wife. She had nothing to do with it at all. She simply did not count in Camilla's reckoning.

All week, from Wednesday to Monday, was a preparation for Tuesday. Nothing mattered except those precious hours spent in his company while he helped her with her book. She did not worry how she looked, did not care about her appearance. There was nothing coquettish about her love, no sirens' tactics were employed. She sat on the chair in his drawing room in her old-fashioned Gor-ray skirt, tattered cardigan over her mother's handed-down *crêpe de chine* blouse, and worshipped him. She asked for nothing more and for a while these visits contented her.

Then one day, when she took a cup of tea from him, his hand brushed hers. That was all. The soft palm accidentally touched the back of her hand and the knuckles of her fingers, and such a shock passed through her body that for a moment she was stunned. Then she wanted with all her heart to touch him again.

It became a game with her. Her Gor-ray skirt was changed for a dress of floral printed cotton with a white piqué Peter Pan collar and she sat demurely in front of him devising a hundred ways to touch him, mostly his hands. She often managed to touch the sleeve of his jacket. Once or twice she had, after the most enormous struggle with herself, plucked up enough courage to lay her hand on his lapel when saying goodbye. It was a gesture she had seen Garbo make but the agony of nerves she suffered before attempting it prevented her from getting any satisfaction from the act. Then one night at the films she saw Joan Crawford touch Gable's face gently and thought she would try that, but Kieron's startled face as her hand moved towards his cheek checked her.

Spring was a long dress rehearsal for seduction. She day-dreamed about him constantly, fantasies of stunning unreality that always ended for her like the movies, in a long kiss and a fade out.

Once or twice Nicole came in to speak to her husband. She saw a scrawny redhead in glasses and old-fashioned clothes. Once she patted Camilla on the head as she passed, as if she were one of their Irish Wolfhounds. Camilla did not even feel her touch.

The days were long, filled with thoughts of him. The nights were restless, endless and feverish. Her nightgown stuck to her body which was aching and unfulfilled. She yearned, needy and pulsating in the heat she herself generated, for it was, as always, cold in Mount Rivers.

But none of it mattered. She was preparing. She was getting ready. She was like an actor waiting in the wings and she prayed her cue would come soon. All the sweated fumblings in the backs of cars, all the moist kisses, the groping hands of her partygoing days, seemed infantile and contemptible. How could she have thought it fun? Thought it grown-up? No, *this* was the real thing. This was love. This was the *grande passion* she had read about in books, and she waited for the inevitable.

Chapter

12

CAMILLA'S book was accepted. The letter arrived one breakfast-time at Mount Rivers. When she told her mother and father, who were reading their mail at opposite ends of the long mahogany table, her mother said, 'How nice, dear. Charles, darling, we'll *have* to do something about the heating here this winter. I don't think I can stand another cold spell without adequate heat.'

Her father was silent and Camilla said in the pause, 'When my book comes out, I could maybe pay for the heating.'

Charles said, 'Don't be silly, Camilla. Caroline, you'll have to work it out. I'm not a magician, you know. I'm not an alchemist. I can't manufacture gold. We'll just have to keep our horns in until I can work out a way ...'

His voice, heavily sarcastic, droned on and on and Camilla rose and left the room. They did not notice.

She went up the wide cold staircase, darkly shadowed, the boards creaking as she went. She remembered, long ago, taking the tart and how she had felt then. She thought now she would burst with joy. She went to her big dark room and, heart thudding, read the letter again.

Dear Miss Vestry,
We are pleased to inform you that we have accepted your novel, *Requiem for Eithne*, for publication ...

Tears of joy filled her eyes. She got off the bed and spun around, hugging herself and yelling: 'Yippee! Yippee! Yippee!'

I need to tell this to someone who'll really appreciate it, she thought.

111

She bathed quickly, splashing cold water on her shrinking flesh, then dressed in her prettiest twin-set and the inevitable Gor-ray skirt. She dabbed a hint of 'Evening in Paris', purchased in Woolworths, behind her ears, and left Mount Rivers.

She bicycled to the station and got the train to Dublin. It was a Friday. Camilla went, feeling odd about the fact that she was breaking a routine, to Merrion Square. The little maid answered the door.

'Mr Kineally's out,' she said triumphantly. Mr Kineally and Mrs Kineally might be ignorant of Miss Vestry's feelings, but Fidelma wasn't.

A hussy, a brazen young hussy, lust written large across her face and not a word will she get out of me . . .

'Where is he?' Camilla asked, well aware of the maid's dislike.

'I don't know and I can't say,' said Fidelma flatly.

'Please, it's very important.'

'Well, now, it may be important to you but that's not to say it's important to anyone here.'

'Fidelma!' The voice was admonitory but gentle. 'Don't speak like that — it is not *comme il faut*. Now, Mademoiselle Vestry, is it not? My husband is at the theatre this morning — can I perhaps give him a message?'

Nicole stood half in and half out of the doorway. She wore a neat little emerald-checked suit with a box jacket and a pill-box hat over her well-cut hair. With a sinking heart Camilla realised how smart she was, and sophisticated. Beside her, Camilla felt ugly and clumsy. Her husky accent was very seductive, but worst of all was the fact that she had called Kieron 'my husband'. It clanged like the knell of doom in Camilla's soul. There was something so final, so all-encompassing about that phrase 'my husband'. It brought to Camilla's mind, weaned as she had been on films, visions of frilly aprons, dinners by candlelight *à deux*, anniversaries, dancing together cheek to cheek, long understanding looks-without-words, a whole history she was excluded from. She did not want to dwell on these thoughts so said: 'Thank you. Thank you, Mrs Er . . .' and went down the steps and away.

Nicole and Fidelma watched her disappear towards Grafton Street, the Frenchwoman with amusement, the Irishwoman with fury.

112

Camilla caught a number eleven bus at the Green. It took her down Grafton Street and crossed the Liffey. She saw Webb's from the top deck and remembered how it had all started. On impulse she got off the bus, which was stationary in a traffic jam, and ran down the quays to Hymie Klein's little shop. She hadn't seen him for some time.

She waved to Kevin Brody in Webb's as she passed. He pursed up his lips and turned away. The thought of how one day her book would be on his shelves gave her confidence and she made a face at him through the glass.

Hymie and Jessica were glad to see her. They were reading a letter when she arrived.

'It's from my grandson,' Hymie explained. 'He writes to us from Florence in Italy. We think he is in love.' His eyes twinkled, and then he sensed she had something exciting of her own to confide.

'What is it?' he asked. 'By the looks of it Cupid may be at work here too.'

She shook her head. 'No, Mr Klein, it's my book. It's going to be published! Can you imagine that?'

The old man jumped up, grabbed her in his arms, and whirled her around and around, yelling for joy.

Jessica clapped her hands and shouted that she would get them a drink. She took out a bottle of sherry and poured it into tiny glasses. Camilla glowed with triumph as they stood in the little shop, glasses in hand, toasting her book. 'To *Requiem for Eithne*,' Hymie said, and they all raised their glasses and drank. Camilla drained hers and Hymie refilled her glass and they all laughed. 'Oh, my dear, I'm so proud of you. So very proud. Are your parents pleased?'

'They're not interested,' she said, tossing off the second sherry. 'I told them this morning and they didn't listen.'

'They will be. You wait.' Hymie filled her glass again. Jessica said, 'Be careful,' and tried to put the bottle away but Hymie grabbed it, saying: 'So she gets a little squiffy. Who cares? It's a great day. It's not every day a book comes out. The world is changed.'

'Oh, Mr Klein, I'm so happy. You know, up to this moment I hadn't quite realised it. It's true, I've got a book coming out. It's true.' She drank and put down her glass. 'Now I must be going.'

'Where ?'

'To tell Mr Kineally. I've got to tell him.' She kissed Hymie on both cheeks and left the shop.

All the way down O'Connell Street, past Easons (My book will be there too, she thought), past the Metropole, the Savoy and the Carlton, past the Gresham Hotel and O'Connell's statue, she thought, my book is to be published, but as the Gate came into view the thought became: I'm going to see him. I'm going to see him. It put wings on her heels and she flew up the steps of the little theatre.

'May I see Mr Kineally, please? It's urgent,' she said to the woman at the box office.

'He's up in the theatre, pet. They're rehearsing.'

Camilla ran up the carpeted stairs and, opening a door on her right, found herself in the darkened auditorium, halfway to the stage. Some actors were wandering about, script in hand, saying lines in a desultory fashion, looking at the ground and interrupting their speeches with 'Here all right?', 'This where you mean?', 'Is this right?', 'Am I OK here? I'm not masking Donal?', 'Hey, Fitz, can you see me?' 'No. No, that's fine — a little to the right.' Voices came from the front row and from the back.

'Who's that?' a small man in the front row asked as Camilla came in. Then she saw Kieron Kineally rise from his seat at the back of the auditorium and hurry towards her. He drew her gently outside, obviously concerned for her.

'What's the matter? Has something happened?'

'Yes,' she breathed, looking up at him with radiant eyes. 'They've bought my book, they want to publish it.'

He stared at her a moment, incredulous, then threw his arms about her, hugging her tightly and lifting her off her feet.

'Congratulations, congratulations, congratulations,' he cried, then looked down.

At that moment he saw her love and desire for him. The passion in her emerald eyes overwhelmed him. He looked and should have fled from the swimming green depths, but he stayed and held her and saw her mouth, half-open, rising towards him, moist, red and ripe. He touched her mouth with his, her lips welcomed him, curved around his, avidly drinking him in. He pulled away but it was too late. He had drowned in that one look, in that one kiss. He was lost.

114

Chapter

13

KIERON was furious. He loved his wife and children; he loved his life, the sweet flow of it, its regularity, its placid beat. He loved Dublin and the leisurely pace of life there. Dubliners did not rush; there was always time for a jar and a conversation full of dexterous twists and turns; an original thought; a meander off the straight and narrow streets of life into the wonderful leafy lanes of the unexpected. His life had been gently structured up to now, but elastic enough to allow for the occasional impromptu meeting. But this was different. This was dangerous. It could sow the seeds of his destruction, yet he had no power to stop.

He seemed to have lost control. It was as if he were ill and unable to function normally. Horrified, he feebly tried to stop the flood of feelings engulfing him, tried vainly to stem the tide of his passion. It was useless. Thoughts of Camilla infected him like a contagious disease. She had given him the fever she carried and their sickness was mutual. When they met their whole bodies underwent a change: their limbs turned to water; their pulses beat; their hearts' unruly pounding caused their brains to empty of rational thought, and madness prevailed.

He had always been careful of his reputation. No drunken genius he. His work, his life, was too disciplined for that. Yet here he was throwing caution to the winds. Everyone could see what was happening, but everyone could also see the futility of trying to use logic or reason against it.

'Sure, the madness is upon him,' the little woman in the Gate box office said, and half of Dublin echoed her.

Naturally Nicole was the last to find out, and although

Kieron knew she inevitably would, he was incapable of being discreet, of hiding his passion. Helpless as a kite in a north-easterly gale, blown hither and thither by the winds of emotion, he felt as feeble as an idiot and about as capable.

Part of the fever was caused by the complications their lustful passion for each other engendered. They were frustrated at every turn, which only added to their heightened emotions, the mounting intensity of their obsession. They met in coffee shops, pretty little places like the Country Shop on St Stephen's Green and Fullers in Grafton Street. They drank cocktails in the Russell and Hibernian Hotels. They had dinner in Jammet's or the Bailey. They held hands, their looks devoured each other, but that was all.

Where could they go? His Merrion Square home was out of the question and Mount Rivers was an impossibility. There was no way he could check into a hotel with her, he was too well-known and there were too many people who would be quicker than lightning in informing his wife. They twisted and turned in the cage of their desire, aching for fulfilment. Kieron could not get away. His play was due to open in the Gate Theatre in a few weeks and he was needed constantly. They sat at the back of the darkened auditorium and held hands. Their fingers were slippery with the heat their bodies generated when they touched. She slid her hand up and down his thigh and he stifled a groan, ready for her, aching for her.

It could not go on. They kissed in doorways, as indeed did all the young lovers of Dublin City, the pub entrances packed of a night with courtin' couples with nowhere else to go. They pressed and rubbed their bodies together, irritated to screaming pitch by the barrier of clothes. He pushed his hands up under her blouse, massaging her full breasts, her nipples taut and sensitive. Their mouths glued together, she stood on tiptoe to place her centre nearer to his swollen sex. They felt short of breath all the time, even with their separate families. Charles and Caroline did not notice their daughter's fevered behaviour; Nicole was aware of the change in Kieron and told herself it was because he was worried over the play, but was uneasy even so.

Then one day, rehearsals having progressed favourably since Kieron's creative energy seemed to have blossomed in a climate of passion and frustration, they took the bus to Howth. Summer had arrived. The Hill of Howth rose gently, purple and gold in the sunlight, draped in gorse and heather, splashed with the abundance of June. The sea, wayward and turbulent, was a surging silver cauldron crashing and tossing its white foam against the grey stones and onto the pier.

They went inland, hand in hand. They climbed the narrow pathways and found themselves on the mossy hillside in a sheltered place of fern and bracken, the honey smell of the rock-rose and the heather all around them. They were alone for the first time since they met. The sun shone warm on their faces and hands and they fell on each other like starving travellers or thirsty desert dwellers. Avidly, greedily, they locked their bodies together and clung as close as two people could. There was no time to undress. Clothes were simply pushed aside in an excitement that made them both cry out, Camilla in pain and then urgent desire, Kieron in an overwhelming need for her body.

Camilla seemed to know instinctively what to do. 'I'm beyond redemption,' she thought afterwards, and gave a cat-like sigh of contentment, stretching her arms above her head and tearing little tufts of heather with her nails. The great mystery is solved and, oh, how wonderful it is.

Afterwards they wanted more and yet more of each other. Their bodies refused to become sated and they consumed each other again with feverish abandon. They returned to the bus, weak-legged and tousled.

Camilla was tired out and content, satiated as she had never been before, her body stilled after its long fever, appeased and throbbing. They sat on the top deck, her arms inside Kieron's jacket encircling his waist, her head on his heart, drowsing in a languid lassitude. He cupped her head in his hand, holding her close to him. The red-gold strands that escaped through his fingers were silky and bright in the evening shadows. She made him feel proud of his potency. He was as delighted as a child at his performance. He had made her cry out in the hills again and again and he had felt spasm after spasm through the depths of her being. He felt young and dangerous.

Camilla thought, so this is it. This beauty and appeasement is what I've read about. Mrs Casey was right. It *is* beautiful with a man you love. And she was right about something else too — *I* am beautiful. Every bit of me is quite, quite lovely. And she sighed and buried her face in Kieron's jacket.

'All right, little girl?' he asked.

117

'Yes. Oh, yes,' she breathed.

She could see lights in the houses as the bus sped past. Beautiful houses, they were, set back from the broad tree-lined avenue. Each front room looked different inside, had its own character, reflecting the owner's taste, and was lit as if to stage a play. Families lived contented lives bathed in those lights, Camilla thought, but at this moment none of them was as happy as she. She doubted very much if any of those people, shut off from the street and the bus by their glass windows and their smartly painted front doors, had ever felt as she had, full of such joy it was painful. She felt sorry for the rest of humanity.

'I love you, Kieron,' she whispered. 'Oh, how I love you.' He smiled down at the tired face looking up at him. She looked so young, her face illuminated in the artificial lights which took all colour from her and left her ghost-like in her weary loveliness.

'I know, my pet. I know,' he said, and sighed.

They went again and again to Howth. The weather continued mild and sunny, full of birdsong and sweet scents, but they were unaware of it. They groaned and cried out in their pleasure and scared the birds away.

Camilla moved as if in a dream. Her body ruled her. She could think of nothing but the wonder of sensual discovery, the world of love which was sex. But Camilla was young. This was her first affair. Kieron, in his forties, was a sober married man and no mature person, he knew, could last at this peak for long. To do him justice he warned her, but she did not care, refusing to take him seriously.

'You know I'm a married man, pet.'

'Oh, hush, Kieron. Of course I know. Don't be silly.'

'Well, pet, there's no future for us.' What will happen . . .'

He did not finish, dared not contemplate what would happen. This girl had become essential to his well-being and he could not bear to face losing her. He closed his mind firmly against the unthinkable thought and Camilla aided him.

'Don't worry about that now, my love. Just don't. Think only of us now.' And he caught the line and held on. She could not see the future either but was sure it would end happily for her, had no doubt about it. It always turned out right in films so naturally it would happen in her life.

Now, when they were with other people, they did not need

118

the constant reassurance of touch. They laughed into the knowledge in each other's eyes, they shared the secret communion of body and thought private to themselves. 'I *know*, you,' their glances said, and all of Dublin knew that they were lovers.

They walked hand in hand through days golden with their love. Bicycling back from the station to Mount Rivers, Camilla never noticed the journey or how she reached home. Full of the smell, the feel, the pulse of her love, she pedalled in a daze, and at home became remote and unapproachable.

Caroline and Charles had discussed her book and now became curious about it. It was not important to them yet, but a glimmer of interest was born and they tried to get some information from their daughter, to no avail. She was preoccupied and answered monosyllabically. Charles hoped she was not sickening for something.

The financial situation in Mount Rivers had gradually worsened. The last of Charles's shares had been sold, the last of his father's paintings had gone under the auctioneer's hammer. Soon there would be nothing left to sell to pay the bills and he was mortally afraid.

His affairs were reaching a state of crisis which Charles could not bear to contemplate. He had developed an ulcer and his doctor had put him on a diet and told him not to worry. Not worry? Dear God, how was he expected to manage that? How in the name of all the saints could he not worry when the home of his ancestors, his whole world, was about to come crashing down around his ears? Damn doctors and their talk! Telling him not to worry about his home and future was like asking him not to breathe. He often thought of taking a gun and going down to the river and putting himself out of his misery.

Caroline was worried about both of them. She knew the strain Charles was under and she pitied him, and would have helped him if she could.

Camilla's behaviour smacked of romance, and Caroline was naturally worried, dreading that her daughter would end up 'in trouble', or fall for someone unsuitable, as she had done.

She bombarded her daughter with questions but Camilla seemed to be shielded by an invisible barrier that rendered her deaf and dumb and uncomprehending. Caroline was frustrated. Her daughter came and went, in and out of Mount Rivers, as she pleased, slippery as an eel and about as graspable.

The summer aided Camilla and Kieron, was co-operative, bringing them long shimmering days of blue and gold and green, warm with the heat of the sun and the fire of their bodies, but it could not last forever. Time, circumstances, conditions were against them. They lived for the moment, taking no thought for the future. But there had to be a tomorrow. It was inevitable. It was certain to bring pain, Kieron knew, but Camilla could not foresee it. She was too young, too raw and inexperienced.

The opening night of his play came and brought with it the first heartbreak for Camilla. It had not occurred to her that his wife must accompany Kieron to the first night, share the success or failure of it at his side.

'I'll get you a seat,' he told her apologetically, feeling despicable.

'Fat lot of good that'll be,' Camilla sniffed, close to tears.

They were sitting in the Country Shop. Middle-aged waitresses milled familiarly about serving afternoon tea. The place was homelike, wooden tables set on a red stone-flagged floor. The china was fine and the food all home-made but Camilla and Kieron did not eat. They sipped strong Indian tea and smoked.

'I'm married. We both knew that.' Kieron sounded resentful. He had not tricked her, not ever.

'I know, my darling, I know. But it will be hard for me not to be with you. Not to be part of your evening.' She smiled through her tears. He patted her hand and immediately, as she turned it into his and palm met palm, wanted her. He sighed, wishing it was not so, but could not stop the darts of desire that pierced his groin and made him clench her hand fiercely in his. She knew, of course, how he felt. She linked her leg around his under the table, their ankles crossing.

'Let's go. The sun is shining outside and . . . Let's go.'

She knew what he meant. They had not planned to go to their hill today, but they had to now.

They got the Howth bus and for the first time Kieron did not respond to Camilla's gay chatter. Before, he would have joined in the heightened gaiety of her conversation and enjoyed the air of being on holiday, like the first day off school. Today he could not. Reality was creeping in. He was frightened by his passion,

120

unwilling but forced by weakness to take this trip. The hill did not appear romantic any more and what they were doing seemed more animal than loving. But he could not turn back, could not now say 'Let's go home.' He had to consummate the act of love with her as soon as possible, or scream like a child deprived of a toy. When she arched her body to his, he again congratulated himself, felt inordinately proud of his quick erection, the youthful strength of his desire. He took her, they took each other, ecstatically. As she came, seconds before he reached his own powerful climax, he thought, she might get pregnant. Jesus, I must be mad.

It was the first time he had thought of it and he was astounded at his stupidity. How could he forget something like that? Probably because he had never had to before. Nicole, as she put it, 'took care of herself'. He who up to now had thought out the pros and cons, the whys and wherefores of every other situation, had not thought about this. He had been behaving like a lunatic. And for what?

He looked at the red-gold head. A fern had caught under the nape of her neck and it irritated him so he brushed it away. She looked up at him, worshipful green eyes darkened to jade by desire, mouth bruised and blurred by kisses. He felt his love for her overcome him again and he kissed her lightly on the nose.

Chapter

14

THE first night of Kieron's play was a festive and exciting occasion, the little theatre packed to capacity. Critics from all the Irish and a lot of the English newspapers were there, leading actors and actresses, writers and politicians — the whole of intellectual Dublin had come. Kieron Kineally was a gifted and talented playwright and the première of one of his plays was looked forward to eagerly. He was the centre of attention, the cynosure of all eyes as he entered the theatre with his wife hanging on his arm. She was tiny, Camilla knew, but beside Kieron she looked diminutive as a doll, as fragile as a china figurine. She wore black, a simple figure-hugging velvet sheath with bead-embroidered and sequinned detail on the shoulders. Her neck rose from it, slim and elongated like a Modigliani portrait, her eyes enormous in her tiny face, outlined heavily in the fashion of the moment.

Camilla had received her advance from the publisher and had splurged on a gloriously luxuriant green velvet skirt and gold blouse created by Raymond Kenna. Though the outfit looked wonderfully flamboyant on her, Nicole's spare elegance made her feel larger than she was, and a little overdressed.

Camilla had arrived early, anxious and full of dread. When she saw Nicole and Kieron enter the theatre, she lurked behind the programme-seller at the top of the stairs until they were parallel with her and then, seemingly by accident, knocked into him.

Then she looked into his eyes, saying loudly, 'Kieron, darling, how lovely to see you. I'm so looking forward to your play. I do wish you the best of luck — not that you'll need it, I'm sure.'

Her voice sounded shrill in her own ears and she turned to Nicole. 'Mrs Kineally — how nice to see you again ...'

But Nicole had lost all colour. Pale at the best of times, she looked now as if she would faint. She knew in that moment, as surely as if it had been spelled out for her, that this girl, this *gamine*, had been to bed with her husband. She knew, looking at his face, seeing the guilt, the lust, the terrible desire and the shame, that they had been together, that they had loved. She plucked at his arm and drew him into the auditorium.

Camilla sat not far behind them, slightly to their right, staring at Kieron's profile all evening. Her heart felt so full of conflicting emotions that she found it difficult to sit still. Jealously raged in her bosom along with anger and a desire to throw a tantrum, break up the auditorium, stand up and scream and tear all her clothes off. She also wanted desperately to put her head in her arms and sob her heart out. She should leave but she was incapable of doing that, she was pinned to the spot, tormented by seeing him but knowing herself incapable of leaving — like a masochist she would suffer it to the bitter end.

Nicole, too, was shaken by emotion. Her usually equable temperament was overwhelmed by a surge of Gallic outrage. How dare he? she thought. How dare he? That must be what's been the matter with him. I probably knew all the time. And with that little slut! That child who came to our house for help. How dare he?

Her face remained cold and calm, her hands still and relaxed. When Kieron heard an appreciative swell of laughter in the audience at one of his comic passages he took her hand in his own and she let it remain there, cool and lifeless as a piece of silk.

Only Kieron was unaware of the turmoil he was causing. He remained in the eye of the storm, unconscious of the havoc around him. He listened keenly and with growing appreciation to his play unfolding on the stage. Concentrating on his work, his creation's first public steps, he was oblivious of the two women sitting so near him, each wrestling with passions which made his characters half-alive by contrast.

The play ended on a second's pause as the curtain fell, then came that deep rumbling roar of approval that every playwright dreams of. It received a standing ovation, and cries of 'Author' sent Kieron up on stage with the actors for the final bows. As he rose and left his seat, the two women in the audience still clapping turned and looked at each other simultaneously. The venom they saw in each other's eyes scared them both half to death.

Camilla was first to leave. She went across the road to Groom's Hotel. She knew Joe and Patti Groom, the proprietors of the place, and was sure they would welcome her. She knew, too, that Kieron would end up there. It was where anyone who was anyone connected with the stage and radio came to celebrate, to bury a flop, to unwind, to be consoled or congratulated. She knew Kieron would go backstage to thank and congratulate the cast, then come here to compare notes with the director, to work out what would need changing or altering.

She sat alone at a small table and drank her sherry. Patti Groom, a large loving woman, pretty and good-humoured, asked her how the play had gone. They chatted and Patti gave Camilla another drink on the house 'To celebrate', then left her to attend to her other customers. A group from the Abbey came in, men in crumpled trousers and duffel coats and women dressed simply in wool dirndl skirts and dark jumpers. They sat near Camilla and spoke in Gaelic, drinking stout and shorts. A group from the film shooting in the studios at Ardmore arrived, curiously alien here, California-tanned, wearing light colours and not smoking. Then at last the Gate contingent started to filter in. Word of mouth had it that the play was a smash and they carried with them that aura of excitement, that hypertension engendered by success.

At last Kieron arrived. He was alone and on his entrance people clapped and held up their hands in salute or tendered a congratulatory grip of greeting. He stopped here and there in the smoke-filled room, throwing his arm around the director's skinny shoulders. He leaned over the table occupied by the Abbey players and said something. They all laughed, and when he straightened up he saw Camilla.

She did not know what to expect. She had not thought the evening through. She had been numbed and shaken by her emotion at seeing him with Nicole and, feeling dazed, had come here unsure what she wanted. He waved and turned away from her. That was all. She knew he wanted to be left alone, to enjoy this evening of success without her or, indeed, his wife, but she wasn't going to let him! She went to the hatch where the barman passed the drinks out and stood behind one of the Abbey players.

'Where's the party tonight, Phil?' she asked.

'I dunno,' he said, exhaling grey smoke as, cigarette in mouth, he picked up a tray of drinks in both hands. 'I'll ask Jim,' he said over his shoulder, 'and let you know.'

He went across to the slim young man who had directed Kieron's play. He was talking to the stage director and the A.S.M. from the Gate. Phil took a gulp of beer, wiped his mouth with the back of his hand and called loudly over the cacophony of conversation and laughter and shouts of greeting: '102; as far as Jim knows. That's where he's going anyway.'

Camilla was content. If Jim was going, Kieron would go too. It was inevitable. They had obviously not had time to discuss the play yet, what had worked and what had not, and Jim loved '102' so would drag Kieron there after him. She ordered another sherry, and when a young critic from the *Irish Times* poured another into her glass she did not complain. The young man, Padrig McConnell, and she compared views of the play. She decided he would be useful to her this evening so cultivated him. She flirted a little and asked him to take her to the party, which he was only too delighted to do. They stayed in Groom's until she saw, at the first calling of 'Time', Jim and Kieron slope off, ducking out of the lounge as unobtrusively as they could. Kieron did not even look back to wave at her, she noticed, and her stomach knotted with pain and tension though she knew he was still pre-occupied with the play. She stayed a half-hour longer then, clutching Padrig's arm, suggested it was time to go.

'102' was a basement in Ballsbridge. When they left Groom's the fresh air hit her, making her feel light-headed. Padrig drove badly, grazing the mudguard of the car parked beside him and careering across the road alarmingly on the way. Camilla did not care. When they arrived, the party was in full swing. The place was tatty, their host a poet, scholar and raconteur who had drunk away the last thirty years of his life and not published a thing since he was twenty. He gave parties here each Saturday, from closing time till dawn, for first nights and any excuse is good enough. He was good-humoured and tolerant of the bizarre, traits he needed as he attracted the most alcoholic and unpredictable elements in the Arts in Dublin.

The guests sat on chairs, on sofas and on the floor. People

were continually arriving and departing. There was a two-barred gas fire glowing meanly in the dim light. People lit their cigarettes from it and drank from cracked mugs and cups. There was a naked bulb hanging from a beautiful crumbling Georgian ceiling but it was off, the room lit dimly by candle stubs in empty wine bottles. There was a naked bulb in the kitchen too, and that one was on. There was a heightened level of noise there, as if the volume of sound was dictated by how much light was available. A group of people stirred a pot full of spaghetti, cut bread, mixed butter with garlic for it and tossed salad.

Camilla saw Kieron dimly, sitting in an armchair in the corner of the room. A spring was poking out from the arm and he was idly plucking it as he spoke earnestly to Jim who sat at his feet. Camilla let them alone, watching carefully from the door of the kitchen where she could see them without being seen. She chatted with Padrig, half-heartedly giggling at his risqué jokes, and allowing him to plant a wet kiss on her cheek now and again. At last she saw Jim look up and Kieron stretch his arms. They were still exchanging conversation but the main body of their discussion had obviously been successfully completed — you could tell that by the way each man's concentration wandered. They let up on each other and started to notice what was happening around them in the room. The play, discussed, post-mortem held, could now safely be left until tomorrow. The time for enjoyment had arrived.

In the kitchen, people were piling spaghetti bolognaise onto plates and Camilla grabbed two fully loaded ones and slipped quickly over to the men. 'Hello, you two. Have this. I'll get you some salad. Back in a tick.' Kieron watched her out of sight. He felt momentarily trapped, and then he saw the curve of her buttocks outlined against the velvet seat of her skirt where she had been sitting. Jim caught his glance, read it accurately, and when she returned with salad took his and excused himself, leaving them alone together.

Camilla sat down on Kieron's knee. She forked spaghetti into his mouth, and into her own. She wiggled her bottom on his lap and pressed her body against his, hating herself for what she was doing but unable to stop. She knew once again she had won.

She felt him grow hot for her and saw the glaze of desire across his eyes. His hands trembled as they touched her skin. She whispered, 'Come on.'

'Where?' he asked stupidly.

'Upstairs. In a real bed,' she said.

'Oh, no. Oh, no.'

'Why not? No one will notice. They won't care anyway. They're always . . .'

She stopped, biting her tongue, for she had almost said. 'They're always doing that here. Nearly every Saturday night someone goes out.' He knew what she meant and every decent instinct in him rebelled, but his desire for her was too strong and he followed her. Their host came reeling over.

'Ah, Kieron Kineally, the poet and playwright who sold out to Mammon, the hallmark of the mediocre. House in Merrion Square, play at the Gate — and will ye look what else he's got. Scarlett O'Hara herself in green and gold. Jesus, what did you do to deserve it?' And he staggered away to insult someone else.

They left their spaghetti on a mantelpiece overflowing with full ashtrays. They crawled over some people on the staircase and found the room. Moonlight made it bright as day. Kieron swept coats to the floor. The floorboards were bare and the bed was covered with a fur rug. They took their clothes off and looked at each other in the silvered light. There was sadness in his face, Camilla thought, and lay on the bed, arms outstretched, pearl-white body open ready to receive him. There was a yearning in their coupling, an unresolved ache in their lovemaking. This time there was no cataclysmic burst of energy and swift explosion but a long slow build up, a crescendo of minor erotic quivers, sweetly unbearable and full of longing. It seemed to Camilla that they were seeking a permanent soldering of body, an eternal melting into each other, when sadly each knew that every joining had to end.

They lay spent in each other's arms for a moment but were in a hurry to dress and rejoin the party. Yet when they did they both found it intolerable and left. Separately.

Two days later Camilla received an invitation to Merrion Square. It was couched more like a command. Mrs Kineally would like Miss Camilla Vestry to have tea with her on Wednesday 16th July at four o'clock in the afternoon. The letter had been posted on Monday and obviously timed to arrive on Wednesday morning, thus giving Camilla no opportunity to duck out without appearing ill-mannered. She felt scared and apprehensive, guilty but defiant.

She dressed carefully and took the train to town. She was simply clad in a pleated olive-green wool skirt and matching jacket, and a holly-red sweater. The weather had turned cold and a nasty east wind whipped down the Liffey and followed her to Merrion Square where it tried vainly to strip the trees prematurely.

Fidelma the maid opened the door, giving Camilla her usual hostile stare.

'Mrs Kineally, please,' she said triumphantly. 'She is expecting me.' Fidelma's jaw dropped.

Camilla had armed herself for the meeting, fantasising a scene reminiscent of those in the novels she so avidly read or the films she saw. She imagined herself facing the wronged wife with courage and dignity, maintaining an air of gentle sorrow and apology for her culpability but standing firm in her love for the woman's husband and her determination that he belonged to her.

She was not, therefore, prepared for the sight that met her eyes. As she entered the room Camilla saw her adversary sitting on the sofa flanked by two boys. The eldest, Camilla saw, in her confusion was nearly identical to his father; the same hair, nose, eyes. Even the way his hair grew was similar. He must be about ten, she thought. The other boy, leaning gracefully against his mother, bore her likeness; small, shy, with a sweet smile. They made an utterly disarming picture. Camilla gasped, and was suddenly totally defeated.

'Sit down, my dear,' Nicole said from the sofa. She wore black again, simple soft wool with pearls. 'Have some tea.' She lifted the pot, which seemed too heavy for her fragile wrists. 'Meet our sons.'

Our sons. What a world of imagery the words conjured up. Sons meant begetting, fathering, night-time vigils, childhood ailments, mutual anxiety, pride in the first steps and words and days at school, joint nurturing and domesticity. The family. The family.

'Sean and Seamus.' The boys rose and politely shook her hand. Sean passed her the cup of tea without spilling a drop, his bottom lip caught between his teeth as he carried it to her ever so carefully. Seamus handed her a plate of fruit cake cut into pieces. Nicole murmured on in her soft accented voice: 'They are home from school — what do you call it? — the long vac.

128

So, they can be carefree and their father can take them to the rugby and that appalling Irish game — what is it?'

Seamus was giggling, poking gentle fun at his mother's ignorance. Sean said: 'Hurling.'

'Ah, yes. Please do not laugh at me, *mon petit.*'

'Oh, Mother, you know the football is over. But Father will take us riding and swimming at Blackrock, and we'll have picnics at Howth.'

A fiery pain exploded in Camilla's chest and she prayed, 'Let me get out of here, oh Lord, without breaking my heart or killing this woman who, after all, is only doing what any wife worth her salt would do for her family. Lord, there is no fight in me at all. I cannot defeat this. I can never win over this — the odds are stacked against me.

She took in the room, cosy against the grey day, lamps lit, tea tray casually untidy, napkins crumpled, crumbs on the embroidered white cloth. The clean fresh faces of the boys looking at her, innocent and guileless, pierced her heart with regret and yearning.

If only it could have been me, she thought. If only this was my home, my children, if only he was my husband.

But they were not and never would be. She was the outsider. He would always cleave to this little family grouped on the sofa. She knew Kieron Kineally well enough to know that. She was his weakness; this woman, these children, his strength.

She rose to go without touching her tea. Nicole rose too. She only came to Camilla's shoulder but might have been made of steel. Nevertheless there was pity and understanding in her eyes as she looked at her rival. She held out her hand. Camilla shook it, dropped it and stumbled out of the room and into the street. She stood there, her face bathed in tears, then walked down Grafton Street sobbing, without seeing anyone or noticing the traffic. She turned into Clarendon Street Church and lit a candle. She blessed herself and knelt and prayed. Her thoughts were hopelessly jumbled.

She demanded that God strike down Nicole and Sean and Seamus and take them to His bosom of love, thus leaving Kieron free to marry her. But she didn't want them or him to suffer so she took that prayer back. She prayed that she wouldn't care about Kieron any more, that she be cured instantly of her passion. She sobbed and begged God to take away her pain. In the incense-filled gloom of the echoing church, she watched the candles flickering in the dark and knew that it was all useless.

Then she left the church and retraced her steps back up Grafton Street. She went into Neary's and ordered a sherry. It was dark in the pub, and it smelled of stale cigarettes and beer, but the atmosphere wrapped around her, warm and reassuring; a limbo for sufferers, a waiting place between the problem and its solution.

She sat at a table in an alcove and sipped her drink and wondered what she should do. She felt drained, and now and again a sob shook her, making her shudder. The barman clicked his teeth in sympathy. He was used to all sorts here. The whole spectrum of humanity and its passions — sorrows, excitements, successes and failures, broken hearts, loves and hates — walked through his doors, drank their drinks, confided or were mono-syllabic, as their natures decreed. It was all the same to him. It was life and that was what a pub was all about. He looked at the redhead. Broken heart, he thought, love trouble, and shook his head sagely. No good ever came of love in his opinion.

She looked up at him. 'Can I have a coffee, please?' she asked, pushing the sherry glass away from her.

'O'course, an' why not?' he said, and started the coffee perculator.

He turned to smile at her but she was no longer looking at him. She had taken a notebook out of her bag and was busy writing.

She did not see Kieron again after the meeting with Nicole in Merrion Square. She avoided his haunts, staying well away from the area he operated in. She realised now that it was a relatively small area: Merrion Square, Grafton Street, Duke Street, the Gate and Groom's. Their whole love affair had been concen-trated into a season and a very tiny dot on the map, she thought. Two dots, for there was Howth. She had not wanted to remember Howth. Her heart twisted within her and she wished, against all logic, that he would try to find her. He easily could. All he had to do was write to her care of Mount Rivers; all he had to do was look for her, Dublin was so small. But he never did.

In her heart she knew he was relieved that his summer madness was over, that he could return to the bosom of his family, his organised, disciplined life. She knew now that he had hated the disruption, the subterfuge, hated the deceit, hated the lies. Headstrong, she had led him on, caring nothing for the consequences. He had stood no chance from the beginning, poor man. He had never told her he loved her, she thought wryly. She had taken his passion for her to mean that he did.

Now left with cold reality Camilla determinedly pushed him to the back of her mind, the place reserved for memories and material for her work. She had a choice, she thought, looking at the facts realistically: she could play the tragedy queen or she could get on with her life, pluck out the pain and the hurt pride, and channel her energies into her work.

She drew in a deep breath every time she saw a tall man in a tweed jacket. Every time she thought she saw Kieron she felt faint, but she was ruthless with herself. She had chosen life. The same could not be said for her friend.

Chapter

15

LIVIA Casey's early death from cancer saddened Camilla though, to her horror, she found herself making mental notes of her feelings for use in her work.

Livia who had shown Camilla great kindness, had always seemed young and invulnerable to her. It did not seem possible that she could be gone. Camilla remembered all the lovely gestures she had made to her daughter's friend, and wished now she had taken more time to show Mrs Casey her gratitude.

Camilla had not even known that Livia was ill. She had not written to Aisling for she had been far too tied up with Kieron. But then Aisling had not written to her either.

Charles and Caroline were shocked by Livia Casey's death. Caroline, who was Livia's age, was stunned and not a little frightened for herself. If it could happen to Livia Casey it could also happen to her. She felt sorry, too, that she had not been nicer to Livia. She had always liked her but had never had the gumption to do anything about it because of Charles' hatred of Big Dan Casey.

Over the years, as things had got progressively worse at Mount Rivers, Charles had again asked Big Dan for a loan, to be told: 'I don't hold with friends borrowing from me. Not people I and my wife socialise with. It doesn't do, y'know. Makes for bad feeling. Embarrassment.'

He found it hard to accept this from a man he considered his social inferior. Well, now Dan's beloved wife was dead and while Charles felt as sorry as Caroline did, he felt too with a flare of self-righteousness that fate had, for once, evened things out.

It was late summer and hot, strange weather for a funeral in Camilla's view. It should be raining, she felt. Slievelea's own little cruciform chapel of grey stones nestled in the lee of the mountains. It was packed. Charles, Caroline and Camilla had driven over from Mount Rivers and crushed themselves into the church where the rest of Caroline's family, the Jeffries, rallied as usual around the Caseys although they did not like them. Few could afford to give such feelings rein.

A lot of Camilla's old gang were there: Georgina Jeffries, her face bloated with crying; the boys she had danced with in those, to her, far off days of their 'coming out'. She looked around the little stone building. The sun shone through the stained glass windows casting multi-coloured patterns on the polished wood floor. Alan Maguire still had a boil on his neck, and she wondered if it was the same one he had never got rid of, or if they came monthly, like her periods. She started to giggle at the thought and her mother stared at her, outraged.

'Shut up, Camilla. Control yourself,' she admonished her daughter, wondering what on earth had got into her.

Andrew McNamara was there with his parents and his hateful sister who was flirting with Emmit Riley. She was smiling across the church at him in a very wanton way, but Emmit had eyes for no one but Georgina Jeffries even though, Camilla thought maliciously, her face was like a punch-drunk boxer from crying. She had never realised that Georgina was so devoted to Mrs Casey, then remembered that the girl was a cryer. Whenever anything at all happened, Georgina either broke into high-pitched laughter or burst into a wailing flood. 'I pity poor Emmit if he wants to live with that apology of a human being', she mused.

She could see, up in the pew at the front, Aisling and her father. Aisling looked distraught and years older, but then she had loved her mother very much.

The change in Big Dan's appearance was even more shocking. His piratical good looks had gone, his face seemed ravaged by grief. She remembered how she had never cared about Dan Casey's reputation. She had always felt that if he could provide such luxury for his family it did not much matter if he was Jack the Ripper. She remembered, too, how she had admired his male handsomeness, his good looks. He cried openly as the organ played and Father O'Brien conducted the Requiem Mass.

133

He was no longer dashing, she thought, as she watched his body stoop and tremble and Aisling catch his elbow. Camilla caught a glimpse of her friend's profile and drew in her breath as she recognised pure hatred in the look she gave her father. How could that be? she asked herself. Aisling had always loved Big Dan, been besotted by her father. Camilla decided she had imagined the look and glanced over at David who was weeping in Sheilagh's arms. The loudest sounds in the chapel were his sobs.

Afterwards, in the bright sunlight under a madonna-blue sky, Livia was laid to rest beside her grandmother and grandfather and the rest of the Rennetts and Caseys.

Slievelea opened its doors then to the County families, and the friends and relatives from Dublin. And Camilla saw as she watched Aisling and Big Dan together that something more appalling than Livia's death had occurred in the family. She tried to talk to Aisling, but she was too busy with the guests.

'Later, Milla. I must talk to you later. Please stay.' She sounded desperate. Camilla was completely thrown by her friend's wild-eyed looks and panicky movements and found herself agreeing to stay the night.

Camilla waited patiently for the guests to go. She wandered about the house, admiring its beauty again, the graceful proportions, the paintings and the statuary, the priceless carpets, the exquisite furniture delighting her eye and relaxing her the way aesthetically pleasing things always did.

I'm not jealous any more, she realised. I can look at these things and not covet them, simply appreciate them. How nice.

She looked out of the dining room window on to the lawns. The sprinklers were shooting starry sprays of water over grass so green, so lush, and a delicious thrill of resolve danced through her body.

I can do it, she thought. I can make Mount Rivers look like this. Well, perhaps not so grand, but certainly in its own way as lovely. I can make it look cared for and prosperous again. Mother and Father don't realise it yet, but I'm going to be able to do it.

She hugged the thought to herself, savouring it joyfully, before she heard her parents' voices in the hall and hurried out.

'We're going,' her mother said, and Camilla noted how truly distressed she looked and she realised that her mother had loved

Livia Casey though she had probably never realised how much until today.

'Are you coming?' Charles asked. He was restless, she saw. He was always edgy in Slievelea. Its affluence made him uneasy, generating a guilt that he did not understand and did not try to analyse. Camilla shook her head.

'No, Father, I want to talk to Aisling. She's very upset.' They left and Camilla went to find her friend. Sheilagh was clearing up in the morning room, her eyes balloon-sized from weeping.

'Miss Aisling's in the library, Miss,' she hiccupped, her body shaking under the weight of her grief. 'And Mr Casey is in his study with Spotty Devlin — you know, Devlin's father. Oh, Miss, I don't know what he's going to do without her. He's distraught, so he is. Sure she was a saint itself, she was, an' never an unkind word. Oh, Miss, I'm that upset. I'm sorry.'

She blew her nose and Camilla hugged her. The maid held on to her for dear life for a moment as if drawing strength from the young body then she detached herself.

'Oh Gawney Mac, Miss. Forgive me.'

'Nonsense Sheilagh. We all loved Mrs Casey. It's natural for you to feel like this. Please don't worry on my account.'

Oh Lord, I sound like my mother, she thought, and went in search of Aisling in the library.

The room was full of early afternoon sunshine. Camilla remembered as she sat and looked into Aisling's grieving face how once she had coveted this room, envied her friend the many books.

Aisling seemed to be making an effort to pull herself together. 'How chic you look Camilla. And you've got so thin.'

'With difficulty. With enormous difficulty, Aisling.' Camilla laughed wryly.

Aisling looked emaciated. Her eyes were enormous, like large wet pansies. Then she lowered her head and for a long time there was no sound in the room save the ticking of the French clock.

How are you, Ash?' The walls of books around them seemed to absorb sound. Camilla's voice barely broke the silence.

'My father hates me, Milla.'

Camilla was startled. Big Dan adored Aisling, everyone knew that. She began to protest but Aisling stalled her.

'You, too. You've always hated me, off and on. Everyone

135

seems to hate me and I can't understand it. I must know, what did I do to deserve it? You see, Milla, it's a mystery to me.'

'I don't hate you. What makes you think that?' Her stomach felt sick. 'I love you, Ash,' she protested.

'Don't lie to me, please. I'm not stupid. And now my father has inflicted such a blow ... She stopped and a look of intense pain crossed her face. Camilla crossed the room and knelt at her feet, crushing Ash's cold hands between her own.

'It wasn't hatred — it was jealousy. Rotten, lousy, craven jealousy! You were — are — so beautiful. You have so much. I hated *that*, not you.

'I tried to tell you but you never seemed to understand. We had no money at Mount Rivers, none at all. So little that a shilling lost could upset the delicate balance of our finances. Here in Slievelea you had everything a human being could desire, and you weren't even conscious you had it. You took it all for granted. Naturally, we were jealous.'

Camilla sighed, 'I wanted to be careless, Ash, just for once to lose something or stain something and for it not to matter. I wanted to be able to afford something small and unnecessary. Many's the time I walked down Grafton Street and lusted after a lipstick in Brown Thomas, but I could never afford one. Can you imagine how I felt when you discarded yours long before they were finished? A whole Max Factor lipstick — think of it!'

Aisling smiled faintly, and Camilla shook her head. 'I sound such a cow, Ash. I was horrid and you didn't know, were completely, marvellously unaware. When you passed by, all the men turned their heads to look at you.'

'They may have looked at me, Camilla, but they cuddled you. You got on with them easily while I just sat and waited.'

'They were frightened of your beauty, your money, Slievelea, Big Dan — all of it. It doesn't matter now, Ash. I'll be a success in my own right. I'll never be you — I don't want to be any more.'

Aisling said tonelessly, 'I feel cold, Milla. Very cold and very lonely.'

Something in her face frightened Camilla. 'Let's get drunk,' she said.

Aisling shook her head. 'I don't drink, or only wine. I don't like alcohol.'

'I do. Whenever the Black Dog sits on my shoulders, when

the screaming meemies rear their ugly heads, when fear and dread gnaw at my guts, I have a drink. We'll have brandy. It's grape, so it doesn't count.'

She crossed the room to where the decanters sparkled in the evening glow. The sun was high but to Camilla it felt like winter. She poured two large drinks and brought them over to Aisling.

'Here,' she said, 'an end to pain. At any rate, for today.' They drank. Aisling coughed when she swallowed a mouthful; the fiery liquid burned her throat and tickled the back of her nose.

'You'll get used to it,' Camilla said. They were drinking in companionable silence when the door opened and Big Dan came in. Camilla rose to her feet and, stretching out her hand, advanced towards him.

'Oh, Mr Casey, please accept my sympathy ...' Aisling had her back to the door, her chair facing the French windows. Big Dan said, 'Thank you, Camilla. Your mother and father have been most kind.'

Aisling had risen. She turned to face her father. 'Get out of here,' she said, her voice venomous.

'Ash! Your father ...'

'Shut up, Milla. You don't know anything about it.' Suddenly she let out a low moan as if she were in physical agony, and rushed out of the room.

Big Dan looked at Camilla. 'Please help her. She needs help,' he said hopelessly.

Camilla picked up the drinks and followed her. She found Aisling standing at the window of her room, staring over the lawns towards the sea. The Sugar Loaf mountain was bathed in gold dust and the Slievelea lands looked fresh and verdant in the mild evening light. Last day of summer, Camilla thought. She sat on the chaise longue and patted the seat.

'Come, sit down.'

Aisling shrugged. 'What does it matter?' she said. 'What on earth does it all matter now Mummy's gone.' Her voice broke.

'You'll get over it, Ash.'

'You don't understand.' Aisling began to bang her head again and again against the glass, saying over and over, 'You don't understand, you don't understand.'

'Explain then,' Camilla said, and put the glasses of brandy on

137

an exquisite little rosewood table. She rose and gently took Aisling by the shoulders.

'Come sit over here,' she said, and when she had pushed Aisling down on the chaise she gave her the drink.

'Drink up.' Aisling took a gulp and coughed again, then finished the contents of the glass as if it were medicine. 'David's here somewhere. I have to help him. He's lost.' She rose to leave but Camilla gently pulled her down again.

'No, don't go. Your brother will be all right. Let's talk.' Camilla knew that something terrible, more terrible even than her mother's death, had happened to her friend. Livia's death would cause weeping and sobs, not this dry and arid agony. Wisely Camilla said nothing. She waited.

Then Aisling looked at her and asked, 'Have you ever loved a man?' Camilla felt her face grow cold and her lips stiff. She thought of Kieron.

'Yes.'

'Well, I loved a man, too, and my father's had him shot.'

Camilla was shocked. Of course she had heard the rumours about Big Dan Casey. In gossip he had often been linked with violence. Big Dan Casey and the Nazis, Big Dan Casey and the Mafia, Big Dan Casey and the sudden disappearance of enemies. This, however, was something else.

'I don't believe it,' she said.

Aisling shrugged. 'Well, don't then,' she said lightly.

'No, Ash, no. I didn't mean that. Tell me, please.'

'It's very simple. I can't tell you why because I don't know but my father had my boyfriend shot. Only he wasn't just any old boyfriend. He was my life, my soul, my heart. There is no life for me without him. I am dead, dead. Deader than my mother in her cold grave outside.'

Camilla did not know what to say or do. Silence fell in the room. The brandy had worked. It had broken Aisling's icy reserve. Camilla let her talk.

'Do you remember, Milla, how I always suspected I would not be able to cope outside Slievelea. I wasn't prepared for the world outside. Do you remember that awful coming-out party? Oh, the nightmare that was! Well, after that I would have liked to stay in Slievelea, here with mother and father and David. I could be an old maid, I thought, and sit stitching in a window and not go to those dreadful balls and parties any more with you lot. Then I'd never have to feel rejected, I'd never have to fake indifference, pretend I was calm and unaffected when underneath my heart was breaking. But that would never have done for Pappy. He was proud of me, wanted to show me off. He never saw my pain. Do you think my father knows about pain? I don't. Well, I couldn't bear the burden of his expectations for me here any more, so when Herbie Goldmyer offered me a role in a film I jumped at the opportunity to leave Ireland, go to London and make a new life for myself. Even that, though, Pappy had fixed. I found out afterwards, he was the chief backer of the film, 'The Lady From Vauxhall'. It was awful trash really.' She smiled wryly at Camilla, who still said nothing.

They were pleased with her at the studios, she said. 'The Lady From Vauxhall' was finished ahead of schedule and she looked good in it. She was well behaved and biddable, did what she was told, was always on time. She ached to please, worried at the slightest show of disfavour. A frown could send her into a panic, a cross word made her anxious.

'You have to be hungry for success', the director would say, and I wasn't. I think that my childhood, the security that Slievelea gave me, Pappy's money, all stopped me feeling the yearning that makes a real actress. I didn't mind that so much, but away from Slievelea I lost my courage.'

Aisling, who had been blessed of the gods, who had known nothing but kindness, been cosetted and protected all her life, was suddenly exposed to harsh reality. People out there, away from the all-embracing love of her home, could be critical of her. She had somehow to earn their respect and acceptance but she didn't know how.

She had no one to cling to, cast adrift in a sea of strangers, the halcyon days of her childhood over. Even her name had been changed. She was now Aisling Andrews, actress, a new identity that held no reality for her.

People in the studios were not awed by her looks. To them beauty was a marketable commodity, to be dealt in like any other. She found herself in a world of lovely women and wealthy men. The men were older, they had large noses and smooth olive skin, smelled of cologne and cigars. They took her dancing at Ciros, and dined her at the Ritz and the Mirabelle. She felt comfortable with them, they reminded her of Big Dan. Although totally unlike him in looks they nevertheless had his mature masculine assurance, were masterful and in charge, made her feel at ease.

They never made passes at her. There was something about her that forbade intimacy, a sort of shield of innocence.

She bought a flat in Paultons Square off the Kings Road. It was small and pretty and she was content there. It was like a womb, a burrow, a place to hide away from the challenge of life.

Herbie Goldmyer became worried about her. She was so distant and she looked permanently tired, as if living exhausted her. It was not natural. Beautiful young girls should have boyfriends, admirers, but she had put up a screen between herself and the rest of the world. After 'The Lady From Vauxhall' was finished, he told her he thought she should take a little holiday.

'Go home to Wicklow, to your Pappy, to that gorgeous house you've got there,' he said, patting her hand, and chewing his cigar.

She shook her head. They sat together on a narrow banquette in the splendour of the Mirabelle. She wore a black velvet gown and her beauty glowed like a diamond. When he danced with her, people whispered about her. She was taller than he by a head but seemed unembarrassed as they moved around the tiny dance floor, the small orchestra playing 'Blue Moon'. When they sat down he asked her again.

'Why, Aisling? Why?'

'I can't. Don't ask me, Goldie. I just can't.'

'Well then, go somewhere else,' he said with a shrug. 'France, Italy. The world is a big place.'

She thought of the de Beauvillandes and the d'Achettas and sighed. 'No, Goldie. The people I know in Rome and Paris and Ireland, they ask too much of me just now. I can't explain it.'

'Well, go somewhere you've never been: Madrid, Granada, Florence . . .'

Her face brightened. Florence. She had visited it once and been enchanted by its beauty. There was no one there that she knew. Why not go? Why on earth not? To get out of London, away from these cold islands, to be alone for the first time in her life, a stranger in a strange land. Aisling smiled at Herbie Goldmyer and nodded.

'I think you're right,' she said.

And so she came to the pink Tuscan town and met him.

140

Alexander. Her face lit up radiantly when she spoke his name.

'He was everything I ever desired in a man, Milla,' she said, 'He knew so much, taught me so much about art, about the world. Up to then I had taken Pappy's ideas and beliefs as my criteria but Alexander introduced me to a whole new dimension of life. He was an artist, and even I could tell he was superb. His paintings were full of compassion and love of humanity. He knew me only as Aisling Andrews, the actress. I didn't tell him about Pappy for he was very socialist-minded, very idealistic, and felt rich people like my father exploited the poor. I didn't want him to know I was one of that despised class. Besides, he was Irish too and might know my father's name. I didn't want anything to spoil it, I adored him so.

'We went everywhere. He took me to the Pitti Palace and the Academy, explaining the work of the masters, Michelangelo, Raphael. Can you imagine, Milla? I was young and impressionable, he was handsome and learned. We were together in Florence, where the air is always balmy, the sun shines all day and at night the sky is thickly jewelled with stars. He gave me a feeling of total security. I trusted him with my heart and soul and eventually my body.

'Our days were filled with excursions on his Vespa, me tucked in behind him, my cheek on his jacket. We went to Fiesole, Padua, Siena, Verona, magic names, magic towns. I felt carefree and enchanted. Every evening he took me back to my hotel, brushing my lips gently with his, whispering, 'I love you, *cara*.'

I told him I loved him too, then rushed up to my room. Then he would phone and tell me again that he loved me.

'Our love affair blossomed and so did I. He took me to his favourite place, Taormina in Sicily. We took a little house on the hill overlooking the sea. I knew he had been waiting, wanting me to be sure. I became a woman in his arms. I grew in confidence and love. Oh, Milla, how can I describe it to you ...'

She buried her face in her hands. When she had recovered she continued.

Taormina was permanently drenched in sunshine yet it was always cool; cool sea breezes on their faces, cool marble underfoot, cool courtyards ablaze with brightly coloured flowers, cool fountains playing in the sun. They learned tenderness and passion on each other's bodies and fell in love more deeply day by enchanted day.

'I was like Sleeping Beauty and he the Prince who kissed me to vital, throbbing life. Yet it was almost as if we were afraid that we had too much, that such ecstasy could not be permitted to last. We savoured every minute, every second together. Then I made an error, a terrible mistake. I wrote to my father to tell him of my happiness and give him my address. No one else knew where we were.'

She shivered, fighting for control.

They planned to marry.

'Will you love me when I'm old?' she had asked him, lying in bed one afternoon with the sunlight shining through the slats of the blinds.

'Probably more than I do now, though I can't imagine that,' he had replied.

'I'm afraid it will all end,' she said. 'It's so good, so beautiful.'

'No, it will never end. You are the most loved woman on earth. Believe it.'

Alexander left the house first that afternoon to race her to the beach. She heard a couple of sharp retorts, like the sound of a car backfiring. For a moment she paid them no heed at all and then an icy shiver coursed across her skin. She ran, blinking, into the sunlight to find Alexander lying twisted on the ground, his cheek pressed to the gravel, chest running with blood.

She was stunned when she lifted his head gently on to her breast, smoothing back his black hair and kissing his pale face. A grave-faced doctor arrived and shook his head, gesturing for two ambulancemen to carry Alexander away quickly. Her cries of agony echoed from the hillside until the white-faced doctor drugged her into a merciful sleep.

She awoke in a white-painted hospital room but all she could see was the colour of blood. Alexander's blood on her hands, on the grass and all the lonely years stretching out, a pain-filled future looming, the loss of her beloved making the living of life unbearable.

She had never really believed the bad things they said about her father, never felt he deserved his reputation for ruthlessness. She guessed the bitter truth on that hillside in Sicily, and when she had seen him Big Dan had not denied it. He refused to tell her why. Not only Alexander was lost to her. In one vengeful swoop the gods had taken Alexander, Big Dan, Slievelea. She could not live there while it was the home of her lover's murderer.

Aisling was exhausted when she had finished. Camilla's heart went out to her friend and she remembered what her mother had said.

'She has too much. The gods are jealous.'

There was silence when Aisling had finished speaking. She leaned back, her face white, utterly worn out. Camilla sipped her drink slowly and let the peace slip over her like a cloak. She held Aisling's hand in hers.

'But why in God's name did your father have him killed?' Camilla asked.

Aisling shrugged. 'I don't know' she said hopelessly. 'But some day I'll find out.'

The door opened and Aisling's brother David slipped in. He blended with the shadows, Camilla thought. 'Is he a goblin, a faery child?'

'I'm scared, Ash,' he said, ignoring Camilla.

'Sit beside me, old fella,' Ash said comfortingly despite her own weariness. They sat there a long time, silent, the three of them, while the dusk fell over the land and darkness closed in. Then Mary, the maid, arrived to take David away and light the fire.

'For it's a wee biteen chilly of an evening,' she said.

David cried and said he did not want to go.

'I want my Mother, Ash. I want my Mother so badly. I can't bear to think of her in the dark damp earth. I can't bear to think of her in that little coffin, shut up. It was so small, so small. She loved the space and the air. I want her back.

Aisling hugged him to her, crooning over him. She was very maternal towards him, Camilla saw. The maid closed the curtains and lit the table lamps. She turned back the oyster satin eiderdown on the bed Camilla had once coveted. Now she would not have changed places with Aisling for all the possessions in the world. When the significance of the thought struck her she was amazed and then felt a great tide of regret for all the years, all the wasted opportunities for love and kindness, all the jealousy, the envy, the corrosive emotions that had plagued her and kept her from her friend. She could have been more generous, she thought. She could have been kind.

Mary left the room, taking a reluctant David with her.

'Your Mammy is in heaven, Master David. You never fret now, alanna, your Mammy's safe with God.'

They heard his voice, plaintive and lonely, receding down

the corridor. 'I don't believe in all that stuff, and anyway I want her here.'

The girls sat quietly together until there was a knock on the door and Devlin came in.

'Dinner will be at nine, Miss Aisling.'

Aisling sat up. Her face was very pale.

'Oh, no, Devlin. I don't want any.'

'But Miss Aisling, Mr Casey ...'

'I do not want any dinner, Devlin. I want to be left alone. Is that clear?'

'Yes, Miss.'

The door closed softly behind him and Aisling slumped back in her seat, giving a bitter little laugh.

'My father is down there, and he is scared of me. After what he has done to me, *he* is scared.' Then she turned to Camilla, 'You said you know about love.'

'Yes, Ash, I know what it's like. My love affair started last spring, with the first cowslips, and it ended just before your mother died.'

'You, too! That's when Alexander ... when we ... We had such a short time, Milla.'

Camilla pressed her friend's hand. 'It's worse for you, Ash, you've more things to overcome than I have, but we will come through I'm sure. Oh, now I feel as if I'll never truly be in love, never again feel that peak of excitement, that total submerging of all my thoughts and desires in another person ...'

Aisling broke in, 'I *know* it, Milla. I *know* I won't.'

'You think that now,' Camilla said. 'I thought that about Kieron. But the worst has passed and life does go on.'

'Why did it end for you?' Aisling's voice was brittle as candyfloss. She sounded remote, Camilla thought.

'Well, he was married with children. It's the same old story, Ash, a married man. Wouldn't you know it'd happen to me? His wife found out about us, and well, she asked me to tea. I went round and found her there with Sean and Seamus their two angelic offspring.' She felt the tears rise in her throat. It was her turn to sound brittle.

'What could I do Ash? She won. Without a fight, without a word said, she won hands down. I was vanquished, defeated. Now, when I think I see him in a crowd, my heart jumps and then starts beating fifteen to the dozen. Or when someone laughs his laugh in a room, or smiles a smile reminiscent of his, or a song we loved is played, or I see Howth Head in the sun, a lump comes into my throat. So many things are painful now that were not before.'

There was a pause then Aisling said, 'Milla, somewhere in the world Kieron *is*, your lover *is*. He exists. Perhaps someday, somehow, you'll meet again and it will work out for you both. There is hope. Your affair might have been a cliché but you had the luxury of choice, and eventually you did the right thing. You were left with your dignity. There was no violence ...'

Her voice breaking, she continued, 'Alexander was more than my lover. Try to understand, Milla. Our meeting was a coming together. We were useless apart, at peace together. We were whole at last. There was fire in our love but it was contained, not consuming but warming, renewing us every day. And my father whom I loved nearly as much as I loved Alexander, had him shot.'

Camilla was appalled to see her so stricken. Her eyes were clouded with grief, black as jet, dark with suffering.

'Mamma might have helped me, but she's gone. That man walks about this house, free, with blood on his hands and I am *sick* with the loathing that is in me. God help me, Milla. God help me.'

In the end the tears came, flooding from her in a stream while sobs tore her body. Camilla held Aisling close, rocked her, cradled her as if she were a baby. When at last the storm was over, Camilla rang for Sheilagh and together they undressed her and put her to bed. Before she left the room, Camilla leaned down and kissed Aisling's forehead.

'Sleep, dear Ash. Sleep heals. Everything passes,' she said.

She said it sadly, regretfully. Somewhere during their conversation she had realised that she did not want Kieron Kineally any more. As she turned to go Aisling said,

'Milla? We'll always be friends now, won't we?'

Camilla squeezed her hand and tucked it under the sheet. She kissed the pale forehead and said, 'Always, Ash. Forever and always.'

As she fell asleep Aisling remembered another voice saying that to her. 'Always my love. Forever and always,' she blinked her eyes, and did as she was to do for many a night to come: she pushed the thought of Alexander away.

145

PART TWO

Chapter

16

ALEXANDER Klein persuaded himself that he loved his little island off the coast of Brazil. He could paint there, feeling himself akin to Gaugin or Rousseau. The faces were alien, the customs strange, the climate extreme and as unlike Ireland and Italy as it was possible to be. There was nothing there to remind him of Europe, of home, of Aisling. Yes, it was an ideal setting for forgetfulness. The past could not impinge on him here, could not hurt him with insidious memories. He did not have to be reminded of her by the sight of bluebells or violets or the vision of a fine blue mist over a green mountain. This was a land of extremes, the colours primary, the temperature hot and humid, and although he hated it it suited him.

And he had his painting. He had moved through life curiously untouched by the things that affected most people. He lived in his head and in his art and nothing else had the power to touch him — except Aisling. Not even the discovery that he was Big Dan's illegitimate son had disturbed him. It seemed to him an irrelevance. His primary concern was his art, always his art. After that came his love for his family. His beloved mother, Jessica, and grandfather, Hymie, gave him a security he happily took for granted. He was used to it, encircled by their love. It had formed a shield between him and an unpredictable world.

Then Aisling came along and the onslaught on his heart and mind shook him to the very core. He loved and was loved so completely. And then suddenly, on a Sicilian hillside, it was over in a blaze of agony and brilliant light.

The physical effects of the mock assassination had been severe enough. There had been the long, feverish journey by sea

149

to Brazil, drugged past the limits of safety and prey to a nightmarish sequence of half-dreams. On arrival, he was dumped in a hospital in Rio. Hymie and Jessica found him there, following him to Brazil without a thought, leaving their beloved little home and shop behind in pursuit of Alexander.

They rescued him from the hospital. Alexander remembered little of his time there or of the voyage until, recovered from his physical wounds, he demanded an explanation of all the events that had brought him here. When the story was told he was determined to find Aisling again.

Then the terrible words had been said. 'She is your sister, Alexander.'

He had been incredulous at first, then furiously angry with himself and Big Dan Casey. He couldn't find it in himself to blame Aisling for her small deception in using her screen name, not after he had revealed his contempt for Big Dan. If he had only told her then about his parentage, all the pain might have been avoided. But so too, he realised, would the ecstasy of their coming together.

Broken, and sick at heart, Alexander channelled all his remaining strength into his painting. What he put on canvas was his soul, and it saved his reason.

His days and nights became a feverish marathon of painting. He felt the inspiration welling within him, impatient for expression. Was this Nature or God healing him? he wondered. Or had sorrow and despair accelerated the creative process? He did not know. He just went with the flow of it.

He hoped that Aisling, wherever she was, had something as potent to hold on to. He realised with a sense of shock that he did not know how she really felt about her acting. There was enormous sadness in the thought.

'We had so little time, my darling,' he thought as he slapped oil on canvas. The brush took life from his emotion, becoming a living extension of his arm, and his arm of his heart.

He hoped that she would heal and he prayed that she would use her art as a means of salvation.

He knew how vulnerable she was, and he could not bear to think of her agony. He cried sometimes as he walked the deserted beach in the moonlight. He railed too and shook his fist heavenward, then, realising how useless it was, took out his paints. By the light of the moon and the stars so near he felt he could touch them, he set to as if his life depended on it. And it did.

The island did not suit his mother or grandfather. It was too far from Hymie's little shop on the quays, and unlike his grandson he had no dark memories of the past. Life had been good there. Martha, his wife, had died, it was true, causing him great sadness. She had been his partner, his lover, his friend, and he sorely missed her. But her death had been in the fullness of time; she had lived a goodly span of years.

Jessica's presence had alleviated the pain of loss. Their daughter, the manifestation of their love, had enchanted him from birth. She was beautiful, and fiercely individual. He had dreaded her marriage and departure from his home. Hymie had tried to prepare himself for the eventuality, for it seemed inevitable to him that a girl as beautiful and voluptuous as Jessica would soon be persuaded to the altar. Instead she had fallen for Big Dan Casey.

Hymie had realised from the first how ambitious the young Dublin boy was, and that marriage to Jessica would hardly be Dan Casey's ideal. He would marry only for money or status.

Hymie had never dared criticise their liaison. He did not want to lose her. When Jessica bore Dan Casey's son Hymie was doubly glad: first, because he loved his little grandson and could afford to indulge that love with Jessica to provide parental discipline; secondly, because Jessica's decision to keep Alexander's existence a secret from Big Dan Casey kept her and the child at home with him. Hymie could enjoy the luxury of the presence of his daughter and grandson without any outside influence. It was a unique situation, which enabled Hymie to live a life of complete content until his beloved Martha died. Then, as time passed, the immediacy of his pain faded, Jessica and Alexander more than making up for his loss.

Hymie was totally unprepared for the tragedy that swept through their lives like a tornado, devastating all before it, smashing and maiming the three of them in its violent passing.

That Alexander should fall in love was something Hymie and Jessica mused over in the amber glow of the little back room behind the shop. They hoped it would be a girl they liked, approved of, but if not they planned to bend over backwards to accept whoever it was. They knew Alexander's gentle loving nature and felt confident that he would attract someone similar.

151

'Like attracts like,' Hymie would reassure Jessica.

Time passed, however, and Alexander, though a hit with the ladies, seemed uninterested in settling down. He was so totally immersed in his painting that he had no time for serious entanglements though there were many love affairs, soon over, soon forgotten.

Until Aisling, Big Dan's daughter, and therefore Alexander's half-sister. How could it have happened? Hymie asked himself. Out of all the world, why did he pick that particular girl? Hymie would look at the ceiling of this unfamiliar room, in this strange land, the fan gyrating around and around, the curtains blowing in the faint movement of air it generated, and ask, 'Why?' There was, of course, no answer. It happened, and it had devastated them all.

Big Dan's violent reaction and its consequences had aged Jessica. She had lost the last of her youth forever during the nights she thought her son was dead. She did not fully recover even when she found that Alexander was alive and Big Dan had shipped him to Brazil. Even when she held him to her heart the joy could not return her youth to her, could not reverse the effect the shock had had on her. At the news of Alexander's supposed death, she had dressed in black, in a throwback to the custom of her Mediterranean forbears. Even when she discovered that her son was still alive she remained dark-garbed and grieving for she too had lost her lover. It was painful for Hymie to see his daughter age, his grandson devastated, and to find himself in his old age, which he had confidently expected to spend in his beloved little shop in the moist, misty city of Dublin, an exile in an alien land among strangers. He felt totally out of place here, a man in a milieu he neither liked nor understood.

However, he made the best of it. He saw his prime duty clearly; to look after Jessica and help her to heal, to be patient and understanding with Alexander's naked grief, shock and horror. And he succeeded. It required marathon strength but he gave unstintingly, with boundless generosity, from his great fund of love.

He was also very rich, a fact he had never given much thought to before. He had been content to live in the little shop, dealing fairly with all his customers. The financial success of his business was not his primary concern, which was probably

152

why he had amassed a fortune. As long as they made enough money each week, to feed his family, clothe them, keep a sound roof over their heads, he was content. The surplus went into the bank, accumulating more and more interest.

He purchased an imposing Spanish-style home, and thus they found themselves part of the social life of the island, invited to dinner, fought over, fussed about because they were new, a novelty. They brought a little colour, a *soupçon* of excitement to lives rendered boring by the heat, the unchanging round of people to visit and be visited by because there was nothing else to do.

Most of the people on the island had good reason to bury themselves in obscurity. They were a rackety bunch, except for the Spanish grandees who had settled here many, many years ago. If the truth were told about the rest, the Johnnie-come-latelys, the island's 'high' society consisted of a couple of international crooks who had escaped with their ill-gotten gains and were wanted by Interpol, an ex-Nazi, who loathed the Kleins but had to put up with them as he did not want to lose his place in the only social life available to him, and a group of tax exiles.

The Kleins dined once a week with one family or another and asked them back to the *hacienda* they lived in. Their homes were all similar; the rooms big and dark, shaded and cool, out of the burning sun; the furniture heavy Baroque or Jacobean, made of rich, dark woods. Portraits of ancient grandees hung in the gloom on the walls, constantly threatened by damp, and the light was never allowed to penetrate. The home the Kleins lived in had belonged to a family which, for reasons unknown but widely speculated upon, had abruptly left and gone to Guatamala. Such events were not unusual here. Sudden arrivals or disappearances were the order of the day. Nemesis sometimes caught up.

Yet Hymie insisted that he desired these people's company and Jessica was amazed. Up until now, he had been exclusively a family man, a gregarious shopkeeper but one who kept the counter firmly between him and his customers. The change to dinner-party *devoté* was out of character until Jessica realised he was doing it for them, for her and Alexander. The society of others, however boring, would force them into the channels of normality. She played the game with him as she had always done. This mess was none of his making. She loved him dearly and she had taken him away from the land he loved and knew, where the grain of living was work, endurance a necessity, laughter the essential healer. Here the tropical climate which he hated engendered lethargy, any effort caused exhaustion, and laughter was low-key. So now, to please him, she found herself caught up in an endless round of parties which none of the Kleins enjoyed. They achieved their purpose, however, forcing them to forget their wounds or at least put them aside in company for one night a week.

Alexander healed despite himself. The strangeness of the environment, the newly acquired depth and vision in his paintings served to occupy his thoughts. Little by little, as the years passed, the memory of Aisling lost its immediacy, faded, took its place in the fabric of his past.

There were visitors to the island occasionally. Hymie and Jessica found themselves greeting newcomers as eagerly as they had once been received. Visitors brought news from the big world outside. Newspapers from Europe were all very fine when you could get them but they tended to be tantalisingly out of date. Radio was informative, but nothing could beat the actual words tripping off the tongue, 'Rome was hot but the fashions, as usual, divine. The Via Condotti is a treasure-trove this year.'

'New York is impossible ... violence has increased so much since Kennedy was shot that one's simply not safe there any more.'

'London is the home of pop music now. No, *not* the States, I promise you, but the Big Smoke itself. All you hear are the Beatles and the Stones.'

'De Gaulle is good for the French. The rest of Europe loathes him, but he is good for France.'

Alexander rarely smiled, but painted incessantly. Jessica kept house, still wearing black, her abundant hair now touched with silver and rolled neatly into a matronly pleat at the back of her head. Hymie watched and prayed. He knew that neither of them would lose the hurt defensive look suffering had branded them with, nor would the inner scars ever heal. They never spoke of Aisling or Big Dan, but their shadows were always present.

It was sometime in the mid-sixties that Alexander met Tatiana d'Olivera. It was what Hymie in his wisdom had felt sure would happen, and Jessica had hoped for but did not believe possible. She knew that Alexander, despite his good looks and attractiveness to women, had not really been interested in any of them until he met Aisling. She was afraid that he, like her, would feel love only once in a lifetime. She had loved Big Dan Casey unremittingly all the days of her life, with her whole body and soul. No other man had ever touched or loved her. She was frightened that the son might be too like his mother.

The d'Oliveras, a prominent Spanish family, lived across the island. The younger son of a grandee, the first d'Olivera had been disgraced, cast out by his family, and had made his way to the island when the first tall ships were bravely crossing the seas to the New World. Hymie liked the old Don, became his friend, finding him unpretentious and gracious. He had lived a buccaneering kind of life though remaining very attached to his home. At eighty years old he still liked to go marlin fishing off the coast in his catamaran, and he still rode like a demon on a black stallion that many a younger man eyed with fear and trepidation.

The family consisted of the old man, his wife, and a spinster daughter. It seemed amazing to Hymie that Don Valesco d'Olivera could have married the cold, proud, humourless woman that Doña Bernarda was, or that Almira could be his daughter. They were like black bats, he thought, hovering in the shadows of Salida, their home, never laughing, their faces set in disapproval. Don Valesco was so gracious, a wonderful host, a practised raconteur, it puzzled Hymie that he could have married such a plain, cold woman.

But, Hymie thought with a shrug, the world was full of strange people who did strange things and he had ceased to be surprised at anything they might be capable of at this stage of his life. All that concerned him was that, of all of the homes on the island, of all the people there, Salida was the place he most enjoyed visiting and Don Valesco the person he liked best. His parties were sparkling occasions.

The night that Alexander met Tatiana started out no different from any other. He had nearly not gone to the d'Oliveras'. Generally, he hated dinner parties, loathed the banal conversation and the quizzing about his work he was forced to endure. He hated to talk about his painting, often finding himself defenceless in the face of crass, uninformed questioning. They ate

155

late on the island; dinner was usually ten p.m. The evenings were cool and it was pleasanter then. The moon shone large and silver, giving the illusion of cool waters drenching the earth, and the stars were brilliant in the black night sky. The crickets crick-cracked and the night-scented jasmine filled the air with its seductive smell.

Around Don Valesco's table that night were the regulars, the little group of people one saw wherever one went on the island, and also a sprinkling of overseas visitors: an elegant French-woman, the Comtesse de Beauvillande and her young son, and an Englishman, Justin Harcourt, a tall good-looking man who said little.

The d'Oliveras' dining room was large, high-ceilinged and dark, lit by candles in silver candelabra. The ornate seven-teenth-century table was surrounded by matching chairs with high carved backs. White-coated servants moved silently behind the guests, and in and out of the buzz of conversation. Don Valesco sat at the head of the table, his silver hair gleaming brighter than the candleglow against his darkly tanned face.

At the other end of the table sat Doña Bernarda and Almira, thin-lipped, heavy-eyed and proud. Around the table, islanders and visitors mingled. The Englishman, Justin Harcourt, talked about the legal battle he was embroiled in in Rio. He was a prominent international lawyer but proved to be a boring speaker, afflicted with a stutter. He chatted to Ruth Krumu-thagen on Alexander's right. She was hard put to contain her boredom and desperate to engage Alexander's attention. She was a superb creature, big-bosomed, small-waisted, round-hipped, the prototype film star. She wore no underwear, was tantalising in a siren's way and had the whitest of blonde hair. She had met Kurt Krumuthagen on her way to stardom, weighed up the pros and cons of life as a star, and life as a wealthy wife, and found no difficulty in giving up the insecuri-ties of her career.

She had married her little Jew-hater, forbearing to tell him that her real name was Ruth Swarchenheim, not, as appeared above the marquees, Ruth Charles.

Now she concentrated on Alexander, deciding that if she played her cards right she might very well make love to him tonight. He looked bored and lonely, but then he always did. She amused herself by picturing him without his clothes, seeing again the long lean body and remembering the sweet taste of it. She had bedded him only once and longed for a repeat performance. He was a beautiful man, she thought, and she was bored and lonely herself. Tatiana was visiting and so Don Valesco was out of bounds, and the Englishman was a bore and not to her taste at all.

She winked at Alexander, and was making a remark about caviar being an aphrodisiac when Alexander heard Doña Bernarda on his left whisper in Spanish: 'The bitch. She has no shame.'

He was shocked by the bitterness of the remark, surprised by the expression of hatred on the woman's normally impassive face. He followed the direction of her gaze and was suddenly glad he had come to the house that night. The young woman looked breathless, as if she had just run downstairs, a lovely dark-haired swallow of a girl. She swooped down on the Don, hugging and kissing him, while she called out to the guests to remain seated.

'I'm so sorry to be late,' she apologised in a softly accented voice, her eyes pleading forgiveness. There was an empty chair opposite Alexander and the newcomer took her place there. She was wearing black, as were most of the women present, unrelieved except by a slim diamond necklace at her throat. Her hair was densely black and floated above pearly shoulders like a thundercloud. Her skin was white as ivory and her brows slanted upwards over big black eyes like the centre of a purple orchid. Her mouth was a slash of scarlet in the moon-whiteness of her face.

She was smiling at him provocatively, yet the look was innocent, like a naughty child. There was a question in her eyes and she read the answer in his: Yes. They ate and talked their way through an eight-course dinner and neither ever remembered what they ate or said. In the flickering candlelight her face had the quality of a Murillo Madonna. He could not take his eyes off her. There was the sound of low laughter beside him. Ruth had been watching him. He had been too mesmerised by Tatiana to pay much attention to her, and this was unlike Alexander who was nothing if not polite. What a pity, Ruth thought, he's lost. She's got him, hook, line and sinker. Ah well!

'She's lovely, isn't she?'
'Who is she?'

Ruth's china-blue eyes widened. 'Don't you know?' She is Don Valesco's *other* daughter. Doña Bernarda quite ruined Almira. This one is different, as you can see.'

'But Doña Bernarda is her mother?'

'On, no he had Tatiana by a Polish Baroness — though she's as much a Baroness as I am.' Ruth laughed and continued, 'She was really a celebrated courtesan, very classy, very old-style, very beautiful, I'm told. She became Don Valesco's alone. He goes to Europe a lot, you know, always has done, except during the war. He still goes to see her, and they say he is mad about her. She lives in Como with Tatiana. Doña Bernarda can do nothing about it. Sour old lemon, she deserves it. Frankly honey, I don't think she cares. If ever I saw a frigid woman ...'

'So that's where he goes. He's always been a bit evasive.'

Alexander looked at Don Valesco. The old reprobate, he thought, the old devil. Then wondered why he had not guessed. Physically, father and daughter were alike: the same large eyes; cloudy soft hair with a life of its own, extravagant lips, red as blood. They had the same dash and brio, Alexander thought and knew he desired this woman more than he had ever desired anyone before. She set his body aflame with a look full of fire and ice, his mind racing with a multitude of unasked questions.

But there could be danger. Don Valesco d'Olivera was a proud and jealous man. His daughter's purity would be as important to him as the illustrious name of his family. To protect it, he would kill without a moment's hesitation.

As dinner ended the guests stood and, following Don Valesco's lead, left the dining room for the terrace where they would drink coffee and smoke, or have a brandy or a liqueur. Alexander tried to move around the table to get to the girl's side, but was forestalled by a hand on his shoulder.

'I say, old boy, like a word with you if I may.'

Alexander saw her slim back moving away from him. Her dress was cut very low, to the waist, and her shoulder blades protruded delicately like wings. She looked over her shoulder at him and his heart turned over. She was laughing, and there was a wicked gleam in her eye.

Oh, God, he thought, and felt his pulses throb.

'Do you mind?'

He realised that Justin Harcourt had spoken to him again. 'What? Oh, no. Of course not.'

'It's just, my brother, Julian — he directs films, movies, you know — is an art lover. Quite a passion with him. He's seen one of your paintings — in New York, I think. Mentioned it not once but several times.'

'Really?' Alexander tried to show some interest.

'Yes, several times. Quite potty about it, he was. I remembered the name. Part of my job, remembering names. I'm a lawyer, not artistic like brother Julian, I'm afraid. Well, Alexander Klein is simple to remember. Other fellows with names like Kotchinka ...'

'Kokoschka.'

'See what I mean? Frightfully difficult. Well, what I'm getting at, old chap, is if you have any paintings to sell ... deem it a great honour and all that. If you have, just say the word. Very, very interested.'

'Oh. Yes. Yes, of course.' She had disappeared. 'Yes, of course, but not at the moment.'

'Why not, old chap, if I may make so bold? Don't you want to sell? After all, art for art's sake can't pay the bills.'

'Thank heaven I don't have to worry about that at the moment.'

If only he could get rid of the man. He felt violent enough to push him though good breeding prevented it.

He could just see the back of her head. Her hair fell on her shoulders, soft as a cloud, and her waist was willowy, pliant and supple. She was speaking to a tall rakish Cockney, popularly supposed to have been part of a bank robbery. She smiled at him and Alexander was swept by an overwhelming rush of jealousy.

'Here's my card. Julian is like a terrier. He's certain to get a Klein eventually, y'know. He sets out after something and he never lets go until he gets it.'

Alexander was only half-listening. 'Well, some day perhaps. We'll talk of it some day,' he said.

'Oh, my brother always gets what he wants. Depend upon it.' He smiled at Alexander, who nodded and managed to escape.

He walked after Tatiana. She had descended the steps of the verandah and at the bottom she turned her head, looked over her shoulder and smiled at him. It was the smile of a wicked angel, provocative but innocent. He followed her, feeling curiously young and gauche, under an archway of frangipani

159

and japonica. He came abreast of her but she did not look at him. They walked in the star-strewn darkness, shivering but not with cold, close but not touching. There was so much to be said yet neither of them spoke. He could see her mass of dark hair, the heart-shaped jewel of her face framed in its moon-touched aureole. They came out from under the frangipanis on to a terrace overlooking the sea. There was a balcony and Tatiana leaned on the stone balustrade, her back to him, gazing over the purple ocean.

'Will we start this?' Her voice was a deep husky whisper.

'Of course, my love. Of course.'

She looked up under her lashes. 'There is no reason not to?'

'None at all,' he said.

She breathed a sigh of relief. 'I'm so glad,' she said, 'because you see, I'm a serious person. You understand.'

He nodded. 'I am, too. I'm not given to...' He stopped himself, realising that, except for Aisling, all his affairs had been casual.

She threw back her hair, sweeping it off her face with her arm, and looked at him fully for the first time.

She really was incredibly lovely. Her skin had the gloss of a magnolia leaf, cream-white tinged with a blush of pink. Her brows were heavy and dark, and she used her lashes as a curtain to veil her eyes, to conceal, to hide their dark splendour.

'You see, Alexander.' She laughed at his look of surprise. 'Oh, I know your name as you know mine. You see, I am not someone who is prepared to be casual. If we continue what has already started ... you know it has started.' He nodded. 'I will ask everything of you.' She spread her hands. 'Everything or nothing. I'm old-fashioned. I am a virgin.'

He drew in his breath, momentarily taken aback by her bluntness, at the spectre of responsibility rearing its head, the magnitude of what she was proposing when they had only just begun to talk. But he was as aware as she was of the impact they had made on each other tonight, and he knew, as she did, that they had already begun to travel down a long road.

'You are surprised? I am twenty-five. This is unusual, yes? Well, Alexander, chèri, I am unusual. What has happened tonight has not happened to me before, and second best was never enough. So —' she shrugged her shoulders — 'I am giving you an opportunity to escape, to uninvolve yourself, if that is possible.'

160

Her hair had descended over her cheeks again, shadowing her face, and she looked at him demurely from under her lashes. It was the only word he could find to describe how she looked, an old-fashioned word for an old-fashioned look.

'You know I cannot,' he said. 'It's too late. It was too late the first moment our eyes met.'

She nodded. They stood together looking out at the night. There was total unity between them, an electric closeness, a warm unspoken communion.

Don Valesco's voice broke the spell. He was calling her name.

'Tatiana. Tatiana. Tatiana. Tatiana.'

They smiled at each other, an ineffably sweet smile. They touched hands for the first time, their fingers ultra-sensitive, tip to tip, then palm to palm. They moved back into the light and the world of others.

Don Valesco greeted them, 'Ah, there you are, Tatiana, my darling, I wondered where you had got to.' His sharp old eyes took in everything and Alexander found himself blushing though absolutely nothing had happened. And yet everything had, his whole world had changed.

Tatiana went to her father and slid her arms about his waist. She laid her head on his shoulder. His gnarled brown hand caressed her soft hair. Alexander watched, jealous of their closeness. Then they went indoors again, out of the moonlight.

Chapter

17

DON Valesco d'Olivera sat in his favourite chair on the verandah at Salida. It was a white wicker chair, high-backed, winged, and covered in white cretonne with a print of large green leaves. It had a matching footstool where he could place his feet and rest, watching the dawn come up or the sun go down over his plantation. Don Valesco had married Bernarda, daughter of Don Pablo Dominquez de Saville, his neighbour. She was plain but well bred and rich, and she brought with her the vast lands and the more beautiful estate of Salida, which adjoined the d'Olivera residence. He had desired more than anything the wooded slopes and the home he now called his own, but the price had been high.

The house was ringed by hills and protected from excessive heat by its high position and the fact that it faced the sea. It stood white-columned in the sun, and when he looked at it, or this view from the verandah, on consideration the marriage always seemed to him worthwhile. Bernarda had given him Almira, a carbon copy of herself. They were devoted to him, obedient to him, dull and charmless. No son had come of the union. God knows he had tried, and the trying had given him no pleasure.

The Don paid visits to Europe and when travel became easier he even thought of returning to Spain, but the bustle and commerce, the noise and sheer quantities of human beings there, appalled him. The gracious age was over and with it the mores and manners he was accustomed to and which still lingered on the island.

On one of these visits he had met the self-styled Baroness

Anouska Vaneska, a Polish emigrée, a great beauty and a courtesan. There were few of her type left; woman of outstanding loveliness, wit and elegance, who gave themselves to the highest bidder. She learned his ways, pandered to his most secret desires, entertained him and enchanted him with her coquetry, carefully chosen clothes, ladylike demeanour and slightly shocking conversation. She expected to be pampered. She lived in the best apartments at the best addresses, furnished lavishly by her lover. She collected jewels bestowed by him, and in general led a life of luxury in return for her favours, her ability to be all things to him.

Anouska was lucky the night she met Don Valesco in the Casino at Monte Carlo. She was attracted to him immediately. He was good-looking enough, she thought, to be living by his wits as she was. Perhaps he was a pauper and not rich enough to provide for someone like her. She thought he was someone with whom she would have a fling while her current protector, the Marquis, was away on business or with his boring wife in Villefranche.

But it had proved otherwise. Don Valesco was in the market for someone exactly like her. He was as attracted to her as she was to him. It was not a *grande passion*, but a much more comfortable liaison that suited them both down to the ground. She was able to jettison the Marquis, who was ageing and boring, and indulge her passion with a companion who excited her, and who was, moreover, rich enough to keep her in the style she found imperative. She had never let her heart rule her head and she was not about to start now.

Don Valesco thereafter made regular trips to Europe, set her up in a chalet in St Mortiz during the war and afterwards bought her her heart's desire, a villa on the shores of Lake Como at Bellagio.

But by that time Tatiana had been born. To her absolute amazement in 1940, at the age of thirty-eight when thoughts of children had long since faded, Anouska conceived and produced a little girl. She was named after her grandmother, and grew so tenderly, so lovely, so adoring of her mother and her natural father, that she lit up their lives. She seemed to have an inexhaustible supply of love within her. Don Valesco thought her more truly her father's daughter, and loved her much more than his tight-lipped legitimate offspring at Salida.

163

He kept Anouska and Tatiana in style, and occasionally, when she had reached the age of eighteen, Tatiana would be allowed to visit him, in the company of friends, to come to Salida and spend time with him.

Everyone knew who she was. Doña Bernarda suffered her with the same silent disapproval that she tolerated most things about her husband, an attitude which she believed ensured her a passport to Heaven when she died. Besides which she knew there was absolutely nothing she could do about it.

Almira, her daughter, had a virulent loathing for her bastard half-sister. Tatiana was both amused and distressed by it. She understood the reason for it, but not the depth of her sister's repugnance. She was sorry for Almira and grateful that the good Lord had given her so much even if she was illegitimate. If being legitimate meant being righteous and vindictive like Almira then she would far rather be happy and herself.

Don Valesco's natural daughter gave him great pleasure. A man who lived by his senses, he appreciated beautiful women as he appreciated fine paintings, good wine and his lovely home, and Tatiana delighted him. In spite of her beauty she had led a very sheltered life and had not, until now, shown any interest in the opposite sex. Her courtesan mother had brought her up more morally and strictly than a Reverend Mother. She had gone to a private school in Switzerland and got her Baccalaureat. She went to University in Milan and graduated with honours.

She spoke German, Switzer-Deutsch, Italian, French and English fluently, the latter charmingly accented. She was very clever, loved her studies and enjoyed most of all History of Art, which was her specialist subject. Don Valesco knew there had been flirtations — she was her mother's daughter, but she had never been serious about anyone. She shrugged men off as amusing dinner-time companions who were not to be allowed to interfere with the business of learning. She had been, Don Valesco thought, in danger of becoming a blue-stocking, a bookworm, which in his estimation would be a shocking waste. Now she had fallen helplessly in love with Alexander Klein. It had been obvious from their first moments together at the dinner table. He could feel the heat of their exchange of glances from his position at the top of the table, could sense their attraction to each other across the crowded room.

164

Don Valesco was in fact pleased. He liked Alexander Klein, found him attractive both in looks and personality, and was a great admirer of his paintings. He had purchased three at the extravagant prices set by Hymie Klein, and thought them worth every penny. But he had to be assured on certain points before he gave his blessing to the couple, and he felt he could trust Alexander to tell him the truth.

He examined his prospective son-in-law closely. As yet nothing had been said about marriage, but Don Valesco knew his daughter well enough to know it would be all or nothing.

Alexander was a man in the fullest sense, Don Valesco thought, tall, handsome in a Byronic way but out of the ordinary run of good looks with his head of thick iron-grey hair, sharp jaw, and the lines of suffering etched on his face. And that was what troubled Don Valesco. Why was the man she had chosen living here in exile? What had he done to keep him away from his native land? Was it something criminal — a crime of passion perhaps? A political charge? He could not believe it to have been something evil. Alexander Klein did not look like a criminal and his painting contained no element of violence. On the contrary, it was full of compassion and pity for human suffering.

But Don Valesco had to know the answers to some questions before he gave his blessing to the union. Then Tatiana would take Alexander to her mother for her approval and permission, and only then would she herself consent to marry the man she loved. He felt sure Anouska would be as pleased with Alexander as he was. She would be, as usual, guided by him. He would write this evening if all went well but first, the interview.

It was cool on the terrace. The cicadas chirruped and the foliage rustled. The fans droned as they circled above the two men. They were shaded from the sun by mahogany trees and each man pulled gently on a Havana cigar, the smoke keeping the insects away.

They had lunched well, Tatiana between them at table. Doña Bernarda and Almira sat at the other end, ignoring Tatiana and Alexander and were, in their turn, ignored. Tatiana's wide black eyes darted continually between her father and Alexander, full of tenderness, pleased that the two men she loved obviously liked each other. Nevertheless she was nervous of their coming meeting in which personal liking might not be

165

at issue. Only after it could she truly relax.

After lunch she left them. She had leaned over and touched Alexander's hand, then risen and crossed to Don Valesco sitting at the top of the table.

'I will leave you two alone together. Doña Bernarda, Almira, please excuse me.'

The other two ladies, who had spoken Spanish throughout the meal, followed her out and Don Valesco and Alexander had retired to the verandah for coffee.

'Well, my boy.' Don Valesco cleared his throat. Alexander waited patiently.

'Without further ado ...' Don Valesco looked at the man opposite. 'Tatiana has implied to me that she would like to think of you seriously, in the role of ...'

'I want to marry her, sir, if she will have me. She says her reply will depend on you and her mother. I perfectly understand.'

'Do you? I doubt it.'

'I think I do,' Alexander said firmly.

'Well, that's unusual for a start. People don't much care nowadays for the old proprieties.

'Whereas I am enchanted by them, sir. She makes me feel very privileged, very chivalrous, very masculine, and very nervous.'

Don Valesco laughed. 'Well, you needn't worry, my boy. I like you, always have. But before I can consent to the marriage, I do need some assurances from you.'

Alexander nodded, 'Of course.'

'May I ask why you came here to the island? It's obvious to me that your mother and grandfather do not exactly love it here, yet you remain. It is also obvious to me that people like Kurt Krumuthagen, Denis Brown, and others we both know, are here because of dark or rather shameful deeds committed in the past. I have never classified you with them and I like to think I'm a good judge of character, but I must have your assurance that you are not here because of some criminal act. I would not blame you for any political misdemeanour but, you see, Tatiana will want to live in Europe and her husband must be able to take his place in society there. This island is not for my daughter. She would not like to settle here and I want for her, quite naturally, whatever will make her happy.'

Alexander paused for a moment then said, 'I would like you to know all about me, about us. I, like Tatiana, am a love-child. It seems our situations are similar. My mother loved one man passionately all her life. He was married to someone else, happily by all accounts, and had a son and daughter of his own. My mother did not tell him of my existence, but later he found out.'

Don Valesco thought of Jessica Klein. That lovely passionate face etched with the bleak cast of tragedy. Yes, he could see, could understand this. He nodded, satisfied.

'Go on.'

'Well, sir, I want you to know that I was happy, very happy, despite my fatherless state. Hymie was father enough for me. I could not have asked for a happier childhood or youth. I wanted to paint, so my mother and grandfather made it easy for me. They sent me to France and Italy. Italy ... was wonderful. I felt I was blessed. Even though my father, Dan Casey, never acknowledged me, that was all right. I had everything I wanted — until Aisling came along.'

Don Valesco saw his face become drawn with pain, but he took a deep breath and continued. 'I fell deeply in love with an actress, Aisling Andrews. I never knew Andrews was not her real name, until it was too late. Her real name was Aisling Casey and she was my father's legitimate daughter.'

Don Valesco did not break the silence which fell but allowed Alexander to take his own time.

'Dan Casey worshipped his daughter. Imagine his horror when she sent him a letter telling him that she was in love with Alexander Klein from Dublin. He knew at once who I was. He's a man much like you, a proud and passionate man. He was determined to separate us. He had to, yet he did not want to acknowledge me. He loved his wife and she would have left him, no doubt of it, if she had known about my mother. He would have lost her and Slievelea, their home, if he had told Aisling the real reason why we could not be lovers.' Alexander looked at his cigar which had long since gone out.

'I expect you can understand, sir, the threat of losing your home, the most beautiful house in Ireland. My mother had told me all of this, she knows him so well. What she had not envisaged was the lengths he would be prepared to go to. Without a word to my mother or grandfather, he contacted some Mafia acquaint-

167

ances in Sicily where Aisling and I were staying. They shot and wounded me but told Aisling I was dead. I was put on a ship for Brazil and weeks later, when Dan Casey had finally told them the truth, my mother and grandfather joined me there. My mother was shattered by her lover's cruelty in letting her think for so long that their son was dead. And then she told me who Aisling really was and it was my turn to despair — until I met Tatiana. She has made me whole again, given me new life. Sir, I want so much to marry her.

'I have told her all this. It was the only honourable thing to do. I have explained that all those events have nothing to do with my love for her, that it all happened a long time ago.'

Heat enclosed them, falling suddenly like a suffocating cloak. Don Valesco fanned himself and Alexander moved his chair directly beneath the whirring blades of the fan.

'I appreciate your telling me this,' Don Valesco said at last, 'it has put my mind at rest. Your poor mother, what a tragedy for her.' He shook his head.

'I am glad too that you told Tatiana. I would have insisted on her knowing before anything was decided. Now, as I see it, you ran away. Or rather, you stayed away. This girl is still an actress?'

Alexander shrugged. 'I really don't know.'

'No matter. Remember, you will go back to Europe with Tatiana. I must ask you, please, to think carefully. If you met this girl again how would you feel? You cannot hide away forever.'

'That is the battle I have been fighting all these years, since I came here. Because our love was so impossible, unnatural, against everything, I have had to pluck it from my soul.'

Don Valesco sighed again. 'Did you succeed?' he asked.

Alexander nodded. 'After a lot of pain, a terrifying struggle, yes, I succeeded.'

Alexander took a white handkerchief from the pocket of his linen blazer, and wiped his damp brow. Tendrils of dark hair clung wetly to his forehead.

'Then that is that. Put it all behind you and start afresh. Enjoy life. Only age is irreversible. Anything else may get better. Your tennis may improve tomorrow, you may go from poverty to riches, you may win the lottery, a man with a death sentence may get a reprieve. There is only one thing you can be sure of:

you will not get younger. So put this tragedy behind you and live your life to the full.'

'I have. I will.'

If I did not believe that you would not marry my daughter. There is just one thing more — money.' As Alexander started to speak he continued 'I imagine you have enough. It's just that you should know that Tatiana will have quite a considerable dowry.'

There was a look of amazement on his future son-in-law's face.

'Even she does not know it, but it is so. Her mother and I arranged it a long time ago.'

'It would make no difference,' Alexander protested, but Don Valesco raised his hand.

'Don't be silly, Alexander. It will make the difference between comfort and luxury. Money, you know, always makes a difference.'

Alexander smiled. The sun shone redly now, painting the land crimson and gold. The old man's face looked devilish as he spoke, illuminated by the bronze haze of heat.

'Money always makes a difference,' he repeated.

'I meant, Don Valesco, that I have enough money now to keep Tatiana comfortably, and enough talent to keep her in luxury. But you are right. Money does make a difference.'

For no reason that he could fathom in this lurid tropical afternoon he thought of Slievelea the only time he had seen it; thought of the sage-green gloom of the woods, the carpet of hazy mauve bluebells, and the sun slanting through the trees obliquely, catching in a beam the slim figure of a slight golden girl, a nymph, Aisling. He shivered and put the thought away.

'Then let us shake hands,' Don Valesco said, and stood up. He stretched out his hand to Alexander. As Alexander rose and gripped the outstretched hand, the older man pulled him off balance, embracing him and thumping him on the back in congratulation. Alexander felt a lump in his throat. Deeply moved, he returned the old man's embrace.

Chapter

18

HYMIE'S warm and loving heart was wearing out. Now that Alexander and Tatiana were engaged to marry, unofficially until Tatiana's mother gave her consent, he felt a great flood of relief, and in that relief he relaxed his hold on life. It seemed that the motivation that had kept him going in this alien land was gone. He had struggled and worked to save his daughter's sanity and his grandson from becoming a recluse. Brilliant painter though he was, Alexander had sought isolation and tried to cut himself off from his fellow human beings. Now all that was changed. He was a man transformed. He went about the house singing. He laughed a lot. He had a twinkle in his eye and a smile on his lips more often than not.

The engagement had affected Jessica deeply too. She loved Tatiana, doted on the girl, and Hymie was delighted to see the affection between them. The two women grew very close. When plans for the trip to Europe were discussed it was Tatiana who insisted that Jessica accompany them. She would hear of no refusal.

'I need you as my duenna. I love Alex so much, but I want to be proper — if I can. You see, I'm so passionate, I despair of myself. But I would like, if I could, to be quite pure on my wedding day. Does that sound silly to you, Jessica?'

'No, my dear. It does not. Different people need different things and we must never be afraid of stating our needs.'

She thought briefly of the girl she had been, undressing for Dan Casey in the firelight. And when she was naked in the fullness of her beauty, that first time, looking at him and saying, 'Now you.'

'Then you will come? To Europe, to Bellagio, with us? Oh, please, you must.'

'But, my dear, you and Alexander do not want an old woman with you. I shall stay here with Father.'

'No, you *must* come with us! You are not old, and we love you. Please, be my duenna and guard me from myself.'

Jessica laughed and Hymie, listening to the far-off murmur of the women's voices and their laughter, loved to hear the sound so long stilled by grief.

'No, I cannot go,' Jessica said regretfully. 'I must stay with my father. What would he do without me?'

Then Tatiana went to Hymie. 'You'll let her go, won't you? Please.'

Hymie laughed. 'Of course, of course. I insist on it. But may I ask something of you? All of you? Please take me with you. I want to go home, to Ireland. Take me just that far with you, then you can go off to Italy in joy and love.'

Tatiana threw her arms around him. 'Of course, you darling! Everyone must be happy and have what they want because I am so happy. And have you any advice for me?'

Her black eyes twinkled and she looked at Alexander under her lashes, but Hymie said seriously, 'Yes. Set him free. If you try to possess him, you'll lose him. Set him free and he'll always be yours.'

Tatiana was to remember his words.

She lived in a dream of happiness, arranging things for the trip. Everything about her marriage must be right, permission sought and given, traditions observed, proprieties maintained. Jessica, like an old-fashioned duenna would act as her chaperone. Deep within her Tatiana knew she had asked this because of her mother's past, and she was ashamed. She adored Anouska but found it impossible to reconcile the genuine love between her mother and father with the unpalatable fact that in the past Anouska had sold her body for money. There was no getting round it. Tatiana was too honest to try, but hated to dwell upon it. Ardent, idealistic, everything in her nature revolted against the wilful commerce in love and favours that formed the fabric of her mother's past. Her mother was practical and matter-of-fact for she felt no obligation or inclination to apologise for her past. This horrified her daughter, and made her feel guilty that she was shocked.

171

Her mother spoke quite frankly about her past, was unrepentant and unashamed; if anything quite proud of what she had achieved. She did not realise the effect her frankness had on Tatiana, this child brought up within the strictest moral codes. The result had been that her daughter had immersed herself in books, turned all her energies into acquiring knowledge and studiously avoided men. Books had given her sustenance and a kind of life at arm's length until Alexander had come along. She had not participated in the hurly-burly of adolescent sexual experimentation, yet her feelings were often in turmoil. She knew she was passionate but did not know how normal that was. Fearful of finding out that she had inherited her mother's immoral tendencies she preferred to stay out of the fray. She guarded herself like a medieval maiden, waiting for the right man and determined to give herself to him alone and only in holy matrimony.

She had more or less given up hope when she had met Alexander. Life for her had settled down into a routine of work and the sort of pleasures usually reserved for old age; good conversation, friendship with members of both sexes, intellectual pursuits, and travel. She knew that people found such behaviour strange in a beautiful young woman, but in time they had come to accept her and leave her to follow her own path in peace.

Looking back now on those years of her life she was glad she had been adamant about not accepting second best. Meeting Alexander, finding within herself a capacity to love so deeply, she knew that all the years of waiting had not been in vain.

Sometimes she had difficulty in restraining her ardent nature and keeping her promise to herself: that she would keep herself for him until their wedding day. Alexander did not try to change her mind, but seemed to feel that one day she would, as he put it, melt. She loved the word and the thought. She would melt in his arms, heated by his passion, at one at last with the man she loved.

There were only a few weeks to go before they left the island, weeks spent in a flurry of packing, showing prospective buyers around their property and saying goodbye to their friends with the exception of Don Valesco who would, after all, become one of the family. He would see them at the wedding and afterwards, for he intended to visit them often.

Jessica was worried about her father. She could see he was failing fast. It was as if he had suddenly let go. She knew that their exile, the great change from the green land of Erin to this tropical island, had taken a huge toll on him.

It was yet another sweltering day and Alexander had crossed to the mainland to collect their tickets and make the last arrangements for their journey. There was no soothing breeze and Jessica thanked God they would leave here soon. She could feel the sweat trickle down from her armpits, dampen her forehead and neck. She would not go to Ireland. She could not bear to. There were memories of her love everywhere in Dublin. She would wait in London, in Brown's Hotel, with Alexander and Tatiana, for they too would not go.

She understood Hymie's desire to see the old shop on the quays, but she was afraid for him doing so. He was going to be so lonely, so devastated when he saw someone else in the home and business premises he had lived in so happily. In the event she need not have worried. On that hot airless day, the old man had a heart attack. She heard his cry and the crash of falling furniture. When she ran on to the verandah she saw him spread-eagled on the floor. Terrified, not knowing what to do, she phoned the doctor and waited for him in a tumult of anxiety.

The servants had helped her get Hymie to bed where he lay grey-faced under the mosquito net. She was horrified to see how thin his body was. He must have been losing weight for a long time.

He did not want to go to the hospital on the mainland, becoming very stubborn with the doctor.

'I won't have them sticking things into me. I won't have them plugging me to machines. Leave me a little dignity. Let me die here.'

Jessica let him have his way. He was old and he had no desire to live half a life from now on, to become a burden, however loved. He did not want to spend any more time yearning for years gone by. He was too old, and tired of being an exile. He was happy that Alexander had found Tatiana. She was a wonder. The way she helped and obviously loved Jessica was a joy to him to watch. He could die in peace now.

Hymie's illness brought Tatiana and Alexander closer together, if that were possible. She proved herself a tower of strength to Jessica and Alexander appreciated all she did to alleviate the strain for his mother.

Hymie's condition worsened, then one evening, when the fiery ball of the sun hit the horizon in the west, he called them to him. His face was calm and tranquil.

'I'm on my way out, on the way to Martha. I want to go, Jess. Don't try to stop me.'

He smiled at her, anxious pleading in his eyes. She reassured him, tears spilling down her cheeks.

'No,' he said feebly, trying to calm her, 'you mustn't cry. Look after Alexander and Tatiana. She's a good one, that one. She'll care for you and make you forget about ... all the rest. She'll heal old wounds for you and Alexander, and give you grandchildren, you'll see. It will be good, Jess. It will be very good, and it makes me happier than you can ever know.'

She sat by his side, holding his hand. Once he touched her wrist and called her name.

'Yes. I'm here, Papa.'

'Jessica, I can't go without telling you, thanking you. You have been so dear to me. You have never failed me. Always remember that. I have loved you so much, my darling.'

'I know, Papa, I know,' she sobbed, but he did not seem to hear her. She remembered his goodness to her all the days of her life, his arms always open to her, his time always hers, his help and support during her youth, her pregnancy, her pain and her love, then her terrible loss. Her father had always been there, a rock, a shield, a haven. She bowed her head to his hand and felt the faint returning pressure.

'Don't weep for me, Jessica. I have had a very good life.'

'I am weeping for myself,' she whispered.

He heard, as if from a great distance, the sound of Jessica weeping. Her beautiful face was the last thing he saw. He felt his body become weightless and a great swell of peace filled him as he slipped gently away into darkness.

Chapter

19

THE journey home was tinged with grief because of Hymie's death, by Jessica's and Alexander's relief at leaving the island of their exile, a place that had remained alien and strange to them both, and by hope at the prospect of a new life. Tatiana too was glad to leave.

'It is home for my father, but not for me. Bellagio is home.'

Jessica went, after all, to Ireland. Alexander went with her. They did not stay long. They brought Hymie's ashes home to the land he loved and scattered them over the grey waters of the Liffey. Jessica didn't know whether it was allowed, but Alexander pooh-poohed her doubts. They simply took the small urn out with them one cool moist morning, and in the curling silver mist trailed the ashes over the dark rippling water Hymie had loved so much.

Jessica could hardly bear to look where the little shop had been. It had been bought for the site and a new building, featureless and functional, stood there now. She was profoundly glad that Hymie had not lived to see it, had not come back and made this journey alone. It would have killed him in a far less kind way, and she was glad that he was spared that. She remembered a far-off day in the sunshine when she had stood on the bridge beside her father's shop and her lover, Dan Casey, had come back from his travels and lifted her off her feet there, swinging her around and around. Her hat had fallen off into the waters below, and her heart had been so full of joy she had thought she might die of it. Those days were long gone. She thought briefly of that man's betrayal and shivered in her hatred of him, longing to be away.

They were glad to leave Ireland behind them and journey to a sunnier clime. They stopped off in London in Brown's Hotel for a few days. Cossetted there, looked after with old-fashioned courtesy, they relaxed. Tatiana did some shopping in Bond Street and South Molton Street. London was swinging, full of noise, loud music and the mini skirt. The roar of the traffic and the stench of the pertrol fumes were overwhelming. There seemed to be a constant blast of car horns, the Beatles 'She loves you, Yea, Yea, Yea' blaring out of every shop — except they were called 'boutiques' now. Alexander saw and deplored London's loss of elegance. The city jarred on him. There was a sense of abandonment in the air, a laxness that Alexander disliked profoundly and Tatiana found disturbing. Having seen a few plays and spent a wonderful evening at Covent Garden, the little party flew to Milan and from there took a car to Como.

They left Como immediately, taking the slow boat up the lake to Bellagio. It was May and spring had arrived. Alexander and Jessica felt their hearts melting and their bodies relaxing at the sight of the beauty around them. It was so different from the noise and bustle of London and the sadness of Dublin, such a contrast to the heat and the lushness of the island where they had lived for so long.

Tatiana watched them, anxious for them to like her home, pointing out the villas that lay beside the lake. Great Renaissance buildings and the beautiful homes of the rich, dotted the shores of the lake, their gardens sloping down to the water or flush with the shore, rising like fairy palaces from the shimmering lake. Sleeping green mountains splashed with pale gold, russet-red and olive, the remote peaks wearing a silver canopy of snow, lay drowsing in the warm sunshine.

The little steamer zig-zagged on its way, crossing the lake from fishing villages where the fisherman mended their nets to pretty groups of houses around stately villas, clustered as if for protection yet slightly apart to allow the villa its pre-eminence. Cernobbio, across to Torno and back to Moltrasio, Pognana, Brienno, Nesso — the names passed in a dream.

It took two hours to reach Bellagio. It had been five o'clock when they left Como, the sun shining and people drinking cappucino or San Pelligrino, Campari soda or a glass of wine at the café tables on the pavement before the Cathedral. While they were on the boat, they watched as slowly, beautifully, the dusk fell. This was the land of azaleas, a riotous glory of pink, cerise, scarlet, crimson and white. The trees grew thick on the mountains. There was lime, for woodcarving. There were horse chestnut, sweet chestnut, castania, beeches, copper beeches, cedar of Lebanon, lemon and orange trees, almond in drifts of pale blossom, magnolia, umbrella and willow. Tatiana whispered that even her mother did not know how many kinds of trees graced the shores of the lake and the woods and gardens of the villas. Candy-floss pink peonies, red, pink and white camellias, pale mauve wysteria splashed colour through the green of the trees and seemed to glow as the light faded. As they travelled the darkness fell and the lights began to twinkle.

Bellagio sits at the tip of the promontory that divides Como from Lecco. As they neared it, the mountains seemed very close, clothed in mottled green velvet. There were lamps at the side of the lake, dotted along it like a necklace of diamonds, shining a welcome in the dusk.

Jessica sighed contentedly. It was going to be all right. The magic of Italy had overtaken her and, although she had never been here before, she felt at home and at peace. She looked lovingly at the two faces beside her, outlined by the first pale rays of moonlight. They were so dear to her, Tatiana almost as much as her son. Alexander's face was peaceful, calmer than she had seen it in years. He looked happy, too, tranquil and optimistic. It was all thanks to the dear and lovely girl beside him, who had so generously taken not just Alexander but his mother to her heart. Jessica felt a flood of gratitude fill her heart, and thought, at last. Here, perhaps, we can be happy.

The girl seemed to sense what she was thinking. Alexander stood with his arm around her, but she put out her hand and clasped Jessica's fingers reassuringly. They stood that way, united in unspoken love for each other.

The mysterious snow-topped mountains on the left were shrouded in a light mist. Lights sparkled at their base where little fishing villages and tiny clusters of houses and villas were lit up against the dark. The odd car, passed along the lakeside road like a comet, a brilliant arrow of light flashing past then disappearing into a tunnel out of sight. The lights were reflected in the sage-green water which turned black under the lee of the higher mountains. The little steamer ploughed its silver furrow across from town to town, Colonno, San Giovanni, Sala

Comacina. The canopy of the sky was aquamarine and starless.

Suddenly, Tatiana pointed excitedly and cried, 'There it is! There is the Villa Salimbeni, my home.'

The little boat had rounded the promontory and they could see the villa, white and brilliantly lit against the sky. Square, perfectly proportioned, patrician, it stood a little above the lake, two great stone stairways like welcoming arms leading to the terrace. Alexander could see servants in white jackets moving about beside a table at which sat a remote figure in red: Tatiana's mother. Alexander felt a moment's panic which the girl correctly divined. She took his hand and pressed it between her own.

The little boat put in at Bellagio and they found a car awaiting them. The housekeeper greeted them at the villa.

'The Baroness says will you go to your rooms to bathe and refresh yourselves after your journey. She would like to see you at ten o'clock for dinner.'

Alexander felt once more the cold hand of fear. The housekeeper was a plump woman with black hair parted severely in the middle and drawn into a bun behind her head. She had a stern face and looked at him appraisingly but her face broke into the merriest of smiles as she embraced Tatiana, called her 'Mia bambino', and Alexander consoled himself with the thought that if she loved Tatiana so much she must want to see her happy.

His room overlooked the lake. It was floored with marble, a cloudy pearl and black, cool under the feet. The bed and furnishings were eighteenth-century. A great gilt-edged mirror hung over the mantlepiece and he found that his luggage, which had gone on by road before them, had been unpacked and his white dinner jacket and his trousers, a shirt and underclothes had been laid out for him.

He was just slipping a flower he had picked from the balcony into his button-hole when there was a light tap on the door and Tatiana came in. She joined him on the balcony. The heavy mane of dark hair that bothered her in the heat, so that it was her habit to sweep it away from her neck and shoulders, was looped high on her head. She wore a coral chiffon dress, short and full about her knees and draped over her breasts softly, clinging lightly to them as she moved. She wore coral in her ears and at her throat and had put some lipstick on her mouth

178

that gleamed on her soft skin.

'Are you nervous?' she asked him, and smiled to see this man-of-the-world with grey in his hair looking vulnerable and tense. She kissed his cheek. 'Don't worry my darling. She will love you.'

They knocked at Jessica's door on the way down and she came to meet them in a high-necked gown of black lace, her white hair piled high and secured with black tortoiseshell Spanish combs. She looked beautiful and frail, Alexander thought, suddenly feeling extra protective of her. Hymie's death had shaken her more than they had realised. Jessica had had a hard time during the past years. Disillusionment with Big Dan, her lover, the shock of Alexander's supposed death, the journey to Brazil and subsequent exile had not been easy for a woman of her age. He felt a surge of love for her and, allowing Tatiana to go ahead, took her arm and led her to the top of the staircase.

It was a light rose-coloured marble and ran directly down to the wide hall where the Baroness stood in a sheath of scarlet satin. As he descended Alexander could see ahead in a straight line from the grand staircase to the lake. The doors were open wide and the gravel avenue swept down to the wrought-iron gates that faced the water, flanked by tall cypresses. For a moment, the glorious vista took Alexander's breath away. He stood still, watching Tatiana trip down the pink marble stairway to her mother. The Baroness's scarlet dress etched her from her surroundings like a splash of paint on a pale canvas. She was very tall and thin, the dress she wore was high at the throat and had long sleeves. Her face came into focus as Alexander, feeling the pressure of Jessica's hand on his arm, began to descend. It was a strange dramatic face, painted and aged. Her eyebrows were plucked away and two pencilled inverted half-circles framed her large black velvet eyes, Tatiana's eyes. The expression in Anouska's was very different. Hers were full of soulful coquetry and self-mockery. They were fringed with sparse heavily mascaraed eyelashes and there was a bold sweep of colour painted on each high Slavic cheekbone. Her nose was long and exquisitely modelled, her mouth a slash of crimson. But despite the make-up and the falsely raven hair, smooth on her head and tightly knotted behind, she had the grandeur and dignity of a queen. A regal lady, used to command, to charm, to fascinate, and one who would not take herself too seriously.

She greeted them, both hands outstretched. 'My dear Alexander, at last! And you do not disappoint. What a beautiful man you are.' She turned to Jessica. 'You must be so proud of him. Would that I were twenty years younger! Jessica, my dear, I feel I know you well. Don Valesco has told me all.'

Jessica winced inwardly. She shuddered to think of the Don exposing all their secrets to this worldly woman who spoke in a light social voice, but looking into the black eyes she found only sympathy and understanding.

Anouska continued lightly: 'But you must be very hungry after your journey, so let us eat.'

She led them into a long light room. Rococo frescoes, pastel and gilt, decorated the ceiling. The windows were closed against the night but uncurtained, leaving the lighted terrace, the flower garden and the lake open to view. A long table was laden with crystal and silver and decorated with light green linen nappery and a centrepiece of lilies and white carnations, with here and there a splash of scarlet.

They dined on *paté de foie gras*, salad and lobster thermidor, cheeses and a stunning mixture of sorbets: passion fruit, blackcurrant and delicate citron. They had coffee on the terrace. It was chilly so Tatiana draped a cashmere shawl around her mother's shoulders and procured one for Jessica. Alexander was aware that during the meal he had been subjected to the closest scrutiny from the Baroness's fine dark eyes. She was judging and assessing him, he knew. She did not appear to be asking questions but her remarks always seemed to elicit revealing replies.

'Your mother must be very proud of you, Alexander. So handsome and intelligent a son, and an artist too. Your work has been exhibited where — Paris?'

'No, I have not had to have a showing yet. My work sells without and I have no desire for fame.'

'But you will wish now to set up house, and Tatiana . . .'

Tatiana smiled at Alexander. Her mother was accepting their marriage.

'My son can afford to keep your daughter as she is accustomed to live without having to depend on his art,' Jessica answered for her son bluntly.

The Baroness nodded, satisfied. 'That is good,' she said. 'Art lovers are strangely fickle. Artists may attain a peak of popularity and then fade, only to rise again, proclaimed immortal, a suitable interval after their death. It is hard for their wives meantime. Are you, Alexander, a modern incomprehensible painter or ...'

'Oh no, Mother. Alexander's paintings are wonderful. Sad and passionate.'

'Like the man himself.' The Baroness smiled sweetly at him and added, 'I rely on Tatiana to remove your air of past sadness before the year is out.'

'Can any of us remove the past?' he asked lightly.

She looked at him intently. 'I sincerely hope so,' she said, and rose, drawing the scarlet cashmere about her. She looked regal against the moonlight and the trees. Behind her the mountains outlined against the sky seemed very near. The lake lay below them, a sheet of silver in the moonlight.

She moved to where Alexander and Tatiana sat together on the white bamboo furniture. She kissed them on the cheek, first Tatiana, then Alexander.

'I give you both my blessing,' she said, 'and I wish you every happiness.'

Then, before anyone could say anything, she went to Jessica and bent low to embrace her.

'I am happy to welcome you to our family, our home, our hearts. My daughter has been brought up the old-fashioned way. She will make Alexander a good wife and you a good daughter-in-law.' She sighed and looked out over the lake. 'I waited for you to come, my heart full of trepidation' — there seemed to be tears in her voice — 'but now I feel comforted. Very comforted. You must have felt the same, Jessica, at first. Our children are so precious. I was so anxious to like you both, to love you both, yet so afraid it might not be so. But it is all right. Everything is good. I am happy.'

Tatiana and Alexander had risen and Tatiana went to her mother and took her in her arms. They stood a moment together, then Tatiana said, 'I'll go with Mother. Goodnight, Alexander. Goodnight, Jessica.'

They watched as, arm in arm, mother and daughter left the terrace. Jessica smiled at her son. 'I quite agree with her. It is good.' She looked at the starlit mountains and said, 'I like this place. I am glad to be in Europe. If only it would rain a little. A soft little shower would suit me just fine.'

181

Alexander laughed with her and she took his hand in hers. 'She is right, Alexander. Our long mourning is over. We can both live again. You will be happy with Tatiana and I shall feel some peace at last.'

Alexander undressed slowly that night. He was very content. He had not seriously thought that Tatiana's mother would disapprove of their marriage, but on the journey here there had been tension and anxiety. Now it had gone. He felt the blissful relaxed state of mind of a man from whom all doubt has been removed. He liked the self-styled Baroness. Her inconsistency amused him: the *grande courtesan* raising a daughter in convent strictness and scrutinising her prospective husband with the authority of a Victorian father. He found it touching and at the same time exciting. This must be how men had felt in olden times to be assured of the virginity of their brides, an anachronism in this day and age when promiscuity was the norm. And yet, in Alexander's opinion, they had thereby lost the great aphrodisiac of waiting for a prize which would be given untarnished by careless use, a pure and unique treasure that no one else could savour or explore. Like Aisling . . .

He pushed the thought away as he had learned to do, and his deep feeling of content returned. Life held promise of great happiness.

He was just about to get into bed when there was a knock at the door. He called 'Come in' and was surprised to see Tatiana in a wrap that glimmered richly in the dark room. She closed the door and flew into his arms.

'Oh, darling, she loves you! I *knew* she would and yet I'm so relieved. Do you understand?'

He nodded. She smelled of a soft jasmine-based perfume, subtle and provocative. Her skin was pearl-white and her lips parted, soft as velvet. As she looked at him her eyes suddenly widened. Alexander caught his breath and drew her to him, holding her as close as he could. He could feel the length of her legs from her thighs to her ankle, and to his surprise she moved her body into the curve of his. Always before she had gently disengaged herself. Now she melted into his arms and threw back her head and opened her lips to his mouth. Thirstily he kissed her, moving his mouth gently over hers and feeling his limbs dissolve with desire.

He disentangled himself from her embrace. 'Tatiana, you wanted to wait '

'Hush, my love. I cannot wait any longer. My body is on fire for you. Take me now.'

He wanted to argue, hear her promise that she would not regret this later. But as she moved against him he knew he could not wait. Nothing could stop him now.

She was breathing fast and she pushed his hands to her wrap which slipped away at a touch. She wore only panties beneath it of oyster satin and lace. Her breasts rose proudly, large and alabaster in the moonlight, and beneath them her waist sloped abruptly to her hips. She put her thumbs into the waistband of her pants and let them slide to the floor. As she stepped out of them she kicked off her high-heeled mules and suddenly was much smaller than him.

He pulled her gently to him again and carried her to the bed. 'Oh my darling, I don't want to hurt you.'

She smiled, her lips glistening now from his kisses, and put her finger on his mouth. 'Shush, you won't. You won't.'

He was firm with her. His first thrust caused a sharp intake of breath but then she sighed and curled her legs about his and his body met only warm wetness and throbbing welcome. It was like a sacrament for them, a total giving, a mutual pleasure. She was as passionate as he. Her body rose to his until at last, biting his shoulder, she came, crying out her fulfilment in a crescendo of little gasps. He lay on her for a while, then raised himself and looked down at her. She was crying, tears spilling from her eyes into her mass of jet black hair. He was filled with consternation.

'Oh, my darling. Oh God, Tatiana.'

Once more she placed her finger on his lips. 'No, darling, I'm so happy. It was so beautiful. Why didn't we do it before? Oh and I asked you to wait and you did, knowing it was like this!'

They both burst out laughing, and he said, 'I didn't, Tatiana. No one does. There are all sorts of reasons why not. You never know until you try. Darling, you're so beautiful, so generous.'

He traced the blue veins on her breast with his lips and she arched her body to him.

'Again, my darling,' she breathed and this time he slid into her easily and felt her tremble with excitement beneath him, felt their climax build, orchestrated by him, until at last, exhausted and sated, they fell apart.

Later, with Tatiana asleep under the white cambric sheet, he rose and went out on to the balcony. He leaned on the cold stone balustrade and gazed out over the lake. A thin mist hung diaphanous on the air and circled the base of the little island opposite the Villa Salimbeni. It seemed to be floating on air.

The mountains, snow-garnished, curved down into the lake, grey vapour wreathing their crevices and clefts. Palm trees stood sentinel, tall and motionless, and below him the azaleas were a brilliant splash of colour in the pastel scene. Above it all the moonlight shone. Suddenly the silver-grey patina of the lake was broken as a little boat ablaze with lights steamed past. Alexander could see its illuminated shape reflected in the still waters of the lake. It left a frill of wavelets spreading outwards in its wake and receded into a pinpoint of light before vanishing altogether. He saw the trees silvered by the moon and as the light wavered in the dark shivering leaves he thought of Aisling.

Aisling. Still she clung to the edges of his mind, a pale ghost, golden-haired, sapphire-eyed, as different from Tatiana as chalk is from cheese. But forbidden. Another aphrodisiacal word. Aisling, Aisling, go away. It was like a sigh, the sound of the sea in his head, the whisper returned from the mother-of-pearl depths of the conch-shell.

Aisling, Aisling.

He had to pluck it out, kill all thoughts of her at birth, ruthlessly censor his mind, for that way lay madness. Tatiana was beautiful, a passionate woman. She was ardent and extraordinarily voluptuous. What was the matter with him? He was horrified to find thoughts of his forbidden love in his head at a moment like this. Dear God was he mad? He shook his head, perplexed. There had been a yearning, a spiritual ecstacy in their union, that would always separate Aisling from the rest of womankind for him. Yet he loved Tatiana, loved her passionately, as completely as he knew how. Their lovemaking, the sexual fulfilment they had just achieved was the best, the most erotic he had ever known. So why these thoughts and why now? He heard the patter of Tatiana's feet as she crossed the room. She came and stood beside him on the balcony.

The moon hung over the mountains, a million stars pierced the blue-black sky. The water shushed gently below and all nature seemed to hold her breath.

'My darling, are you all right? What are you thinking?'

184

He circled her slim strong waist with his arm. 'I'm thinking how much I love you,' he said, and they went indoors again.

Chapter

20

THE first time Alexander did his disappearing act and vanished from their home for six weeks, Tatiana was distraught. The note he left her was cryptic:

> Don't worry, my love. I need to be by myself and work. I have gone to Rosia and do not want to be contacted while I'm working.

Nothing else. Nothing at all. She was devastated, but she remembered Hymie's words: 'Set him free. If you try to possess him, you'll lose him.' He was an artist, she told herself, a creative genius. He must be unfettered to do his work in peace, undisturbed.

But she minded very much and she was angry. She tried to quell her anger, pluck it out, but to no avail. She was a passionate woman and possessive by nature and she resented Alexander's high-handed treatment of her.

They had been so very happy, so in tune with each other. Tatiana could not believe that life could be so complete. It was as if all the pieces of a jigsaw had fallen into place, revealing a picture so breathtakingly beautiful that it amazed her. She was stunned by how completely they complemented each other. They found joy in the same things, laughed together, were deeply moved by the same injustices. They enjoyed similar foods, neither liking meat too much, preferring fish, fruit and poultry. Both admitted their favourite lunch was fresh bread, cheese, tomatoes and wine, and whichever fruit was in season.

They read the same books, discussed new movies, and were

restful in each other's company, content and at peace on a level deeper then either had ever believed possible. In bed at night they explored each other in delight and learned how to please each other, experiencing whole new worlds of love.

Tatiana had been so supremely happy that when she found she was pregnant she had a moment's fear that everything might change.

'Oh, dear Lord, please don't let it make a difference.'

But it did. It made things even better. A cocoon of love enveloped her. Alexander's joy surrounded her and she felt beautiful and complete and contained within it.

They bought the Villa Donatello deep in the Tuscan hills above Sienna. The birth of their daughter, Anouska, called after Tatiana's mother, was easy. Everything in her life seemed to be like that now, and Tatiana was superstitious. Deep within her she worried about the ease of things. Could life really be so free of problems? Could one really have ones heart's desires without difficulty, without pain?

In their bedroom, the dim night light glowing in the darkness casting a roseate glow over everything, she would hold Anouska to her breast and feel the greedy little mouth suck, full of drowsy sensuality at the sensation. She would turn her head to look tenderly into the face of her sleeping husband. A chill of fear at the magnitude of her happiness would steal over her for she was terrified of losing it.

They had a studio built for Alexander. Set a little away from the house it overlooked the valleys and the warm pink roofs of the villages below them. He was working on a series of paintings there but Tatiana discovered the existence of a second studio, a secret little house of his somewhere deep in the hills, she did not know precisely where. He called it Rosia and she was not welcome there. He was not dictatorial about it, never frowned at her or forbade her to go there, but she knew she should not. It had never surprised Tatiana that Pandora opened the box or that Bluebeard's wife entered the forbidden room. She understood how one could become preoccupied by a banned and secret place.

When Alexander's canvasses and equipment arrived from Rio Tatiana had gone with him to the studio and watched him unpack the crates. He did it all himself for he was too nervous to trust it to anyone else. The studio was simply a roof and three walls of glass sliding doors, giving the painter light and space. They had had it air conditioned for Alexander did not believe that physical discomfort helped the artist.

'The images I receive, the pain I see in others, my receptivity to others' anguish and my own, helps, of course it does, the creative process. It is in everything I do. But hunger, starving for your art, impedes rather than contributes. Anyhow, my darling, it is not for me.'

Tatiana sat on a packing case swinging her legs, watching the man she loved. Looking at him gave her so much pleasure; the curve of his neck, his strong wrists. He wore tatty jeans and an open-necked shirt and looked healthy and vigorous.

She jumped from the crate and looked at the paintings he was stacking against the back wall, the wall made of stone. Most of the paintings she knew and loved. She admired her husband's work, gave him her unswerving support and was proprietorially proud of him.

As she looked at the familiar finished and half-finished work she came across a portfolio that she had never seen before. Alexander was busy, grunting with the effort of unpacking a large case, scattering sawdust and straw about. Tatiana untied the strings that held the portfolio's stiff boards together. Curiously she rested the folder against the wall and flicked through the paintings it contained. They were quite different from Alexander's usual work, but obviously his. Oil on canvas, painted in the Impressionist style, much sweeter and more romantic than he normally was, they depicted a woodland scene. Dark greens superimposed on pale, golden light on shadows, a tree-filled place, a girl. All the pictures contained a girl in half-flight, a golden-haired nymph with wide startled violet eyes. The painter had made her indistinct yet she was obviously very precious to him. Tatiana could see, from every gentle stroke of the brush, how much Alexander had loved this girl. It was Aisling. It had to be.

She stood frozen to the spot. She felt suffocated, she could not breathe. Then she heard him shout and felt the portfolio pulled away from her.

'Never touch those,' he said. She had never heard him speak like that before, his voice so harsh and cold.

Still she stood, unable to move. 'Who is she? she said. But she knew, and he knew she did. 'It's her, isn't it, the one you

188

loved? Your sister.' She spat the last words at him, horrified by her vehemence, at how ugly she sounded. She had not realised before how much she minded the thought of the woman in his past that had caused him so much pain, that he had tried so hard to forget. She still could not say the name, had never said the name; Aisling.

'Yes,' he said quietly.

'She's still there, somewhere within you, isn't she?' Tatiana whispered, wishing she could put time back so that nothing need ever have been said. If only she had never opened that cursed portfolio, never seen the beautiful face of his lost love. Now she knew that no matter what happened that face would be with her forever.

Alexander shook his head, 'Tatiana, don't be foolish. Of course she's within me. All my life is within me. Hymie, mother, you — and, yes, her. I *am* my past. But I love you, you know that. Don't make me have to persuade you of it. It shouldn't be necessary.'

In her heart she knew he was right yet she could not help but be jealous. Hymie's words echoed over and over in her mind: 'Set him free. If you try to possess him, you'll lose him.'

Soon after this Alexander must have bought himself the cottage, Rosia, somewhere in the hills on the other side of Sienna. He simply said he needed complete privacy to work, that he was impossible to be around when he was in a creative phase, when a style was in its inception. There was a certain point, he said, when he could work on the canvasses in the studio at the bottom of the garden, but not in the beginning. She had fondly thought he would work under her nose, but he explained it was not possible.

'Nothing must interrupt me at that time. I hate to be interrupted, but it's more than that. I become immobilised if I am interrupted, the flow is broken. It's a disaster. I eat, sleep, whatever, only when I need to, sometimes not at all. I'm impossible and you would worry about me up there at the villa if I did not come to meals or bed, and I would worry about you worrying about me. I would make an effort, because I love you, and then I would be horrendous and you'd hate me, my love.'

He grinned at her and she smiled back, fighting the desire to hold on to him for dear life. She wanted to tell him that she wouldn't bother him ever, that he could eat whenever he wished, sleep all day and work all night if he so desired. But she did not say it because she knew that what he said was true. She would fuss over him. She would want to interfere. Not at first, of course. She would have such good intentions and she would battle to keep her word. But as time passed she would not be able to refrain from poking her nose in, trying to be helpful, anxious about his nourishment and his well-being, needing him too in the bed beside her. He was right. He would feel her presence willing him to come to her, irritated and lonely and, God forbid, martyred when they did not break bread together, did not sleep in each other's arms. So she said nothing.

Now he had gone to the hideaway, to Casa Rosia, and she felt bereft, full of loneliness made more devastating because of the completeness of their happiness before. What could she do? Inevitably, Hymie's words returned. She wanted to keep him so she set him free.

Chapter

21

TATIANA grew used to Alexander's absences. They were part of her life, a condition of having his love, and his children. The birth of their daughter Anouska had been followed by the birth of a son whom Alexander loved intensely. He worshipped the boy. Tatiana smiled on them, her heart full of joy as she saw Alexander's pride in his son develop as he played with Alexi, read to him, showing infinite patience with the child.

In the softly lit bedroom, arms and legs entwined in the aftermath of lovemaking he would bury his face in her scented hair and murmur, 'You have given me everything. You have given me the world.'

And yet. And yet. The dryad, the nymph with the name like a sigh; Aisling came to haunt her. Ever since she had seen those paintings the Irish girl had lurked somewhere in the corners of her mind. She was a memory for Alexander, buried with youth, as darkly dangerous and seductive as first love, forbidden love must be. Forbidden things had a sweeter taste, an allure that she could not hope to rival.

Often she chastised herself, for it was obvious that Alexander loved her, loved Anouska and adored his little son. They were a happy, tranquil family, content, at peace with each other. Why then this doubt? She was a confident, assured woman. She knew her husband loved her and she was secure in his love.

She knew, though, that there was an element in Alexander that she had never possessed, and she was jealous of that independent core. She believed that Aisling had penetrated that secret, private part of him, that she was mistress there.

She felt this and resented it most when he went to the Casa Rosia. He had left that first time after she had discovered the paintings of the girl in the wood, the golden girl, slim and startled as a fawn. They were not his best paintings. They came nowhere near the technical excellence of his other work for, it seemed to her, these paintings were born of passion and were painted in a hurry, then left, incomplete. He had not needed to finish them for he had found the model for them and they had become one. He had told her in brief, clipped sentences of his love. But he had nearly lost his reason. He had taken years to recover from Aisling and Tatiana knew he would not forget her. Most of the time Tatiana did not mind. Her world was cloudless as the blue Italian skies. The sun shone on the beloved faces of her children and her husband. Their lives unfolded serenely. There was no drama, no turmoil.

Then Alexander would become silent. The day would be no different from any other day, but she would know. There would be a slight frown, a tiny irritability, a click of his fingers, a sigh, an infinitesimal withdrawal of himself from her. And she would know. And she was always right. He would go, and her life would be as empty as a leafless tree, an uninhabited house, an unlighted street, bare, empty, dark. And she would remember Hymie's words and repeat them over and over again, 'If I want to keep him I must set him free. If I want to keep him I must set him free.'

And she did. He was her life. He was essential.

She never knew how long he would stay away; sometimes a month, six weeks, once it was for as long as ten. Sometimes he sent her a brief note, sometimes not. Afterwards he would say, 'You know where I am, what I am doing.'

He always came back exhausted, with a pile of brilliant canvasses, so dynamic as to take her breath away. Mostly they would be unfinished and he would complete them in the studio, in a sunny mood, never minding interruptions, as if all the hard labour was behind him. She knew she could never complain. He would not understand, he considered his behaviour normal for an artist.

'I'm quite impossible to be with at times like that my darling,' he would say lightly, and she knew that if it were not for Aisling she would not mind. She would have accepted his absences as the children did, if it had not been for the fact that he had taken the portraits of Aisling to his hideaway and never brought them back. In that hidden place he fled to to work, Aisling was always with him.

192

PART THREE

Chapter

22

DUBLIN critics were very unkind to Camilla. They said her book was derivative, a one-off. Like a flock of tutting hens they picked on this word and pecked on that sentence, worrying at her prose and condemning it as flimsy. The public, however, loved it, and, more importantly, bought it. She was suddenly a celebrity.

At first her parents were disbelieving. Charles Vestry came to the breakfast table one day and, picking up his *Irish Times*, almost choked as he saw the face of his daughter under the caption 'Irish writer heads Best Seller List.' Then, when the penny dropped, he demanded the cheque she had received in part-payment for her work. Camilla handed it over meekly and endorsed it, Charles breathing down her neck in excitement as she did so. He was very surprised at the size of the cheque but he was not about to let Camilla see that.

His manner to her changed after that. He became more courteous as if, Camilla thought, she had suddenly become someone of account. Charles became uneasy in her presence; he simply did not know how to treat her. He knew how to behave with a wife, children, servants and friends, businessmen and workers, but a daughter who was a successful writer was someone outside his experience and baffled him. He treated her as if she were some strange alien thing, a different species that had suddenly pitched up at his dinner table and who was quite unpredictable and might behave in an odd way, bite your hand or something. He sometimes jumped when she spoke to him, and seemed, to Camilla's amusement, nervous of her.

Caroline was proud of her daughter. She had become cynical

over the years and no longer hoped for great changes. She knew Camilla's earnings would ease things a bit, but could not quite come to terms with the fact yet. Then one day at breakfast, Camilla said, 'I really think it's time we had this room re-decorated and painted. Oh, and the roof retiled, and the gardens relandscaped.'

There was a stunned silence. Charles, who had a spoon half-way to his mouth, spluttered and put it down with a clatter. Camilla looked at him unblinking.

'Camilla, don't be ridiculous. Your cheque helped, true, and I'm, er ... we're grateful, yes, grateful. But what you suggest would cost far more than that. It would be well out of our scope.'

Camilla smiled. She was enjoying herself. 'Oh, no, it's not. I've sold the book to a movie company for a huge amount, and they want me to help them with the script.'

'You wouldn't know how,' Charles said, not meaning to put her down, but in his usual way doing just that.

'I'll learn, Father. I've got an agent now, Betsy Bright. She yo-yo's between London and Dublin, picking up Irish talent. She's in with all the right people. She promised me that if I gave her the sole rights to my work she'd sell it for far higher fees than I could hope to get. She certainly did with the book! She's sold the film rights to an independent producer, and persuaded them to employ me as part of the script-writing team. I couldn't believe it when she told me. It knocked me out. Whew!'

'Your language, Camilla, is apalling. You sound as if you were educated in the Grand Central Cinema instead of St Dymphna's. If that's the way you write, I cannot imagine what they want with you.'

Camilla tried not to feel hurt. Her father still hadn't read her book. 'They're not concerned with perfect syntax, they just want speakable lines that sound natural and Irish. They have two other script writers, veterans, but they're American and want me for "authentication", as they call it. I have to make sure the dialogue is colloquial and the whole *ambience* of the thing is Irish. And, Father, it *is* my book, my money, so I want improvements to Mount Rivers started without delay.'

Charles and Caroline stared at her. Her father swallowed a couple of times. There were tears in his eyes, and to her horror Camilla heard the dry rattle of a sob in his throat.

196

'You mean, we can have this place fixed up?' His voice was a whisper.

'You can send all the bills to me. Don't stint, and don't worry about it. We can afford it now,' Camilla said.

Charles's shoulders were shaking, his whole body bowed. She was suddenly filled with a tide of love for him so unexpected that she rose involuntarily and went to him. She put her arms around him, holding him tight.

'There, there, Father. It's okay, really it is. Everything will be all right from now on. You can set Mount Rivers to rights and Mother can buy a whole new wardrobe.'

She thought with astonishment, I love them. I really love them and I guess I always have. Only I never knew it before.

One evening in the Grand Central Cinema she bumped into Kevin Brody from Webb's. She had to climb over his legs to get to her seat. Filled with mischief she winked at him in the dark, and noticed his discomfort with glee. She settled in a seat beside him to watch the movie, an old one, and could not resist offering him a toffee. They chewed companionably together until 'The End' came up. Camilla had been watching him covertly and realised that the pimply youth had turned into a brown-eyed serious-faced man. He had even white teeth and he smiled easily. He seemed shy so she suggested they have a coffee. They went to the Paradiso and sat for hours, talking and talking. They had a common love of literature and argued over Flaubert and Stendhal, Rousseau and Proust, Jane Austen and Laclos, and inevitably James Joyce. The time sped past and they were old friends in an evening. They laughed about their first meeting.

'I was furious with you,' he said. 'I'd guessed you were stealing books. I was so self-righteous then. I felt that if you couldn't pay you shouldn't get and I couldn't wait to catch you.'

She laughed. 'You were right, Kevin. I was very immoral. Anything I couldn't afford, I took. It's no way to behave. But, I promise you, I don't do it any more.'

'Did you hate me?' he said.

'I thought you were a meanie and Mr Klein was God. It's funny to think of now. I looked forward to the day when you'd have one of *my* books in the shop just so I could say "Ya, boo, sucks to you".'

'Well, you can now, Milla.'

'Yes, but I don't want to any more. Do you know what became of the Kleins, Kevin?'

He shook his head. 'Search me. One day they were there and the next gone.'

Together Camilla and Kevin did not set the world on fire; there was no heart-thumping, weak-kneed reaction, no birds sang nor trumpets blew, but they were content. They met daily. Camilla worked all morning in Mount Rivers then took the train to Dublin. They had lunch together, held hands, walked through St Stephen's Green and fed the ducks. When Kevin went back to Webb's, Camilla often went with him and would spend the afternoon browsing through the books, doing research for her writing or just enjoying herself reading the works of minor poets. After he had finished in the evening and the shop closed they went to a movie or a theatre, or had a meal or a drink in Davey Byrne's or the Bailey.

After a few months of renovations at Mount Rivers, Camilla called a council meeting in the big cold dining room. It was odd to see her father concentrating all his attention on her, actually listening to what she had to say. Her mother's beautiful face had a worried crease between her fine gold eyebrows and an anxious expression. Camilla realised for the first time how much of a strain her father must have been under. He had not deliberately kept herself and her mother short of money. He had not had it to give. And no doubt he had worried, grown frantic at times in the struggle to keep Mount Rivers going and give her the education and her mother the life style he felt a Vestry should have.

Ah, dear God, I have so much to learn, she thought, and said: 'Father, I want to put a certain amount, whatever you think is fair, into a special account for the running of Mount Rivers, separate from the renovation work.'

He blinked and looked at her in amazement.

'As I told you, I intend to pay for initial repairs to the house and grounds. After that, there will be money in the bank for your use. And, Mother, I've opened an account for you, too, to save you having to ask me.'

A sob caught in her throat as she saw her mother's eyes fill with tears. 'Darling Milla,' she said, and opened her arms.

Camilla ran to her and, wrapped in her embrace, blurted out: 'And, Mother, do you remember how you said you wished you

198

could have oodles of soft fluffy towels, and buy new things and throw away old things and not be careful? Well, you can now.'

They were both crying and Camilla felt her father's hand on her head. She heard him say very quietly 'Thank you, Milla', and he left the room. It must have been hard for him, she thought, then concentrated on her mother's plans. Caroline wept and laughed and arranged to go to Brown Thomas the very next day and have a spending spree that would make an Arab potentate go white with envy.

Mount Rivers bloomed and blossomed like her parents with the influx of new money. Regiments of cleaners, plasterers, painters and plumbers, duly arrived to work. Drains were cleared out, the plumbing modernised, a new boiler installed. Gardeners arrived to clear and tidy, landscape and plant the pleasant gardens. Paint was stripped and restored, and paper renewed. Living in a sparkling rejuvenated home was a constant excitement to Caroline and Charles. The garden put on a summer face and summer spirits invaded Mount Rivers. There was the sound of laughter in its rooms once more, and Camilla was delighted to hear her mother singing as she went about the house, moving from room to room, happily checking things and running her fingers over some pretty new fabric as if she couldn't believe her luck.

She would shiver and smile and burst out, 'I wanna be loved by you, by you and nobody else will do, I wanna be loved by you alone. Boop-oop-e-doo.'

The years that followed were happy for Camilla. Her friendship with Kevin Brody ripened, but not into love or sex. He seemed content to take her to theatres and intimate little dinners when she was in town for she was often abroad. Her first book reached the best-seller list in Dublin, then England, and Betsy Bright was not slow in selling the book to the U.S.A. When the movie came out it boosted her sales and the book sat at Number One in Dublin, England and America for two months by which time she had completed her second novel and written a television play about Dublin for the B.B.C.

She loved her work. It absorbed her and she began to imagine that perhaps there was no room for a man in her life. The thought depressed her so she did not dwell on it. Her writing preoccupied her to the exclusion of all else.

She saw Kieron once. She was lunching with Betsy Bright in

Jammet's. It was cold outside and she wore the red fox fur coat that matched her hair. Artificial lighting in the daytime gave the popular restaurant a romantic gloom. Cutlery clinked and the buzz of chatter filled the packed room. As Camilla stood still to take off her coat she saw Kieron sitting at a table, and simultaneously he saw her. He half rose, seemed embarrassed, then sat down abruptly. He smiled uncertainly at her and turned back to his companion who, Camilla saw, was the young director, Jim something-or-other, from the Gate Theatre.

That was all there was to the meeting. She felt nothing. She was astonished for she had visualised the scene many times, acted it out in her mind, written a script. Never, in her wildest dreams, had she anticipated a total absence of feeling. It was sad but hardly tragic. She shrugged her shoulders and turned back to Betsy, feeling suddenly very relieved and strangely carefree. She spent a lot of time in London and Europe, enjoying her freedom, her free-wheeling existence. She enjoyed being an anonymous observer, part of a crowd, free to watch how others behaved, drawing inspiration from people who were unaware of her existence.

She often thought of Aisling. There were occasional notes from her interspersed with long silences. When they did arrive the communications were stilted and short. Camilla learned from one of these brief missives that Aisling had married. She was hurt not to have been invited, but then discovered that the wedding had taken place far away. Reading the London papers she found out that Aisling had married one of the richest men in the world, Ali Al-Mulla, and she could not resist a wry smile. The blurred press photo showed them together on his yacht, the *Sea Witch*. The man was indistinct, could have been anyone. All Camilla could see for sure was that he was not quite as tall as Aisling and looked slim and dark. Aisling's head was thrown back and her hair was blowing in the wind. She had one arm up to push it out of her eyes. She looked tanned and fit and very lovely. She wore shorts and a T-shirt and one foot rested on the other in a curiously little-girl stance.

For some reason Camilla thought, she's still isolated, separated from life by her looks and her money just as she was when we went to our first parties. She still seems like a person apart, even with her husband's arm around her.

Time passed and there was another missive, a printed

200

announcement that caught up with her in Paris. It stated that Samantha Al-Mulla had been born in Colombia Presbyterian, New York City, New York, on the 27th of January 1967. There was a note on the back in Aisling's writing:

> Isn't it wonderful, Milla? Please be godmother. Ali is Muslim so I don't know how to manage it, but we'll think of something.

Then silence. Aisling, Camilla thought, lived in another world, a world she had no desire to enter.

A year later she went to Rome for the second time. She had written a book set in the Eternal City, a love story, and now the B.B.C. wanted to film it for 'Play of the Week'. It should adapt itself very well to the format but Camilla wanted to do some authentication of her own and as she had the time, could work anywhere and had a craving to visit Rome again, she decided to write the script on the spot.

She got a little apartment off the Campo de' Fiori. A friend of a friend in the B.B.C. had gone on location with a film unit for six months and they were anxious not to leave their home empty. They were happy to let Camilla stay there for the few months she expected to be in Rome.

She set to work exuberantly. She loved Rome and the Romans and her work went well. One day, sipping a cappucino in the Caffè Greco on the Via Condotti, she was picked up by the most delicious young Italian. She was amused by him, lusted after his body, liked his astonishing good looks, and immediately started an affair with him. He was wonderful in bed, insanely possessive, quite useless in any practical way, and not all that bright. He bored her sometimes, his mental capacity being strictly limited. He shocked her by never having been to the Villa Borghese. To live in the same city where the Canovas and the Bernini marbles were, and never to have bothered to see them, was beyond her comprehension. But he was beautiful and a terrific lover and he did not intrude on her working life. She did not allow him to. The situation suited her perfectly.

One day a card arrived with the brief message:

> Will be in the Excelsior on Thursday. Please meet me for lunch. Expect you around 1 p.m.
>
> Aisling.

Camilla always left a forwarding address with Betsy Bright in London which Aisling was aware of. Camilla, remembering that she had not seen her friend since Livia Casey's funeral, looked forward to the meeting, wondering whether Aisling would still be as beautiful and as sad.

When Camilla entered through the great swing doors of the Excelsior she felt immediately incorrectly dressed and clumsy. She wished she could conquer this insecurity and knew deep down that one day she would be able to saunter through any hallowed hall with panache. Not yet, she told herself, not yet. Have patience.

She saw Aisling at once, uncurling herself from the deep chair she sat in, in the lounge opposite the entrance. The mirrored room caught and reflected her a hundred times over as she stood to greet Camilla. She looked incredibly lovely in a cool white linen dress, with a dark brown leather belt secured loosely around her waist and low-heeled dark brown shoes. A big brown and white Gucci bag lay on the table before her. She looked curiously vulnerable, a little tentative, as if unsure of her welcome, but Camilla, losing all self-consciousness, bounded up the stairs and hugged her. Aisling put her arms about her friend and responded, after a moment's hesitation, by warmly kissing Camilla on both cheeks.

'Oh, Camilla, it's good to see you.'

Camilla laughed. 'And to see you, Aisling. And to see you.'

'Shall we eat here?' Aisling nodded over her shoulder to the elegant restaurant behind her. It was all cool pink and white; a great chandelier, the twin of the one above them, hung over white damask tablecloths, centrepieces of pink carnations, and great mounds of fruit glistening in silver bowls.

Camilla shook her head. 'No, Ash. It's far too grand to have a heart-to-heart. It's been so long.'

Aisling looked uncertain. She was lost outside the confines of places she knew. It never occurred to her to venture anywhere new.

'You choose, then,' she said.

'I want to take you somewhere really Italian, La Carbonara in the Piazza Campo de' Fiori. It's near where I live. Come on, let's go.'

She felt bad about putting Aisling, in her pure white linen, into her scruffy little Volkswagen but shrugged mentally. Aisling would not give it a thought. Camilla was more concerned about her friend's clothes than Aisling was. It came, she supposed, from her childhood.

They drove down the Via della Tritone and into the Piazza Venezia, past the great wedding cake of the Vittoriano and down the Corso.

The girls laughed and talked as the little car manoeuvred its way through the traffic, re-establishing their easy familiarity. Now and then Camilla leant out of the car and yelled, 'Basta! Basta!' to a passing driver who had aggravated her in some way.

Aisling looked at her in astonishment, then burst out laughing, 'Oh, Milla, you've changed! You could never have done that before. You hadn't the nerve.'

Camilla shifted the groaning gear. 'Yes, I've changed, Ash. Haven't we all?'

Aisling sighed, 'I'm afraid so, Milla.'

Camilla parked on the pavement of a tiny side street and triumphantly dragged Aisling into the Piazza. The square was crowded. It was market day and the scents of the different produce greeted them: onion and garlic, strawberries and flowers, all mingling. The awnings over the stalls were fresh and white, the stall-holders smartly dressed and smelling of perfume and aftershave. They wore clean jeans, brilliant white T-shirts, pretty blouses and skirts, and the inevitable widow's black. The friends were greeted with a cacophany of cheerful badinage. Camilla led them over cobbles slippery with squashed tomatoes and the discarded outer leaves of vegetables, past the gesticulating stall-holders and the seductive perfume of the fruit, to the far end of the Campo.

There did not appear to be a restaurant there, but she parted the fuzzy hanging curtain at a doorway and they stepped into the cool dark interior of Camilla's favourite Italian eatery. The proprietress, sitting at the rear keeping one watchful eye on the comings and goings of her staff and customers and the other on the newspaper she was reading, waved to her.

'Buon giorno,' she called.

The place was full of Italians gossiping loudly, laughing and slapping each other on the shoulders.

Aisling gazed around, wide-eyed. 'This place is *amazing*, Camilla. I never saw the like.'

Camilla was irritated, 'Oh, come off it, Ash. You've been to places like this before.'

Aisling shook her head. 'I've never been anywhere like this, honestly, Milla. I'm not adventurous like you. You always had more excitement in your life than I did. I don't go to new places, just the same old haunts. Oh, well!' She shrugged. 'I like it here, though. Thank you for bringing me.'

Camilla, again a little irritated, remembered how terribly well-mannered Aisling had always been. She hadn't changed. Camilla ordered for them both at Aisling's request *gnocchi verdi*, tiny green dumplings made with spinach and cottage cheese and served with melted butter and grated cheese, then when they had finished they helped themselves from a selection of stuffed red, yellow and green peppers, aubergines, courgettes in batter, deep fried marrow flowers and a wedge of the huge cold omelette full of mushroom, onion and tomato. They finished with a slice of *tarte aux pommes*, the most delicious Aisling had ever tasted, the pastry crisp, the apples sliced thickly and covered with apricot glaze.

During the meal they talked of Mount Rivers and Slievelea, of childhood and those lost green years. Camilla was glad they were over, relieved that painful time was behind her; Aisling felt only the ache of regret for vanished happiness and misplaced trust.

She wanted wine which Camilla ordered for her, refusing to take any herself and drinking mineral water instead. Aisling seemed irritated by this until she had had a glass, then she seemed to forget that Camilla wasn't drinking.

'Do you remember that day in Mount Rivers we talked about getting married, Milla?' She said, turning the stem of the wine-glass in her fingers, 'Well, it turned out differently for me. No Pappy. No party on the lawn. Just a million of Ali's friends on a yacht miles away from home.'

'Sounds fun.'

'Don't be flip, Milla. You know what I mean.'

Camilla said nothing.

'I've settled for half a life but it's better than none, I suppose. How about you?'

'Camilla smiled ruefully. 'Me, too. But who do you suppose gets it all? Are there such people? I wonder. I used to think you were such a one but it didn't last. As for me, well, work seems to take up all of my energy.'

'I can't really say that of anything. I've got Samantha, though. She's beautiful, Camilla. I love her so, but —' she leaned over the table and touched Camilla's arm — 'I'm afraid to get close to her. It's too dangerous.'

'For whom?' Camilla asked.

Aisling shook her head, 'For both of us. I lost all the people I loved in one fell swoop. I don't want Sam ever to have to go through that.'

'But Ash, surely you can't deprive your child of ...'

'She's not deprived! God, Milla, what do you think I am? She's deprived of nothing. It's just that I don't want her ever to rely too much on anyone. Oh, dear, Camilla, I can't seem to do anything right.'

Camilla put her hand over the beautifully manicured one still resting on her arm.

'But you, Ash?' she asked, 'What about you? How are you really?'

Aisling put down her fork and looked Camilla full in the face. 'I'm well, Camilla, or as well as I seem able to be.'

'Why not happy? Why never happy? God gave you everything a woman could want.'

'Except the right man. The only man.'

'Oh, Ash, can't you forget about that? It's been a very long time.'

Camilla was irritated again. Half of her hated Aisling's tenacious grip on the past. The other half pitied her obvious inability to let it go. She thought of Franco, who waited jealously for her at home, certain she was meeting another man despite her assurances that Aisling was a woman.

Aisling said sadly, 'Do you think I like being unhappy?'

'What about ...?' Camilla could not remember her husband's name.

'Ali? Oh he's fine. Poor man. Sometime I feel ashamed of the way I treat him. He needn't put up with it, though. Sometimes I wish he'd hit me or something. I fell for the first kindness, Camilla. The first person to be really loving and kind.' She sighed and said almost as an afterthought, 'And he has more money than me.'

'How did you meet him?' Camilla asked.

'In the South of France. I'd been drinking a lot. When I went back to London after I saw you last, Milla, I went a little mad. I don't know what happened to me.' She laughed nervously. 'Or rather I do. I know what happened. I lost the will to live, to go on.'

She covered her face with her hands. How to tell Camilla how she had been, what she did?

She had been in full flight, from her father, from Slievelea, from the memory of Alexander, from the pain of the loss of her mother, and most of all from herself. She could never remember the exact sequence of events that led to her meeting Ali. They were too blurred and fuzzy in her memory.

She had tried so bravely to pick up the threads of her life. It had taken all her strength, all her courage, to return to London, to the film industry, to where she had been before she met Alexander. She had dutifully made a movie which had been a big success. In it she played a rich girl living a hopeless life on drink and drugs in the jet-set. She smiled ironically to herself when she thought of it. She had tried to draw strength from somewhere to give her the energy to go on. She dug deep within herself for hope and found only despair.

She remembered Camilla's words — 'Whenever the Black Dog sits on my shoulders, when the screaming-meemies rear their ugly heads, when fear and dread gnaw at my guts, Ash, I have a drink' — and followed her friend's advice. She found that a brandy or two helped her to sleep. The doctor recommended sleeping pills and tranquillisers so she took her prescription Mogadon and Librium not instead of alcohol but as well. She needed so badly to sleep at night for the horrors came then and she lay in a hunched-up ball, her arms over her eyes, trying to blot out the memory of a blood-stained body on a wild hillside in Taormina. The memory kept coming back, accompanied by a sense of loss so overwhelming that she thought she would drown in black despair. She ached to die but lacked the courage to commit suicide, choosing instead a longer, more agonising path to self-destruction.

She tried everything. She stayed out late, sometimes all night. She drank and drugged and used sex to try to still the turmoil within her. It was the right time. The permissive society had arrived. Mini-skirts and smack, beehives and hash, pop groups and sex, everywhere people were casting off the old morality and liberating themselves from fear and guilt.

But it did not work for Aisling. She was using the drugs, the drink, the sex, to help her forget and it did not work. She held her head high, twisted the night away, and clasped the warmth of another to her in the vain hope she could take a few hours off the carousel. She tried faster music, stronger wine. Pressing her fingers to her temples she prayed for surcease and none came. She hated herself and what she was doing, but there seemed to be no alternative. She sank so quickly into a world of booze and drugs, of casual affairs, unfinished work, broken promises and closed sets, untidy living that often ended in untimely dying. Without success she plundered London, New York and the South of France in her wild pursuit of anaesthetic, forgetfulness. People said she was on a self-destructive course. They predicted an early death, or at least collapse. They said that what Aisling most desired, courted, desperately searched for, was descent into the gutter and oblivion.

Then she met Ali Al-Mulla. He was different from the other men who had drifted in and out of her life like so much flotsam and jetsam.

She had been to a party in St Paul de Vence and the people she was with took her to the Hotel du Cap in Antibes for a nightcap. There she had met the film star, Rocky Steele. He was dazzlingly good-looking, and spent most of his time pumping iron in the gym. He was very big, had the pectorals of a Mr Universe, and not much in his head except the upkeep of his magnificent body and the ambition to make it out of 'B' movies into what his agent called 'Quality Stuff'.

Aisling Andrews appealed to him. She looked vulnerable and beautiful, and he felt, too, she might be useful to him. If she liked him she might insist on having him co-star with her, and her last movie had been an artistic success. He turned his full attention on her and assumed that as she accepted his offer of a lift home, she was accepting his body as well. He liked to screw and thought he was good at it, did it a lot to prove how good he was.

He was staying on Ali Al-Mulla's yacht which lay moored in the sapphire blue waters off Cannes harbour. Rocky took Aisling to the boat in the tender, thinking to himself how great her body looked. She was wearing a crocheted mini dress with nothing beneath but the briefest of briefs.

In his cabin he threw himself upon her without any preamble and she suddenly seemed to come to life. She started to shout,

'Hey! Hey, not so fast — hang on.' He was horrified lest anyone appear and enquire what the matter was. The thought of Rocky Steele being seen to be rejected made his blood run cold. To shut her up he slapped her sharply on both sides of her face. She started to whimper. He had not meant to hurt her, for Christ's sake. He'd never done anything like it before, never needed to, but suddenly he found himself tremendously excited. He had never got hard so fast so he hit her again, blackening one eye.

By this time he could not stop himself. He ripped off the crocheted dress and raped her, holding her arms out in a cruciform grip and pounding into her viciously. She was silent throughout but when he came she suddenly let out a piercing scream. The next thing he knew the cabin door burst open and Ali and two of his crew were standing there. What happened next was very fast. Ali knocked Rocky across the room and told the crewmen to throw him overboard.

They protested he might drown but Ali said, 'Let him.' He went to Aisling who lay on the bed, spreadeagled, her nose and mouth bleeding. He gently wrapped her in the coverlet and lifted her in his arms, speaking to her as if she was a child. When the tide of shock receded she sobbed in his arms. He rocked her until she was quiet but for dry, hiccupping sobs, It was the first time she had cried since her mother's funeral.

Later he carried her, still wrapped in the coverlet, to the bathroom off the cabin. He ran a bath for her and lifted her gently into it, waiting till the scented waters closed around her before removing the protection of the cloth. He washed her gently all over with the big yellow sponge, then patted her dry and put her into his own bed.

Ali never took advantage of the situation. He was solicitous and tender, caring for her and asking nothing in return. He set sail for the Greek Islands, giving her time in which to heal. Physically, she recovered quickly. Her skin turned pinkly brown under the rays of the sun. She swam constantly, not in the pool on board but in the grape-coloured sea. They stopped at several islands and strolled about the chalk-white villages, eating cheese and tomatoes, black olives and hard butterless bread. It was enough for Aisling. Indeed, it was superb. She wore shorts and a bikini top faded by the sun, and one day on Mykonos she slipped her hand trustingly into Ali's as they walked along. He pressed it but said nothing. It was difficult for him to leave her alone but he had the wit to know what was best for her and to want her to have just that. She healed under his tender care and consideration.

One night, on board the *Sea Witch* after supper, she asked him why he had never tried to make love to her.

'I didn't wish to rush you,' he said.

'Well, it's all right now,' she said, and leaned across the table to touch his hand.

She wanted to repay him. She wanted so much to show him how grateful she was. Aisling was too impetuous, too impulsive to take her time. Now she had some respite from her inner turmoil she grabbed at the man who had provided her with that peace, the one anchor in her life, the person who enabled her to sleep, to rest once more. She grabbed at him as a drowning person clutches a straw, not seeing that she was grasping at the escape he provided rather than the man himself. She looked to him to make it all better, not realising that the only person who could do that was herself.

Making love with him was good, fulfilling and satisfying. If it lacked earth-shaking excitement, that was par for the course, Aisling figured. She felt very safe, very protected with him, so when he judged the time was right and asked her to marry him she agreed instantly. She could not imagine anything she wanted more. It sealed the future for her, guaranteed her emotional security, she thought. He had replaced her father and Alexander; blunted the memory of them both. She felt now that she was another person, that she had begun a new chapter in her life. The Aisling who had fallen heedlessly in love with Alexander had vanished forever.

They were married on board the *Sea Witch*. Ali was too afraid of losing her to wait. He flew in his friends from all over the world and was surprised when Aisling told him there was no one she wanted to attend. She had no intention of inviting her father. She thought of Camilla but was deeply afraid of her friend's honesty. Camilla knew her through and through and she was nervous of what her friend might see in her eyes.

They stayed on the *Sea Witch*, happy and heedless, until reality broke the rhythm of their tranquil blue days at sea. Aisling discovered she was pregnant.

She told Camilla as much of this as she could. The sad little story came out in muddled sentences but Camilla got a clear picture. Aisling was still isolated. She was a poor little rich girl who could not manage her own life, who drank too much because she could not face reality, had never been prepared for it, who did not love her rich understanding husband enough.

'And Samantha?' Camilla asked.

'I wanted . . .' Aisling's eyes filled with tears and she brushed them away with the back of her hand. She filled her glass. She had nearly finished the bottle. The wine had loosened her tongue but her diction was perfect.

'I wanted you to be her godmother, but I never got around to asking. It's sad to think how many things I never got around to. She's lovely, my daughter. So lovely. Yet I feel, I don't know, distanced from her. Not able to reach her. I love her too much, you see. I'm afraid to let her know too much.'

'Why?'

Aisling's eyes flashed. 'I don't know why. Really, Camilla, what a thing to ask.'

'I'm sorry, Ash. I didn't mean to upset you.

'Milla, she's a wonder.' Aisling slurred a sentence for the first time. She was not drunk, Camilla knew, but neither was she sober. Suddenly she said, 'I must go, Milla. It was nice to see you again. Nice to talk to you.' But she made no move to leave.

'Have you any friends here in Rome, Ash?'

She shrugged. 'The gang. The usual crowd. They're the same everywhere. Same people in different places.'

'Can I drive you anywhere?'

'No. Really I'd prefer . . . I'll grab a cab.' She seemed suddenly in a hurry. She was nervous but still desperately trying to please. She gripped Camilla's hand.

'It's not a pretty tale, is it? But you don't think badly of me, do you?' she asked anxiously.

Camilla's heart flooded with love for her. She put her arms around her. 'No, how could I? Oh no, I love you dearly.'

'Because I couldn't bear it if you did.' She gave a little sob then rushed out into the sunlight, into the noise and bustle of the square.

'The proprietress said, 'Your friend, bellissima, eh? So beautiful.'

Camilla laughed at her enthusiasm, 'Oh, yes, she's beautiful.' But she added to herself: I wouldn't change places with her for a million pounds. She thought of Aisling's Rome, her circuit: the

Excelsior, the Via Condotti and Farnese, of dining in the exquisite Raneri and the Hassler with 'the gang'. But where was the real Rome in that? She sighed for her friend and followed her into the sunshine, home for siesta and a pleasant afternoon in bed with Franco.

Chapter

23

CAMILLA did not see Aisling again until she asked her to be matron-of-honour at her wedding.

She had not thought it would happen to her; falling in love, marrying. She consoled herself by thinking that in any event she was not too enamoured of the condition of matrimony, not with her mother and father's example before her. She could see, too, that Aisling was not as happy as she could be with Ali, and though Georgina was contentedly married to Emmit, she seemed more interested in the state of marriage rather than in Emmit himself. Did she love being Mrs more than she loved her husband? Camilla often wondered.

It was the summer after her Roman interlude, as she called it to herself. Franco had been devastated to see her go, but she had a pretty strong idea he would not remain broken-hearted for long. By now he would have fixed himself up with another girlfriend to admire him. Although, to do him justice, she felt sure he would not exactly have forgotten her, nevertheless she was equally sure he did not give her much thought nowadays. She had received a letter a day from him at first, heartbroken, inconsolable letters, swearing his undying devotion. They had dwindled to one a week, then one a month, and finally stopped altogether.

When Camilla returned to Mount Rivers from Rome she was disorientated. She missed the sun, the security of knowing it would be there every day in the blue sky, the thought that when she got up and showered she could slip into a T-shirt and jeans, or a cotton frock and sandals, and that would be that. She left Rome in the late autumn and came back to a dismal soggy

October, prematurely cold, grey and wet.

Camilla did not like London at the best of times so she finished her business with Betsy Bright as quickly as she could and came home to Mount Rivers to find her father ill. His ulcer was playing up and he had lost a lot of weight. Caroline was distraught and Camilla exasperated at the way her parents, since her success, had cast her in the role of problem solver. As a child she had never been consulted over any family problems, only strict unquestioning obedience was expected of her. Suddenly, overnight, she found herself playing the part of the elder statesman, her advice sought on everything. Money had given her an authority she did not desire.

Her father recovered but found he had enjoyed the role of invalid and from now on was to adopt the airs and self-pitying attitudes of the professional patient. On important occasions, dinner parties and hunt balls, he was always well, upright, dapper. But his day-by-day existence was shadowed by the helpless air of the not quite well. He deferred to Camilla in all things, was pathetically dependent on her where before he had been a dictator. The change was very marked and she often thought, when she was being fair-minded, that the financial strain over the years of her childhood had sapped his energy and left him too nervously drained to cope with the changed financial situation. It was sad to see him like this. Her success had come just a little too late to benefit him in an emotional rather than a material way. He was beyond taking positive pleasure in their newfound affluence and could only accept it gratefully.

Her mother did not help. Caroline was in a state of soporific dependence on Camilla, and blissfully happy to be so. This irritated her daughter beyond reason. That such euphoria could be induced by nothing more uplifting than a wardrobe full of new clothes! Her mother had got her wish. She could be as careless as she liked, throw things away, dress differently every day, revel in her silks and satins and the newness of them all. Camilla found it pathetic, yet she knew she was being unreasonable to expect it to be otherwise. Caroline had always been like that. Useless to expect her to change now. But it grated on Camilla's nerves, as did so many things.

Far from congratulating herself on the fact that she had brought them happiness, Camilla found herself vexed beyond belief by their tranquil acceptance of their new prosperity. It added to her general malcontent and made her edgy and irritable. She wanted sometimes to lean on her parents, to turn to them for guidance and comfort, feel the sweet irresponsibility of youth. She was young still, for heaven's sake. But it was not to be and Camilla found herself coping with the management of the estate as well as having her own work to do. She had a manager, a secretary, and a very clever accountant, but there was still a lot more paperwork than she liked, and the final decisions were always hers.

Winter passed into a cold damp spring with a continuous east wind blowing in off the sea. That became an irritant, too, grating on her nerves, humming through the house, setting everyone's teeth on edge with its persistent howling.

When she thought about it, she had every reason to be happy. Her Italian script was being edited, another film script in production in Kerry, though in the last analysis there were only about three of her ideas and four of her lines left intact in the shooting script. But she had been paid a fortune, and her latest novel had received very creditable acclaim in papers like the *Irish Times*, the *Guardian*, and *The Times* and *Observer*. She could not complain on that score.

Mount Rivers blossomed in the spring sunshine. The sound of the waters gently lulled her to sleep at night. The trees flanking the drive were bursting into bloom, the gravel newly turned before the great oaken door, now polished, its locks and latches oiled. The roof was sound at last against the cold and damp of winter, the gales and scurrying winds. Inside the house was comfortable at last. Hot water was always on tap, a washing machine to leave the Kilty twins bemused and strangely insulted. There was central heating and a full deep freeze that took away all cook's anxiety and made life more luxurious all round. Yet, contrarily, as she listened to the increasing murmur of the two rivers, Camilla hankered after the old hardships. She could not understand herself. What was the matter with her?

One day she suddenly decided to drive to Howth. It was the first beautiful day they had had in a long time. It was warm, hot even, and a lovely soft breeze was blowing. Why she was suddenly filled with a burning desire to revisit the scene of her old love, the scene of her passionate introduction to sex, she did not know.

Her love-life was non-existent and she felt curiously averse to men, strangely disillusioned and soured by her experiences with them. Kieron, Kevin and Franco, not the most auspicious bunch. Kieron had been obsessed with her, as she had with him, but little more. What had she known of his likes and dislikes? What had she known of his habits, the ones you grow to love and hate in a close relationship? Kevin was a biddable and correct escort, guaranteed to behave well always, polite but boring. And Franco, beautiful Franco, was narcissistic in the extreme; casual, endearing, childish, he was wonderful in bed but otherwise superfluous.

She jumped into her little Volkswagen, pulled the roof open and put her foot on the accelerator. She intended to drive fast by the coast road to Dublin. She did not know why she wanted to go to Howth, simply knew that she was determined to get there as quickly as possible. The wind in her hair and the sun blessing her face did nothing to dispel her cross-patch mood, a mood she realised she had been in for a long time. She felt at odds with the world, without any reason to be. She wanted desperately just to enjoy the day, accept the sun's benediction and the sweetness of the heather-scented air on her cheeks, but her red Irish anger kept flaring up. There was anger at the stupidity of the Dubliners who had allowed their city to open its arms to bulldozers and Wimpey Bars. She wondered at the people who had permitted the destruction of the exquisite Georgian houses, the façades of which had pleased her eye ever since she was a child.

She felt distaste for, a horror of, the raucous cry of the modern world with its screech of brakes, the blare of trannies, the continual hum of 'musak' in public places. She felt sometimes, in London particularly, that she was caught up in a relentless race, which killed time, and drowned silence. When she could not stand the media world any more, she fled to Mount Rivers as a monk to the chapel.

This time it had not worked and she did not know why. She told herself that happiness, tranquillity, the stillness of mind and soul and spirit she yearned for came from within, could not be bought or grabbed at, that tumult could not be evaded but had to be plucked ruthlessly from one's own soul. Her restless feelings were her own fault, she was the author of her own malaise.

She didn't know why the car stalled. Perhaps she had

215

handled it too roughly in her anger, or perhaps her mother who did unspeakable things to her own car had borrowed it and was to blame. Camilla could never work out afterwards what exactly happened. She remembered the car stalling at the traffic lights in Duke Street in the heart of Dublin, utterly refusing to start. When she grabbed the gear stick it came off in her hand entirely.

There was a lorry behind her. The driver had his hand on the horn and was blaring it. The shrill unpleasant sound jangled her already strained nerves. It was the last straw.

She jumped out of her car and purposefully walked to the articulated lorry behind. The driver looked down from his pulpit-high seat as she beckoned him. He stared at her, astonished, still blasting the horn. She beckoned again. Reluctantly he shrugged and removed his hand from the horn, opened the door and jumped down beside her. She was very much shorter and had to look up at him, a freckle-faced red-haired giant of a man, looking down on her with amazement.

Nothing daunted, full of righteous fury and flame-cheeked from agitation and bravado, she lifted her arm and slammed the offending gear-lever into his palm.

'You fix it,' she said belligerently. 'And I'll get up there —' she pointed to the driver's seat — 'then I'll blast that bloody horn and you see how you like it!'

She jumped, grabbing the handle of the door and pulling herself up into the cabin. Quick as a flash she was in his seat, looking down on his astonished face.

He stood for a moment, nonplussed, then shrugged and went to the little yellow car. He heard her yell out, 'I can't wait. I'm taking this pile to Howth. If you want it back, fetch it at the end of the pier. I'll be in the tea shop up the hill on the right.'

She had driven vans in Mount Rivers but she was not at all sure she could handle this lorry. However, she turned the key in the engine and the powerful machine sprang into throbbing life. She pulled on the wheel, backed out from behind the Volkswagen and drove off, waving to the lorry driver who stood gawking after her.

The little tea shop in Howth served home-made brown bread, crispy bacon and brown eggs fresh from the hens in the back plot. They had home-made scones and salty butter, and you were served by a dumpling of a girl or the owner herself, all smiles and *caed mile failte*. The tea shop in the living room of the owner's cottage was crammed with tables covered with flowery paper, and decorated with various religious pictures on the walls, all rather bad reproductions procured in Rome or Lourdes from one of the many stalls trading in such monstrosities. There were sea shells on the tables for ashtrays.

Camilla sat at her table, munching bacon and eggs and drowning the new-baked brown bread in butter, reflecting how much better she felt. She had acted on impulse, without thinking, and had derived enormous satisfaction from what she had done. She smiled at the memory of the lorry driver's face, then laughed aloud in the tiny room. The merry sound caused no surprise at all, for weren't happy lunatics a lovely class of person to have around, for God's sake? It was the first time she had laughed in months.

The only other customers were a family — plump, rosy-faced mother, balding father and freckled little son, with thick Cork accents — and a tweedy wind-blown hiker with a blazing red skin and a peeling nose who smiled at her when she laughed and murmured in Gaelic.

A ginger cat, sleepy from the sun, came in and rubbed itself with sinuous grace against the legs of the tables and chairs. The proprietress had taken away Camilla's empty plate and was in the act of putting a comb of Howth heather-honey in front of her, along with some soda scones hot from the oven, smiling at her and saying, 'Sure isn't it a grand life and no mistake?' when the doorway was darkened by the gigantic silhouette of the red-haired lorry driver.

'A right bloody dance you've led me, you exasperating apology for a woman,' he announced loudly to the room in general. Everyone knew exactly who he was talking to. The Cork woman studied them slyly, all interest, from beneath her lashes. Her husband blushed and choked and licked his lips in anticipation. Never having the nerve to quarrel himself, he got a vicarious pleasure out of watching others at it. Their son gazed, frankly delighted, at the ensuing conversation. The walker looked from Camilla to the lorry driver as if he were at an absolutely gripping play.

'If you dare to insult my womanhood, my femininity, you'll never see your precious truck again!'

'Haven't I just, down on the marine front? Haven't I just

seen it blocking everything all the way back to Dublin? And you'll give me the keys, or I'll take them from you, don't think I won't.'

'And what makes you think I'd mind? Is "bloody" your favourite word, or is your vocabulary a wee bit limited?'

Their audience watched with open mouths and avid interest, fully aware they were watching a flirtation, an intricate verbal, sexual dance. They were eager to hear the outcome, too interested to dissimulate.

'You're a brazen hussy,' he said with relish.

'And I won't give you your key so you'll have to take it from me! I'll give you that pleasure free, gratis, and for nothing.'

'You bloody well will! You'll hand it to me as lady-like as ye were brought up to be, Miss High-an'-mighty.'

'Sit down, you great shambling eejit of a man, and tell me your name.' Then, suddenly anxious, 'You won't lose your job, will you?'

He threw back his head and gave a great bellow of a laugh. It rose from deep within him, demanding that everyone join him. It carried everyone in the little room with it on its crest of merriment. In that one moment of unaffected joy, Camilla was lost.

'Ach, no. Don't you worry about that.' He stopped laughing and covered her hand on the table with his own large freckled one. She did not move, but caught her breath, suspended in a moment of wonder. Then she realised the nonsense of it. She was a writer, an educated lady, Miss Camilla Vestry of Mount Rivers. But then she remembered the thief, the little girl outside Webb's on the quays, and how she had felt then.

She smiled at the man before her. His eyes, merry and blue as agates, twinkled back at her like the waters at Mount Rivers with the sun on them, a million sparkling pinpoints of dazzling light. There was something wicked in their depths.

'You are exactly like Tiziano Vecellio's "La Bella",' he said. His mirth threatened to overcome him so he held his arms across his chest as if hugging himself. He watched her slyly, awaiting her reaction. She had spluttered involuntarily on the mouthful of tea she was drinking. Dumbfounded by his remark, ashamed of her assumptions, she was nonplussed.

She took a deep breath and looked at her lorry driver again.

'Oh, I'm sorry,' he said. 'You shouldn't jump so quickly to conclusions. But your face is beautiful, beautiful, beautiful ...

You are beautiful, but you are also funny.'

Her face flamed. 'Watch it, mister. Just watch it.' She felt discomfited, very embarrassed at being shown up so.

He threw up his hands as if warding off a blow. 'God, yer a terrible woman entirely. I'd be nervous of the likes of you.' He had mockingly put on the gurrier Dublin accent and she let out a little squeak of fury, but he kept smiling and their audience waited breathlessly, hanging on to their every word.

The proprietress of the little tea shop was leaning on the plastic cover that shielded the cakes from the flies; fat éclairs and hard meringues stuck with a lurid cherry, little buns covered in melting icing decorated with bright green angelica. The Cork man was wiping his plate, cleaning up the bacon grease and remaining egg yolk with a thick piece of buttered brown toast. His wife was cleaning up her resisting son's face with a large red handkerchief and a heavy hand, but her eyes were on Camilla and her companion. The hiker rested his chin on his knuckles and sat, mouth open, forgetting to make any pretence of polite disinterest, and the plump maid held the ginger tom in her arms and looked under her lashes at them, an avid expression on her face.

In this country we are all desperately interested in each other, in the daily commerce of our neighbours, Camilla thought. There are so many places where no one would look, no one would care, even if one were being murdered. But here they hang on our every word. She felt suddenly so full of joy and content that she had to blink her eyes to conceal her tears.

The lorry driver looked at her anxiously, his face wiped clean of laughter. He has understood my every thought and mood before I myself have known what I was thinking and feeling, she thought. Oh there's a thing!

'I'm sorry,' he said, full of concern. 'I shouldn't have ...'

'No,' she said. 'It's not that. I'm happy, that's all. And it's been a long time.'

She didn't care that they had an audience, didn't bother to lower her voice. She shook her head. 'I don't know what's happening,' she said wearily.

'You don't know what's happening?' he echoed in disbelief, shouting to her and the whole assembly. 'You don't know, an' you a woman, with all that intuition? We're falling in love, woman, that's what's happening.' And he leaned over the table and kissed her softly on the lips.

A sibilant sigh of satisfaction ran through the room. The encounter had reached a satisfactory conclusion, and as if some-one had pressed a starting button or flicked a switch everyone was galvanised into action. The hiker clicked his fingers for the bill, and the proprietress hurried to get it for him. The girl in the sunny doorway dropped the cat who landed softly and ran outside while she went to the hiker's table and started to clear it. The Cork family stood up, collecting their belongings, all the paraphernalia for a day out: bucket and spade, a string bag with oranges, Coca-Cola cans, magazines, tissues, a flask, and a waterproof bag no doubt with bathing things, towels, jackets and plastic raincoats against sudden inclement weather. Well, you never knew, an' the sunniest day could end in heaven's tears.

The lorry driver said, 'My name is Gerald Fitzgerald of the Fitzgerald Clan, and anyone who loves me calls me Fitz.'

She said, confused, not really in command of herself at all, 'Oh, Fitz . . .'

He smiled at her and tenderly lifted a strand of her hair out of her eyes. Then he said loudly, 'And will you do me the honour of dining with me tonight?'

She nodded. 'Of course,' she said.

There was a cheer, led by the proprietress.

'Good on yourself,' said the hiker.

'You should have kept him dangling a bit,' said the Cork woman. Then, to her husband, 'Yerra will ye get offa your back-side, aren't we missing the best of the day?'

'My name is Camilla Vestry.'

'Sure aren't you a famous woman writer now? Well, I'll be . . .' He burst out laughing again, spreading good humour about. The Cork woman looked at him fondly and the sting went out of her voice as she addressed her husband, 'Hurry up now, alanna.'

'Your car is outside. It's fixed,' Fitz said. 'Here are the keys.'

'Here are yours.'

'What, no tussle? Ach, well, maybe later.'

He stood and went to the door. Everyone in the little café waited with baited breath. Camilla's face turned to him expectantly.

'Seven-thirty in the Hibernian. Don't be late. At least I'll

always know you loved me, even though you thought I was a
lorry driver and you a fine lady,' he said, and left.

Chapter

24

IT turned out that Gerald Fitzgerald of the Fitzgerald Clan was in the haulage business with a fleet of trucks and the car hire business with a successful countrywide chain, and myriad side ventures stemming from these. One of his drivers had phoned in sick that morning — the hand of God, in Fitz's opinion — and the spare driver they usually had on tap was at his sister's wedding so Gerald himself had taken the truck out, only to meet this termagant of a woman, he said, this shrew of a colleen who had frightened him out of his wits and brightened up the whole day.

For their first proper date they would have dinner in Jammet's. They met in the Hibernian at seven-thirty for drinks first and Camilla was incredibly nervous. She had changed her dress six times before she was satisfied and ended up wearing her first choice after all, an apple-green silk frock printed with white rosebuds, crossed low over her full breasts, the skirt draped and wrapped around her hips, splitting to the knee when she sat. She knew she looked very pretty in it. She had brushed her thick red hair until it shone like burnished copper. She felt like a teenager on her first date.

He was waiting for her in the lounge. He uncurled himself from his chair, looking unfamiliar in his beautifully tailored dark suit, white and blue striped fine cotton shirt, and navy silk tie. He looked huge and distinguished, an imposing figure of a man. He had smoothed back his hair but the twinkle was there in his bright blue eyes, she was relieved to see.

He put out his hand and formally shook hers, then burst out laughing and everyone nearby smiled.

'Christ, I'm nervous,' he said. 'I was so scared you might not come. I was here at six o'clock.' She immediately felt at ease. 'What will you drink? Gin? Whiskey? Why not Champagne?'

They laughed together and she knew it would be wonderful. The evening progressed and they told each other all about themselves; the words spilling out, the similarities of taste and opinion causing them to gasp in unison at the miracle of it. She knew as they stuffed themselves with *tournedos garni*, and ice cream with hot chocolate sauce, that she was happier with Fitz than she had ever been with anyone in her life. With Kieron it had been lust, pure and simple. Kevin had shared her interest in books and films, and little else. Franco was like a loved child, not her own but someone else's that you wanted to send away when the serious things were happening.

With this man she felt a complete woman. There was a little bubble of joy within her that felt as if it might explode. She was excited and stimulated. She felt she could share everything with him: her thoughts, her hopes, her fears. She longed to touch him, to hold him, but it was not her predominant desire.

They talked about books and films but also about politics and football. She found they were in total agreement about the state of the world and what should be done about it, and in the hope that Ireland would win the Triple Crown for rugby.

He said over coffee, 'You know I lust after you?'

She could not be coy. She could not flirt with this man, or play a game. All the little tricks she had at her fingertips had to be discarded. Here nothing less than total honesty would do. Besides, the urge to touch him was overwhelming. His hand lay on the table and she desperately wanted to caress the golden down on the wrist below the pristine white cuff. His nails were square-cut, the hands themselves large and strong. All she had been able to think of as they drank their coffee was how they would feel on her body. There was no time or need for silly games between them. They had 'clicked', as they used to say at the hops long ago. 'Clicked' meant more than just liking, more than lusting, more than finding common interests, more than falling in love. It meant a soul to soul connection, a feeling of intuitive understanding of the other without speech, a meeting of mind and heart in joyful recognition. Oh, yes, they had 'clicked'.

She nodded. 'Me, too.'

'Then let's get it out of the way and start the real business of living together.'

She felt foolish saying, 'Isn't it a little soon to decide that? To live together, I mean?'

He shook his head. 'I don't think so. Do you, really?'

'No,' she whispered. 'No.'

They left the restaurant and strolled into Grafton Street. It was a bright starry night though the pavements were wet and glittering with the reflected shine of the street lamps.

'It must have rained while we were eating,' she said. He linked his fingers in hers and she felt the familiar shock of physical longing course through her body. She slid her arm around his waist under his jacket. Her whole being was weak for him, but there was much more this time. Much more.

'I have a little pad, near here, in Dawson Street. I use it when I'm working late. It's not very nice ...'

She squeezed his hand reassuringly. 'It doesn't matter. Let's go.'

They walked in silence through the cool fresh evening. He opened the door with a key and they walked through the untidy outer office full of typewriters on littered desks, phones, overflowing ashtrays, rolled up balls of paper in wastepaper baskets.

'The cleaner comes at the crack of dawn each morning,' he said. 'I'm sorry. I didn't anticipate ...'

He sounded anxious, but she giggled. 'I feel like a burglar,' she said. 'Oh, stop being a fuss budget. It's all right, really.'

Behind the office was a small room. It was neat, almost spartan, but cold and bare.

'I'm not here much, except to crash when I'm exhausted. It's not very glamorous, is it? The bed is so small.' He pulled at his tie.

'Sure what do we need with space? That's not the purpose.'

Her breath caught and he took her in his arms. 'Are you sure about this?' he asked.

For reply she kissed him. Her mouth opened under his as their passion grew and she slid out of her dress, then had a sudden attack of nerves.

'I'm not Marilyn Monroe, you know.'

She had never thought much of her body, always comparing it detrimentally with Aisling's. Now she was suddenly unsure of herself. In front of this man she was vulnerable, something she had never been before. She wanted to be perfect for him.

Please God, let him love me, she prayed silently.

Once more he divined her feelings and gave a little shake, looking really cross.

'I don't want to make love to Marilyn,' he said. 'I want to make love to you. I want to get to know *your* body, every inch of it. I'm not interested in anybody else — and don't ever put yourself down like that again! Don't you understand? I'm not looking for perfection, I'm looking for you.'

He undid her bra, touching the heavy globes of her breasts with warm, trembling fingers.

'You are ravishing,' he said. 'But, if by chance *you* are looking for perfection, I'm not so great. I'm hairy. Ever so hairy. Look.'

His body was covered in a slight golden-red down which excited her. She thought he was the most beautiful man she had ever seen. She understood what he meant. There was no reason to be self-conscious, not when they loved and wanted each other this much.

Their lovemaking had the added dimension of people who like each other, and care about each other's feelings, even engulfed in a tidal wave of passion they instinctively responded to each other's needs. At one point, his body deep within hers, he said, 'Oh, Camilla, my darlin', I love you. God, how I love you.'

Her body, aching for him to continue, stilled a moment and she said, 'Oh, Fitz, me too. Me too.'

She arched herself to him, and he took her to her coming and his with a triumphant shout.

Afterwards they showered together, joyfully sharing the tiny cubicle and the icy water, then drying each other. They both felt energised and full of love.

'Let's get out of here and never come back,' he said.

'Ahhh, I'm mad about this little room, the room I found my love in. I've grown very fond of it.'

They left the building and walked the moonlit streets of Dublin, hand in hand. They walked over O'Connell Bridge, staring down into the Liffey's dark inky waters. They went up past the Customs House, where the ships came in, and looked at the names on the hulls and smelled the oil, taking care not to

225

trip on the coils of ropes that seemed to be everywhere. He sat her on a bollard. He could not stop touching her. Gently, he brushed her hair from her cheek.

They could hear the swash of the water against the wall below them.

'There are stars in your eyes,' he said.

'It's love,' she replied.

'I'm going to live with you, love you, take care of you all the days of our lives,' he said.

She nodded. 'I know.'

'When every hair on your head, every pore on your skin, every sinew and line of your body is familiar to me, I'll learn you all over again and take delight in you every day of my life.'

They talked the talk of lovers the world over, and she was full of such happiness that she felt she could not contain it.

'Where will we live?' he asked. 'For we must live together, from this moment on, always.'

'Forever and always,' she said. 'So you choose.'

'No, you.'

'Oh, darling, if I touch you again I'll ravish you here on this bollard.'

'Let's have some breakfast. I'm starving.'

'And I only fed you last night! God, the wench is going to cost a fortune. She *eats*.'

'Nowhere will be open yet.'

'Ah. That's where you're wrong. Remember I'm a lorry driver? I know a little all night transport café in Dorset Street where they serve a mean fry. Come on.'

They ran laughing down the quay, hand in hand.

Chapter

25

CAMILLA and Fitz decided to get married. It was the logical thing to do.

Fitz's head office was situated in Santry, to the north of Dublin, and he had the smaller one in Dawson Street. He lived mainly in a house beside his headquarters and it was here that their affair had its first home, but it was not satisfactory. It was a small surburban house with no room for Camilla to work.

Mount Rivers, although it would ultimately belong to her, was not a suitable place for them to live. Caroline and Charles were very anxious to have the young couple there. They talked about dividing the house and giving the Fitzgeralds their own entrance. Camilla felt that her father was nervous that if she left Mount Rivers she might discontinue her financial support of the place. He had got into the habit of worry and there was no changing him now. Camilla reassured him as best she could, and told her parents she would be happy to arrange things as they suggested but explained gently that she and Fitz wanted another home as well. She had already bought a small house in Peel Street off Kensington Church Street in London. She hated hotels and as she had to be in England a lot these days, what with her script-writing and her television work, she had found it more conducive to comfort, more relaxing and better for her work, to have a home there.

Fitz did a lot of work in the Cork/Kerry area and Camilla and he decided that that was where they would live while in Ireland, deep in the heart of the country. They loved to be alone together, needing little company. In any event Fitz had to wine and dine a lot of clients and Camilla was involved in constant and rather fraught script conferences, so what they both wanted more than anything was a haven, a sanctuary that they could escape to and be alone together. Kerry's fuchsia-lined lanes, deep lakes and purple mountains lured them both.

In the harmony of their love, Camilla forgot about the past and lived very much in the present. Their house in Kerry was a converted thatched cottage with a little land around it. They had a large living room, comfortably furnished with a couple of glorious paintings by Agustus John on the wall, both Fitz's, and a piano that he tinkled on. He loved Scott Joplin and improvised on the keyboard while Camilla cooked. She delighted to hear him playing in the next room as she prepared their evening meal. She would put down the knife or the cooking utensil on the kitchen table and pause a moment, looking towards the mountains, amber and green in the distance, and wonder at the joy that was in her. She felt topped up with the bliss of life and would whisper a prayer that it would never stop, that nothing would ever be allowed to spoil their happiness. The days and weeks fled by and they were sufficient unto themselves. Life slowed when they were together, time moved at a calmer pace. They found solace and sustenance in each other's arms and company.

When Camilla was with Kieron she had had to keep touching him in her insecurity. This was not necessary with Fitz. The surety of oneness was there, the profound confidence of deep mature love.

Camilla bloomed, there was no other word. Her skin took on the special glow of women who are secure and confident of being loved, and unconditionally loving in return. In their tranquillity her eyes looked like polished emeralds. Her hair shone with life, and her laughter spilt over with joy. It seemed sometimes as if her laugh came just seconds before it was due or expected, as if she was constantly ready to burst into merriment.

When Fitz was not with her there was no violent loneliness. She knew they would be together again. She remembered with a rueful smile her long vigils outside Kieron's apartment in Merrion Square, and knew there was no need to have Fitz in the flesh beside her to feel he was part of her and she of him. But when they were together, life was more fulfilling and happier than she had ever thought possible. They laughed a lot, sharing the same sense of humour. A lot of their time together seemed pure fun.

She thought, This is how life should be. This is perfect, and crossed her fingers suddenly cold as she remembered her mother's voice: 'When the gods give you so much, they become jealous and demand a high price.' The feeling of trepidation was only momentary. She knew that, unlike Aisling's, her love was firmly rooted in reality, her joy was of this earth.

She did not often think of Aisling. Her friend seemed as remote as a star in the heavens. She thought of her sometimes as she sat looking at the mountains drenched in a blue mist, or watched the dawn come up over the sea in a tentative spilling of molten gold, or watched the sea, the surging Atlantic waves, green and white-crested, heaving themselves on to the pebbles only to suck and sigh their exit, dribbling back diminished from the shingle. Or sometimes, sitting in the shade of the willow near the water's edge at Mount Rivers, throwing stones into the scrabbling, gurgling river, or arm in arm with Fitz in the winter, walking down a boreen in the rain in their wellies and oilskins, silent for long companionable moments broken suddenly by a laugh or a kiss, or in the spring, the soft drizzle nourishing her skin, the purple shadows and the silvery light creating enchantment everywhere, sometimes then the thought of Aisling would slip into her mind like a shadow, but it was soon lost in the reality of her own happiness.

She talked to Fitz about her friend.

'A beautiful unhappy creature,' he mused, 'she sounds to me like the author of her own discontent.'

'Ah, no, she isn't. She couldn't help it, poor love. Not at all. In her childhood she had everything too easily. She thought life would always be like that. She was unprepared. In any event she has the illness, poor dear. The Irish illness. She drinks too much. She tries to find solace that way.'

'I've seen her in a film — I can't remember what it was called. She looked glorious but unreal.' Fitz smiled at Camilla and squeezed her waist. 'I like my women real.'

'Are there more of us then?' she quipped, and they started to laugh.

Even in the hurly-burly of London in the seventies, Camilla found peace in Peel Street. There, typing her scripts, watching the sun cast shadows over her little patio garden, pleasing her eyes by occasionally looking at the bright geraniums, the camellias in tubs or the laburnum in the corner, she would think briefly of Aisling's butterfly existence with pity and compassion.

To the public it looked as if Aisling Al-Mulla had an enviable life. Her lovely face featured often in the pages of *Tatler* and *Harpers & Queen*. There she was at the Monaco Grand Prix, skiing in Gstaad, at premières at the Met in New York and Covent Garden in London, at charity balls and benevolent functions. She looked out of the pages, her beautiful face smooth as glass. Sometimes, if a shot had caught her unawares, a close observer might see the fixed quality in the smile and note the pain deep in her eyes.

Camilla, though, when the question of marriage arose, knew that she wanted Aisling to be her matron-of-honour. The intensity of her desire surprised her. It seemed that her life had reached a peak and she wanted to share her happiness with her friend. It would be incomplete without her.

Chapter
26

AISLING was wrapped in fur when she stepped off the plane at Dublin Airport. There was no mistaking her, with her exquisite long legs, blonde hair blowing across her face, she stood out from the crowd. As a genuine work of art is easy to distinguish from the thousands of bad copies displayed by touts outside galleries all over the world, so Aisling, as usual, was set apart. For a terrifying moment Camilla wondered if she had made the most appalling mistake introducing such beauty to the man she loved. Then, as if he had sensed her feelings, Fitz's great freckled hand closed over hers. He looked down at her a moment, with love in his eyes and sympathy lurking at the corners of his mouth.

Feeling more secure she waited at the barrier to greet Aisling. She saw her moving effortlessly through the crowd, a porter following with her cases. People made way for her, as they always did. The friends hugged each other and Camilla felt with some alarm how thin she was.

Fitz grasped her hand. 'So you're the one who saved my darlin's life. I owe you one.'

Aisling looked confused for a moment, then gave him her ravishing smile. Once more Camilla felt the old familiar tug of jealousy at her heart.

She brushed the disloyal thought away. Aisling was more to be pitied than envied now, she thought, as she glanced at her friend's taut, strained face.

Aisling sat in front with Fitz on the drive to Mount Rivers. There were awkward silences in the car at first. The Rolls, usually driven by Marty Tullough's son, Seamus, with a pride and a delight that made him near impossible to endure, was in Fitz's charge today. Camilla had given in to her father's status-conscious urge. It was important to him to show their neighbours, those people who had looked down on him and pitied him in the past, how times had changed for the Vestrys. The Rolls epitomised his good fortune in a way nothing else could. Its almost vulgar opulence gave him the feeling of cocking a snook at the whole country.

It was April, and cold. The familiar lanes slid past but Aisling would not be going home. Camilla had told Fitz she would be staying in Mount Rivers and he could feel her sadness as she sat silently beside him.

He looked at her perfect profile, the exquisite skin, the faint arch of her brows and the sweep of her golden hair. She was as beautiful as Camilla had said, and more, but remote as the moon. Her loveliness had an untouchable quality about it.

Aisling pushed her sable coat off her shoulders and seemed to come to life. She said, suddenly bright, 'I'm looking forward to this so much, Milla. It's going to be funny, though, staying at Mount Rivers.'

'You did it often enough when we were little.'

'Yes, I loved it then, but I went *from* Slievelea. Have your parents seen Pappy lately, Milla?'

She was ashamed to have to tell Aisling the truth, that Charles and Caroline had never darkened the door of Slievelea since Livia had died. They had never liked Big Dan and now that his wife had gone did not bother to hide the fact any more.

'No, Ash,' she said. 'Mother and Father ...'

Aisling sighed audibly and nodded, 'They never liked Pappy, I know. I never understood before.'

'There are faults on both sides, Ash.'

'Well, I shall visit him, Samantha wants desperately to come and meet him. She never has, you know, because of me.'

'Why don't you phone her and fly her over for my wedding? I'd love to meet her. Get her over and then she can meet Big Dan, too.'

'Perhaps. But Ali won't like it. It's school, you see.'

'Oh blow school for once!'

But Aisling was concentrating on the view ahead. They had rounded a corner and were approaching Mount Rivers, following the river.

'Oh, it's beautiful, Milla! It's taken my breath away. You've had it all spruced up.'

Camilla glowed with pride. Yes, Mount Rivers did look beautiful.

Camilla settled Aisling into her room.

'It's all changed, Milla,' she said wonderingly. 'Yet it looks familiar ...'

Camilla threw back her head and laughed. 'That's because it is! It's a copy of your room in Slievelea. I so envied you that room that when I was having Mount Rivers restored, I tried to have my bedroom decorated exactly as I remembered yours. But it was folly, I realised it as soon as it was finished. It reflected your taste, not mine. I had the fittings and the furniture moved here to the guest room. Oh, Ash, it's good to have you here!'

Camilla sat on the bed, playing idly with the ropes which held back the fourposter's curtains, thinking how much time had passed since she and Ash had last talked. One thing puzzled her; during their last conversation Camilla had understood that Aisling hated her father and never wanted to see him again. One of her main reasons for inviting Aisling to Mount Rivers was to get round the problem of where she would stay as she had seemed adamant about never going to Slievelea ever again. Something must have happened to change that. Camilla wondered what.

Also she was worried by Aisling's appearance. Oh, she was exquisite still, but she could feel the tension emanating from her friend. 'While Caitlin unpacks, let's have tea downstairs before the fire in the drawing room,' she suggested. 'Let's talk. I want to catch up on things.'

Aisling left her sable coat on the bed. She was wearing a cream cashmere dress, long-sleeved, with a draped neckline. The soft wool outlined her slim body, emphasising how thin she was. She followed Camilla downstairs, admiring the changes in Mount Rivers.

'Remember how cold the hall used to be? We always have a big log fire burning here now. Come on.'

Camilla led her guest into the drawing room. It was elegant where before it had been shabby. The walls were papered in eau-de-nil and cream stripes, and the sofa and chairs covered in a light green tapestry. The beautiful Waterford cut-glass chandelier hung from the newly cleaned ceiling, and the room

233

seemed light and airy where before it had been heavy and dingy. A cheerful fire burned in the large grate surrounded by a Louis XV serencoline marble fire-place, over which hung an enormous antique mirror.

Aisling sat on the sofa in front of the fire, warming her hands.

'I'm so cold, Milla. Can I have a drink?'

'Of course. You're cold because you're too thin.'

'I know, but I can't seem to put on any weight.'

It was ironic, Camilla thought, that even now Aisling's problem was one most people would envy.

'You're too tense,' she said, handing Aisling a brandy and soda and ringing for some tea for herself.

'What can I do, Milla? And please don't talk to me about drinking. I can't bear it if you do. You see, Ali and I have grown so far apart. I think he has someone else, maybe more than one. It's not his fault. I haven't wanted him for so long . . .'

'That's not what you want to tell me at all, is it, Ash?' Camilla knew by her friend's hesitant speech that there was something else on her mind.

'No, Milla, this is going to sound unbelievable but it turns out Alexander is alive.'

She said it bluntly and at that moment Tansy Tullough came in with the tea. Nowadays she wore a starched uniform and a smug expression on her face.

'I'm sorry, Miss Camilla. Caitlin is busy unpacking and the rest of the staff are seein' about the weddin'.' Her voice had assumed a much grander accent, a tone of hauteur to match their new found affluence.

Camilla poured the tea when she had left. She sugared and milked it automatically, stunned by Aisling's news.

'Have you seen him?'

'I don't know where he is'

'Well did you look for him?'

'No, Milla, not yet. I'm too frightened. Can you understand that?'

'Yes, I think so.'

Camilla could see at once her friend's dilemma. She had clung on to this love for so long, probably idealised it out of all proportion, that to deal with Alexander in the flesh might now require more courage and clearsightedness than she was capable

234

of. Her friend's sensitive face revealed that she had been right in her surmise.

'Oh, Milla, I don't know what to do.' She gulped the brandy and Camilla noted the effect it immediately had on her.

'You see, it was all so long ago — as you once said. It's not that I'm afraid that *my* love hasn't stood the test of time, I'm sure it has. I've never really loved anyone else. Even if Alexander is changed I wouldn't care. What I'm worried about is whether *his* feelings for me have changed. He might be married.'

'He probably is,' Camilla said. 'Heavens, the man can't have remained celibate all these years, carrying a torch for you.'

'No, I don't expect that. Not at all. If only, deep down, he loves me as he always did.'

'Gosh, Aisling, I don't think you can expect that. After all, he made no attempt to see you.'

'Well, Milla . . .' Aisling was pulling at her handkerchief. She tucked it away and held out her glass to Camilla for a refill then sat looking into the dark liquid reflectively.

'You don't know everything,' she said painfully. 'What I told you before — about Pappy and his Mafia connection being responsible for Alexander's shooting — I didn't know the reason. I didn't find out myself for years, not until Pappy became ill. Did you hear about that?'

Camilla shook her head, 'I must have been in London.'

'They said he was dying and must see me once more. I'd hated the thought of him for so long, but when I got the news all I could think about was how happy my childhood had been — Pappy was a sort of god to me then. I'd vowed never to set foot in Slievelea again, not while he was there, Alexander's murderer. But when Devlin called me in Switzerland with news that he was dying, of course I went.'

She smiled ruefully and looked down at her glass. 'Devlin met me at the airport, ready to drive like the devil to get me to Pappy — but I couldn't face it, not without a few more drinks inside me. I'd had quite a few on the plane.'

She drained her glass with shocking suddenness and Camilla hesitated for a moment before pushing the heavy crystal decanter towards her. Aisling poured herself another generous measure and continued her story.

'I went to the Gresham. My mother's confessor, Father

O'Brien, was there. He was very mysterious. He took me to the presbytery. I couldn't think why. He said that he had something to tell me. It seemed he had a message for me, from Mummy.

'Apparently many years before she had confessed to him that I was illegitimate — she didn't say who my father was. Just before she died, she called Father O'Brien to her and told him, if it should ever be necessary, he could tell me the truth about myself.'

Camilla was shocked. Incredulous, she said, 'You mean, your mother ... Livia Casey ... I don't believe it!'

'It must be true, Milla.' There was conviction in Aisling's voice as she continued, 'Mummy would never have lied in the confessional. 'Father O'Brien drove me to Slievelea. I left him in a daze. For years I'd hated Pappy, blamed him for all my unhappiness, and now to learn he wasn't even my father ... I saw him the next day. He looked so sick and old, new lines of pain on his face and sorrow in the eyes that used to be so devil-may-care. I could have finished him then, hurt him worse than the illness by telling him about Mummy and me, but when it came to it, I just couldn't. I found I couldn't hate him. But he was dying. He needed to make peace with me.

'He admitted the great wrong he'd done me in ordering Alexander to be shot but for the first time he told me why. It seemed that for years he'd conducted a secret affair with Alexander's mother and they had a son It was a well-kept secret, even from Pappy for a time,' Aisling said. 'But eventually he found out, and believed that Alexander was my half-brother. When he heard we were having an affair, he was desperate. He arranged to have Alexander shot, and for me to be told he was dead. He wanted us to be parted irrevocably without having to explain why. Mummy would have made him leave Slievelea if she had ever found out. In fact, Alexander was still alive when they spirited him away to South America. Pappy even had an address for him there but it is years out of date.'

'You mean, all these years Big Dan has believed Alexander is your half-brother?'

'Whereas in fact Alexander wasn't my brother at all and neither was he dead. Alexander's family had no reason to doubt that Big Dan is my father so he must think, if he thinks of me at all, that I'm his sister but Milla, I'm not.'

It was an incredible story but, as a writer, Camilla had long since come to terms with human frailties, and realised only too well from her own experience that many families concealed bizarre secrets from the outside world. The most important thing now was for Aisling to find some peace, and to do that she must find Alexander.

'I've searched for him and found him in my imagination. I've played the scene over and over again and it always ends with me in his arms, at peace ...' A sob caught her throat. 'But, Milla, I'm terrified to look for him! I'm so much older now. I was eighteen then. Look at me now. I'm so changed, so ... flawed. I don't think I could bear it if he rejected me. I think I would die.'

Camilla went to her and put her arms around her.

'Listen, love, no man in his right mind would reject you. But if Alexander is married to someone else he might not think it, shall we say, honourable to desert wife and family for a woman he has not seen for years. But until you find Alexander, and you mustn't procrastinate about that any more, you'll have no peace. Don't you see it's the not knowing that's the worst part? Once you've found Alexander you'll sort things out. When the wedding is over and you leave here, start immediately.'

She could see as she spoke that Aisling wasn't really convinced. She looked indecisive and tentative, an excuse ready on her lips.

'It won't be so difficult to get hold of him — all it takes is courage. He's an artist. You can find out his address from Sotheby's or some art dealer in London. The better galleries should know or could tell you how to contact the people who *would* know where he is. Find him and sort it all out and then you can find some peace.'

She did not add that she knew there would be no real peace for Aisling until she had sorted out her drink problem too. She could not imagine that Alexander would rush into Aisling's arms; things like that did not happen in real life. But then, she corrected herself, people like Livia Casey were not supposed to be unfaithful to their husbands either, so perhaps she was wrong.

'There, there, Ash. It will be all right,' she said, but she did not believe for a moment that it would.

237

Chapter

27

CAMILLA was married in Mount Rivers two days later. The sun shone. The day could not have been lovelier. Aisling was matron-of-honour but all Camilla and Fitz could see was each other.

Mount Rivers looked beautiful. The guests milled about the hallway; stood, glasses in hand, on the staircase with its new carpet. They strolled the driveway to where, on one side on the lawn, a marquee had been erected. It was a jolly affair with a little Irish flag flying from the pinnacle and inside, behind a long trestle table, uniformed maids served champagne and helped the guests to cold salmon, caviar in silver bowls set on ice, lobster in aspic, and the inevitable tarts, pastry wafer thin, fruit-filled and drowned in glistening glaze. The glorious feast had been singlehandedly organised by Tansy Tullough in her brand-new fully equipped kitchen.

'I can use a lavish hand now,' she boasted to Marty and her helpers and the staff, and in her pride her cooking had reached new heights of delectability. Caroline, plump in her yellow silk dress and cartwheel straw hat, looked lovely, content and relaxed, and Charles in his morning suit was an insufferably benevolent host.

'Do have some more caviar. The champagne is Bollinger, there's plenty of it.'

Camilla wished he wouldn't but there was no way to stop him. She mentioned it to Fitz who laughed.

'Oh, let him have his little gloat. He's loving it,' was all he would say.

It was a lovely day and a lovely wedding. The Kilty sisters

wept with joy and hugged Camilla and Aisling both. An orchestra played on the lawn, silly romantic pieces that nevertheless brought tears to the eyes of the bride, her mother and Aisling. Camilla was horrified at being moved by them.

'Oh dear, how soppy. I must love you very much to be affected by such drivel.'

Fitz chuckled. ''Course you do. What's more we're going to build up quite a repertoire of sentimentality from now on. "They played this at our wedding, didn't they?" "Remember the first time I saw you?" "You wore that perfume on our first anniversary." I'm not ashamed of stuff like that,' he said.

Camilla did not wear white, to her mother's and father's consternation. She wore pearl-grey satin and looked very lovely. Aisling wore old rose, a wild silk suit that matched the fat bouquet of roses Camilla carried.

Aisling kissed her after the ceremony, her sapphire eyes full of tears. 'Be happy,' she said. 'Be happy, Milla. I'll pray for it with all my heart. And forgive me for being so awful. You will, won't you?'

Camilla nodded. 'You're not awful, Ash, you just think you are. We all love you but don't be afraid to find your own happiness. Promise?' Aisling nodded.

When the time came Camilla changed into a neat little jade-green suit, and climbed into the helicopter that was to take them to Dublin Airport. She threw her bouquet down from her seat. The wind from the propeller carried it sideways and Camilla saw the tiny pink posy virtually launch itself at Aisling's chest. She had a vision of her friend's startled face as she clutched it, and then the helicopter circled and bore them off over the mountains.

Camilla and Fitz went to Porto Heli for their honeymoon. The blue waters of Greece enchanted her. They spent their time out in boats, swimming, eating, sleeping in the sun and making love. Everything there made Camilla feel sexy; the heat made her feel sexy, the water and the swimming made her feel sexy, eating Greek food made her feel sexy, and the wonderful smell of the jasmine at night made her feel sexy. But most of all Fitz made her feel sexy. They were sublimely happy in each other's arms, at peace in this bright blue and white world where the light was crystal clear and there were no shadows.

Aisling had phoned New York and asked if Samantha could

239

fly out for the wedding, but Ali had said no. Aisling was furious with him for she knew Samantha desperately wanted to come to Mount Rivers, but Ali was adamant.

Aisling went over to Slievelea the day after Camilla's wedding. The house looked serene in the early spring sunshine. There were buds on the trees, the daffodils were out in yellow carpets and snowdrops clustered around the base of the trees, with the crocuses and primroses. Everything was as usual, reassuring, opulently cared for. Her old room greeted her unchanged, and she wept her heart out on her bed as soon as Sheilagh left her there; wept for lost happiness, lost dreams, lost loves.

Sheilagh came back and cuddled her, cradling her in her fat arms as if she were a baby again.

'Hush, alanna, hush. Why must you take it all so to heart? I know. There, there, I know. It's not the same since your mother died, and Master David gone off too, no one knows where. And the master himself so sick, so ill ... it's pitiful to see. Ach, the best times are gone and that's for sure.'

Aisling found her father sadly changed. Only his will kept him going, Devlin said. He survived by willing himself to.

'There's something keepin' him here, Miss. I dunno what it is, truly I don't. Maybe something unfinished.'

'Do you know what that could be, Devlin?'

'Ach, no, not a clue. If I did wouldn't I tell ye?' He looked at her slyly. 'An' what'll happen to the house when he does find his rest, that's what I want to know?'

'Well, let's not worry about that just now. Let's wait and see.'

'That's all very well for you to say. Easy if it's not your livelihood, beggin' your pardon, Miss Aisling. But will you be comin' back here to live? Do you think there's a chance maybe? I think it may be on the master's mind too.'

'I don't think so, Devlin. But don't look so crestfallen. It will be all right, I promise.'

'I'm sorry, Miss. I'm worried, that's all.'

Big Dan greeted her almost shyly. They'd reached a kind of peace on her last visit, at the beginning of his long illness, but he had no hope of recapturing her former trust and affection. Nevertheless, there was a request he was anxious to make.

240

'I'd like to meet Samantha. Could it be arranged, pet?'

'I'll try, Pappy. Ali refused to let her come for Camilla's wedding, but maybe he'll agree to this.'

'Say I'm dying! For God's sake, it's true, isn't it?'

Devlin sniffed in the background. He cried a lot these days, Aisling noted. Well, he was not the only one.

'Oh, stop snivelling, Devlin, for pity's sake,' Big Dan growled. 'I don't know what he's more worried about — my death or his own future.'

'Ach, sir, sure that's not fair now, is it?' Devlin gave a squeak of outrage.

'Ach, man, I didn't mean it. Just shut up the din and go! Leave me with my daughter.'

When the butler had left the room Big Dan continued matter-of-factly: 'Now tell me about the wedding. I can't get over Milla Vestry making a fortune scribbling! So Mount Rivers is gussied up? Can't imagine it. It was dingy, as I remember, and shabby. Charles Vestry always was feeble. Couldn't keep body and soul together. No wit, no get-up-and-go, didn't know how to capitalise on his assets. Silly bloody fool! Kept Caroline Jeffries in penury all her life. She was a pretty woman once, lovely. Deserved much better, but the Jeffries were snobs. Preferred to marry her to an old name and let her wither away in poverty than take a jumped-up Johnnie-come-lately like me who would have given her a good time and a decent roof over her head.'

'But there was no one else like you, Pappy, that she could have taken,' Aisling said.

'True,' he chuckled. 'Ah, well, they all hated me. To be sure it made no odds. I couldn't have cared less one way or the other.'

He lay back in his chair, tired and grey-faced. How old he looked, Aisling thought. Old and in pain. She remembered his handsome laughing face, teeth flashing, blue eyes twinkling, the smell of healthy male sweat mingling with his cologne as he lifted her high over his head.

'Pappy. Pappy. Pappy,' she whispered.

'My love, I'm so lonely sometimes,' he said gruffly. 'There is a lot of pain. I tell myself I deserve it.'

'No, Pappy! We all do what we have to, I know that now. It seems as a family we aren't very good at finding happiness.'

241

'I had it so many times, me darlin'. Or had I? Sometimes I think it was all an illusion. I was always on to the next thing.' There was a pause then he said suddenly. 'Do you ever see David?'

She shook her head. 'Not often. Sometimes.'

'How is he?'

'All right as far as I know.'

'Is it true that he's a pansy, one of those?'

'Yes, Pappy, I think so. It's not so bad, you know. It's not his fault.'

'Is it mine, do you think?'

'No, Pappy. It's no one's fault, it just is so. He was born that way.'

'No one ever was in Foley Place. It was never so in the old times!'

'Oh yes it was, Pappy. You just didn't know about it. It was kept hidden, you see. Under the carpet.'

'Better so, don't you think?'

'No, Pappy, I don't. I think the truth is always better.'

She thought suddenly that he was not really her father, and if he knew the truth of that it would probably kill him. It was too knotty a problem for her to think about now.

The evening fell and she sat before the fire after Devlin had taken Big Dan away to bed. She sat dreaming, remembering happier times, a golden childhood, the beautiful green years and how her life had turned sour. She felt as old as the shadows that darkened the corners of the room, and as insubstantial.

Three days later Aisling left Slievelea for London. Before Camilla's wedding she had received a letter from David telling her that he was at Paultons Square and would very much like to see her. It was unusual for David to make any kind of direct request and Aisling felt guilty about not having responded before this. But she knew before she saw him what the burden of any conversation with David would be: how lonely he was, how unloved, a miserable failure in his father's eyes. She had delayed seeing David until she had seen Big Dan. Perhaps his attitude to David might have changed, one never knew, and she could have been the harbinger of good news to her brother. Most of all, she knew, he longed to be accepted by his father. But Big Dan would never change, and neither would David.

Aisling was exhausted when she reached London, and felt

lost and lonely. She took a taxi to Ali's flat in Kensington Road where she bathed and changed into a cream linen suit and a caramel-coloured silk camisole. She fastened a thick gold necklet around her throat and stepped into bronze sandals, low-heeled and comfortable. She thought she would do some shopping, visit Brown's in South Molton Street, have lunch in the Connaught, wander down Beauchamp Place and pop into Janet Raeger for her underwear. She would have afternoon tea at the Ritz, in the pink and gold miasma of old-world Edwardian elegance, then she would go to Paultons Square and check up on David.

The shopping gave her little pleasure. Part of her seemed to be somewhere else. She kept remembering Camilla's face, and how she had looked at Fitz. The day passed in a daze. She sat in the Ritz, a mountain of carrier bags at her side, and thought, soon I'll look for Alexander. Pappy is all right for the moment. Samantha is fine at school. Camilla is right. I must face up to it once and for all. I'll fix my hair, and my face, maybe spend a few days at a health farm. And then, rejuvenated, I'll look for him, and find him.

She took a taxi to Paultons Square, confident that David would be there. London never changed, she thought. The red buses and the square black taxis were so reassuring. They shot around Sloane Square and down the King's Road. Home soon. The driver helped her with her parcels. They always did. It was something she took for granted.

She rang the bell of the flat but no one answered. Her hand shook as she put the key in the lock. The house was in darkness, very cold and silent. David must be out, she thought, and tried to shake off the nameless apprehension that gripped her.

The clock in the living room ticked loudly. She left her parcels in the hall and turned on the lights. There was no one there. She stood immobile, every sense alert. A chilly feeling crawled over her skin. She forced herself to be calm, making every gesture slow and deliberate. She opened the kitchen door. David had been there, and recently. She felt a flood of relief and didn't understand her emotion. There was bread on the table. The slices cut from it were hard but the loaf itself was springy to her touch. There was a half-drunk cup of coffee and some cheese. The cooker was unusually dirty and there was a pan in the sink. David had obviously fried himself some bacon and eggs, and, typically, left the washing up to Mina, who came in weekly. Aisling smiled again, wondering why she had felt so terribly apprehensive.

She took off her jacket and went into the little bathroom. The lavatory faced the door and she sat on the fancy seat, staring at her orange satin dress with diamanté straps still hanging on the back of the door. She remembered the last time she wore it. It had been the time she went to Annabel's and got drunk and had a row with Ali. She'd returned to her own flat and passed out on the sofa. David had found her the next morning and they had nursed hangovers together. The dress had hung on the door where she had put it in exchange for a terry-towel robe. Mina, the Philippino girl who 'did' for them, would leave it there forever unless specifically instructed to remove it and put it in her wardrobe. Aisling felt a moment's irritation with the girl, then shrugged it away.

She sat on the lavatory feeling numb and disconnected from life, thinking about herself as if she were someone else. She decided to have a bath and began to peel off her clothes. Naked, she turned to run the bath, and saw David. He lay in the bath, below the water. It was brick red and his face was still and set as a statue. The water was cold. He must have been dead some time.

There was no note. She wandered about the flat, still naked, looking everywhere for some message from him, but there was none. She felt sick and immeasurably weary. David, poor unnoticed little David. He'd been a pale shadow, always following her at a safe distance. She remembered holding his small body in her arms while he sobbed out how afraid he was: of school, the dark, life without his mother ... He was too fearful to live, she thought. Life was too much for him. He could not survive without nurturing, without constant reassurance, and there was no one to give him that so he had slit his wrists. He had written to her but she had delayed. He must have thought she had abandoned him. Poor, poor little David. She wept for the sadness of it all, the waste, the might-have-been. She went to the cupboard and got out the brandy bottle and poured herself a large drink. She tossed it back and poured another. She dialled 999 and told the police. Still she wept. Tears coursed down her cheeks. She looked at herself in the mirror over the fireplace and went on crying, rubbing her eyes like a child. Her running mascara gave her the look of a clown.

The doorbell rang and she rushed upstairs to the bedroom and grabbed a bathrobe out of the wardrobe.

'I want Ali,' she said to the police. 'Please get me Ali.' They were very kind and sent for her doctor. She was put to sleep with two Mogadon and her upstairs neighbour was asked to sit with her. The woman, who ran a homeopathic shop on the King's Road, had never spoken to Aisling in her life and did not approve of her. She sat in her long Indian printed cotton dress, hands clasped tightly in her ample lap, and pursed her lips in disapproval.

The police notified Ali who hurried to London to be with his wife. He obeyed Aisling's call as he always had and always would.

David was to be buried in Slievelea. Ali had contacted Big Dan, who said that they should bring his son home. He seemed more resigned to the news than upset by it. So David left the world, hardly missed, a fleeting shadow who had drifted through a short uncommitted life, rejected because he asked to be.

PART FOUR

Chapter

28

The geometrical skyline of New York was studded with golden lights as evening fell. In the apartment overlooking Fifth Avenue, Samantha Al-Mulla, Aisling's twelve-year-old daughter, stood looking out over Central Park, leaning forward against the uncurtained window. She saw the tawdry city begin to dress, putting on her sparkling camouflage for the night; she watched the car lights winking below her in the dark, moving like an illuminated centipede along the main arteries of Manhattan. She had not turned on the lights in the apartment, but stood there in the gathering gloom gazing at the superb panorama below her.

The sound of a door slamming roused her from her thoughts and she saw her father come into the spacious living room. He turned on the lights.

'Hello, Daddy,' she said.

Ali Al-Mulla froze. 'Samantha? What are you doing up at this time?'

'Grandpa is sick and Momma wants me over there and I want to go! You must let me go this time. Please, Daddy. Please.'

Ali shook his head. 'Samantha, listen to me.' Then he hesitated. When she looked at him like that, brown eyes begging, his heart melted and he usually gave in. She was very dear to him, nevertheless ...

'No, Daddy, you listen to me. I love you but I've never met Grandpa. I've never seen him once. I've never even been to Ireland. You wouldn't let me go last time. I want Momma. I haven't seen her for a while and I miss her. Daddy, please.'

'Samantha, don't. You've got school. You've got to ...'

'Oh, Daddy, I *know*. You don't have to say. But just now I want Momma. My Uncle David is dead and I'd never even met him. My Grandfather Casey is dying. I want to go to Slievelea and meet him before it's too late, don't you see.'

'I suppose so.' Ali sounded doubtful.

'It's only fair.'

Ali thought about it. God alone knew how Aisling was at the moment, what with her brother's death and the situation with her father ...

She had seemed, on the surface, happy for the first years of their marriage. He had always known that she was not in love with him, just as he was realistically aware that she needed him. He had thought it would be enough. She was like a broken reed, or a bird whose wing had been damaged. She always seemed to him a vulnerable helpless creature, in need of care and protection, and he was happy to afford her the refuge she had craved.

They had been happy for a while. He remembered the good times. She was not drinking then. Yet he had to admit to himself that even when things had been at their best there was a part of Aisling he could never reach.

When her father first became ill she had gone to Slievelea. She had not been there at all since they married and when she came back she was drinking again. Her unhappiness had returned like a dark cloud hanging over her.

She was best only with her daughter. They loved each other, those two, more than they realised, he thought. But they could not seem to reach each other. There was a barrier, a constraint, something holding Aisling back even from the daughter she adored. Ali did not know what it was, but perhaps the barrier could be breached in Slievelea.

Aisling was still upset over David's death. Samantha would help with that. In many ways she was more grown up than her mother.

One of Ali's greatest assets in business was the ability to change tactics, to admit he was on a wrong course and to change his mind and adapt. He did that now. Making a lightning decision he said, 'Okay, Samantha, you win. Go to Slievelea. Go to your mother.'

'Oh, thank you, Daddy.' She swung from his neck and kissed

250

him. He hugged her, laughing a little at her intensity. She was so like her mother.

'I'll be back soon, I promise,' she said, but somehow, his heart heavy within him, he did not believe that she would be. He turned quickly away from her and went to his room.

Samantha shook back her short blonde hair and turned off the lights again. She sat down on the window seat and looked at Manhattan's dazzling panoply of lights, sighing happily.

She turned her back on the smart apartment, the priceless carpets, soft beige leather furniture, the Lipschiz on the marble-topped table, and the Mondrian, Modigliani, the De Stael and Dubuffet on the walls. She sat, eyes closed, hugging her thin legs to her chest. She was going to Slievelea. At last she would tread green fields and there would be space and time.

She had longed for this for so long that she could hardly believe that her father had capitulated so suddenly, so easily. He had always been against it before. She knew he was afraid of her mother's past. Samantha was curious about that. No one told her anything. She guessed her mother was unhappy. Sometimes she wondered if it was her fault, but deep inside her she knew it had to do with the past, her mother's secret past.

Samantha adored her mother. Aisling was always gentle and loving with her daughter, but there was a remoteness in her attitude that prevented their ever being really close and cosy together. Perhaps at Slievelea Samantha prayed, perhaps at Slievelea they could snuggle up together and really chat. The bubble of excitement within her swelled to bursting point and Samantha opened her eyes and she yelled: 'Yippee!'

Then she went to bed and straight to sleep.

The following morning Ali Al-Mulla tip-toed into his daughter's bedroom and found her sprawled across her bed like a rag doll. She was still fully dressed in last night's faded blue jeans and Marilyn Monroe T-shirt. He bent and kissed her tenderly on the cheek. She did not stir. He went downstairs and left a note on the kitchen table: 'Hassan is getting your ticket. Safe journey. Love you. Daddy.'

The noise of the door slamming behind him as he left the apartment woke Samantha. She sat up, saw by the bedside clock that it was eleven-thirty and pulled on her loafers, the only article she had removed last night. She brushed her teeth, ran her fingers through her hair, and, slinging on her bomber

251

jacket, left the apartment.

She turned off Fifth Avenue down Fifty-ninth Street and crossed Madison and Park until she reached Third Avenue. Turning right she headed into the wind until she reached J.G. Melon's.

Her face was blue with cold, her teeth chattering, as she slipped on to a stool next to a boy with soft dark hair and a pimply adolescent face.

'Hi, Charlie.'

'Hi, Sam. How're ya doin'?'

'Okay, Charlie. Fine.'

He looked into her eyes, seeing the glow of excitement in them. 'Hey, what is it, Sam?'

She told him what had happened; first the phone call, then her father at last agreeing to let her go to Ireland. When she had finished they chewed on their hamburgers and french fries in silence and watched the people around them with cool unblinking stares. Samantha loved the warm smoky atmosphere of the diner. She loved the sight of people coming in out of the rain and cold of the awful April day, stomping their feet on the doormat and removing their wet macs; the relaxation from tension as they moved into the warm, noisy, friendly ambience, and the inevitable smile that appeared at the prospect of good food.

Charlie broke the silence. 'I like your Dad.'

'Oh, Charlie, what do you know?'

'I know I like him. He seems okay to me. Anytime I talked to him he was real nice, treated me as if I existed, ya know? Not like some dumb kid. Your Mum, now, she doesn't even know I'm alive.'

Samantha's lips had become a straight line and her eyes had narrowed to slits. 'Okay, Charlie, that's it!' she stood up, 'Lemme go!' she said as he tried to stop her. 'I don't want to talk to you any more. You just don't understand.'

'Sit down, Sam, and cool it. Just simmer down. I know your Mom's beautiful. The most beautiful woman I ever saw in my whole life, and that includes Linda Evans! But it can't be easy for your Dad.' This was a new thought for Samantha, who sat down again. 'You don't know very much about it, do you?' Charlie said.

She shook her head.

She's just a baby, he thought tenderly, looking at the small heart-shaped face dominated by the huge brown eyes, so like her father's. She had always been too thin for her age, too small, too alone. 'Anyhow, don't think about it now,' he said gently. 'What time does your plane go?'

'Nine o'clock tonight'

'I'll take you to Kennedy.'

'Oh, Charlie, you're ace!' she yelled. 'Hassan would take me in the Merc but I'd rather you took me on the Carey bus.'

They both burst out laughing, Samantha nearly choking and Charlie banging her on the back. Some people looked at them disapprovingly.

He had once borrowed his father's car and got stopped half-way to Kennedy by the cops. They thought, in retrospect, it had been the greatest.

'I'd better call Hassan,' she said. 'He'll insist on travelling with us, two seats behind ... We can pretend he's a private dick, can't we?' And we'll spend the day together, hanging out. Oh, Charlie, I'm so glad I've got you!'

They spent the day wandering about New York City. They went into Bloomingdale's and Charlie bought her some psyche-delic nail varnish and a hairband, a narrow blue elastic one she put round her wrist and swore she would not remove until she saw him again: 'Not even to wash, Charlie.' They had eggs over easy and hash browns in a diner on Fifty-ninth Street. At last, cuddled together on the Carey bus they had boarded at Grand Central Station and followed as predicted by the tall black Hassan, they bumped and rattled their way to Kennedy. They were silent on the bus, all bravado gone. They held hands and gazed out of the window, speculating on the lives and characters of the drivers of the cars whooshing past in the rain. At the airport they kissed chastely, Hassan watching from a discreet distance.

Charlie wasn't sure if the moisture on Sam's cheeks was rain or tears. He joked 'Courage, mon brave' from their favourite Tom and Jerry cartoon, The Three Mouseketeers. Then she walked away from him into the garish terminal, a waif-like, curiously vulnerable figure. Hassan called a cab and took Charlie's arm. Together they rode back in silence to New York.

Samantha's journey was uneventful. Because she was slight —

'A slip of a thing' Devlin called her when he met her at Shannon Airport in Limerick — she had been able to sleep comfortably on the flight over and give the movie a miss.

Ireland delighted and astonished her. It was so small and green, she thought. Just the right size. She had spent holidays in the South of France where the shimmering sun, the brilliant sea, the classy hotels, delighted the senses. Winter in Switzerland was like something out of a fairy tale, utterly enchanting but unreal. Ireland was what a country should be, she thought. Houses cocooned in trees snuggling into the land, not a skyscraper anywhere. The people were so helpful and on the verge of a joke or laughter all the time.

Devlin chatted with her all the way to Slievelea, telling her all about Big Dan, her grandfather, and the great house itself. He stopped at Durty Nellie's for a pint to help him on the journey home and see him from the boundary of Clare with a smile on his lips.

'It's the only way to leave anywhere,' he said.

She saw the house long before they reached it. The lights shone through the trees, like welcoming beacons in the dusk, and the grace and beauty of the building caught at her heart.

'It's beautiful,' she breathed.

'Yes, Miss.' Devlin's eyes flickered sideways to look at Slievelea. 'It hits ye,' he said. 'In the solar plexus. Hits ye right there.'

'How is my Grandfather?'

'Ach, Mr Casey waxes and wanes, but sure he's not at all well now, God help him. He has one foot in this world, and one in the next.'

'Oh, Devlin, don't! I want to get to know him, talk to him. I'm so excited to meet him.'

Devlin shook his head sadly. He doubted whether the little miss would have that much time to spend with her grandfather. The old man was very low. Sheilagh had said that the Banshee had cried out three times in the night, according to Corny O'Callaghan, but sure who'd believe him? Wasn't he three-quarters gone by six of an evening? Sure, how would he be *compos mentis* enough to hear anything after nine or, at the optimistic best, ten? Yerra he loved inventing and spreading portents of dire happenings, did Corny, all products of his fevered alcoholic imagination. Or so Devlin hoped.

He heard the child draw in her breath as the car turned

through the gates, up the drive, and Slievelea was revealed, pearl-grey in the mauve twilight. She leaned over the back of the seat.

'Please show me round now, just a little. Please, Devlin.'

He shook his head. 'They'll be waiting tea for you, Miss.'

'Oh, just a little, a tiny teensy little bit.'

He laughed and shrugged. 'Yerra, all right. Sure what's the harm?'

Aisling was with Big Dan in the library when they arrived. Evening had fallen. Sheilagh came in to build up the fire; Mary, her daughter laid the table for tea. She placed the table near Aisling, and covered it with a damask cloth. She laid the china, the violet-strewn cups and saucers, then the silver teapot and milk jug and sugar bowl, with deft, silent movements, while Sheilagh watched approvingly. There were hot buttered crumpets, barm brack and toasted scones. Aisling poured the tea.

'Have something to eat,' Big Dan said.

'No, thank you, Pappy.'

They sat quietly, one on either side of the blazing log fire.

'I wish you'd eat, Ash,' he said again plaintively.

'I'm all right, Pappy.' Her voice was weary.

The clock ticked and a log fell. There was the sound of a car in the drive.

'That's them,' he said.

Aisling nodded but did not move. It was nearly a half an hour later, and Big Dan was getting edgy, when the door opened and Devlin came in with Samantha. Or rather she erupted into the room, full of vitality, like a breath of very fresh, very heady air. Her mother and grandfather blinked at the energetic intrusion.

'Momma, Momma, I'm here! I'm actually in Slievelea. Oh, Momma, it's ace! It's lovely, lovely, lovely! I made Devlin show me round. He didn't want to, I *forced* him. He's so cute! How could you ever leave here, Momma? How could you? It's the most beautiful place in the world.'

She turned to Big Dan, holding out her hand. 'I guess you must be my grandfather. Forgive me if I've been rude, it's just that I'm so excited. I'm Samantha. I don't want to be Al-Mulla any more. I want to be Sam Casey of Slievelea.'

Big Dan laughed.

'Please,' she said.

'You may if you wish. But you must do what your mother and father think best.'

'Well, I'm sure here is a great deal more suitable than New York City.'

'We'll stay here for a while,' Aisling said soothingly.

'No, Momma forever. Have I ever asked you for anything in my life before? Seriously, have I?'

Aisling realised with surprise that Samantha never had. She had never wanted anything very much.

'Well, I'm asking you now. I want to stay here in Slievelea. I belong here.'

Big Dan knew that one day, very soon, he would die. But now, at this moment in time, he had Aisling with him in this his favourite room in Slievelea, his beloved home. He had Aisling and her enchanting daughter.

Aisling sat across from him, firelight on her beautiful sad face. Did she know, he wondered, that the only place she would ever find rest was Slievelea? And she had brought him the present of this delightful American child. The old world and the new. Sam Casey. How truly miraculous that was.

He nodded over his tea. The child took a footstool and put it beside him. She sat on it and rested her head on his knees. Gently he stroked her silky hair and she turned and smiled up at him.

Samantha's arrival held pain as well as pleasure. The astonishing rapport she had instantly felt with both the house and its owner was dampened by the fact that Big Dan was dying. In her young life death had so far had no place. It was an awesome experience to endure and Samantha walked the woods that winter and spring, tears on her cheeks, as she cried, 'Why? Why? Why?'

Then to a half-believed-in, superstitiously-needed-to-be-appeased God she said, 'Don't you see how much I love him?'

Perhaps this shadowy God heard her oblique request, for her grandfather had a remission.

Meanwhile, Aisling was drinking all day. Sam often heard her mother about the great house, crashing into walls, falling over. She saw her stagger on her way to bed, her beautiful face blurred and marred, defiled by excess. Sam's heart was bruised to its soft centre but her grandfather comforted her, understood

256

all. They talked endlessly.

Sam pushed him out in his wheelchair one day, tucking his mohair rug around him, though the day was warm. He said to her, looking down to the sea, 'I love this view. Look at Slieve-lea, Sam Casey, me darlin'. Look at that old grey stone. It's protected the family for hundreds of years — it has weathered the winds and the snow, the sun and the soft rain of Ireland. Look at the grass as green as emeralds and the wood yonder — the bluebells you'll see here make sapphires look pale and paltry in comparison. I love the lake, every leaf on every tree, every blade of grass here. I fought for them, Sammy. I've cheated and I've murdered even. Are you shocked?'

She had shaken her head, her eyes sparkling with excitement at the thought.

'You've got Livia's heart-shaped face and so many of her expressions,' he said. He sighed then and Sam gently stroked his soft white hair. She knew her face was not at all like Livia's and her eyes were brown. She had minutely examined the family portraits which hung on the walls above the curving staircase. The faces were so revealing and her grandfather told her all about her ancestors: Lord Rennett, lace at his throat, shot beside the lake; Lady Rennett, his wife, pale and gentle, who lost her reason when Lord Rennett died.

'Nowadays she'd have a shrink, be neurotic and probably marry again,' Big Dan had said.

She loved the portraits of Lady Deirdre Tandy-Cullaine. Samantha thought she had never seen such a beautiful face. There were two paintings of her; one when she was eighteen or thereabouts in her first ball gown of pure Brussels lace with tiny silver threads running through it. She wore pearls at her throat that Samantha had seen her mother wear, and her hair was dressed with flowers. The second portrait showed Deirdre as a magnificent old woman. Dressed in black velvet, back straight as a ramrod, she was formidable, proud, aristocratic. It was a face that demanded to be painted and the artist had obviously loved his task.

I wish I'd known you, but I wouldn't have been frightened of you any more than I'm frightened of grandfather, Samantha thought.

Her grandfather laughed fit to be tied when she told him what she was thinking. He had taken her hand in his and held on to it very tightly.

'I feel very possessive of you, little one,' he said. 'It's been a great fault of mine. I fought for Slievelea and I got it — I won first prize. There's not a house like it in the length and breadth of the land.'

Samantha nodded, her heart swelling with love for this old man, and the place they were in.

'Do you feel the same? Yes, ye would. I had to learn so much to make myself worthy of Slievelea. "Lord of the Manor" is a far cry from the back-street slum I was born in — a little Dublin gurrier, I was. I started as a barrow boy, would ye believe?' He threw back his head and yelled out something she could not understand. 'That's the street cry I used. Slowly, it's "Any ould pots an pans, bedlinen will do".'

Devlin had appeared from the side of the house in response to Big Dan's shout. 'I want to see Spotty again,' Dan said as the butler came over to them. 'Devlin, get in touch with your Da for me — I want to see him before I die. Now, where was I?'

'You're not tired, Grandpa, are you?' Samantha asked.

He shook his head impatiently. 'No, no, no, no, no. You've given me back my life, child, for a while anyway. If only you knew ...'

She heard the sob in his voice, thought it an old man's sentimentality and patted his hand. His skin was soft and dry. She and Devlin pushed the chair around the house and into the rose garden. Here they were sheltered from the breeze and out of earshot of the sun. The air was soft and warm and some early roses turned their faces to the pale platinum sun, reaching for warmth. Dan imitated their gesture and Samantha told Devlin that he could leave them for a while. She sat on a stone bench and held her grandfather's hand.

'This was Deirdre Tandy-Cullaine's favourite place to sit and dream. She was your great-great-grandmother. I met her when I was a young man and she made owning Slievelea possible for me.' He gave a triumphant laugh, slapping his hand on his knee.

'Dammed if I don't think she's here now, telling me something. Of course, of course.' He looked at Sam and patted her hand.

'I must do with Slievelea as she did and give it to you.' He paused then said, 'I loved her very much, Sam, maybe more than I've ever loved anyone — except perhaps you.'

She pressed his hand to her cheek.

'I've always loved women,' he continued, 'it's been the only softness in me all my life. Psychologists now would say it's because my mother rejected me, didn't notice me much, cold woman that she was, a great Irish patriot. Well, whatever the reason, I've loved the women in my life though I've been too possessive of them. Jessica must have no one but me. Livia must be mine and mine alone. However, you know nothing of that, a cushla, so pay no attention to an old man's ramblings.'

He dozed a little and silence settled comfortably over the rose garden except for the sweet song of the birds, the rustling tissue paper sound of the wind in the rose leaves, the barking of the dogs in the distance and the reed-thin voice of Mary, the maid, as she sang an Irish song over and over, always stopping on the same line as if she had forgotten the rest.

> My young love said to me
> My mother won't mind,
> And my father won't chide you
> For your lack of kind,
> Then she moved away from me and this she did say
> And this she did say and this she did say ...

Samantha loved these breaks in the old man's stream of memories. She could dwell on what he had said, piece together the jigsaw of the past, ponder on its ambiguities. She loved the old man's hints of a mysterious and violent past.

Then Dan opened his eyes, gave his stooped shoulders a little shake and continued, 'I destroyed Aisling.' Samantha started to protest, but he waved her to silence. 'Oh, yes. Your mother belonged much more to me than *her* mother, and that was wrong. It smothered her, gave her a sense of false security. She wasn't prepared for life, for men. Life's not fair, Sam, remember that and you'll be all right. Never expect life to be fair. Aisling did and it ruined her. Please God she'll get better ...'

His voice broke a little, but he continued, 'It would make me so happy if she got better. I feel so much to blame for your mother. It was as if all the love dammed up in me, allowed no outlet in my childhood, drowned the women I loved — except for Lady Deirdre and yourself. Perhaps because I had no real power over either of you, I left you both free. You seem sensible, child, a child of a wiser generation. I didn't do so well with my life.'

Sam laughed. 'I don't know how you can say that, Grandpa! All this money and power from — where did you say? A slum? I think you did okay.'

'Oh, yes, materially. But I lost everyone I ever loved in the process.'

'The secret is, Sam, to live your life. If I had mine all over again I would probably do everything I did exactly the same. It's easy to be wise after the event. I made mistakes but I lived my life to the hilt. Remember that, won't you?'

She nodded and he looked at her shrewdly, his bright blue eyes sharp as a bird's.

'Perhaps you know it already. With your mother and father, I reckon you might have some glimmer of what I'm talking about.'

Samantha nodded and smiled and they were silent. It was always like that between them; the comfortable rambling conversations lapsing into a silence full of mutual content and companionship.

Samantha did not simply listen to his ramblings but confided in him, too, everything about her short life before they had met.

They watched as the spring dusk fell, shadows creeping over the land, deep purple, velvet green, pale mauve and salmon. The roses, tired from their straining towards the sun, drooped on their stalks and a star came out over the russet hills. Samantha tucked the rug over the old man's legs and pushed him slowly back to the great stone house.

Chapter
29

The room was small and full of cigarette smoke. It spiralled around the heads of the men around the table and lay heavy in the air, a thick dense fog. All the windows were shut, and hermetically sealed with black plastic stuck to the frames with drawing pins. There was a naked electric light bulb overhead. The room contained a mattress in one corner, an army blanket covering a comrade who was sleeping there. He looked like death; white-faced, open-mouthed, motionless. The chairs were straight-backed and the table around which the men sat was covered with a plastic cloth, patterned with the brown rings of a thousand damp coffee mugs. There was an electric kettle plugged into a socket in another corner of the room and in front of it lay a tin tray, the original design scratched off, on which stood chipped mugs, a carton of milk, a bowl of sugar and a plate of McVitie's digestive biscuits.

The men around the table looked at Derry Devlin who sat with his eyes downcast, hands loosely clasped between his knees. The men were all thin, he had noted, there were no fat ones here. They had in common, too, a certain coldness in their eyes. They were men of few words. It seemed to Derry as if they communicated telepathically. In the dark centres of their minds there was no light. Like machines they went inexorably on their way, incapable of stopping. To stop would be too frightening. Their thoughts might wander then, ask unanswerable questions, give them pause for thought. Derry knew all this and it neither attracted nor repelled him. He simply accepted as inevitable the path he was treading.

He knew they were going to ask something big of him, and

that it was because he knew the Caseys of Slievelea for whom his uncle worked. He did not mind. These men were his real family. Since his mother died there had been no place to go except to these people. He belonged here, was part of a close brother-hood.

Some of them talked of 'the Cause' and that made him laugh. Inwardly, of course. He never laughed aloud. He knew there was no 'Cause' any more, that it had been buried some far-off day when the first, twentieth or hundredth murder had been committed in the name of freedom. Now they fought because they were an army, for that reason alone. They did not know how to do anything else. They fed off danger because they had been weaned on violence and they were hooked on it. If Ireland were united tomorrow, how many of them could live in peace, settle down and send up a grateful prayer? None, Derry knew, nary a one. The next day, off they'd be to fight in Palestine or some South American country, and it would not matter on which side they fought. Some of the men had been mercenaries all their lives, as far back as the Congo years ago. The newer ones had been trained in Syria. Oh, yes, there were a few fanatics, and all of them held little green Irish passports. They were the ones who truly believed in a united Ireland, men with a chip and a violent nature whom the South had not been kind to. You found very few Southerners with homes, a family or money up here in the Bogside. There were some in the I.R.A. but they were old hat now, old men wanting to become respectable in old age, to join the politicians and go to the media and explain themselves. No, the true I.N.L.A. were indigenous to the North and had British passports. They were tense men whose lives ran to a pattern. They lived underground, away from the light, or slept in remote fields, alone most of the time. Terrorists, he thought, were themselves terrified but could not admit it even to themselves. Death was inevitable, a violent lonely death probable.

The S.A.S. were as bad, trigger-happy bastards. The North was a breeding ground of violent jumpy men. They never won the game but the tension and the excitement, the sheer animal will to survive, kept them going like a drug.

They were angry today, Derry knew. They were also planning something big. He had heard talk. Just a sentence here and there, but enough. If they were monosyllabic, he was silent. A

Cistercian monk could not be less talkative than he. They valued his mute obedience.

He remembered his first job. A young family, all in bed. The instructions were that he and Gerry were to get the man, the father, and if there was anyone else there, too bad. The man had been seen going into the police station. He had been around the periphery of the organisation for a few months and was a danger, even with his limited knowledge of people and places. He had to go. When they broke in he had been asleep in bed with his wife. They were both naked and there was a babby beside them. They got him spot-on. His body leaped like a landed fish and fell to the bed, bloody and exposed. The wife had screamed and so they shot her and the babby. He was never sure why he shot the babby. Reflex action? A sense of incompleteness if they hadn't? The room must contain only death before they left.

The men were speaking softly to each other and dragging deeply on their cigarettes. Eamonn McClusky wore a patch after losing an eye when a bomb he was planting blew up in his face. The men admired him for that but he was a mean man, full of fury, with a hard Belfast accent.

They were angry now because a schoolboy member of the I.N.L.A. had been gunned down by the S.A.S. a few days ago. He had been part of a group on their way to attack an army patrol. They were masked and carrying rifles and a rocket launcher. The S.A.S. had pinned them down and shot them, no questions asked. The boy had called out: 'For God's sake, don't shoot me' before they sprayed over a hundred bullets into him and the others. The I.N.L.A. were making a big deal about the inhumanity of it all which was silly, Derry thought, silly and stupid. They themselves never gave a tinker's whether their victims were young or old, whether they wanted to die or not. What was sauce for the goose, Derry thought, and left it.

Eamonn fixed his good eye on him and said: 'Are ye ready?' Derry nodded. 'At's hamself — the head mawn.'

Derry knew this meant Lord Bristow, an English industrialist with extensive business interests in Eire.

'When that mawn was in Stormont, in the Government, he did us damage. At'll show tham.'

Who? Derry wondered. He had heard them speak about Bristow's past connections with Stormont and the Government of

Northern Ireland, and now of his connection with Big Dan Casey. It appeared, they said, that Big Dan Casey, the son of two of Ireland's greatest patriots, was selling out his business interests to this man, their enemy. Lord Bristow had been to Slievelea often in the past months.

This was the place to nail him. One of the others at the table said, 'We want ham. He made pledges once, he didn't keep them. Now he's encroaching on Gaelic territory, siphoning off Gaelic money.'

'Yas, he has ta go,' Eamonn agreed. 'You see?' Derry nodded again. 'The oul fella, yer Uncle's boss, is dyin'. Bristow's around there all the time. Keep yer eyes open. Ef Dan Casey dies, an he'll have te soon, the funeral might be the time.'

A man with a shaven head and a hard mouth said, 'See, ye'll not be noticed, not there with yer uncle. No one'll suspect you.'

'Any problems then?' Eamonn asked. Derry shook his head again. 'Okay, then. Go and wait to do it. That's the contract. That's the contractual agreement.' He stood and put out his hand. Derry shook it and left the room.

Outside he lit a fag. The tension drained from his body. For a long while now he had known that there was something big afoot and now he knew what it was. They had chosen him as executioner. He had been singled out for the honour. His connection with Slievelea had a lot to do with it, but nevertheless it was a great honour, a great trust. He tested his feelings for a reaction. As usual there was none.

Chapter

30

Samantha met Derry Devlin that first spring at Slievelea. She always remembered the feel of that day, the fresh spring air, the cool salty taste from the sea breeze that agitated the leaves on the trees and blew the soft white clouds swiftly across the sky. She felt totally at peace. She and Big Dan had shared lunch in the dappled light of the dining room. They had been silent, in harmony with each other.

Afterwards, as usual, Samantha enjoyed a walk through the bluebell wood. The silence there matched the stillness within her. She had never felt so at peace. She slouched along, fists deep in the pockets of her jeans, whistling tunelessly the song Mary sang:

'My young love said to me
My mother won't mind
And my father won't chide you
For your lack of kind,
Then she moved away from me
And this she did say,
It will not be long love till our weddin' day.

She liked the words. They were somehow reassuring and serene like the woods around her and the day itself, particularly the words Mary always forgot:
'It will not be long love till our weddin' day'.

The spring air was bracing and the carpet of bluebells proved Dan right — sapphire was a cold, limited colour compared with the endless number of hues reflected in the sea of flowers, tints ranging from lilac and violet to cobalt. The sun peeped and danced through a lattice of tender young spring leaves and the lake beckoned, glimmering in the distance, enchanting, sparkling. Samantha loved it, spent hours alone here while Dan tossed and turned the disturbed sleep of an invalid.

Samantha wandered towards the lake, trampling through waist-high bulrushes in her wellington boots to untie the remaining rowing boat. There were usually two and she wondered idly where the second had gone before pushing herself through rushes and reeds and on to the still waters. The ever-changing lake was sometimes pearl-grey with mist-scarves like chiffon catching the trees and wafting across the dove-coloured water. Sometimes it was so blue it seemed indigo and the white swans sailing the surface were reflected in its depths; sometimes it seemed a green continuation of the wood, the leaves, the grass, the silver fish stirring in the depths and the olive sea-grass swaying beneath the lapping wavelets; sometimes it was azure matching the pale blue sky, sometimes, and Samantha liked this best of all, it was purple; a pool mirroring the heathered mountains and wine-red hills, golden sky and dark green leaves. Today it was an expectant powdery blue with touches of buttercup gold from the cool spring sun which washed the sky yellow.

She saw the gazebo resting like a mirage on the shimmering surface. She untied the boat and poled slowly to the Greek temple pushing through the weeds that sometimes clung to the oars. She sat on the steps near the edge, feeling like a tiny speck in the radiant world. She prayed Big Dan would not die. Not yet — not just yet. That her mother would get well, mentally and physically; and that Charlie would come this summer or next. Somehow he must persuade his Mom.

She sat there quietly. The world seemed caught between evening and twilight. She heard a sound behind her. Unalarmed, she turned her head. There was a young man standing motionless, leaning against the gazebo's pillared portico. He must have been there all the time, she thought, seeing no reason to be afraid of such a slip of a lad. His face was thin and fine-boned and oddly closed. Only his eyes moved. He stared at Samantha as if ordering her to speak first. She did.

'Who are you?'

266

'I'm Derry Devlin — me uncle works above.' He jerked his head towards the wood.

Samantha was proud of herself for being able to interpret the sharp nasal twang with which he spoke. 'You have a Northerner's accent,' she said.

'Aye. Me Mam was a wee Northern Catholic.' He pronounced it 'Caitholic'. 'She married me da when she worked here as a skivvy but soon got bored with the life. Even a bit of a skirmish with the U.D.A. seemed better than this deadly dull place. Nothin' happens here, she said.'

'We don't have skivvies here — unless your mother is a hundred years old.' Sam was stung by the implied slight on the family, and the derogatory use of the term for maid.

'Well, it seemed to me mam that's what she was. She had a livelier time in Belfast.'

'Some excitement — death and killings!' She couldn't keep the sarcasm out of her voice.

'I thought ye'd understand it, bein' American.'

'How did you know that?'

'I have big ears, and me uncle said. You're Big Dan Casey's granddaughter from the U.S.A. The land of Al Capone, Jimmy Cagney and gun law.'

Sam shrugged. 'Oh, the movies.'

'Movies nothin'. All America carries guns. Everyone knows, it's a fact.' His voice was passionless. 'In my job we carry guns too. It's a nice feelin'.' She shuddered. He said after a pause: 'Americans are all fascists at heart, only they haven't the honesty to come right out and say so. You should know. They're jealous of the Brits who are the only true democrats left.'

She couldn't follow his reasoning.

'But they are your enemy, surely?'

'We've no love for democracy,' he said with a shrug.

The cold spring sun coloured the world pale gold. It hovered above the edge of the lake. Birds sang, sublimely unaware that an enemy of life itself stood motionless leaning against the Corinthian pillar.

'Have you ever killed anyone?' Samantha asked.

'None of yer business,' he said, and his voice was still and cold and dead and she suddenly knew that he had.

'Do you hate the English, the Brits, so?' she asked after a pause.

267

'Ye don't understand, it's war. Hate has nothin tae do wi' it, not any more. It's inevitable. If you grow up Catholic in Belfast it's all ye dream of becoming, a member of the I.R.A. or, if ye're really committed, the I.N.L.A. Conditions are so bad it's all there's left te aim for. Like the gangsters in the Twenties, it's the only chance of glory.'

Samantha looked at his hard young fearless face. Despite the savagery of his words she wanted to put her arms around him, to hold him, to make him smile. She blushed and hung her head. He flicked the end of the cigarette into the lake where it hissed and sank.

'Don't you regret the suffering you cause?'

'I only regret an ejucation. I'd have liked an ejucation,' he said, 'but there was no chance of that. Me mam would have helped but she was blown up — so were me sisters, and the babby. I was comin' back from school and the bomb went off. I saw the front door go up, bits of me mam and the babby and Ellen and Maeve all over the garden — they must have been in the hall, someone musta got them there — an I laughed. I laughed.' His voice held no other emotion than vague surprise. 'I never laugh,' he added. 'I don't know why people do it, but I did it then. I couldn't stop. They tried to keep me from the garden but I went past them. There was a crowd of neighbours there. The women were keening, moaning like souls in torment, and I saw me mam's arm lying in the grass all by itself, just an arm. I picked it up and I took off her weddin' ring, see.'

He held out his hand. The plain gold band caught the sunlight. His hand was small, the nails dirty and bitten. There were callouses on the side of his thumb and first finger.

He must be left-handed, she thought.

'I held her arm and they couldn't get it away from me. It was all that was left of her, ye see. I was twelve years old.'

He remembered the smoke and the acrid smell that seemed to be everywhere, and him holding that arm to his breast, and the struggle he had with the ring. He had pushed away the kindly neighbours who tried to surround him and take him in charge. From somewhere came a terrible noise, like the sound a rabbit makes in a snare. He realised it came from him.

Then two strange men had materialised beside him. One of them had put his hand on Derry's shoulder, calming him. Everyone else was rushing about. There was confusion everywhere, and a small fire had broken out. He could smell it. People were shouting and Mrs Tomblety from next door was screaming.

Her daughter said, 'Quiet, Ma. God help her, Mrs Devlin. She wouldn't have hurt a fly, poor woman.'

The man with his hand on Derry's shoulder gestured for him to follow. He knew who they were and he went. He didn't care what happened to him then. He still didn't care.

Mrs Tomblety had stopped screaming and was sobbing on her daughter's shoulder. 'The babbies, the poor babbies! Jesus, Mary and Joseph, the poor babbies!'

He took a last look at the bits of pram scattered about, and left with the men.

'I never went to school again. I went on the run. I joined the I.N.L.A., learned to fight.'

'Why did you come down here?'

'To see me uncle and get some money, then I'll go back. Ye can't live without money, ye know. Mickey gives us bread.'

'Mickey?' She thought his use of the last word very old-fashioned.

'Devlin, your butler. Christ, ye don't even know his name!'

'Does he know what you do?'

'He guesses, he doesn't want to know. Very few Southerners do. It's "I'm all right, Jack" for most of them. They don't want to be involved in the North's schizophrenic struggle. There is no personality conflict here in the South — ye are easy in yer own skins. The North is psychotic country — Belfast is an English town and the people are at war with themselves, never mind each other! But ye don't know what I'm talking about!'

He looked at her closely. 'Yer not goin' to tell them I'm here, are ye? That I visitin' me uncle fer bread? Yer not te say a word about me or ...'

She looked at him defiantly. 'Or what?'

He shrugged. 'Ach, it's not important. Yer only a kid an' they'll never believe ye. I'll deny I'm anythin' but a wee Belfast lad on a visit wi' a relation, me uncle. Mickey Devlin. I'm not on the wanted list. They don't know me.' He seemed to be persuading himself, giving himself the argument.

'Grandpa would.'

'Maybe yes, maybe no. I don't care anyhow if I do get caught. It's all the same to me. I dont't care much about anythin'. Ye'd

269

get my uncle in trouble, though, *if* they believed you which they wouldn't. An' maybe yer Grandather too.' He was silent, his head turned away. 'Ye won't grass will ye?'

'No' she said quietly. She didn't know why she said it, why she agreed to the promise of silence. She just knew she could not split on anyone.

'I didn't think ye were the sort to grass.' He looked at her and the glance was edged with wistfulness. 'Ye hate me, don' ye?'

She shook her head. 'I want to but I can't.'

He looked younger even than she. He was playing in a grown-ups' game and was frightened, she could see. Oh, he might not know he was scared, but he was.

He whistled tunelessly, his eyes avoiding hers. She looked away from his face, white now in the dying glory of the sun, and gazed into the lake. Her eyes pierced the shimmering surface, penetrated the undertow where grasses swayed in slow motion. Her pupils dilated suddenly.

'Look,' she said. 'Bones!'

He saw the chalk-white skeleton at the bottom of the lake and shrugged. 'It's been there for ever,' he said. 'From Druid times mebbe. Or perhaps it was murder: a Catholic priest for his religion, a Fenian for a bloody Brit, a jealous husband, who knows? Anyway it's a peaceful resting place. Better than being sprayed over half a mile by a bomb.'

The sun had left one golden shaft dividing sky and lake like a sword. They stood in near darkness, face to face. He could see the tiny freckles on her tip-tilted nose and at the corners of her eyes. His lashes were white-gold in the draining light, the colour had gone from his eyes which now looked silver. Samantha could smell tobacco on his breath from the cigarette he had smoked, and she shivered. He put his arm around her and squeezed her thin shoulders. It hurt but she did not mind.

'Come on,' he said. 'Look, there's the moon. Ye must get back.'

She nodded and he smiled at her. It felt funny to be doing it, as if the muscles of his face were reluctant to go that particular way. She caught her breath at the sweetness of it, the sadness of it.

'Ye forget it can be like this,' he said. 'Nothin' to fear. No explosion waitin' in the next minute or hour or day. Yer always

270

waitin'. Ye learn to live expectin' it. Ye forget it can be like this.'

She looked up at him in the silvery dusk. He pushed a strand of her hair away from her forehead, then abruptly left her and climbed into a boat, holding out his hand.

'Come on, they'll be sendin' out a search party. The likes of you can't be missin' for long before there's a hue and cry.' They took the boat he had crossed in, leaving hers moored on the island. They journeyed back in silence. The lake was a silver mirror sparkling under the stars. The oars cleaved the water leaving a spray of shining spangles dancing far behind them. Derry helped her out at the small jetty on the house side of the lake. He tied up the boat and gripped her arm again, so hard it hurt. Then he put his fingers to his lips, abruptly let her go and ran off through the woods.

She had raised her arm to wave but he never once looked back. She let it fall rather forlornly and, plunging her fists into the pockets of her jeans, trudged up the path through the woods to the house.

Samantha told her grandfather everything about her life, but she wouldn't tell him about the meeting with Derry down by the lake. She would not break her word. She could not bear for Derry to be caught, punished, imprisoned. She would not be responsible for that.

She knew how little sympathy Big Dan, her mother and father had with terrorists. Her father was virulent about the Palestinian Liberation Organisation and Big Dan and Aisling were equally anti the I.R.A.

'My mother and father were active in the Irish Revolution,' her grandfather had said, 'the old I.R.A. But this lot — no, Sam, it's not the same thing at all. This lot behave like the old Black and Tans here used to when England sent her convicts and criminals to subdue the rebellious Irish savages. They raped and killed innocent women and children, weren't too fussy who they murdered as long as they generated terror. This lot's the same. Throwing bombs at England is no answer. Slaughtering innocents is shocking and murderous and not to be tolerated.

'Things have changed Samantha. There was no Frenchman, German, Italian or Spaniard who did not understand the old I.R.A., the old war, and there's no Englishman who ever will. They have not felt the march of foreign boots across their land, the hot breath of oppression over their dreaming towns. Journey through the villages of Britain and you can feel the undisturbed peace of centuries.

'Amputate the North, I say. Belfast is an English town. Cut that poisoned gangrenous limb of the Holy Land of Ireland and set it adrift in the North Sea. We in the South do not want it. Let them keep their British passports. Let Paisley, the I.R.A., the Brits, the Prods and the Catholics, all of their bigotry, drown! They are ignorant men and women all and ignorance is the very worst crime.'

No, Sam would not speak of Derry Devlin to Big Dan Casey.

When she got back to the house Devlin was nowhere to be seen and Sheilagh told her that Mr Casey was not too well and had retired early. She was to have dinner alone in the dining room. Then Sheilagh winked at her and said, 'But sure ye might feel like a little lost colleen there all by yerself, so I thought we could sneak you a tray in the music room an we could pop on a video — "Mary Poppins" mebbe, or "Star Wars"?'

Samantha smiled at Sheilagh, glad of her consideration. No, she did not want to eat alone in that big imposing room tonight. Yes, she'd love a tray in the music room and the companionship of a video. She did not tell Sheilagh she would much prefer to watch "Kramer versus Kramer", but sat stoically through "Star Wars" until Sheilagh had taken away the glass bowl that had held her ice cream with hot chocolate sauce.

'Goodnight,' the maid said, 'and don't forget to turn the machine off.'

When she had gone Samantha stopped Darth Vader in his tracks and replaced him with Dustin Hoffman and Meryl Streep. She curled up on a sofa under Big Dan's mohair rug and promptly fell asleep. Devlin looked in later, shaking his head at the sight of the unconscious chocolate-smeared face and the tug-of-love scene on the screen. Worried by his nephew's visit and Big Dan's condition, he sighed deeply and carried Samantha up to her bedroom. Depositing her on her bed and covering her with the duvet, he sighed once again and left her in peace.

Chapter
31

Aisling had had to get away from Slievelea, though she longed to stay, to remain in the house she loved so well. She longed to share the warmth generated by her father and her daughter. They exuded an atmosphere of loving and belonging, of peaceful content in each other's company. They did not exclude her, far from it. By speech and gesture but, most compellingly, by the expressions in their eyes they begged her to join in, to complete the circle of their love.

But she could not. Though she wished so much to relax into that soothing love she found to her horror that she could not any more. She could reach no one. She felt as if she was behind glass, screaming silently.

Once, when she had left herself short of drink in her room, she had gone downstairs to get some from the library. She could hear her father and Samantha talking, or rather could hear Big Dan's gruff voice rambling on and on as he seemed to do perpetually with Sam. Samantha was laughing at what he said. It was a chuckle of deep merriment, of total enjoyment. Aisling had not heard her laugh like that for many years.

Aisling had paused for a moment, longing to join them, but she knew she could not. She needed a drink too badly. The door to the music room was open. She scuttled out of a shaft of light into shadow, a thief in her father's house. She opened the library door stealthily, hoping not to be heard. As she glanced around she saw Devlin, a tray of sandwiches and hot chocolate in his hand, looking at her. He was obviously going to the music room with a snack for Dan and Sam, and stared open-mouthed at her strange behaviour. Aisling said nothing but slipped into the library, closing the door behind her. She reached the blessed liquid in the cut-glass decanter with a sigh of relief.

Another day — it remained etched on her mind in every detail — Samantha stood in the open doorway watching her pour a drink at ten o'clock in the morning. The sun shone obliquely through the dining-room window. The servants had cleared breakfast from the table and from the sideboard, but on the latter there always remained decanters and glasses. The sideboard stood between twin French windows which were open on this crisp sunny day. Everything in the room was gleaming and sparkling in the springtime freshness; the Constable and the early Turners on the wall, the dark polished wood of the tables and chairs, the dancing tongues of flame in the wide fireplace, the glow of brass fire-irons, bright yellow daffodils in a huge bowl. Shafts of golden light from the sun hung over the lawns.

Aisling saw none of it, too intent on picking up the brandy decanter with hands that shook uncontrollably. She took a tumbler and managed to pour some of the spirit into it. She brought it to her mouth with both hands, teeth chattering against the glass, and drank greedily. As she put down the glass she saw Sam standing in the doorway. They stood for a heartbeat, motionless, looking at each other.

'Mother, you're sick,' Samantha said. There was no condemnation in her voice, which made it worse. She sounded mature and pitying and Aisling could not bear it. She shook her head and left the room, walking on to the terrace away from Sam. It was colder out there than she had thought.

Borey Nugent brought the chestnut mare around from the stables and she pranced restlessly in the driveway, waiting for Samantha. She came running past Aisling, small and neat, in jodhpurs and bright yellow polo-necked sweater. She struggled into the tweed jacket she was carrying, put her black hat on her head and tapped it secure with the palm of her hand.

'Hi, Borey,' she called as Aisling turned back into the dining room, relieved. Now she could have another brandy. She felt alien to the pair, her father and daughter, an outsider, an embarrassing onlooker. They pretended not to notice her erratic behaviour, her trembling hands, her unsteadiness. But they could not help seeing her as she was, though they tried to make allowances, to forgive, to sympathise.

It was intolerable, this pity from her own father and daughter. Aisling slammed the glass on the table with such force that a hairline crack snaked up the side of the thick crystal. She would go to London. Perhaps there, if she could see Ali, she could sort herself out, do something to extricate herself from the mess she was in. A small voice, instantly stilled, told her she was simply trying to run away, to escape from the restraints Slievelea imposed on her. In London she could drink herself to death and be damned. A great wave of relief engulfed her as she went to the telephone.

Aisling left Samantha at Slievelea with Big Dan and a highly qualified tutor, the latter to appease Ali, and ran away to London. She had postponed her search for Alexander, and postponed it still. Incapable of facing him or herself, she had lost her long battle with alcohol. Once she had drunk to still her fears but now she had to drink to survive. She had no choice in the matter and hated herself for her weakness. How could someone who had spent such a magic childhood at Slievelea, had the best possible education, been brought up to be a lady, behave so? Frightened and out of control she paced the Kensington Road flat and drank compulsively because she could not stop. She felt she was searching, searching for something just outside her grasp.

Memories came flooding back, unbearably sweet. She could see Big Dan holding his arms out to her, feel again the beating of his heart under her cheek. She remembered her mother's sweet face, her hand covering her mouth when she laughed, and the day she had crowned Camilla with daisies.

Camilla had been there then, was always there in Aisling's memories. She must see Camilla now. Only Milla could help her.

Chapter

32

The houses in Peel Street had originally been terraced workers' cottages inhabited by the staffs of the big houses in Kensington and Mayfair. More recently the middle class had turned them into fashionable town residences. They were like dolls-houses, Aisling thought, homely and prosperous. Pretty window boxes full of flowers, fresh paint in pastel shades, pink and blue and lemon. The interiors visible through sparkling windows looked like advertisements from glossy magazines. Every house looked cared for and inviting.

Camilla answered Aisling's ring. She looked surprised then her expression changed to a welcoming smile. Taking Aisling's sable coat from her, she ushered her into the living room. It was furnished with pretty pink and white chintz-covered sofas and armchairs. There was a glass-topped coffee table. Glazed cotton Roman blinds drawn halfway and fine lace covered the windows, and there were masses of flowers everywhere. It was a room of pale light colours. A white piano stood in one corner with sheet music scattered on it. Although the room was over-crowded it was comfortable and homely, providing the reassurance Aisling craved.

Camilla looked quizzically at her visitor for a moment then said, 'I'll get us some tea.'

Aisling bit back the words on her lips. When Camilla left the room she crossed to a shelf where a collection of bottles stood and took the stopper out of a whisky decanter. There was no brandy. She raised the bottle-neck to her lips and took a swig, then another, then one for luck. Wiping the neck of the bottle with the palm of her hand she froze, paranoiacally certain that

Camilla was spying on her from the doorway. She looked over her shoulder, saw no one, and replaced the bottle. Then she walked quickly and silently across the room and peered into the hallway. There was no one there. She could hear Camilla's voice speaking in French.

'*Quelques biscuits avec le thé, s'il vous plaît, Yvette.*'

Aisling's heart was pounding. She felt the whisky firing her blood and, with trembling hands, closed the door and stood with her back to it. She heard footsteps coming upstairs and quickly crossed the little room, sitting down just as the door opened.

Camilla entered the room with a laden tray in her hands. There were mugs, incongruous beside the dainty tea things, a Wedgwood plate on which sandwiches were arranged, matching sugar basin, fluted milk jug and graceful teapot. Aisling knew she could not hope to hold anything, despite the stolen drink, her hands shook too much. Camilla seemed to divine her state. She poured the tea into the mugs and, as if it was the most natural thing in the world, put Aisling's near her on the table rather than in her hand. She obeyed her guest's nod and added milk and sugar. Camilla pointedly picked up her mug with both hands and Aisling, following suit, found she could get the mug to her lips quite safely that way.

Camilla examined her. There was understanding in her eyes, though Aisling couldn't think why. Her old friend was married and happy, mistress of this peaceful, pretty house. What did she know of the demons inside Aisling's head?

Camilla assessed her friend's precarious mental balance at a glance but noted too that it did not seem to have affected Aisling's looks unduly. She was as elegant as ever. The pleats of her beige skirt just covered her knees and her incredibly long silk-stockinged legs ended in soft coffee-coloured leather shoes with high heels; Aisling had never been afraid of her height. Her cashmere sweater looked touchable, cuddly even, but her face quivered with tension.

Camilla looked at her own legs, short Irish legs she always called them, and fingered the fabric of the Indian-type smock she wore over a Marks and Spencer polo-necked sweater. She sighed ruefully and said to Aisling: 'Well?'

'Well, Camilla.' Aisling looked down and laughed nervously. 'I've just arrived in London for a break from Slievelea. Pappy is dying this time, and after David — you heard about that, I suppose?' Camilla nodded and Aisling continued in a rush: 'Sam's with Pappy. She's much better with him than I am. It's easier for her. I had to get away for a while but I find myself a wee bit lonely and thought I'd pop in to see you.'

'My dear, I'm so sorry for your trouble. Poor David — and your father.'

'I'm sorry to disturb you, Milla. I'm sure you must be busy working. I hate to burden you with my problems like this. Is Fitz here?'

'Not at the moment. He has his work and I have mine. He comes over for weekends, then in a month or two we'll have a lovely break in Tralee.'

'How lovely.' Aisling's voice sounded mechanical.

'Yes, it is. Look, why don't you stay here a bit? There's plenty of room.'

'Oh, no, I couldn't.'

She could have only a month ago, but now Aisling always needed another drink very quickly and she was afraid to be anywhere where her drinking might be noted and perhaps stopped. The strain would be too much.

'No,' she said again, 'I'm happy to stay in Ali's flat in Kensington Road.' There was an awkward pause. Aisling suddenly realised she had sounded rude and ungracious. 'I'm sorry, Milla. I didn't mean to sound ungrateful. It's just that . . .'

Camilla sighed. She could see that Aisling was near breaking point. It's arriving, she thought. She's fought to keep sane but she's on the brink of disaster. All her adult life except for the magical time she had spent with Alexander, Aisling had been fighting, an exhausting inner struggle. Now that is coming to an end. Oh, I hope I can help her, Camilla thought, please God, let me be able to help her.

Aisling had begun to cry. Tears flowed down her cheeks as if a dam had burst and her breath rasped in her throat. Camilla went and sat on the floor beside her, stroking her hand and plying her with tissues. Finally Aisling sobbed herself to a stop. She blew her nose, drew in a shaking breath and suddenly looked at Camilla.

'I don't know why I came here today. It's awful, arriving unexpectedly and crying all over you. Forgive me, please.'

'There's nothing to forgive. There never is between real friends. We're "Friends forever" remember? Just remember you can count on me. If you need me, I'll be here.'

Aisling stood up, suddenly full of purpose. She dried her eyes and hurried to the door.

'Thank you, Milla. Thanks a ton. I'll remember, though why I should need you . . .' Her voice petered out and she could not meet the clear gaze of her friend. 'I must go. Really I must,' she said.

In the hall she looked around wildly. 'Have you got my coat? Ah, there it is. Goodbye.'

She pulled at the door as if she couldn't wait another minute. Camilla drew back the chain and undid the Banham lock. Aisling was out on the path in an instant, opening the tiny gate and waving goodbye. She practically ran down Peel Street and disappeared from sight.

Camilla closed the door and returned to the living room. She sipped at her tea, but finding it cold called Yvette, the young French student who worked for her part-time, and asked her to make some fresh. She made indifferent tea but that did not concern Camilla now. She sat and thought about her friend who was drowning every bit as surely as she had nearly drowned that day at Mount Rivers when Aisling had saved her life. She knew she would be there for her friend when she needed her, and she knew too that it would not be long now. She decided to explain it all to Fitz in case she had to devote more time to Aisling. He would understand. She felt a sudden surge of gratitude for her man and said a quick prayer of thanksgiving.

Their lives seemed so complete, she thought, but there had been tough times for them too. When they first married she had felt that her cup of joy was filled to overflowing with Fitz and her successful career. She could never wish for anything more. But she did. She wanted children.

Fitz had mentioned what fun it would be to have a family, and suddenly it had seemed the most desirable thing in the world.

'A boy like you and a girl like me,' she had said, laughing up at her husband.

'Even if it's a girl like me and a boy like you, I don't mind. So you can stop taking the Pill.'

'But, Fitz, I'm not. I've never been on the Pill,' she told him, a chill of fear in the pit of her stomach.

'I assumed you were,' he said, surprised. 'I don't know why. Male chauvinist piggery, I suppose. Sorry, darling.'

And then she had seen the dawning realisation in his eyes.

'Don't worry, my love. If it's not to be, it's not to be . We have so much. Maybe the gods don't think we need anything else. I know I don't.'

She had gone to the doctor the next day. They had done tests in Dublin and in London. It had taken months. The answer came up the same: she was infertile. How horrible those words were to her. They repeated themselves over and over in her mind:

'You are infertile.' And the worst, 'Barren.'

She had spent weeks in a pit of depression, paying no attention to her husband's reassurance that it did not matter. She felt diminished, a failure as a woman.

She saw Fitz's worried face, the distress in his eyes and the shut-out look he wore, and she could not help him. She knew she was being selfish but could not help herself.

Then one night when he had drawn near to her in their big bed in Kerry, to put his arms around her and comfort her, she had turned away, isolating herself from him in her misery. He had pulled her into a sitting position quite roughly and shaken her until her teeth rattled. She was so surprised that she had just stared at him aghast, and he had shaken her again.

'Now listen to me, Mrs Fitzgerald, and listen well! I did not marry you for children. I married you because I loved you, because you were the dearest thing to me in the whole world and I wanted to have you with me to be part of me all the days of my life. You loved me, too, or said you did, and we created heaven between us. Yes, my love, heaven. If you think I'm going to sit here and let you wantonly destroy what we've got, this special precious love, then you're an eejit and a fool. How dare you? I ask you, Mrs Fitzgerald, how dare you?'

She saw to her surprise that he was really angry with her and felt a sob rise in her throat.

'How dare you play around with our love? How ungrateful can you be? Don't you know you're playing with fire? Don't risk the perfect thing we've got. You might damage it beyond repair. So don't, I beg of you, don't.'

She saw that his eyes were full of tears. He touched her

tentatively, as if he were afraid she might rebuff him. She felt ashamed in front of him. She opened her arms wide to him, holding on to him for dear life, wrapping her arms around him and almost hurting him with the strength of her hug. She felt his body shake and realised he was crying.

'I love you so. Darlin' I love you so and I thought I was losin' you,' he said. She held him and they rocked on the bed together, comforting each other, consoling and soothing until their bodies melted into each other and they became one, their act of love an act of healing.

They hardly ever spoke of it again. There were, the doctors said, adoption and all sorts of other avenues to explore but Fitz and Camilla put aside any such alternatives. They came to a deeply satisfying conclusion that they did not really need children, that they were sufficient unto each other. Camilla told Fitz that it was the stigma of infertility that had bothered her much more than the fact that she could not have children. She told him, and she meant it, that the actuality of little ones underfoot did not appeal to her at all.

It had deepened their love for each other. What had been joyous and true was now profound. Camilla thought of her husband, her heart full of love and gratitude.

I'm so lucky, she thought, so very lucky. Ash has drawn all the lousy cards and I've got all the aces. But I'll wait for her. She's going to need help. And soon.

Chapter

33

A flood of loneliness washed over Aisling as she entered Ali's apartment. It felt empty, cold and impersonal. She shivered, fighting despair, and took off her coat, hanging it in the hall closet. She kicked off her shoes and drew the curtains in the living room. Feeling small and very alone she poured herself a drink and turned on the hi-fi. Mahler's Fifth Symphony flooded the room, melancholy erotic music.

'I can't stand this,' she said aloud. 'I'll phone Ali.'

She pulled the phone towards her, dialled the New York apartment. Ali answered. He asked her about Samantha. She told him Sam was great and safe in Slievelea then could think of nothing more to tell him. After all, what did she ever do now but open fresh bottles of brandy? She opened another when she had said goodnight.

She got up the following morning, or rather fell out of bed, and made the loo just in time to throw up. It was hard dry retching. For a time she knelt on the floor, leaning her head against the cold rim of the ceramic bowl. Then she shook her head and the walls seemed to be moving. For a moment the motion of tossing her head to and fro had caused this phenomenon, she thought, then found she was mistaken. The walls *were* moving. They were covered in ants. The ants were moving. The ants were everywhere. She lay on the floor, too petrified even to scream. She would have to tell Ali. He would get Rentokil to exterminate them.

She crawled away from the lavatory, but the ants were everywhere. She kept brushing them away yet, when she looked at her bare legs there was nothing there. She stood, hauling herself upright by grasping the rim of the wash basin. The ants were in the basin too. She ran the cold tap to drown them then, cupping her hands, filled them with cold water and splashed some on her face. She did this a few times, gasping with the shock, then filled her hands yet again. Holding them to her mouth, she lapped the water with her tongue. She felt better as she sucked at the pure clean liquid and slaked her grim and raging thirst. She raised her head slowly and looked around. The ants had gone.

She sighed with relief then shuddered as she caught sight of herself in the mirror over the basin. She had two half moons of black below her eyes. The eyes themselves were bloodshot and swollen. Her lipstick had smudged and dyed the skin around her mouth.

There is no name low enough for me now, she thought. Suppose Alexander were to see me like this? Oh, Jesus, no. Please, no. She thought of Camilla, then shook her head sadly.

'It's too late,' she said aloud. 'Too late.'

She bathed, scrubbing herself until her skin was red and raw. She shampooed her hair twice, used an expensive perfumed conditioner. She cleaned her teeth twice, gargled with Listerine, sprayed Gold Spot on her breath, bathed her eyes in Optrex and a second time in Couleur Bleue. She dusted herself with fine Guerlain talcum powder, sprayed herself liberally with Shalimar. She still felt dirty and used. She dressed herself in a cashmere polo-necked red sweater, grey flannel pleated wool skirt and matching jacket. She made up her face carefully. She left the apartment with no idea where she was going.

She walked along Kensington Road and crossed into the Park. It was a cold clear day. A snappy wind tugged at the children's kites and stung their cheeks rose-red. The sun sparkled remotely in an ice-blue sky. The trees had a sprinkling of leaves and the grass was stiff with frost. Aisling shivered. She was usually insulated from this kind of cold by her fur coat. She wondered why she had been so foolish as to dress so lightly. This suit was meant for warmer weather. She always forgot London could be cold.

She was not going to drink today, she had made up her mind. She was going to prove to herself that she could do it. She had planned her day carefully. She would walk in the Park until noon then she would have a light lunch in Fortnum and Mason and go to a movie in the afternoon. She would walk up Piccadilly and into Leicester Square and pick some light and glamorous film to see — a James Bond, a Woody Allen. After that she would dine in the Grill Room at the Savoy. Then home, a sleeping pill and bed.

She told herself she could do it. She gazed enviously at the couples in the Park. Everyone looked happy to her. A boy and a girl passed, young and obviously in love; they were oblivious to anyone but each other.

There were anxious-faced mothers with children 'Don't *do* that, Amanda. How many times must I tell you?' 'Leave it *alone*, James. Put it down. You never know who had it.' 'If you hit Davina once more, Jonathan, I shall tell your father tonight and there will be *no* MacDonalds or video.' Aisling wished she could be one of them. She saw a dirty old tramp lying against a tree. He was putting newspaper under his tattered coat. He had a green bottle in his pocket. She shuddered and walked swiftly away.

She wandered towards the children's playground. Tears came into her eyes as she looked at the Fairy Tree. The magic of it touched her. She crossed the road to the tube station and took the Central Line from Queensway to Oxford Street then changed on to the Piccadilly Line. She was unhappy in the tube. She felt trapped, claustrophobic. She got the escalator at Piccadilly and looked upwards, eager for escape. Then she saw him — Alexander! His back was to her. She could see his neck, his head. It was unmistakable the way he held his head tilted fractionally back. His once dark hair was steel grey but still soft and abundant. It *was* him. There was no one like him in the whole world.

She thought she would faint. Her knees gave way and she fell on them. They were grazed and her tights laddered. She barely noticed.

'Alexander,' she called. 'Alexander,' she screamed. The man was ahead of her, disappearing out of sight. A woman behind her was trying to help. 'Leave me alone,' she cried. 'Alexander!'

'Well, really! I was only trying to help.' The woman sounded hurt. 'Probably drunk,' she said, sniffing self-righteously.

Aisling ran out into the multitude at Piccadilly Circus. She looked backwards and forwards distractedly. There was no one even remotely resembling Alexander. She was going mad. What had the woman said — 'Probably drunk?' Well, she might as well be. What did it matter? She would have a drink — then she would forget the pain. Forget Alexander for the moment. She strode purposefully towards the Café Royale.

After that things became hazy. She lost track of time, her actions, what she said or to whom. She remembered bars, bright lights, and sometimes people's faces turned to her in pity or in disgust. She remembered going round and round and round on the Circle Line, not knowing what she was doing in the Underground or where she was supposed to be going.

The nightmare reached its climax in the Hammersmith Underpass. How she got there she never remembered. She found herself sitting there with someone else. It was a man. He stank and his face was bloated. He had scabs on his forehead, Aisling saw through a blur. His hair was matted and he had a filthy scarf knotted around his neck. His eyes swam in their red sockets. His jacket was shiny with grease and dirt, and looked ancient and foul, yet beneath the dirt and sores his face was young. The smell of sweat and stale alcohol came from him in waves.

Aisling shook her head. She felt numb, paralysed. She couldn't move, couldn't feel. She looked at the neon-lit nightmare graffiti on the concrete walls. There was a painting of a dragon snaking sideways across a wall, psychedelic green, its eyes terrifying. Aisling sat on the filthy floor of the cold grey tunnel and tried to scream but could not, tried to move but found she was unable to.

Then suddenly a cry rose from her body, from the core of her being, from her soul. 'Dear God, help me now. Help me, my God. Help me, please.'

She found herself walking on unsteady legs, her high heels click-clacking on the stone floor, down the tunnel as she followed the zig-zagging shape of the dragon to the entrance. She emerged in front of the tube station, saw a phone box in front of her. She could recall the phone number clearly yet she had not memorised it. In her pocket she found ten pence. She dialled the number. Afterwards she was dumbfounded that she had managed it; that she had remembered the number, that her fingers worked, that she could cope with the tricky business of putting the money in and pushing the correct buttons. Afterwards she found out why, understood how. It had happened to many others, that vital burst of energy prayed for, reached out for in the dark night of the soul. Somehow she knew Camilla would be there.

Aisling whispered through stiff lips, 'Camilla, please come for me. I'm in Hammersmith Tube, at the phones. Camilla, help. Oh God, help. Oh my God, help me. Camilla, help me.'

Chapter

34

Aisling was never to forget Camilla's kindness to her. Her dedication and care during Aisling's nightmare days and nights of drying out was above and beyond the call even of love. She held her hands through the DTs when the ants swarmed over her again. She bathed her face with towels dipped in ice water. She held Aisling's convulsed and sweating body in the pangs of withdrawal. She whispered the Serenity Prayer over and over to her, the prayer of Alcoholics Anonymous.

'God grant me the serenity to accept the things I cannot change, the courage to change the things I can, and the wisdom to know the difference.'

When the worst was over and Aisling's body was sponged down and gently patted dry, the linen on the little bed in Camilla's spare room changed for the umpteenth time, her friend lay exhausted and pale between the sheets. Her body ached in every limb but the worst agony was over. Camilla gave her the first drink of orange and tepid water. They smiled at each other when Aisling did not heave it up at once. Then she sank into a deep sleep, hardly shifting her position in the bed, to awaken eight hours later and drink a cup of weak sugared tea. She managed a Digestive biscuit and slept again, deep, undreaming, soul-refreshing sleep.

Later they talked — God, how they talked — all the barriers gone. Camilla took Aisling to A.A. meetings. She had prepared well to help her friend. She had phoned the General Service Office and kind people had told her what to do. Aisling would do anything to get well so she agreed to attend meetings. Part of her mind rejected the simple slogans, and she was daunted by the rigorous programme of self-honesty, but she saw it was the only way.

And it worked. She did what she was told and the compulsion to drink, that awful enslavement was taken away. She could actually say she did not want a drink; she whose every day had been permeated with the craving for alcohol, did not want it any more. She attacked the programme fervently. After all, it was saving her life, bringing her to a normality she had never known. For the first time she began to see things in perspective and to lose the terrible nameless fear that had dogged her night and day for so long.

Aisling's ardent nature took to the A.A. programme. She found that the only person she could change was herself and that she must change or die. She helped others. She gained tranquillity, confidence, peace of mind and, above all, humour and freedom. It all took time. But as she gained control, she was happy for the first time since she had lost Alexander. Then, her happiness had depended on him, now her happiness depended on no one but herself. Within her was a well of peace and although she could be upset by the vicissitudes of life she could never again be shaken by that terrible numbing fear. She had done battle and she had won.

Summer turned to autumn. Aisling had never seen such colours before. For her it was as if the world was new. The texture of every leaf, the play of light on water, rain shimmering in little pools on the pavement, was a revelation. She remained in London, recovering. Camilla came and went, giving Aisling generously of her strength but constantly going home to her Fitz, and Ireland, and peace. Samantha stayed in Slievelea, happy with her grandfather.

Ali came to London. He found Aisling very changed. Physically she looked terrific, but it was more than that. Something inside her had altered. His butterfly had become a dove. She was calmer, humorous, more gentle than he would ever have believed possible. She explained about A.A. and the programme. He did not understand, but that did not matter. It worked for her and the result was spectacular. She looked older, it was true, but wiser, ready to laugh at herself, take life more lightly, live more fully in the here and now. Nor was she prepared to do penance for the past. After her initial apology she left the past where it belonged — behind her. There were

288

no fears for the future.

'I live life on a daily basis,' she would say.

They lunched in Sambucca and San Lorenzo, dined in Harry's Bar. There was a tentative quality in their approach to each other; a watchfulnes, too. Ali could not quite trust her yet, she saw. His gaze would be upon her as waiters wandered about with glasses and bottles, but she did not mind. She would nod as their eyes met. In fact, she had begun to find his constant company a bit of a trial. She found it difficult to admit to herself how boring she found his conversation. It was a new husband she was seeing through realistic eyes. He was kind and generous to a fault, but interesting? Unfortunately not.

She said, 'I'm finding it a bit difficult, Milla — I'm glad you and Fitz are coming to Gstaad. I don't think I could bear it otherwise.' The four of them had planned to go to Gstaad in February.

They were sitting in Camilla's cosy little kitchen. It was perfectly in harmony with the sitting room upstairs. Aisling thought, with its flagged floor, and blue and white tiled walls. There was a blue and white tablecloth on an old scrubbed pine-wood table. There were bunches of herbs and dried flowers, ropes of garlic and Breton onions hanging from the walls, a grandfather clock from Mount Rivers and a jolly wood fire burning in the little iron grate. They drank coffee in thick pottery mugs from Davos Platz, pottery the colour of a speckled egg painted with butter-yellow primroses.

Camilla never offered advice, for which Aisling was grateful. The women simply listened to one another and shared their experiences and shaped their thoughts as they talked.

'I don't think, Camilla, that there is any way I can stay with Ali. I don't want him any longer, physically or mentally. He used to be my saviour, the knight in shining armour who came to my rescue when I called. But I don't need rescuing any more. What shall I do, Milla?'

'I don't know. You'll have to make up your mind about that. It often happens, you know. You were an addict — a dependent person. You aren't any longer. You have no further need of Ali, perhaps. You've become strong. When is he going back to the States?'

'The week after we get back from Gstaad.'

'Then let him go and you stay here. Give yourself a break.

You can sort it out then. Leave the problem of Ali for now and a solution will come, you'll see. The moment of decision will present itself and you will find the words and the determination to act. Meantime don't fret about it.'

They sat till twilight in front of the kitchen fire, peacefully drinking their coffee and talking in a desultory fashion. They laughed together and rose eventually, hugging each other. Aisling waved farewell at the little gate, and with a last smile towards her friend's dark silhouette in the lighted doorway she ran into Kensington Church Street. She remembered, as she always did when she left Camilla's home, her first visit there, and smiled as she always did when she thought how things had changed since then. Contentment flooded her. All was well. She could cope. She would let Ali go, then she would find Alexander.

They flew to Geneva at the week's end, the four of them. Camilla was blissfully happy to be with Fitz but careful not to flaunt her contentment before her friend.

Gstaad is one of the most fashionable and delightful skiing resorts in Switzerland. Nestling prosperously in a circle of snowy-breasted mountains, it wakes up at Christmas and closes its eyes again in March. During the winter it is a fairy-tale world of snow.

They were a happy party, the Al-Mullas and the Fitzgeralds, staying in Chalet Blanc across from the Palace Hotel.

The chalet was an old building with low-ceilinged rooms, wood-panelled and cross-beamed. There were hand-painted flowers on every wall. Logs of sweet-smelling pine burned in open fires. The wooden house groaned and creaked, shrinking inwards from the cold and outwards from the warmth within.

Gstaad was a world dominated by the weather. When and if it snowed, if it rained and, oh horrors, if it got warm, heads were shaken and there were long faces, but the social round continued irrespective of the weather. Ali's Volkswagen Passat was capable of getting them through the snow wherever they wanted to go. They dined in the Olden, listened to Heidi sing, went to Rougement to Le Cerf to eat fondue and raclette and listen to the playing of the zither and the saw. The big parties that Aisling had loved were a trial for her now and she and Camilla and Fitz found their dinners out together much more enjoyable.

Ali and Fitz were excellent skiers.

'Where shall we go today?'

'The Wispile.'

'No, the Eggli. It's quicker, we can do more runs.'

Sympathising with Camilla, who did not ski, Aisling often sat it out or went for quick easy runs. She sat with Camilla at the top of the Eggli. Fitz and Ali waved to them as they set off with Hassan. The sun illuminated everything and cast blue shadows to the left like a frown. They sat on the bench, ski-suited against the cold, elbows akimbo, drinking a café Hag and nibbling a Caller *chocolat au lait aux noisettes*, eyes squinting against the sun behind sunglasses.

On the last day of their visit Hassan drove them to the cable car which they took to the top of the Wasserngrat. They were high as kites on good humour and *joie de vivre*. Tall pines were heavily laden, the snow forcing the branches low over the ground. Their breath steamed up the inside of the lift, condensation hanging in pendant drops from the roof and streaking slowly down the perspex windows. Fitz cracked silly jokes and Ali and Camilla giggled over nonsensical things. Aisling smiled but said little.

When they reached the top the world was a blanketed place, muted and wreathed in cloud. The men went skiing while the women waited at the Eagle Club. Angelo, tall and smiling, greeted them, and they sat and drank capuccinos and looked out over the magic mountains.

Camilla said, 'Ali doesn't know what to make of you now.'

'I know.'

'What will you do, Ash?'

'I don't know, Milla, I really don't. If it wasn't for Sam . . . He's so good with her. I still have to win her trust.'

'You will. Don't worry, Ash.'

'She *wants* to put me on a pedestal. It would be easy for me to climb up but disastrous if I did.'

'You won't. You'll stay on terra firma now and it'll all work out, never fear.'

'Suppose so.'

The men arrived, Fitz in his usual high good spirits. Aisling liked him immensely. He was not in awe of her and obviously loved Camilla very much. He had a zestful, uncomplicated enjoyment of life. They ate salad from the buffet and finished with fruit tart. Camilla remembered the day she stole the apricot pastry at Mount Rivers. How long ago it seemed now, and how far they had travelled.

Camilla and Aisling took the cable car down while the men skied again. It began to snow heavily and they descended into a shroud of mist. When they reached the bottom Hassan was there with the Volkswagen. Aisling told him to wait for the men. She and Camilla walked back in companionable silence.

The sun came out after the snowfall. Everything was covered in snow, even the undersides of the bare boughs of the trees, which traced a black lacework against the ice-blue sky. The whole world was covered in a sparkling eiderdown of white, and melting snow fell from the heavily-burdened trees, dropping now and then on top of their heads. They walked by the little river; a babbling rushing stream gurgling and rushing forward at breakneck speed. They crossed the little hand-bridge and walked back to Gstaad through the woods. It was magical there, a silent white world, snow everywhere, sparkling with a million silver rays.

They came into the chalet red-cheeked from the cold, laughing and stamping the snow off their boots. Aisling called for tea: '*Quelques biscuits avec le thé, s'il vous plaît, Rosa,*' and wondered where she had heard the sentence before. Then she remembered so long ago in Peel Street and Milla down in the kitchen and she a trembling wreck listening. She shivered.

'Is anything wrong, Ash?' Camilla asked.

'No.' she replied. 'It's just that sometimes I remember, and I'm ashamed.'

'You mustn't be. It wasn't your fault. It's an illness, never forget that, an allergy.'

'I know. And thank you, Milla. It's been wonderful here, and . . . you know.'

Camilla kissed her. 'Yes, it's been wonderful. And it's going to get better, Ash.'

'I know. I have such faith now. The bad days are over at last, the Black Dog has gone.'

'I'm so glad,' Camilla said, and went to her room.

Fitz came in as she was showering. He stripped off and joined her under the deluge of water. He soaped her and she soaped him and they teased each other and indulged in infantile horseplay that soon turned to passion. Legs intertwined, bodies arched to meet in the rhythmic ballet of sex, they now knew each other well enough to pleasure each other ecstatically. Their mutual orgasm was long and intense and exhausting and they fell asleep afterwards, twined in each other's arms.

Ali and Aisling waited for them in the living room. The fire blazed and the clock ticked. There was silence. It was a long silence that eventually grew embarrassing. They both knew why Fitz and Camilla were not down. They were both aware of the awkwardness of their position. Ali wanted to tell Aisling that it was all right really, that he no longer wanted to make love to her, that somewhere along the line he had lost his desire for her in that way.

Aisling was embarrassed. Fitz and Camilla's physical attraction to each other was obvious to everyone despite their care not to draw attention to their mutual passion, their closeness. They gave themselves away in a thousand ways, however. Aisling noted their consideration of her feelings with gratitude but it did not alter the fact that something had to be done, and done now. She could no longer go on living a half-life. If she was going to become really well, whole again, then she must act. This short holiday in Gstaad had helped to stabilise her, and living at close quarters with Camilla and Fitz had shown her how love could and should be.

'Ali, I want a divorce,' she said suddenly, surprising herself. She added, 'Please.' Camilla had told her not to be afraid of action as it rarely produced the expected reaction or result. She was correct, Aisling thought now as she looked at Ali's face. Astonishingly he seemed relieved and glad. She had expected a quarrel, pleading, begging, even bribery. Instead, there was relief.

He does not love me any more, she thought. She knew he would always be fond of her, be her friend, but she realised now that he had wanted to leave her as much as she had wanted to leave him. It was a humbling thought. She smiled ruefully and held out her hands which he clasped between his strong brown ones. What a very nice man he is, she thought.

'You want it too, Ali.' It was not a question, but a statement.

'Yes. It's been difficult, Aisling. You are better now I know and I should tell you ...'

She put her finger to his lips. 'No. Don't say anything. Let's leave it. We'll get what they call an amicable divorce with no

293

fuss and no hard feelings. Okay?'

He nodded and kissed her cheek gently as Camilla and Fitz burst into the room, apologising for their tardiness.

They made a high-spirited party that night in the Olden. There was an undercurrent of festivity in the air. Ali and Aisling seemed more carefree than usual and Fitz and Camilla were in the jolliest of moods. For some reason she could not understand Aisling felt happier, younger and more carefree than ever in her adult life. There was a free-flowing tide of joy surging through her veins and she did not know its source until Camilla whispered in her ear: 'Freedom.' Then she knew. She was, at last, her own person. She was capable of making decisions, of being in charge of herself and her future happiness. She felt wonderful.

Chapter
35

Samantha was stunned and felt guilty when Aisling called her about the divorce. Her mother told her that was foolish.

'Don't you see, darling, there is nothing you could have done. There was nothing anyone could have done. It was inevitable. Please don't let it make any difference to your relationship to Daddy or me. Perhaps, my darling, we can all live more peaceably with each other now. Let's at least try.'

'Okay, Momma, if it's best I'll try.' Then the inevitable pause, and the question,

'You okay Mom?'

'Yes, my darling. Milla and I are coming back to Ireland and I'll see you soon. I love you.'

'Love you too, Mom. Very much. You sure you love me?' She sounded very young, very vulnerable.

'Oh, my darling, so much, so very much.'

'That's all right then. 'Bye, Momma.'

Sam told her grandfather. They had a long chat about it which helped her a great deal.

'Your mother never should have married Ali,' Big Dan told her. 'She was in love with someone else and I messed it up — for very good reasons, mind. But Ali was a mistake made out of loneliness and despair. Not his fault at all, Sam, and you must remember that. No sitting in judgement on your parents. You'll make all the same mistakes in your own life, so bear that in mind. I wondered for years why they had married. I know now. Can't you see the purpose of it, me darlin'? If they hadn't married there'd be no you. An' that's not a happy thought, now is it?'

They chuckled together.

'Listen, my pet, you'll see both your parents whenever you and they want. All you'll miss are the quarrels. That's not a bad deal, is it?'

She shook her head and thought what a comfort he was. She had told him all her thoughts, all her feelings, everything about herself, and he had mended and soothed, sorted out and patched over all her pain and perplexity. Yes, Big Dan helped her with the news of the divorce but it did not prevent her feeling sad sometimes. She felt all the confusion of a teenager in changing circumstances. Her world had been lonely, it was true, but it was a world she was familiar with, a world she knew. Now the winds of change were blowing and she felt fearful and rather apprehensive.

Derry found her crying in the wood one day. He was wandering around the grounds, haunting the place with his dark presence.

'My Mom and dad are divorcing,' she said by way of explanation.

'I never thought of you with a father.'

'My father is Arab.'

'Arab?' Derry sounded incredulous. The Arabs were their friends. The thought put Sam in a new light for him, a strange light.

'I suppose I should be with them,' she wailed, 'but I don't want to leave here. I love it here so much. Maybe I could have stopped them.'

'Wha' could ye have done?' he asked reasonably.

She looked back at him. He wore old patched jeans and an anorak. He looked pinched with cold and the tip of his nose was pink.

'Nothing, I s'pose.' She smiled at him through her tears. 'Momma said that too but it didn't hit home. You saying it sorta helps. There was nothing I could do.'

She wiped her face with a tissue. The ground was sparkling with frost. There was no snow yet, no rain, just hard hoar frost and patches of ice. The trees were bare, barren February trees, and the earth was sleeping. A rook flew overhead and Sam shivered.

'One for sorrow,' she said. Her breath froze in little clouds. She dug her hands deeper into her tweed pockets. She wore thermal tights her mother had sent her from Marks and Spencer under her jeans, and she was wearing an Arran sweater. She doubted Derry was as warmly clad. He had scuffed sneakers on his feet and a tartan cowboy shirt open at the throat. He hopped from one foot to the other. He seemed embarrassed.

At last he said 'Sam, will you be my friend? No matter what, will you?'

She was surprised.

'Sure I will,' she said. 'But what you do, though, it's not right.'

He nodded. 'I know.'

'Can't you stop?'

He shook his head. 'No. You can' stop or they'll get ye. There's no escape, no way out, no hiding place.'

'Can't you leave the country? I'd help you.'

He looked at her again. 'I believe ye would. Mebbe ...'

'Maybe what?'

'Mebbe this'll be the last time. Then, ye never know.' He sounded infinitely wistful.

'What do you mean — the last time?'

'Ach, nuthin', Sam, nuthin'. I must be off. I'm sorry about yer Da. It's crazy, ham bein' an Arab.' He shook his head.

'There's nothing crazy about it. It's a big world outside, Derry Devlin. Perhaps you should see some other parts of it besides ... where?'

'The Bogside, the Falls Road, and Tripoli, Libya, with the Arabs. And here, Slievelea.'

'Well, that's not much. There's the U.S.A. to see and — oh, lots of places.'

He shrugged. 'No time,' he said.

'Look, it's a new moon.' Samantha pointed to the thin crescent in the sky overhead. 'Oh, it's beautiful — make a wish, make a wish.'

'What fer?' Derry asked.

'So it'll come true, of course.'

Derry started to walk away, then stopped. He looked at the moon. 'If only it could be different,' he whispered, and blinked his eyes swiftly as the moon became blurred.

Samantha ran to his side. She took his arm but he instinctively pulled it away. She leaned forward and kissed his cheek then turned and walked back through the wood towards the house.

Derry could feel her kiss on his cheek still. A sob caught his throat. He leaned his forehead against a tree-trunk and curled his arm over his head.

Chapter

36

Aisling came home to Slievelea and spent a couple of weeks there. She found Samantha in good form, but realised for the first time how insecure her daughter was.

Why, she's just like me, she thought in wonder, and hugged the thin little girl, who hugged her back. Her embrace was fierce. She clung to her mother, and Aisling's eyes filled with tears at the evidence of her child's need.

Mother and daughter grew very close. Samantha did not need to ask any more, 'You all right, Momma?' She could see for herself that Aisling had changed, was over the terrible symptoms of her illness.

Camilla had not, after all, returned to Ireland with her but had stayed in London at her agent's request. Betsy Bright was negotiating a film deal in one of her books and urged her to stay in London until it was 'in the bag'.

'Listen, darling, it's Julian Harcourt. I mean, he's the *crème de la crème*. His last two movies won awards from Cannes to Hollywood. We're not talking mini-series here, we're talking Art with a capital 'A'. So stick around, huh? I want you on tap when the guy talks business.'

'*If* the guy talks business.'

'Oh, he'll talk all right. Listen, honey, you're so wrapped up in that gorgeous husband of yours that you haven't realised how big a name you've become. Right now you're hot stuff. You can't pass a book-shop window without seeing *Requiem for Eithne, The Meeting of the Waters, Tim Taylor's Triumph*, and a huge picture of you.'

'That awful one!'

'Whatever. So don't leave town, as they say in the movies. Okay?'

'Okay, Bets. You win as usual.'

Aisling returned to London to sell Paultons Square. She never wanted to enter the apartment again. Camilla suggested that she stay at Peel Street while she tied up the sale and decided what she wanted to do next.

Aisling loved the Peel Street house, its brightness and freshness, and was only too glad to accept her friend's kind offer. In the back of both their minds was the important question-mark of Alexander.

In the spring, when Kensington Gardens were playing host to little clumps of pale mauve and yellow crocuses, when the cherry and apple blossoms scattered their lacy petals on the wind, when the children were free of the trappings of winter and the ducks sailed on the pond leading a flotilla of fluffy offspring, Camilla and Aisling walked along, arm in arm, in contented silence.

When they reached the Round Pond Camilla opened a bag of crumbs and scattered them on the grey water, watching as the pigeons plunged to grab some of the bread only to be hustled away by the hungry ducks. She looked at Aisling, who had gone to sit on a bench. She had never been more beautiful. The classical bone structure was clearly visible under the fine porcelain skin. There were lines around the clear violet eyes and silver in the golden hair but the face had a radiance and optimism it had lacked before, and there were tiny dimples at the curve of her lips when she laughed, which she often did.

Camilla joined her on the bench. 'They're filming my last book,' she said.

Aisling hugged her. 'Oh, Camilla, I'm so glad. How wonderful.'

'Yes, it is. The thing is, they say I can write the screenplay and I have *some* say about the casting.' She glanced sideways at her friend's still face. 'Aisling, I wondered ... The mother in it. It's a great part, comic and tragic, would you like to play it?'

She saw the tranquillity leave Aisling's face. She frowned, looked scared for a moment, then questioning.

'Do you think I could, Camilla?'

'I don't see why not.'

'No — neither do I. Not now. If there's a chance, I'd love to try.'

'I'm glad. It's time you worked again. It'll be another part of self-discovery, a testing time, and it will help you get over this divorce thing. I know you weren't in love with Ali any more, but you miss him just the same. And you need to stretch yourself. It's part of recovery.'

'How marvellous it would be, Camilla. And you would be there to give me encouragement . . .'

'Listen, I've given your name to the backers. There's been some talk about your past reputation — rumours of unreliability, you know. But the director is a youngish bloke — very gifted, keen on you. He's seen 'Lady From Vauxhall' and 'The Rag Doll'. I've made noises about the sixties and weren't we all like that, but we've all changed, calmed down. Yesterday's punk is today's Conservative. They seemed to accept it.'

'Should I maybe tell them . . .' Aisling said uncertainly.

'No.' Camilla was firm. 'Alcoholics *Anonymous*, remember? They wouldn't understand, you can't expect them to. Anyway, the guy's very excited about the idea. He wants to meet you.'

'What's his name?'

'Julian. Julian Harcourt.'

'Do we have a date?'

'Well, yes. I said I would ask you if lunch in the Connaught on Tuesday next would be okay?'

Aisling nodded. 'Lovely. How do I come? Glamorous? Dowdy?'

'Come as you are. Julian's no fool. Come as your own beautiful self.'

The lunch in the Connaught was Aisling's first tentative resumption of her social and professional life in London. She was nervous enough about that without the added strain of being looked over with a view to employment.

Camilla encouraged her remorselessly. She had to take steps forward.

Aisling was excessively nervous while getting ready, trying on half a dozen outfits, applying her make-up with extra care. Camilla, knocking on her door, found her only half ready. 'Come on, we'll be late.'

'Do I look all right? I'm such a mess. This skirt makes me look too thin and the coat is . . .'

'Look, Aisling, he's coming to meet you, your coat doesn't matter. *You* are enough.' She gave Aisling a hug and they exchanged smiles.

'Courage, Ash, courage,' Camilla said. 'And there is something you have done that I haven't been able to manage.'

Aisling looked at her enquiringly.

'Samantha.'

'Oh, Milla. Darling Milla.' Aisling pressed her hand and they left the apartment together.

Julian Harcourt was a director on his way up: prematurely grey-haired, good-looking, incisive and ambitious. He disliked the idea of the big studio set-up — the multi-million dollar movie, the star system, the showbiz razzmatazz — and only used it when he had no alternative. He believed that small was beautiful, and was determined to make little works of art. His gods were Ingmar Bergman, Renoir, Marcel Carne.

Camilla Vestry's book, with its images of cool green-shaded lanes and bicycles and buttercup meadows and sex in the grass, appealed to his highly developed visual sense. Her casting suggestion of Aisling Andrews for the mother who lives alone in the big house, possessive of her son, and loses both him and her reason in the end, intrigued him. He had Aisling's old movies re-run in a Soho studio. He sat in the dark, long legs slung over the back of the seat in front of him, alone except for the bored projectionist. He watched, fascinated, as a very young, over-made-up Aisling, looking incredibly beautiful and artificial, wary and stilted, simpered her way through 'The Lady From Vauxhall'. He ran through the other movies she had made of a similar stamp. There was a marked change in her in 'The Rag Doll'. She still seemed edgy, almost as if she were on something, which she probably was, but sexier, more in tune with the camera, a latent talent beginning to reveal itself. There was a stunning five-minute sequence at the end of the film, the scene that had nearly won her an Oscar. Aisling Andrews was worth a try, he decided.

He went to the lunch engagement in the Connaught full of anticipation. He seated himself at the table Monsieur Chevalier suggested. He was dressed in a soft blue-and-white check Viyella shirt and silk tie, a French blue cashmere jacket and beautifully-cut cord trousers. He smelt of Gauloises, and Pierre

Cardin cologne. He smiled at Monsieur Chevalier, the maitre d', who had known him and his brother Justin for years.

'I'll have a look at the wine list while I await the rest of my party,' he said, then realised that Aisling Andrews must have made her entry. Camilla had warned him of the effect she had, and she had not exaggerated. The people at the next table, two businessmen or politicians, stared at her, mouths open, forks raised. A husband and wife turned round to study her more closely, and so did Julian. The buzz of interest in the room was too powerful to resist and, like Lot's wife, he looked behind him.

His first impression was of her height. She was so tall, so upright, held her head proudly on her slender neck, her body beautifully poised on long elegant legs. She wore high heels. She was dressed in a grey suit made of finest suede and trimmed at the wide medieval-style sleeves and neckline with silver fox fur. She wore a tall Russian fox fur hat and stood in the entrance, calmly waiting.

Camilla had seen him and plunged into the stately wood-pannelled room. 'Julian', she squealed, manoeuvring her way between the tables towards him. He stood up, kissing her on both cheeks, but his eye was held by Aisling's smooth glide towards them. He met her marvellous eyes levelly. The chink of cutlery, of bottle on glass, of muted discreet conversation, became remote. He stood for so long looking into those velvet eyes that Camilla, already seated and shaking out her white damask napkin, said louder than she had intended, 'Come on, Julian, sit down. Aisling's cast her spell upon you too. It's the usual pattern.' She smiled at him to take the sting out of her words but Julian had not even heard them.

Aisling sat. The waiters moved efficiently about her. She peeled off her grey suede gloves, her graceful movements fascinating Julian. Each finger plucked at the tip, then the smooth unveiling of the long pink-nailed hands. Right hand, left hand ... A huge square-cut diamond masked her wedding ring, reflecting the gleam from the chandeliers and the spring sunshine filtering through from Carlos Place. Julian watched as she pulled off the fur hat and shook out her shining gold hair. A waiter took her jacket and gloves and hat, another handed them their menus.

Camilla chattered non-stop as Julian studied that unforgettable face. The eyes perusing the menu were clear, a rich violet colour. Her bones were traceable under the matte-pored camellia skin. Her silk shirt had a stock wound high around the throat and pinned with a square diamond pin. She fiddled with it as she looked at the huge parchment covered folder before her. Julian watched her with the eyes of a man stricken but also with the detachment of an artist. He saw the pale sheen of sweat on her upper lip, the fine lines at the corners of her eyes, the faint puffiness beneath them. There were tiny blue veins at her temples.

A waiter made as if to pour some wine into her glass. She quickly covered it with her hand and said, a little too loudly, 'No alcohol, please. May I have Perrier water?'

Camilla said, 'Me, too. Some Perrier with ice and lemon and lime, if you have it.'

'But of course, Madam.'

Julian had the impression Camilla was trying to help her friend, though why precisely he could not think. He looked at Aisling's cameo profile. She looked a good deal younger than her years, he thought.

He's hooked, Camilla realised. Oh, hell. Oh, help. Oh, damnation. No, don't think like that, Camilla. Don't think negatively — think positively. It may be all for the best. Julian is no fool. He's not going to ruin the film for anyone.

They lunched on excellent foie gras and toast, had superb roast beef with vegetables and a little salad to follow, and finished on a perfect Stilton and fresh fruit.

Camilla let Julian talk. Aisling listened attentively to what he said. Camilla allowed her mind to wander.

'Well?' said Aisling at last.

Julian nodded. 'I'd like you in the film,' he said. 'I'd like you to play the lead.

Camilla smiled. 'I knew it! Anyone with eyes could see you'd made up your mind the minute she walked in here.'

Julian blushed and looked angry, but Aisling laughed. She did not laugh often, but when she did it was enchanting and surprising at the same time.

I'll use that in the film, he thought. I'll keep her serious and then halfway through, in the sunlit field with her son, she'll throw back her head and laugh like this and it'll work like a dream.

'We have to go to Rome in June,' he said.

'Rome?' Camilla said, surprised.

It was his turn to laugh. 'You don't think I'm going to trust the Irish weather for all those idyllic scenes in the grass. Heavens, it would cost me a fortune to wait upon the Irish sun. We'll shoot some scenes in Italy just to make sure we have the key scenes in the can, then go to Ireland in the summer for exteriors. Interiors are here in London. However, we're only reconnoitring in June — shooting proper doesn't start till next year. I'd like you with me Camilla to advise about what is typically Irish, or as near to it as we can get. And I want to pick up a painting there from an artist friend of mine. Can you come?'

'Love it,' she said. 'If my Fitz can join me later.'

He paid the astronomical bill, which always seemed worth every penny, and they left the building. Julian shook hands with the two women, promising to phone Aisling. He repeated that the film was due to start shooting in March of next year, and he would be in touch with her. Aisling smiled and said if she would not be in the way she would like to come to Rome with Camilla. He said nothing would give him more pleasure. The two women stood side by side, watching Julian step into the taxi that the doorman had procured for him, then strolled into Grosvenor Square. Camilla squeezed Aisling's arm.

'Well?' she asked gently.

'Lovely. I feel fine. Very good, dear Milla. Much better than I thought.'

'Good,' Camilla said. 'I hate to say I told you so.'

Chapter

37

Derry stretched his arms over his head. His body constantly ached. Most of the men suffered similarly. It was the damp, they said, sleeping rough. Your bones got rusty, like an old man's.

The woodcutter's hut, more a hovel really, was deep in the bluebell wood at Slievelea. No one knew it was there except Samantha. Those who had once known about it were long dead. At any rate he could not imagine anyone from the big house, from Slievelea itself, coming down here. For the moment it was his earth, his home. Until the job was done. He had known worse. It was a shelter, at any rate, which was more than could be said for the ditches he spent half his life in, rain dripping down the back of your collar and fingers numb with cold.

Samantha had brought him a blanket but the real joy was the sleeping bag. He did not know where she had got it. It did not seem a likely article for them to have in the big house. God, it was grand. He slept so deeply in it that he was frightened and thought he was dead. He couldn't remember having a night's sleep like that since he was a child at home in his little bed. He remembered his home. It wasn't too great but it was bloody Buckingham Palace compared to this. And this was better than a ditch. It was all relative, he thought, and hated himself for thinking. He had not thought at all for years, and now he thought all the time. Since he had met Samantha. He didn't like thoughts, they were dangerous and disturbed his calm. They made him feel and he didn't want to feel. Thinking of his home made him feel. Two square rooms below four square rooms above, furniture courtesy of plywood. And his mother: plump, warm, round-breasted. A place to lay your head when you were tired, to find comfort. Like a home in itself, it was, her breast. Then horrifically he had held her arm, her detached arm. Could anyone imagine what that was like? he wondered. Could Samantha?

The longest conversations he had had in his whole life he had had with her. He thought of her world and how it must be, but he could not get to grips with it at all. He had no yardstick by which to judge it. But Samantha took it for granted. She lived in Slievelea, woke to the sunshine, the light in a pretty bedroom, the warmth of fires, the smell of good food.

He remembered the last time he saw her, down by the lake. Her hair was clean and sweet to smell. He knew he mustn't think like this. It was dangerous and debilitating. He must think of the job.

The nearer the job loomed, the more reluctant he became. He wanted to put the whole thing off. Now he just waited, not thinking of it, unaffected by the terror that he would one day perpetrate.

Sam came. As if mesmerised, and partly against her will, she was drawn irresistibly to him. It was partly from pity for him. She had never met anyone like him before.

He did not care why she came. She was warm and human and reminded him that there was a world outside his, a world he had lost. In that world there were mothers and fathers, sisters and brothers, families and friends. In that world there were birthdays and Christmas, summer holidays and laughter. There were tears too, but there were people to wipe them away, to comfort, to heal. In his world there was nothing. No family feelings to confuse the issue, no happiness to cloud his icy purpose. Even hate was a complication he could not afford. An absence of feeling was the ideal.

And now there was Samantha, confusing him.

'Why did you come?' he asked. 'I told ye not ta.'

'I brought you some food. You gotta have food.'

She had brought some sandwiches, an apple and a bottle of beer. The sandwiches were delicious. They held thick hunks of meat, white chicken, nearly half a breast, in one, and ruddy beef squashed up with moist tomato and crisp lettuce in the other. He ate hungrily, tearing the meat and the soft white bread with his teeth, and gulping the beer greedily.

She watched him with a soft expression in her eyes.

307

'Why de ya look like that?' he asked. 'Why did you come today?'

She shrugged. 'I dunno. I guess I didn't like to think of you here, cold and alone.'

'Well, that's best for me. I don't need nobody ner nuthin'.'

'Everyone does, Derry. Everyone.'

'In your world, mebbe. Not mine.'

She looked at him a moment, his thin face, narrow nostrils, and wide empty eyes. She shivered.

'Could I tell Grandfather about you?' she asked. She meant it innocently enough. Perhaps she could ask Big Dan for help. She was ill prepared for Derry's reaction. He grabbed her by the shoulders fiercely, hurting her back, his thumbs bruising her flesh through her tweed jacket. His eyes looked wild, like the eyes of an animal at bay.

'Don't ye dare, d'ye hear? Don't ye dare.'

'Stop, Derry, you're hurting me. It hurts,' she sobbed, tears of pain in her eyes.

But he had her in a vice-like grip, and he seemed to be having difficulty breathing. The pain shot through her body, spiralling down her back. It was dark in the little hut. He pressed her closer to the damp floor, the weeds growing through the cracks in the flagstones, the smell of woodland animals and damp foliage. Then, just as abruptly as he had violently gripped her, he let her go. He covered his face with his hands.

'Oh, God, forgive me. I didn't mean to hurt you. Not you. Never you.'

She sat still as a statue. She wanted to cry. There was a huge unmanageable lump in her throat. Although she felt sick with the shock of his violence, she knew her face was expressionless.

'It's okay,' she said at last, her voice a whisper.

His head was bent and for some reason beyond her understanding she reached out and touched his soft fine hair with a touch light as a butterfly. He felt it. He looked up and for a moment they stared at each other. She could hear the wind outside, sadly sighing.

She was the first to break contact, drawing her eyes from his, tracing the edges of a flagstone beside her with her finger. It felt rough beneath her hand and her shoulders still throbbed unmercifully.

'It's okay' she said again softly. 'I know you didn't mean to do it, Derry. But you know I wouldn't betray you. You know that.'

He nodded. 'It wasn't tha', I trust ye. I was thinkin' of you. You could be hurt bawd. They might have got ye''

'How would they have known?'

He nodded sagely, 'Oh, they would. They do.' He lifted her hand from the flagstone and held it between his own. His clasp was warm. He looked at her hopelessly. 'Ye better go,' he said.

She stood up. The hut was not high enough for her to stand upright. He did not rise. She brushed the back of her pants and looked at him a moment, then she left. With her going the darkness fell, outside, inside and within him.

Chapter

38

As usual, Alitalia was late landing at Fiumicino. The hostess shrugged resignedly, accepting it philosophically, and took one last drag on her cigarette behind the galley curtains.

At the airport, Julian shepherded them into a waiting limousine which drove them to the Hassler, their hotel at the top of the Spanish Steps. As Aisling heard Italian spoken for the first time in years, the memories came flooding back. When she reached her room she ordered some tea and gratefully lay down on her bed. It was good to be here. It was good to feel the warm Italian air in the streets, the scents, and the sounds of Rome in her ears. She drank her tea, bathed and dressed, refusing to dwell on the past.

Julian buzzed her room to tell her that Camilla and he had thought of going for a little walk on the Via Condotti then dining in Maestro Stefano's afterwards. Wasn't that a good idea? Didn't she agree? She was more than agreeable and hoped all arrangements would be taken out of her hands similarly. She just wanted to flow with the tide for a while.

They left the hotel an hour later. Rome was beautiful in spring but then, Aisling thought, so was everywhere. Spring held a breathless expectancy, a promise, an excitement, the pledge of a passionate summer and idle days just around the corner. Travelling towards it was much more exciting than its actual arrival. But Rome was enchanting in the spring. The Spanish Steps were ablaze with flowers, like the Via Condotti where it seemed a sin not to buy something for surely it was the most beautiful and tempting shopping street in the world. Bulgari. Gucci. They stopped for a coffee in Caffè Greco.

Aisling had that liberated feeling she always had when she left a chilly climate for a balmy one. No stockings, she thought. Bare legs and arms. She wore a simple silk dress and carried a cashmere stole. The dress was white with black polka dots and Julian thought she looked eighteen in it.

The Italians were used to beauty. Their standards were high but their admiration open and unaffected. 'Bella! Bellissima!' They shouted after her, and she and Julian and Camilla giggled.

They took a taxi to the Piazza Navona. Maestro Stefano greeted them affably and they sat gazing in the glorious Bernini fountain as it grew darker and the lights came on all over the square. The little lanterns that flanked the restaurant burst into light as suddenly as shooting stars. They ordered melon and soft pink Parma ham, small *tagliatelle verde alla crema*, *fegato alla Venezia*, and finished with *Tartufo*, the mortal sin of an ice-cream sweetened with chocolate sauce. They were easy and relaxed together but acutely aware of the undercurrents in the situation. Julian was bewitched by Aisling, that much had been obvious from their lunch in the Connaught. Camilla wished briefly in this magic Roman night that Fitz were with her. It was not that Aisling or Julian had given any intimation of anything untoward, their conversation was politely general, but there was an underlying excitement in their most innocent exchanges. She remembered that Aisling must have felt something like that in Gstaad when Camilla and Fitz had been so happy. Julian had set himself out to charm, and though he concentrated equally on both women Camilla was well aware that the real target was Aisling.

The usual tourists thronged the square. As the sun went down behind the church, its setting rays turning the windows into squares of gold. Lovers sat on the stone benches near the Bernini fountain and kissed and touched as if they could not bear to be apart. Who were they, Aisling wondered, that they had nowhere else to go?

As Maestro Stefano's got more crowded, the waiters moved the pink-clothed tables along the cobbles nearer to the little black grille that shielded them from the square proper. Street artists sketched and sitters giggled at the implausibly flattering results. Balloons drifted airily to and fro, carried by a laughing black-eyed girl with a heavy belt around her waist. She shouted their price in a raucous cigarette-impregnated voice. The splashing of the glorious fountain underlay the other sounds in the Piazza.

A tour guide led a group of Americans, pointing here and there, his voice lost in the vastness of the place. Beautiful young Italians of both sexes greeted each other affectionately with kisses and hugs. 'Ciao.' 'Ciao.' Gypsies with babies strolled by selling faded single roses. A boy with the face of a Renaissance cherub, and the faded and torn jeans of a beggar, blew into a hollow reed attached to a miniature keyboard. It was Mozart, though barely recognisable. Aisling gave him some coins and Maestro Stefano was not pleased. The boy probably plagued the restaurant and she had done them a disservice. A painter moved swiftly across the square and set up his easel. He was very old, his skin wrinkled and brown as a fisherman's. A *carabiniero* chuntered by on his motorbike. Birds sang out their farewell to the day. The lovers' shadows blended into one other. The waiters in their white coats stood with folded arms and talked, shrugging their shoulders to the lilting cadence of their language as they waited for the customers to leave.

They walked part of the way back under a velvet sky pricked out with stars then took a taxi to the Piazza d'Espagna and sleepily climbed the steps. They felt full of good food and bonhomie. They had a coffee in the hotel on their return, sipping in silence, each content with their own thoughts.

Julian went to make a phone-call. When he returned he was rubbing his hands together and seemed full of an elation that made the women look at him enquiringly.

'I've got Umberto Perdoni,' he said, and saw only incomprehension on their faces.

'Oh God, what a couple of ignoramuses!' He laughed, too excited to be cast down. 'He's the greatest cameraman in the world! Well, he and — Oh, never mind. Put it this way, Fellini and Zeffirelli both adore him. We're so lucky! The dates just happened to be right.'

He waved his hands in triumph, then ran them through his hair. 'As the weather is so good, I thought we might drive through Tuscany for a few days and look for good locations. Also, I have a date to see my artist friend and pick up my painting. Is that all right with you two?'

312

Camilla and Aisling nodded. Julian crowed with delight, rubbing his hands together. 'Poppy-fields, here we come,' he said.

Camilla threw back her head and laughed. 'Oh God, Julian, I can't believe you're planning to turn Italy into Ireland. They're so different.'

'Look, if Polanski turned France into Hardy country in "Tess", I can do it here. You should know, Camilla, it's the poppy fields that are so important. Three of the major scenes take place there, and that's where we last see Maeve when she's mad. So as long as I get some really magical shots of a poppy field, *any* poppy field, I'm happy. Do I make myself clear? Do you still want to come?'

Camilla said: 'I want to, but it depends on you, Ash — how do you feel about it?'

'I'd love it. Perhaps not Florence ... Not yet. Oh, well, we'll see.'

Aisling looked at Julian and saw his eyes narrow. Nothing was said, but they both knew they had turned a corner.

She lowered her eyes from his face. Camilla, aware of the change in the atmosphere, said, 'Well, that's that then. We start tomorrow?'

Julian reluctantly withdrew his gaze from Aisling. 'Yes, crack of dawn.'

Camilla rose. Aisling was still staring at Julian. 'I'll go to my room now' she said. ''Night all.'

Aisling rose to follow her and Julian put out his hand to stop her.

'Will you come with me?' he asked. She nodded. He took her hand and held it between his, then lifted it to his lips and kissed the palm. Aisling smiled at him again, that rare and dazzling smile.

They went to Julian's room. He held her in his arms, soothing her body, wrapped her in his warm embrace. Instinct told him she was nervous, needing calm reassurance. He kissed her soft lips, rained little kisses on the corners of her mouth. He caught her bottom lip softly between his teeth and heard her quick intake of breath. Her arms went around him and she responded to his kisses hungrily.

They undressed and made love in silence. Their lovemaking was warm and satisfying. Their bodies fitted and they led each

313

other to a long slow shuddering climax, and in the languid decrescendo they both laughed and lay back, satisfied.

At breakfast next morning Camilla announced that she was sending for Fitz. She had seen Julian holding Aisling's fingers between his and said, exasperated. 'It's obvious what you two have been up to, and if you think I'm going to play gooseberry all the way to Tuscany and back, you're making the mistake of your lives!'

Julian laughed and Aisling blushed. 'Sorry, Milla. I didn't mean . . .'

'I'm thrilled for you. If you two want to have a fling, by all means do. I'm *not* upset, I just feel left out and lonely for Fitz.'

'Well, Umberto will be with us tomorrow . . .'

'I don't want Umberto! I only crave my lovely Fitz.'

'Wire him then,' Aisling told her friend. 'Send for him. Why not?'

'He can catch us up,' Julian said. 'The bags are in the car. I reckon to drive to Sienna today. We'll stop for lunch on the way and stay there overnight. Tomorrow we'll pop in for tea with my friends. I've phoned them.'

They piled into the Volkswagen Golf Julian had hired from Hertz and set off in a holiday mood. Aisling still felt curiously detached and happy. Carefree as a child, she was only interested in the feel of the sun, the breeze on her face, the scents of the countryside, the promise of the next delicious meal, the thought of gentle lovemaking, body on body, mouth on mouth and the deep dreamless sleep that would follow. There were no problems; for the moment everything was shelved.

As they neared the glorious Tuscan countryside they passed through little towns of red-rose stone. Tiny pink villages pressed themselves into the sides of the hills, and the spears of the ever-present cypresses reached to the blue sky. Julian and Umberto noted the scarlet poppies strewn across the moist green fields and made notes. They had picked up Umberto in the Traste-vere district of Rome, a big teddy bear of a man. He sat in the back beside Camilla, saying little.

Mist on the hills, green fields and olive trees, warm sleepy towns where stones were cool to touch and splashing fountains played a gentle decrescendo from open cherubs' mouths. Dogs slept in the sun and grey-haired women with weather-beaten faces peered between the lace-curtained windows of small upper rooms little changed since medieval days. Once wimpled women looked out on the same cobbled narrow streets, and men in doublet and hose strolled, swords at their sides, pageboy hair under plumed caps. Now Vespas roared past and fat tourists walked the same streets complaining of aching feet, wanting to get on with it and over it and back to the comfort of home.

They lunched in a little *trattoria* where the *padrone* sang Verdi loudly to the hills. They ate Parma ham and melon, veal cutlets, and the most delicious home-made strawberry ices. They fell asleep in the field behind the restaurant, Julian cradling Aisling in his arms, Camilla with her head on Umberto's stomach, which gently rose and fell to the rhythm of his breathing. They woke laughing, covered with grass and itchy from bugs, good-humoured and ready for a cooling drink. The *padrone* gave the women a home-made lemon drink and the men had a beer. Then they piled into the car and drove onwards towards Aisling's destiny.

Chapter

39

The euphoric mood lasted. Sienna was explored the following day. The medieval town enchanted them and they whiled away the morning in the Piazza del Campo, gazing at the splendour of the Piccolomini and the San Sedoni palaces and drinking coffee under the umbrellas in the square.

They had lunch at the hotel and Camilla called Fitz then went to join the others in the square for coffee. They lingered while the sun crossed the sky. Finally, Julian hustled them together.

'Come on, I promised Tatiana I'd have you there for tea. You'll have to forgive us, Umberto. You know how the English are about tea.'

'And the Irish,' Camilla said, laughing. 'Don't forget us.' Aisling smiled and Umberto made a face. He hardly ever spoke and the others teased him about it as they drove up into the hills. He said only, 'My camera talks for me,' and was silent again.

'Here we are,' Julian said at last. The villa was set into the side of a hill, its terracotta roof just visible above the trees. An old man answered Aisling's pull at the bell and she jumped back into the car as the wrought-iron gates were opened. The drive was long and winding and reminded her for some reason of Slievelea. The villa, when they reached it, was a graceful Palladian building, all fluted columns and flights of steps leading to a huge front door. They were admitted by a uniformed maid who ushered them through a marble vestibule. A white marble staircase led to the upper floors.

The maid crossed the foyer and led them through a vast cool

316

living room, full of regal crimson-and-gold-upholstered furniture, to some French windows. In the shaded courtyard beyond a beautiful woman waited. She had masses of black hair held behind her head with a comb. She wore a simple black silk dress, pearls at her throat, and had the most elegant legs Aisling had ever seen. She looked beautiful and sexy, in an elusive way.

She greeted them graciously and seated them around a white wrought-iron garden table covered with a linen tablecloth. In the centre of the courtyard a fountain splashed softly, a restful sound. The old stone walls were covered in ivy and mosses. There were giant terracotta pots of azalea and hibiscus, splashes of vivid colour against the green. In a niche in the back wall of the garden, lined with brilliant green moss, stood a beautiful statue of Aphrodite floating in a shell.

Formal introductions were never made for just as Julian began an old lady arrived, white hair covered in a lace mantilla, clothed all in black and leaning on a thin malacca cane topped with silver. There was a shuffling of seats as the men stood, and Tatiana said, 'Mamita, how lovely to see you. You're just in time for tea.'

The old lady suddenly stopped and stared intently at Camilla.

'Camilla? Camilla Vestry!' she said. 'As I live and breathe, it's Camilla Vestry.'

Aisling, for no reason she could think of, was filled with apprehension. She shivered suddenly and Julian said, 'I'll get your cardigan from the car.'

'No, I'll go,' she said, wanting to get away, and slipped back into the living room behind her as if fleeing from some threat she could not see. She tugged at the door in the lobby but it was too heavy for her to open.

In the courtyard Camilla was hugging Jessica Klein. She clasped the old lady to her, muttering all kinds of questions, jumbled and tearful.

'And where is Hymie? Where is my darling old Hymie? You disappeared one day in a flash — you left no forwarding address, and I missed you all so much.'

'Hymie is dead, dear. A long time dead. Oh, but it's good to see you, to see someone from the old country. Sit down beside me and tell me all the news. Is the Liffey still peat-black Irish, and how are you doing with the writing?'

Jessica pulled Camilla into a chair beside her, holding on to her hand for dear life, and ignoring the others in the surprise and excitement of rediscovery began to converse.

Tatiana poured the tea and Julian said, 'I'll go and find Aisling.'

Tatiana nodded absently as he turned back into the house.

Aisling heard someone on the other side of the door. She retreated into the living room. It was unsophisticated and silly, she thought, to lose her cool like this. It was not like her. Why she had suddenly become so panicky she did not know but she was going to stop now, take a few deep breaths and return to the garden.

The room was shadowed and cool, the sunlight forcing its way with difficulty through the slats of the Venetian blind in one corner, casting a trail of gold over the floor. She heard footsteps outside in the lobby, perhaps a servant bringing the tea. She stood very still in the centre of the room, fighting to calm her wayward nerves, looking at the portrait above the marble fireplace. It was the face of the woman she had just met, Tatiana, a lovely face, warmly seductive, intelligent and beautiful. She was suddenly struck by the portrait itself, its style. The technique was curiously familiar, something about it that she recognised.

For a split second recognition trembled on the threshold of her mind. She put her hand to her mouth as the door opened and Alexander walked in, a letter in his hand.

He saw her half in shadow, half in the shaft of sunlight. The golden rays picked out her hair, illuminating it, casting a nimbus of light around the beautiful vulnerable face he had tried so hard to forget. He dropped the letter on the floor and they gazed at each other, aghast. He moaned, a cry of pain and longing, and there was nothing in the world that could have prevented him catching her in his arms, folding her to him, reclaiming the other half of himself.

'Alexander, Alexander, Alexander.' She cried, like a chant, over and over again, and sobbed in his arms and kissed his eyes and cheeks, caressing his hair and skin as if to make sure he was real.

'Alexander. Alexander. Alexander.'

They clung together, touching like blind people, desperate

318

for the reassurance of each other's physical presence.

'Oh, God, I've waited so long for you. So long.' Alexander covered her face with kisses, then took a step back from her the better to see her face.

'Don't let me go,' she cried, 'I'll fall if you let me go.'

He held her to him again, his arms wrapped around her. 'I keep thinking I'm dreaming,' he said, kissing her hair, running his hands through the golden strands. 'I can't believe you're really here. You've haunted my dreams for so long.' Then he groaned, his face stricken. 'But, God in Heaven, Aisling, you're my sister . . .'

She shook her head vehemently. 'No,' she said. 'Don't worry, I'm not. Please let me explain.'

'Yes, but we can't stay here. Let's go. My car is outside.'

For a second she thought of the others, Julian and Milla, but he was holding her again and kissing her lips and her mouth scorched beneath his and she wanted to consume him.

He did not think at all. He took her hand and led her outside into the sun.

Julian had entered the French windows unnoticed. He stood still, stunned by what he saw: his friend, Alexander Klein, holding Aisling as if he would never let her go. He was sobbing, Julian saw, and they clung to each other as if they would die of joy, totally unaware of his presence, crying out their love in words so tender, so passionate that Julian shivered. He stood in the shadows a moment, transfixed, then turned and left, shutting the door very firmly behind him. So that's it, that's Aisling's sadness, he thought, understanding only part of it.

In the little walled garden, tea was being sipped. Umberto was drowsing on a bench a little away from the others, petals falling on his face.

'Did you find your friend?' Tatiana asked tranquilly.

'Oh, yes. She'll be along in a moment.' Tatiana did not seem to mind one way or the other. 'Sit down and tell me how you are, dear Julian,' she said. 'Is this woman your latest inamorata? She's lovely.'

'She's an actress in my next movie. I'm making a film of Camilla's book, and she is to star.'

'How nice.'

'But you, Tatiana, you and the children. How are you and Alexander?'

'You'll see him when he deigns to come down. The children are fine. Alexander's work is a great success. The critics are catching up with him, and about time, too. Not that he cares. He's as content as he can be, here with me and the children. He still disappears for weeks on end, but you know how he is, I don't need to tell you. Why don't you tell me about your film.'

Julian felt it was safer to let her chatter. He knew something momentous was happening in the house behind him but he could not think what to do about it. What could he possibly say to Tatiana? He cursed himself for bringing Aisling here.

The sun slanted on to the warm stones of the little courtyard. Jessica Klein and Camilla had plenty to talk about. Julian listened to Tatiana's gossip and came to terms with the fact that he had lost Aisling. For the first time he felt middle-aged. Camilla, in her excitement at seeing Jessica again, had devoted her full attention to the old lady. It was only when tea had been drunk and Julian rose to leave that she noticed Aisling's absence.

'Where's Ash?' she asked.

'She didn't feel well. She said she would wait in the car,' Julian replied.

'Oh, you should have told me,' Tatiana said.

Camilla was immediately concerned. 'I must go to her.'

Julian shot her a warning glance and Camilla felt the first clutch of alarm. They said their last goodbyes and left. In the driveway Julian told Camilla what he had seen.

'They were in another world,' he said. 'I can't explain it, Camilla, it was a kind of mutual exclusivity. They were totally immersed in each other.'

'My God, so she's found Alexander! Then there is nothing anyone can do, nothing. Poor Tatiana.'

The little party which had set out so gaily dwindled into a sad and fretful duo. Umberto disappeared back to Rome, full of ideas for the film. Julian was more upset than he cared to admit. He had never before been abandoned. He was peeved and his pride was hurt. Camilla, too, felt a little angry and let down by Aisling but perhaps her feelings would have been less intense if Fitz had been there with her. She missed him desperately but phoned him to tell him not to come to Italy after all, that she would come home at once.

Aisling and Alexander had disappeared, no one knew

320

where. Tatiana phoned Julian and said her husband had done one of his disappearing acts but she was used to it; she would phone Julian again when he resurfaced. When he did he was bound to have some new work with him. That was usually what his disappearances heralded. In the meantime she would send on the picture Alexander had left in readiness and Julian could mail the cheque to them. Was his girlfriend better?

Yes, she heard him reply, Aisling was all right now. Well, another time. Goodbye and many thanks.

The phone clicked and went dead, and so did Tatiana. All feeling left her body, it was as if she had been anaesthetised. Her knees then went weak and she could not stand. She collapsed on her bed, their bed. Aisling!

She knew what had happened. She knew now why her beautiful guest had not come back for her tea and why her husband had disappeared. She felt the world stand still. Fear coursed through her, prickling her skin, churning her stomach.

Aisling. You could not forget a name like that. There were times when Tatiana had wanted to scream, to do violence to that other woman, yet in her heart she had always thought of her as a ghost to be laid to rest. Now the thing she had dreaded had come to pass. Aisling was here in her life.

Tatiana tried to be positive. It would be good to have the lingering shadow put to the test of light and exorcised forever, if that was to be the ending ... Secretly she was terrified. She might lose him. The ghost might prove the stronger. She dared not think of it, unable to face even the possibility. As the days passed her head ached with the constant tension, and her temper became short. The children were unhappy. They had never seen her like this. Their laughing, loving mother was suddenly sharp as a knife, cutting and unkind. She tried not to reveal her terror but children are shrewd.

'It's because our Papa is away,' their son Alexi said one day, rocking to and fro in the hammock.

Anouska shook her head. 'No, he has often been away. Mamma is sick or something. I'm frightened.'

Tatiana heard them from her bedroom where she sat immobile, unable to act.

There was a phone in the Casa Rosia but she dared not call. Suppose that woman answered? Tatiana felt she would not trust herself if that were to happen. She might say something she

321

shouldn't, drive Alexander away forever.

She heard the chorus of birds and the splash of the fountain in the sun, the chatter of her children's voices. She could smell the sweet fragrance of flowers on the air. She felt the soft satin of her *robe de chambre* against her legs and saw her beauty reflected in the mirror; the dusky cloud of her hair and the soft curve of her mouth, no longer laughing. It had gone now, the joy in her heart, the smile on her lips. A bleak darkness, an apprehension invaded her life.

Jessica was her only support, the one who stopped Tatiana from despairing and filled her heart with hope. From the first she was wise, tactful and supportive.

'That family have brought little good to the ones that loved them,' she said, and patted Tatiana's hand. 'He'll come back. I know my son, and he'll come home.'

'But in what condition, Mamita?' Tatiana asked. 'He will have been with *her*.' She did not want to go into the complexities of their relationship, did not even want to think about them. In the dark reaches of the night, black thoughts set her tossing and turning in the bed that had been a haven of joy and delight until now. There was nothing she could do then, caught helplessly between sleep and wakefulness. But now, in the daytime, her mind shied away fastidiously from thoughts of Alexander and the other woman.

'How will I feel? How will he be?'

'A *gra*.' Jessica used the Gaelic words tenderly. 'Listen, you have to be strong. You have to decide exactly what you want and go get it. Is your priority Alexander or are you going to allow a shadow, a ghost from the past, to destroy all you have built? Listen to me for I know all about it. If you want him, your husband, the father of your children, then get him back by fair means or foul, keep him, cherish him, and forget all about the past. He'll cure, he'll mend. I know he loves you. He will never be happy with the Casey girl. He will find that out, I'm sure. When he comes home, welcome him. Asking him nothing. Begin again.'

'Oh, Mamita, how good you are. How wonderfully you console me. I don't know where I am going to get the strength, but I'll try. He is all I ever wanted, you know. All that has ever really mattered to me.' She hugged Jessica and the old lady patted her back with her gnarled hand. 'Of course you are right. I must be strong for the children's sake, if for nothing else. But, oh, Mamita, if I lose him I think I shall die.'

'You won't,' Jessica said with finality, 'Not as long as you hold the trump card.'

'What is that Mamita?'

'Alexi. My son will never leave his children. There is no power on earth will separate him from his son. Remember that in the long hard time to come.'

Chapter

40

'There is no part of me that is not yours, not a tiny nerve in my body that does not respond to you.' Alexander cupped Aisling's face between his hands as she spoke.

'I was so afraid that you would find me old,' she said.

He laughed. 'Old? What has age to do with it? We were fashioned from the same piece of earth.'

He had heard her words incredulously: 'Big Dan is not my father.'

He remembered Jessica saying a long, long time ago, in another country, another time: 'She is your sister, Alexander.' He felt again the tropic sun on his back, the sound of the sea and the intensity of his agony and rage.

He remembered his grief, his madness. Once again the world tilted on its axis.

'Big Dan is not my father.'

'Are you sure, my darling?'

'He doesn't know it himself. My mother never told him. She told her confessor to tell me when the right time came, and it did, because you see Alexander I am not whole without you. My life's been such a mess without you.'

A sob caught in her throat and he held her tight and knew the awful truth — even if she was his sister, it would not matter. The years flashed past as they were supposed to do when you were dying and he saw Aisling in the wood. Aisling in her ludicrous sports car on the street in Florence, Aisling with the dappled light on her golden body lying on the white cover on their bed in that room in Taormina.

He looked into his beloved's face. There was such anxiety in her eyes, such love, hope, vulnerability, he felt as though someone had hit him in the chest. He stumbled across the room and into her arms. He thought of the phrase he had so often repeated to himself: she is your sister, it is forbidden.

And now it wasn't. She was here, alive, warm, infinitely precious in his arms.

They had driven all evening through the champagne-coloured twilight. He took her to his small cabin, Casa Rosia, surrounded by olive and cypress trees. It was far away from the sounds of man. The bird song was loud there and it was oddly reminiscent of their little place in Taormina. Two rooms, kitchen and shower, flagged floor, wood and white linen.

'It is home,' Aisling said and Alexander nodded. They ate bread and cheese and he drank wine. He offered her some but she refused.

'I can't,' she said, and he nodded.

They said little, the silence broken only by the call of birds as they prepared for rest.

'I've been so lonely,' she said.

'I know.'

He held on to her. They felt infinitely familiar yet strange to each other. It was as if they had never been apart, and as if they were complete strangers.

They lay in each other's arms, wanton yet reserved, then all barriers were down and they were home, where they belonged. Aisling thought, it was all just waiting until this. All other men had simply appeased her desire, this is love. His body and mine are the meaning of my life. If I never have another moment's happiness in my life it will have been worth it just for this.

They slaked their passion, rediscovering each other's bodies. 'There is no part of me that is not yours,' Aisling said. 'No nerve in my body that does not respond to you.'

They spent the summer together in the hills above Sienna. It was Taormina again, same sun and loving and laughing together.

No one knew exactly where they were. Aisling phoned Camilla who, ashamed of her initial irritation, was warmly understanding. Back in Dublin with Fitz she was content as a brown hen and urged Aisling to take her time to sort things out with Alexander. Next Aisling phoned Julian in London, apologised and tried to explain. He was now immersed in the script and pre-shooting schedule and Aisling, for him, had become Maeve, the character she would play in the film. With the ruthlessness of the artist he had relegated her to her proper place in the scheme of things. He was gracious and tactful with her, and ten minutes after he had replaced the receiver he had forgotten her call.

Alexander sent a note to Tatiana.

They avoided discussions of outsiders, of others. They were selfishly in love, happy and engrossed in each other. They put off all talk of decisions while they walked, arms around each other's waists, through the poppy fields that Camilla loved so well, or picnicked under a fig tree. The world was theirs, a Paradise, but each knew that a day of reckoning lurked.

Aisling was the first to mention it. 'You must never do anything for me you'd be ashamed of, Alexander.'

'I'll have to talk to Tatiana.' It was the first time her name had been mentioned. Aisling nodded and they did not pursue the subject. They both knew how the other felt. There was no need to explain that all other relationships paled in comparison with their love.

But time passed and when Aisling made her weekly call to Slievelea, Samantha sounded worried. Eventually Alexander said one night when after lovemaking they lay silent in each other's arms, feeling the great stillness of content. 'Aisling, we must make decisions. I want to marry you, for us to be together for the rest of our lives. Oh, my love, we are useless apart. You must go back and I'll sort things out here, then come to you.'

He made it sound so easy, the end of a marriage, parting from his children. She knew it would not be.

She clung to him when they parted. 'I am lost without you.'

'I know. I am lost without you.'

She watched Alexander leave, tears blurring her vision.

Chapter

41

Big Dan lay in the oak bed he had inherited from Lord Rennett and had favoured since Livia died. He lay propped up in grandeur, finally dying. Samantha held one of his hands between hers, wetting it with her tears.

'Sam, are you never going to take that piece of string off your wrist?'

'Oh, Gramps, you know I can't — I promised Charlie,' she sobbed.

'Then of course you mustn't.' He coughed and sighed. The pain had gone, with the drugs. It had been a struggle, but the end was in sight. He had wrested this final year from the black figure of Death, to spend with Samantha, just as he had always ruthlessly grasped from life exactly what he wanted.

'They were good days, Spotty, weren't they?' he whispered. Big Dan's early companion and comrade at arms was weeping copiously, the one man who had loved and served Dan faithfully all his life.

'Yes, Dan, they were grand sure enough. Da McCabe's barra', God bless us, and you feckin' it from under the Archbishop's nose.'

Dan smiled faintly. It all passed through his head. Such a good life until he ruined it. And where was Aisling, his beloved Aisling?

'Aisling,' he called.

It was dark now, the faces around the bed blurred and indistinct.

'I'm here, Pappy.' She said with a sob and knew he would always be that, her Pappy.

327

'Aisling, I loved you. I always loved you.'

'I know, Pappy, and I loved you. It's okay.'

Big Dan sighed and it seemed to them that he fell asleep, but the light had gone out and he was dead.

PART FIVE

Chapter

42

Alone, waiting, the cold was bone-biting. Derry's hands felt slippery. What was different this time? he wondered. Perhaps it was being in the South. He was ill at ease below the border. Violence seemed misplaced here in this sleepy countryside. And there was Samantha. Now there was always Samantha. He wished he could take a pot-shot at the bloody birds! He set his sights on the little church.

In his imagination he visualised Samantha's face, seeing her honesty, her puzzlement. He knew she had no conception of his life, any more than he had of her cushioned existence inside Slievelea.

He remembered a poem he knew. His mother had often recited it to them, and it had stuck in his head:

Oh to have a little house
To own the hearth and stool and all.

He couldn't remember any more but he often thought of those lines. He knew he did not really want a little house. What would he do with it? He could not *live* in it, that was for sure. But the words echoed in his head, and he remembered his mother and their little front door and the room which they sat in, constantly drinking tea. The rug on the floor was worn through in places, and the table they sat around was covered in oil cloth patterned with apples, pears, oranges and bananas. Their pottery mugs were cracked and the plates were odd, purchased by his mother from jumble sales and charity shops. There was one plate he'd loved particularly. It depicted a little

Japanese bridge over a stream. A willow tree wept into the water and a Japanese lady crossed a bridge. Because he had been on the run since his mam died, his memories were fast fading. He seemed to be losing his hold on himself as they dimmed. His body was there. He still needed to feed and clothe it, though it mattered little to him what he put in or on it. Maybe he was disappearing too.

He had little idea what he looked like. He could not see himself, or recognise his reflection in the mirror if and when he looked. The face that looked back at him lacked identity. It had eyes, a nose, a mouth, but no reality. Maybe he had died along with his mam and family and was really dead and undergoing a series of long and complicated tests to qualify for the Heaven his mother spoke of. His mouth drew back over his small teeth in a mirthless smile. By now he must have earned his credentials for the other place.

He had never thought like this before and it unnerved him. He knew it was because of her, Samantha. He had no choice, that was the trouble. People thought you had a choice.

Once, in the hut, a star had shone in through the crack in the door. It was a small crack and the star was big. Even from that great distance it was big as a fist in the sky, and it was brilliant. It shone with cold remote radiance into the little room where he lay in his sleeping bag. For a moment he had thought of running away, but even as he thought it, he knew how silly he was being. They never let you get away, they never let you escape. There was no refuge.

No, the only escape for him ever was death. He thought of the grim reaper, the tall dark figure with a scythe whom he did not fear, thought of as a friend. That dark cloak would one day wrap him round and shroud the emptiness where his heart should have been. One day. Maybe soon.

Chapter

43

ALEXANDER drove his car towards Slievelea. The countryside was unfamiliar. He had not been here since that visit so long ago when he had first seen Aisling in the wood. He remembered the moment as if it were yesterday; an azure carpet of bluebells, the leaves on the trees in constant glittering motion where the sunlight penetrated the verdant shadows. He remembered her startled face as she became aware of another presence, the breathtaking beauty of her. He remembered his journey back to Dublin on the train, how bemused he had been. He thought of those magic days in Taormina and just recently in Sienna. Was he doing the right thing? He wondered. Coming here to Big Dan's funeral to tell her this way?

The trees in the narrow road made an arch overhead, a gold and bronze tunnel through which he drove. He thought of his mother, Jessica. What must she be feeling? he wondered. The man she had loved all her life was dead.

He had gone back to the villa, in body if not in spirit. He had refused to discuss matters with either Tatiana or his mother. He could not. He was incapable of discussion even though he knew he was causing pain.

His mother had said, 'You must make your decision as soon as possible, Alexander.' He knew full well the decision she thought he should make but he was incapable of it. He felt he was being pulled apart and wondered at the jealous God who gave him such a choice to make.

'I wish you would go away and make your decision, for you see, my darling, I cannot bear it.'

Tatiana's face was pale and tragic. The strain he had put her under was terrible and he hated himself for it. Regrets, however, were useless, a waste of time. What he had to do was come to terms with the problem, reach a decision, and act.

333

They were a sad little household where before there had been such happiness. Strangely enough Tatiana was almost relieved. She knew that the end was near, Alexander would either go or stay. Either way she would be out of limbo. Knowing him as well as she did, she knew that if he stayed Aisling would have been truly exorcised, and felt deep in her heart that he would choose his family. After all, she held the trump card, Alexi, his son.

If he left her, she thought she would die. It would be the end of her life, of sanity and happiness, but she held on, trying not to think like that, trying not to contemplate the possibility.

Jessica was a tower of strength to her during these dark days, while the sun shone and the birds sang and the household continued its placid routine and everyone was acting a part. She said to Alexander, 'Remember, I know about love. Try not to choose the wrong way.'

They sat in the sunlight in the courtyard while Tatiana pruned roses, the sun slanting on to paving stones worn smooth with time. Little plants grew between the cracks: lavender, herbs, sweet-smelling verbena.

Anouska was reading. Her soft brown hair fell to her waist and her skin was tinted by the sun. She wore a white broderie anglaise pinafore dress and her plump pink arms and childishly short neck looked warm and curved as the stones. His son Alexi ... The boy was the light of his life, his heart, his constant joy. He loved Tatiana and Anouska but had faced his innermost self and acknowledged to himself that he was, for some mysterious reason, inextricably tied to Aisling. He had said to her, 'You are my life, you are my love. You are my home, my hearth, my fire. You are the heart in my body, the smile on my lips, my blood-stream. You are the best part of me, my other self, all that's positive, creative.' His emotion for her was similar to what he felt for his son. But with her there was passion and complicated and disturbing feelings that did not intrude on the warm totality of his love for Alexi.

Aisling loved him beyond reason. She had abandoned herself to him, and he loved her in the same way, to the same degree. But to leave Tatiana and his family? Most important of all, the children? Could he, should he, had he even the smallest right to do that? Anouska would survive, be bruised, but she was close to her mother, they would draw together in their pain, they would support and strengthen each other and grow strong. There would be bitterness, heartbreak but, he felt confident, not total destruction. But Alexi? Ah, that was the rub. Could he survive without his son?

He drank his coffee and glanced across to where his tall, eight-year-old son sprawled on the garden sofa, book in hand. As Alexander stared he looked up and smiled at his father.

'Father, what exactly is honour?' Alexander's heart leapt within him. 'It says here: "was a man of courage and honour". I know what courage is, but honour is more difficult.'

'It certainly is, Alexi.' Alexander looked at his son. Jessica adored him, too, and Alexander knew why. Alexi was a carbon copy of Big Dan. His son looked at him from thickly fringed cornflower blue eyes. His grin was lopsided and charming. He looped his arm gently about his son's waist and explained to him about honour, knowing he had reached an irrevocable decision.

He could not leave Tatiana, his family, his home, his honour. He knew, too, that thoughts of honour would have flown out of the window if Alexi had not been part of this family, and yet he would never have been at peace with Aisling without it. He would have to tell her face to face. Their arrangement had been that if he came to Slievelea he came to her forever, and if he didn't it meant he chose his family in Sienna. But he could not leave her in a whirlwind of doubt and speculation; delayed planes, accidents, the illness of a child, all might have prevented his arrival. He hated to think of her, waiting and wondering.

He decided that the honourable thing to do would be to face Aisling with the decision he had reached. He knew she was incomplete without him; he was incomplete without her. Nevertheless the sacrifice was essential for the well-being of a child; he had to tell her that, face to face. It was an unnatural thing he was doing to himself and her, it was unnatural to separate two halves of the same object, but it had to be done. Tears blinded him. His heart felt like lead in his breast. Driving through the regal arch of trees he kept seeing in his mind's eye Alexi, tall as a sapling, the trust and tenderness in the clasp of his young hand.

It could break my heart, Alexander thought, but for his sake I won't let it. But, oh, my darling, I hope you understand. It's asking a lot of you. Perhaps too much.

335

Chapter

44

The Mass was high, a requiem in Latin. The Taoiseach, Ireland's Prime Minister, stood at the end of the left-hand aisle, flanked by two body guards. There was a sprinkling of politicians from both camps, Finn Gael and Fianna Fail. Lord Bristow was there, gently courteous to Aisling, the big man's daughter. The little church was full of businessmen, some who had hated Dan, some who admired and envied him, few who loved him.

Aisling knelt in the family pew. Samantha wept softly to one side of her, and Lord Bristow sat on the other.

Camilla had said, 'She needs a man beside her for support,' and the elderly businessman-cum-statesman had gallantly filled the breach. Camilla was on Samantha's other side, her arm about the girl's shoulders. Behind them the Devlins, Spotty and his son Michael, the butler, also wept. Spotty's clothes smelled strongly of mothballs, his clear-eyed innocent gaze showed sadness and disbelief. He had not quite grasped the fact of his boyhood friend's demise, for he had thought Big Dan indestructible. He kept shaking his head from side to side in disbelief. At his side, clinging to his arm, was his plump pretty wife, hair no colour nature ever invented, make-up with more enthusiasm than skill, her round good-natured face perspiring in the crowded candle-filled church. She had had a little brandy before arriving this morning and was therefore feeling more kindly disposed towards Dan Casey than usual. The organ played and people stood and sang, 'The Lord's my Shepherd, There is nothing I shall want.' They knelt and Father O'Brien said the De Profundis: 'Out of the depths I have cried to Thee, Lord. Lord hear my prayer.'

Aisling knew without turning that Alexander had come into the church. She felt a surge of joy so strong she thought it would choke her and stared at the coffin at the foot of the altar. It was covered in flowers. She looked at it and smiled. 'Did you do this for me, Pappy?' she whispered. She turned in her seat. Alexander saw her and their eyes met in a glance of such mutual sweetness and surrender that joy filled her eyes with tears and onlookers thought she grieved.

He is mine now. We are each other's. We are whole again. He has committed himself by coming here to see me. He has, as we agreed, thought it all out carefully and come to the decision that I am worth the world to him.

The pallbearers carrying the coffin left the church, Aisling following, arm around the weeping Samantha's shoulders. The child's face was blotched and red with crying. They grouped themselves around the open grave; Aisling stood behind the priest and behind her Lord Bristow and the politicians. On the other side stood the Devlins, Camilla, Julian, and Alexander. It seemed that all the birds of Wicklow were singing a requiem. The sound filled the air, competing with the priest's words. 'Ashes to ashes, dust to dust,' Father O'Brien said as the sun burst out on Slievelea, bathing everything in a dazzling spotlight.

Pappy would love this, Aisling thought. She could see the house, tall and stately against the amber sky. The mountains rose, purple and plum, dark-breasted in the edge of the light. She could hear the dirge of the sea below them, see the sparkle of the lake deep within the verdant mass of trees.

She looked across the grave as the men lowered the coffin and met Alexander's eyes and smiled over the body of his father, her Pappy who was now privy to all secrets.

Derry tasted fear. The sun momentarily blinded him. His hands shook. His eye sought the target, Lord Bristow, but Samantha was in the way. His finger trembled and a leaf fell from a tree and touched his ear. He jumped like a scalded cat, shook his head and trained his sights again. Why was Bristow so close to the family? Aisling was in his way, then she moved. They started to fill in the grave. His finger tightened on the trigger. Sam leaned forward to throw a rose on to the coffin, leaving Lord Bristow exposed. The shot rang out as Aisling leaned side-

337

ways to support her daughter . . .

Derry dropped the gun and ran. He had messed his pants and little moans tore from him as he fled the scene, not sure what he had done.

Aisling felt the impact of something alien in her body. She was stunned and numb and cold and saw the dawning horror on the faces around her. She searched the crowd for Alexander. When she met his eyes she smiled.

'My darling, you came back to me. Thank you.' She closed her eyes.

Alexander screamed, 'Get her indoors. Get a doctor! There must be a doctor here.'

The bullet had winged her shoulder and she had lost a lot of blood. She came to for a few moments to find Camilla standing over her, her face full of concern.

'Oh Milla, Milla, he came back to me. He came back,' she whispered.

Later, in the library, Samantha clung close to Camilla and Alexander drank a large whiskey and soda. It was dark and the last mourner had gone from Slievelea. It was typical of Big Dan Casey to have had a drama enacted at his interment. 'God bless us, he shoulda been alive, he'da loved it!' they said.

They had come to Slievelea for Big Dan's wake, to eat the food and imbibe lashings of drink. A little thing like a shooting wasn't going to stop them. The Gardi Siocanna were everywhere. Information gleaned during the course of their questioning elicited the fact that there had been someone lurking about the grounds for the last weeks, even months. No one seemed to know who it was.

Camilla told the Gardi that she thought Samantha knew the identity of the mysterious person but Samantha, to her own astonishment, denied any such knowledge. She was appalled by her deceit, felt implicated in her mother's wounding, yet to her horror was reluctant to tell the police anything she knew. She was certain it was Derry Devlin who had shot her mother. She was equally certain that he had made a mistake. She thought the Taoiseach must have been the target. She had nothing in her heart except contempt for the despicable act, especially as it had gone wrong and her innocent mother had suffered. But the nagging question remained, why had Derry, a practised shot, missed? Deep down she believed that he had lost heart at the last moment. She felt sure that was what had happened, and she too at the last moment lost heart and courage and could not tell on him.

She kept hearing his flat Northern voice saying, 'I saw me mam's arm lyin' in the grass all by itself, just an arm.' She kept visualising the empty lost look in his eyes and thought she knew where he would be. She decided to slip away and see him, talk to him before she told the Gardi all she knew.

They were everywhere. There were cordons up all over Wicklow and they were searching the grounds and the environs of Slievelea so Samantha stayed with her mother until she was quite sure Aisling was sleeping comfortably. Later she accompanied Camilla, Alexander and Julian downstairs to the dining room where a grand buffet was spread out for the mourners.

Though one could hardly call them that now, Camilla thought, for there was a party atmosphere in the room. People laughed and shouted greetings to each other across the room. Someone was playing the piano in the music room, 'Kathleen Mavourneen', 'Danny Boy' and 'The Mountains of Mourne', and an unsteady chorus of slightly out-of-key singers joined in. Only the servants were in tears, sniffing and wiping their noses on their sleeves. It was a scene Big Dan would have appreciated.

Slowly they decimated the whole poached salmons, the lobsters, the salads and the mousses, the pâtés, the mounds of Beluga caviar in crystal bowls resting on crushed ice. People laughed and joked and swapped memories of Big Dan's villainy. There were few people there who sounded as if they had loved him, Camilla thought, and many a one was heard to say, 'Ah well, sure the money he had didn't save him from the grave in the end, now did it?' with relish and a wink.

Camilla saw her mother and father on the other side of the room, talking to Georgina and her husband Emmit. Their children ran around and around them in a circle, grabbing at the women's skirts with grubby hands, but were not reprimanded by their mother.

'Will you be all right, Sam?' Camilla asked. 'I must talk to my parents.'

'Of course Camilla. I'd like to be alone for a bit.' She was thinking of Derry and how soon she could sneak off to find him.

What would happen then she neither knew nor thought about.

Samantha thought Camilla's mother looked very beautiful but plump. Her red hair was exactly the same colour as her daughter's. She remembered what Camilla had told her about thinking she would never be as beautiful as her mother. How ridiculous that was.

Big Dan had told Samantha that people change, every situation alters, despite the human insistence that some things are immutable. She guessed he was right.

She saw Alexander Klein talking to Lord Bristow and wondered about his connection with her mother. In another corner Samantha saw Spotty Devlin and his wife weeping, too distressed to feel uncomfortable in the company in which they found themselves. They were Derry's relations, she thought, though he said he had never met them. Devlin, their son, was on tenderhooks, jumpy as an unbroken pony, a desperate expression on his face. He looked like a trapped animal and she knew why.

'Are you all right?' Camilla said to her mother.

Caroline grabbed her arm. 'Darling, what is going on? You're in the know. Tell me, what have the police found? And how is poor Aisling? Is she all right? Why would anyone want to shoot her?'

'Aisling is resting upstairs, Mother,' Camilla said soothingly. 'I don't thing anyone wanted to kill her. I think they were aiming at the Taoiseach or one of the politicians or Lord Bristow. I think they got her by accident.'

'Well, they skedaddled off like a bullet from a gun — Oh sorry, darling. You know what I mean.'

Charles said sanctimoniously, 'Dan Casey was always involved in violence. It's no wonder it has erupted at the man's funeral. I'm not at all surprised.'

Camilla did not bother to comment. To her surprise, Georgina greeted her like a long lost friend, kissing her on both cheeks.

'Darling Milla, how lovely to see you. Emmit and I often talk about you, and I remember our happy, happy days at St Dymphna's. Lovely times we had! And where's your husband? We'd love to meet him.'

'He's not here, Georgina. He's at home, keeping the place warm for me until I return.'

340

'You must bring him to see us, you really must. We have a lovely new house on the Vico Road, Windy Hollow. It's gorgeous with everything modern. So labour-saving, you know. Emmit doesn't like me to wet my fingers, do you, dear?'

Camilla excused herself and went over to Alexander. 'I want to talk to you if I may. Privately,' she said.

'Of course. Excuse me, Lord Bristow.'

'Come to the library. I doubt if we'll be disturbed there.'

As they left the room Camilla saw Samantha slip out through the French windows. She looked rather furtive, Camilla thought. The she focused her attention on the man beside her. It was no wonder Aisling was in love with him. His mouth was sweet and vulnerable and there was passion and idealism in the dark eyes. Any woman would want to touch the greying hair, soft and abundant, and kiss away the shadows from his face.

She closed the library door behind them and faced him. 'I want to know what is going on,' she said.

Alexander had sat down in Big Dan's chair. The old man's rug was still on the back. Camilla sat opposite him. The fire burned merrily in the grate, casting a mellow amber light on the leather-bound books.

'It's not idle curiosity, I assure you. I love Aisling. I don't want her hurt any more. So what's the score?'

'Can you take it?'

'Try me.'

'Well, in a nutshell, we had a pact.'

She nodded. 'I know.'

'If I did not turn up here I was staying with Tatiana, my wife.'

'And if you came here you would be coming to Aisling?'

He nodded.

'Then you are leaving Tatiana?'

He looked at her levelly. 'No, I can't leave my family. But I needed to tell her face to face. It would have been all right except for the shooting. Now she thinks . . .'

'You must tell her, Alexander. She must not hope in vain. Any more of that kind of tension, or half-hearted love, will kill her. Do you understand?'

He knew she was right but nothing had worked out as he had planned. He still wanted to return to Tatiana and his children, but Aisling's look, the glory in her eyes at what she thought was his decision to stay with her, reproached him beyond endurance.

341

There had been an end and a beginning in those moments he had held her in his arms, limp and seemingly lifeless. He loved her, he knew, but they had both held on too long to the past, to the magnitude of what they had felt for each other and the cruel way it had ended. He loved the total consuming passion she had for him but he found it irksome, too. He had not realised it until now. He did not want to be possessed. He needed space, air to breathe, room to move out of the orbit of others and into his own creative sphere. Tatiana allowed him that.

He thought of her tender care of him all these years, of the infinite variety of her personality, her wild warm love for him and her generous understanding. He remembered her gifts to him: their two children to whom she had been a wise and loving mother, her deference to his beliefs. How tactful she was, how gracious an hostess, how passionate a wife, how understanding of his art. He knew now he truly loved her. He loved the texture of their lives together, what they had built. He loved the home they had jointly created in the Tuscan hills, their children's tears and laughter, the casual conversations they had had, their shared worries, mutual activities.

He loved the tiny things that made the smallest stitches in the tapestry of their life together: the placing of the bowl of flowers in the hall on the table where letters waited collection. The cracked tooth mug that held the children's toothbrushes, one blue, one pink, in the nursery bathroom. The kitchen tap that dripped. The chaos of the table in the patio after Sunday lunch. There was something about the thought of that table that wrenched his heart. It was a symbol of their love, their life together. The broken bread, sustaining, life giving. The half-empty wine glasses, the bowl of fruit with the grapes, red and white, apricots and peaches, the ice melting, the coffee half drunk. It would be hard never to have Sunday lunch there again. No, not just hard, impossible.

He loved Tatiana as he loved himself, his life, his art. Aisling had been the fragile ghost at the feast of his life. What he had had with her belonged in another time, another place. It had been an idyll, a joyful romance made tragic by fate and because of that they had both elevated it out of the realms of reality. He would not diminish it but it had nothing to do with his life now. He could not pick up where they had left off, for what of the years between? Years that had held Tatiana's love and faith, her trust through a thousand domestic upheavals, little tragedies and joys.

It would have to be faced. The problem of Aisling would have to be dealt with courageously and truthfully. He owed her honesty. If he remained with her, left Tatiana, Anouska and Alexi, he would break not only their hearts but Aisling's as well, for he knew that in the fullness of time she would recognise that he did not love her enough, that his thoughts inevitably drifted back to his family, and then she would surely go mad and despair.

Yet he dreaded telling her. There had been no opportunity as yet to approach her. She lay in bed, weak from her wound, and when he tried to see her Samantha had been there. The right moment would come, he knew, but waiting was hell.

Chapter

45

Samantha was in torment. Her lovely mother was lying in bed, suffering. It was her fault, and hers alone. Her mother could have been killed but still Samantha could not tell on Derry. Why could she not give away a terrorist? She had no simple answer. She did not understand her own feelings. Derry had understood her. Derry had trusted her. Derry had loved her when she had been lonely but for Grandpa Casey. Above all he had needed her, and no one else in her life seemed to do that. Derry had made her feel special, a little different.

She wondered where he was now, what had happened to him, how it felt to be hunted. For even though the Gardi didn't know the identity of the gunman, they would hunt him remorselessly. Derry had been a fugitive for most of his life. Samantha felt the sympathy of the secure for the loner outside the pale.

Her feet led her naturally to the woods. She did not hear the sounds of stealthy pursuit, did not see the shadows slip from tree to tree behind her, the watchers marking where she went.

A soft rain had started to fall. She walked the familiar path as a chill wind blew in from the sea and the clouds grew angry and slate-coloured above, tussling with the gale, running hither and yon over the floor of heaven. The wood obscured her view of the house and Samantha felt isolated, cocooned in the cathedral of trees which met high over her head, cutting out the world of sounds. She felt quite alone, but she was not.

She turned up the collar of her windcheater and slipped on the slushy ground. Trickles of rainwater fell heavily from the leaves overhead, dislodged by her passing. Water slithered down the back of her neck, sending a chill over her. She longed for the sounds of voices and laughter, the silence oppressed her. She heard a rustling in the wood and thought it was the trees in the wind.

She saw him before she was aware she had. It was as if she had always known he would be there, outside the hut. His body swung from a tree which creaked under his weight. His feet dangled limply, the sneakers wet and tattered, the laces broken. His arms seemed short, his jacket sleeves almost up to his elbow. In his right hand he clutched the blue hairband she had given him. It trailed from between his fingers, soggy with rain. His face was bloated and grotesque. Samantha tore her eyes away from the mottled visage, the protruding eyes and tongue, the extraordinary horror that was Derry Devlin yet was not.

There was a yell behind her. She jumped, staring around her, scared out of her wits.

'He's there! Get the little sod. It's all right, Miss. There now, it's all right.'

The Gardi were all over the place. One of them held her but she struggled away and tried to pull the band from Derry's fingers. The policeman grabbed her again and pulled her away, saying, 'Easy now. Easy.'

She threw up into the bracken beside them and the Gardi held her head.

'I'm all right,' she said.

'Yer not, Miss, y'know.'

Her mouth tasted awful and she said to him, 'I won't run away.'

He smiled at her. 'Yerra it doesn't much matter if you do.'

The policeman followed her down to the lake. All the other men were busy with the body and the hut. A photographer had arrived on the scene.

Everything seemed grey. The waters of the lake were a dark bluish black and the trees were ghostly in the wet pearl-grey mist that floated over the surface of the lake like a cloud. Samantha knelt on the jetty. She cupped her hands and splashed icy water on her face. It was so cold that she spluttered and gasped with the shock of it, but she did it again. And again. And again. Then she rose, and sighed.

The kindly officer said, 'Come with me, Miss,' and obediently she walked to the house.

She told Aisling everything about Derry, and Aisling told the Gardi. She was sitting up in bed drinking some tea that Sheilagh had brought, looking very much better. Sparkling, in fact. It did not dawn on Sam until much later how well her mother looked. Aisling had not reacted to the story as she had expected. There was no scolding, only warm understanding, kisses and a great big hug.

'I'm so glad you told me, dearest,' her mother said. 'We'll say no more abut it. The Gardi can make of it what they will. They're happy they've got their man. The poor boy paid a heavy price for missing his target.'

Samantha whispered, 'Momma, I think it was my fault.'

Aisling shook her head. 'You don't know that, my darling, no one ever will. Remember, his life wasn't worth a penny, whether he was caught or not. If he was captured he would end up in Portlaoghaise, and if not — well, the I.N.L.A. make no secret of what they do to those who betray or fail them. His inaccuracy would be counted a betrayal, make no mistake. His failure to kill was an unforgivable crime.

'How or why Derry missed we'll never know. Deliberately or by mistake? Seeing you there? Remembering something you said? Perhaps you struck a chord of tenderness in him he did not even know he possessed. He was a sad boy, like my brother. They are both better off out of this world. Neither of them was happy here.'

Samantha breathed in raggedly.

'Sorry, my love, I know it sounds harsh. But one thing is sure: he must have loved you very much to have died holding your hairband. No matter who is the giver and who the recipient, love is always a good thing. But didn't Charlie give you the hairband? How are you going to explain it to him?'

Samantha looked at her mother. The dimples at the corners of her mouth were dancing in and out. She saw the twinkle in her mother's eyes and they both burst out laughing. It was like a clearing of the air, clouds parting and the sun coming out. The laughter turned to a sob in Aisling's throat. Tears gathered in her eyes and splashed onto her cheeks. Samantha drew a great quivering breath and felt her heaving shoulders caught in her mother's arms. They laughed and cried in each other's arms, clinging to each other in the storm, murmuring to each other, shushing each other and wiping each other's tears away. When

346

it was over they smiled at each other, full of tenderness and understanding.

'Oh, Momma, I love you.'

'I know, my darling. And I love you.'

'I know now. I didn't before.'

'How could you know? I drank to escape my feelings, even my love for you. No more, darling. Even when I stopped drinking I was fearful of your rejection. I had made such a mess of my life. I felt you would be ashamed of me. I had not realised that love is not measured that way.'

'Oh, Mom, I'd never have rejected you.'

'I know that now. Please forgive me for not trusting you.' Samantha hugged her, and Aisling said briskly, 'Ring for some more tea, Sam, will you?'

When Sheilagh came in she saw them chatting and laughing together, and thanked the Virgin Mary for answering her prayers.

Aisling felt well enough to join Camilla, Alexander and Sam downstairs for dinner, Julian having slipped away quietly at the end of the wake. Alexander noticed that she and Samantha were both animated and full of good humour. Camilla had been on the phone to Fitz.

'He's missing me like hell,' she said. 'He's phoned me three times today at Mount Rivers. He couldn't get through here because the Gardi were monopolising the phones.'

They were served by a grief-stricken Devlin but served with the splendour for which Slievelea was famous. The glasses were fine Waterford, the nappery thick and white, the chandelier cast its bewitching light on the guests and the paintings.

Alexander thought, she belongs here. It suits her beauty as nowhere else does. I wonder if she knows.

Tonight Aisling did indeed look beautiful, more beautiful than Camilla had ever seen her. She wore a black velvet gown, cut low over her breast in a 'V', long-sleeved with skirts flaring to just below the knee. One arm was in a sling, but it did not seem to bother her. She looked radiant. There was a glow to her skin, a patina like the sheen of the pearls at her throat, and her eyes made the sapphire on her hand dim by comparison. She kept referring to her daughter and they often touched each other, Alexander noticed.

Camilla, too, looked lovely. She was saying, 'In any event, I must get back to him. I miss him so. And I'm happy about you now, Ash. You seem fine to me.'

She nodded. 'I'm fine, just fine.' She smiled at Alexander. 'I want to speak to you after dinner, if I may?'

He nodded apprehensively. The moment had come sooner than he thought. Camilla tactfully took Samantha upstairs.

'I'll stay tonight but tomorrow I'm off to Tralee. If you need me later tonight, Ash, pop in to see me. I won't mind.' She gave her friend an encouraging smile and went upstairs.

Aisling rang for Devlin. 'Bring some brandy for Mr Klein into the library, and some more coffee for me,' she said, and crossed the great hall ahead of Alexander. His tension was mounting and he tried to train his soul in patience. Devlin poured him a drink and Sheilagh came in with some coffee. It seemed to take forever before he was alone with Aisling.

The room was dimly lit and full of shadows. It smelled of fine leather and beeswax. A bowl of chrysanthemums stood on the table, filling the air with their curious musky scent. A huge fire crackled in the grate.

Aisling sat in her father's winged chair and motioned Alexander to the one opposite. It was not what he had been expecting at all. He had imagined her putting her arms around him.

'Aisling,' he began, but she interrupted him.

'Let me speak, Alexander. Hear me out first. I must tell you, you'll never have any idea how happy you have made me.' She held up her hand as he started to protest. 'No, listen. You don't know how necessary you were to me, to my happiness, my health, my reason. Your coming to me like this has made me whole again. You have given me back my life. And yet, please don't be hurt, I see now that there was something sick about my obsession. All those years I was drinking, I thought it was because of you. But it was me, my own damaged personality condemning myself to hell and using you as an excuse. I never tried to forget you, but fed on the memories until they began to poison my system. I allowed myself to live off old experience at the expense of everything new in my life — like my daughter. *I* spoiled my own life. You didn't do it. My father didn't do it. All by myself, I did it. It was my sickness.'

She looked at him, eyes pleading for understanding.

'I'm well now, Alexander, but my life has changed and so has yours. We are neither of us young star-crossed lovers any more.

348

I love you. I'm doomed, I think, never to love anyone but you for all the days of my life. No. Don't come near me or I won't be able to go on.'

She took a deep breath. 'I want you to understand that I can't live with you. You are married. You have a wife and children. She probably loves you as much as I do. I can't break her heart and live at peace with myself. Your two children probably adore you as you adore them. I can't tear their lives apart. It would be wanton selfishness only permissible in the young and foolish. I couldn't do that.

'I have reparation to make to my daughter whom I love as you love your children, but whom I have neglected as I'm sure you never neglected your children. She *needs* me, Alexander, you must understand that. I must be with her, help her grow into adulthood, be aware of her problems, be there for her. She's been through such a lot on her own, had some terrible shocks. She's behaved with touching gallantry. I need to be with her, to be her mother, not because I *should* but because I *want* to. So what I'm trying to say, I suppose, is goodbye.'

He felt an enormous relief, not because he did not love her but because she need never know his rejection of her, and he need not hurt her.

'My dearest, I do understand. You are brave and good and right.'

'I don't want to talk to you about it any more now. I wanted you to understand, that's all.'

'I understand, Aisling, and I love you. Remember that.'

She had never looked more beautiful, he thought, full of love and gratitude. Her eyes were shining with tears and she had an exhausted air about her. The day had worn her out but she obviously drew strength from the rightness of her actions. Momentarily he wished he might never leave her, this exquisite woman who loved him, momentarily he wanted to stay. But the moment passed.

'Goodbye, my darling. Thank you for your gift of love.' She smiled as she spoke, but there were lines of strain at the corners of her mouth.

'Goodbye, Aisling. My love, my friend.'

He kissed her forehead lightly and left her standing there in the firelight.

Alexander left Slievelea immediately and took the last flight from Dublin to Heathrow where he spent a restless night in an airport hotel. He could not wait to get home and put Tatiana's mind at rest. He took the first available flight to Pisa and drove hell for leather to Sienna. When he saw the pink roof of the villa he heaved a sigh of relief.

Tatiana heard the car arrive. The pain in her heart gave a last excruciating stab and then died forever. She had suffered intensely in the last weeks and months but she had believed in Alexander. She had waited for him to come home and reached the conclusion that if he did not he would be unworthy of her love. She could not love a man who would desert hearth and home, wife and family, for an irresponsible passion. The Alexander she loved was incapable of such callousness and she had never really doubted that one day he would come. But when? She had not known that, and the waiting was hard.

They were sitting in the garden under the shade of the huge umbrella. She heard the sound of a car on the drive. It could have been anyone, but Tatiana knew it was Alexander. Her heart rose within her, beating so strongly she thought it would tear her breast apart. She looked at the children; Anouska as usual was sitting in the shade of the mimosa in front of the mossy niche where Aphrodite stood. Her sweet face was drawn to a frown of concentration and she swung one thin brown leg over the other. Alexi was as usual in the hammock, playing lazily with a battery-operated plane.

'Zurruum, zurruum,' he murmured, circling the silver toy. Jessica sat knitting, her silver hair gleaming under the sun. She glanced across at Tatiana at the noise of the car and saw her face, instantly realising what was about to happen. She gave Tatiana a reassuring smile and watched compassionately as she rose and left the garden.

Jessica stood up, her bones old and creaking, the movement tiring her. She walked up the steps with the aid of her stick, and crossed the marble floor tap-tapping her way across the dim interior. The door to the hall was open. Through it she saw her son and his wife enfold each other in their arms, melting into each other as if carved from the same substance.

Tatiana's eyes were closed and Alexander's expression was that of a voyager who has at last reached safe harbour. Jessica felt a lump in her throat. It was all right. The ghosts were laid.

Aisling's spell was broken. The fatal attachment of Kleins to Caseys was over. Big Dan was laid to rest. Alexander had come home. Peace reigned in the quiet Tuscan villa. Her old heart lifted in a song of praise to God and she tap-tapped her way back to the sun-filled garden and the children.

Camilla took off her shoes and wiggled her toes. She sighed deeply and looked at Fitz. Her remark was heartfelt, 'Oh, love, it's so good to be home.'

'You can say that again. I've missed you like hell. I just can't be doing without you.'

There was a contented pause.

'Is Aisling all right?'

Camilla nodded, 'Yes. At last Ash is at peace.'

Fitz rose and stretched. 'Good,' he said. 'Now I want a certain Titian-haired lady in my bed without delay. There are bits of her I want to re-explore. I was in terrible danger of forgetting some of the delights she offers big men called Fitz.' Camilla giggled, rose and put her arms around his waist.

'I love you, me darlin'.' His voice was unusually serious. 'I want you to know that.'

'Me too,' Camilla murmured contentedly, a great peace in her heart. 'Oh my love. Me too.'

She looked back over her life and wondered what she had done to deserve such a blessing. She looked at Fitz and shivered at the depth of her love for him. He was the vessel of her love, contained her contentment within him and lovingly nurtured it. Sometimes, remembering her turbulent childhood, she could not believe her quiet content.

After they had made love she said, 'Heart of my heart, do you know how much I love you?'

'Listen, woman, I know. Why do you think I cherish it, our love? I know how precious it is, how lucky we are. The sun and stars shine out of you and me, and without you there is nothing. Come here and kiss me again.'

It will be like this forever, she thought, because we are satisfied, because we are not greedy. She said farewell to the last vestige of sad little Camilla Vestry of the green years, far away from another world, bid her a happy farewell and turned her face to her husband.

Night fell over Slievelea. The twilight was purple with shimmering pearly shadows. Samantha and her mother walked the terrace after dinner. Devlin would bring them coffee in a moment and they would have it together in the music room. He was more cheerful these days. His face grew brighter day by day. The house had not been closed as he had feared. In fact, it promised to be busier than ever with Miss Aisling and Miss Samantha there all the time. Aisling had taken command with an authority that surprised everyone, including herself. Devlin had promptly switched his allegiance. Now it was 'The Mistress says . . .' as if he were quoting from the Bible.

Samantha took her mother's hand. They walked together, staring at the sliver of new moon in the midnight blue sky. Aisling pulled her cashmere wrap closer. So much had passed, so much had ended and so much begun. She felt blessed and curiously tired, as if she had been running in harness for a long time and only now was untethered and free to rest.

'Momma?'

'Yes, my darling.'

'Can we stay here for a long time?'

'Would you like that?'

'Oh, yes.' Then, anxiously, 'Would you?'

'I'd love it best of all,' Aisling said, and hugged her daughter. She looked at the little peaked face and the huge brown eyes, Ali's eyes. The habit of anxiety was hard to lose but Aisling's mission was to erase it forever from her daughter's life.

'We'll stay here, Sam. Big Dan wanted us to. He knew it would happen. He left all this in our care. We'll stay in Slievelea for as long as you like, in peace at last.'

A faint breeze blew in from the sea, smelling of salt. The land around them was so still and quiet that Aisling could hear Samantha's breathing. The gentle sound filled her with hope. She put her arm around her daughter and together they went into the house.